SHOW ME THE WAY TO GO HOME

SHOW ME THE WAY TO GO HOME

A NOVEL

BY SIMMONS JONES

Algonquin Books of Chapel Hill   1991

Published by
Algonquin Books of Chapel Hill
Post Office Box 2225
Chapel Hill, North Carolina 27515-2225

a division of
Workman Publishing Company, Inc.
708 Broadway
New York, New York 10003

Library of Congress Cataloging-in-Publication Data
Jones, Simmons, 1920–
    Show me the way to go home : a novel / by Simmons Jones.
        p.   cm.
    ISBN 0-945575-41-6 : $19.95
    I. Title.
PS3560.O538S48   1991
813'.54—dc20   91-3413
                                                        CIP

10 9 8 7 6 5 4 3 2 1
First Edition

For Morehead and Johnny and Bob

This novel should be played on an upright piano,
slightly out of tune, and very late on a summer night
with all the windows thrown open.

SHOW ME THE WAY TO GO HOME

PART ONE

THE MOON WAXING

Be not forgetful to entertain strangers; for thereby some have entertained angels unawares.

—Hebrews 13:2

CHAPTER ONE

Just before the sun came up on a day in the middle of June, newsboys with the voices of raucous songbirds pitched the *Milford Morning Herald* onto porches all over town. They flew in and out among the silent houses and leafy trees, calling out to each other in the half dark, standing high on the pedals of their bicycles like messengers from the gods.

They had not awakened Mr. Clyde Diggs, however. Mr. Diggs had waited flat on his back in the dark of his bedroom for more than an hour, impatient for the thump of the *Herald* on his front porch. He sat now at the kitchen table, dressed for the day except for his bedroom slippers and the disorder of his thick white hair, studying with grave misgiving the newspaper spread open before him. Peelie Diggs was at the stove cooking his grandfather's breakfast as he did every morning of the world, except Sundays and holidays, before going out to deliver the mail.

"PROMINENT MILFORD REALTORS VISIT ROME," Mr. Diggs read out to his grandson, piercing him with his ice-blue eyes, as if he

3

were responsible for the outrage. "Now, listen to this one, Peelie," he instructed, continuing to read from the text. "Milford Realtor Julian Warren announced Friday he has invited his younger brother, John Thomas Warren of Rome, Italy, to join the family firm, Warren and Company, Realtors, in the very near future. Mister Warren and associate partner Skinner Bates left for Rome last week to complete arrangements." He reared back in his chair, stricken by disapproval. "Invited!" he said, piercing his grandson a second time. "If Julian don't quit inviting John Thomas to do first one thing and then another thing he ain't going to do, I hesitate to predict what might happen, you've cooked the eggs too stiff again, Peelie."

"Yessir," Peelie said, perfectly agreeable.

Mr. Diggs began to eat his breakfast, resigned as usual to unsatisfactory eggs, and at the same time continued with the enlightenment of his grandson.

Nor had the newsboys awakened Miss Evelyn Black. Miss Evelyn was getting ready to go to bed in her expansive, heavily curtained house on a forgotten street. She hung her sparkly black gown in the closet along with all the other sparkly gowns, one for each night of the week, and sat down at her dressing table. She studied her face in the mirror for some time and sighed. "Thank you, Gloria, honey," she said to the young girl in a wrapper who had come in to bring her the morning paper. "You girls try to get you some rest."

"Yes, ma'am," Gloria said, perfectly agreeable, and left Miss Evelyn taking the paint off her face and reading the newspaper at the same time.

Miss Evelyn put out her cigarette and turned the page. "PROMINENT MILFORD REALTORS VISIT ROME," the headline announced. "Oh, my heavenly stars and body—Julian!" she cried out and laughed like a girl, knowing better than most the long and actual history behind the printed words. For an instant, her youth returned to her in all its sweet and foolish bliss.

Over several generations, current events had come to be the lifeblood and chief export of Milford North Carolina, due possibly to the restless character of its natives and its pleasant and occasionally perilous situation on the Atlantic seacoast. It wasn't that the headlines and hard-fact stories in the newspaper were thought to have much more than passing significance so far as real life was concerned. They served as the dust jacket and hard cover of the actual book in which were written current events as they actually happened in the curious lives of the people of Milford that everybody knew and had always known. Some of these events were remarkable, some of them probably not, some of them were carried in the *Milford Morning Herald,* others were not:

ROME—In a pensione on the Via Due Macelli run by a German countess with the voice of a trombone, Julian Warren sat on his bed in his pajamas and wondered where Skinner had found to go that he could stay out all night like a damn alley cat. What's more, Skinner was married to his first cousin, Susan Johnson, and was not at liberty, so to speak. Today, Julian had decided, was to be the day he would inform his little brother, John Thomas, that he, John Thomas, had no choice but to return home to Milford North Carolina where people knew who he was and what he came from. Otherwise, the checks issued each month by the Trust Department of the Milford National Bank would cease by Julian's instruction, he being guardian. There was no satisfaction for him in this thought, only a great weariness that, by inheritance, the obligation was his to take action.

MILFORD—Father Elvin Flowers, pastor of St. Matthews Catholic Church, met his sister Nell, with her broad, pleasant face and a rosary wound among her pale, fleshy fingers, at the railway station. She had come to help her brother at the rectory, as there had been a record number of conversions in the region recently. She had dreamed, dozing on the day coach, that a fine man from the country would come to ask her hand in marriage. She thought it best not to discuss this dream with Elvin.

BLADENS BEACH—Ernie Dexter in his mattress-ticking shirt rambled through the old barn of a house, knocking on doors and shouting, "Rise and shine, rise and shine, let's get up and make magic time," in the affected voice his apprentices detested. They were not surprised he had never made it as an actor and had had to resign himself to being production director at the Bladens Beach Playhouse every summer. They emerged reluctantly from their dreams of sex and fame, about which they knew next to nothing, and faced another day of hauling furniture and painting flats.

NEW YORK CITY—Crazy Dick Harteman decided he was tired of living with the drunken fag on Central Park West. So he took a long shower, gave himself a fix, put the packet of skag and his rig and his clothes and the fag's leather box full of watches and rings and cufflinks in a small suitcase and departed hurriedly for the West Side Terminal. He caught the first bus south.

MILFORD—At 814 Ransom Place, Laura Warren gave instructions from her bed to Annie Davison to get down all her suitcases and the small trunk. She did not feel at all well. Annie stood at the bedroom door for some time, regarding with somber resignation the frail, red-haired woman in the great Victorian bed before she spoke. "Mislark, I don't want nothing to do with you moving yourself over to Bladen Beach with that houseful of strays calls theyselfs actors. Ain't a thing in God's world I can do about you stepping yourself out on the stage for all to see, but I ain't going to help you pick up and move out to such as that."

"For godsake, shut up, Annie, and get my suitcases down," Laura Warren pleaded from the pillows.

"Who going to take care of poor Jubie?" she asked.

"You are and Julian when he gets home," Laura told her.

"I ain't got the strength and Julian ain't got the sense," Annie said.

"Goddam it, Annie, get my suitcases down and tend to your own damn business," Laura screamed and sat up in the covers looking wild.

"Dear Lord, help us," Annie said and left the door empty.

ROME—Skinner Bates and John Thomas Warren found themselves together in John Thomas's bed in his apartment in a seventeenth-century palazzo at the angle of Vicolo delle Cinque and Via del Moro. They did not feel at all well. They had left the Piazza Navona at midnight after a terrible argument and had been followed by Luis Martello, second-rate bullfighter turned third-rate actor, and Carmella Moon, the most beautiful black girl in the world, and Sidney Lauren, the most beautiful white girl in the world, and predatory night creatures from all over old Rome. Music had throbbed in the crooked alleys of Trastevere until almost dawn. The apartment was beyond rescue and there were no cigarettes and probably no coffee. The cat was complaining bitterly, sitting like a doorstop on the balcony overlooking the disastrous living room. Skinner Bates was mute with consternation.

MILFORD—In her small cathedral house at 1213 Ocean Front Drive, Susan Johnson Bates answered the telephone hoping it was a call from Rome Italy. It was. But not the one she had hoped for. It was from her cousin Julian Warren and not from her husband of just under a year. Julian saw it as his duty to inform her that his beloved brother John Thomas had fallen from a window of his apartment and disappeared off the face of the earth in the middle of a talk about going home to Milford North Carolina.

"What was he doing in the window?" Susan asked.

"That's where he always sits," Julian said.

"Jackass," Susan said. "Where the hell is Skinner?"

"He's out looking for John Thomas," Julian said. Susan could hear the waves through the telephone wire crossing the Atlantic Ocean.

"Look here, Julian. You go look for John Thomas and send Skinner Bates home to me," she said sharply over the sound of the waves. "I don't give a hoot in hell about John Thomas."

"Good-by, Susan," Julian said and was drowned out in the rush of waves over the wires stretched across the Atlantic Ocean.

GROVER—Doris Ann Hawkins pulled herself up into the seat of the

battered pickup truck beside her father, prepared to hear the lecture he
would deliver for the entire forty miles to Bladens Beach. There was country mud on her father's heavy shoes. The lecture was a small price to pay
for another season, her third, as an apprentice at the Bladens Beach Playhouse, where there were boys from the cities and in-person stars from the
movies she had gone to see every Saturday since she could remember. "If
your momma was still living, I don't know what she'd say about you
running off from home to be with these show people ever summer, Doris
Ann," the lecture began. Doris Ann gazed at fantastic dreams straight
ahead through the windshield, the light breezes from the distant sea blowing the curls about her round, bespectacled, cherubic face.

"I don't know what Momma would say, Daddy, I wish she was here
to tell us," she said to him, giving him the cue to continue. Doris Ann
loved her father more than she could say, he was all she had in the world.

MILFORD—It was nine o'clock sharp, and Ned Trivett, already delighted, was easing himself through the screen door onto the front porch
of his house on Hooper Street. He held a cup of coffee in his hand. The
sleeves of his black silk kimono stirred gently in the mild morning air.
"*Ah! Buon giorno, ragazzi! Come sono fortunato trovar tal deliziosi amici sotto
il mio tetto stamatina!*" he exclaimed, lifting his coffee cup in salutation.

The two young men in white wicker chairs looked around at Ned
as if they had heard distant thunder and were mildly curious as to its
source. "Rome Italy," Brother Reeves announced in a voice loud enough
to be heard as far as the street, apparently returning to the subject under
discussion.

"Good morning, dear boys," Ned said to Brother Reeves and Jake
Cullen who appeared to be discussing items from the *Milford Morning
Herald*.

"PROMINENT MILFORD REALTORS VISIT ROME," the *Herald* insisted, lying flat on its back.

"Good morning, Ned," the dear boys said as Ned settled himself
with considerable care into the white settee.

"How splendid it is to start the day in the company of two such stunning accomplices," Ned went on, peering across Jake's knee at the rejected newspaper. "And I see you have come upon some local gossip in the morning news."

"Here comes old Peelie," Brother interrupted.

"Well, good morning, Ned, hello, Brother, hello, Mister Cullen, welcome back to Milford," Peelie Diggs said in his high and penetrating voice as he came through the gate and up the front walk.

"Ah, good morning, Peelie," Ned said. "Do come join us."

"I ain't handed you one of these purple packets in a long time, Ned," Peelie said, standing at attention on Ned's porch studying the extravagant scrawl across the face of the letter. "This here's from Rome Italy like the last one," he said and surrendered the lavender envelope with the family crest stamped on the back as if he were giving up his last chance for indescribable adventure.

"You see there, Jake. Rome Italy," Brother confirmed.

Ned decided Peelie looked like an escapee from the Milford Military Academy in his postman's uniform. "Parade rest, Peelie," he ordered. Peelie shifted his weight smartly onto his right leg. "Oh my," Ned went on, "another battle plan from the Princess Graziella. I wonder what war she's waging now. I had thought the prince might lock her in the castle tower to keep the world safe for peace of mind. However, I should have known that was too much to expect, nobody has ever dared keep Graziella in confinement for more than a minute or two at a time, sit down, Peelie."

"I wish I could, Ned," Peelie said. "I got to get the rest of the United States mail delivered before noon." In spite of which, he malingered for a moment longer, shifting his weight onto the left leg, perhaps in the hope that he might divine the contents of the impressive packet in Ned's hand.

"Sit down, Peelie," Ned said, holding the envelope against the hazy morning light.

"You ain't come down to the Post Office to renew your passport lately," he told Ned, playing for more time. "If I recall correctly, you would be about due."

"Sit down, Peelie, I'm not at all sure I can survive another of Graziella's reincarnations without a touch of cognac in my coffee," Ned said. "Won't you join me and the boys in an early morning toast to my salad days, Peelie?"

"I reckon not, although what part of your salad days I was privileged to witness was worth a whole lot more than a toast," Peelie declared, shifting his mail sack onto his shoulder.

"Too true," Ned said, dimpling.

"Well, so long, boys, I better get the rest of the mail delivered before they start pitching rocks at the U.S. Postal Service," Peelie sighed. "Don't forget about the passport, Ned, it don't do to let the salad days run all the way out." He stepped down from the porch into the familiar and predictable round.

"Certainly not, dear boy, give my best to your grandfather," Ned called after him, weighing the lavender packet on his hand. "I wonder if Graziella has finally managed to get herself burned at the stake," he said to Brother and Jake.

There was no response.

However, "Rome Italy," Brother Reeves announced again, that being the subject of the day, this time loud enough to be heard across Hooper Street. Ned and Brother and Jake Cullen were drinking coffee on the tiny front porch of Ned Trivett's tiny, salmon-colored house overlooking the pocket-handkerchief lawn which Brother manicured on a regular Saturday basis. He sat now with the hedge clippers in his lap, instructing Jake Cullen with his earnest and guileless face. "That's where John Thomas got up in the dark to run off to, and I guess Julian and old Skinner went over there to bring him back to Milford again, even if he was bad for business when he was here," Brother explained, filling in the details left out by the hard-fact story in the *Morning Herald*.

"I see," Jake said in his early morning voice which was to stay early morning throughout the day and night.

"What it was," Brother rolled on, picking up momentum, "after a while everybody started leaving Julian. First, his beloved brother run off to Rome in the dark, and then his wife, Miss Laura, throwed him out so she could go on the stage. So Julian rambled around till he found old Skinner to keep him company around the clock like he always wanted John Thomas to do but John Thomas wouldn't."

"I see," Jake said again and almost did.

There was a brief pause for consideration.

"Ah! An astonishing history beautifully conceived," Ned took up again, much refreshed.

Neither stunning accomplice paid much attention to this compliment, having grown accustomed to hyperbole on this little porch with the spindly columns and ornate balusters. "I guess I better get started on the hedge," Brother said, frowning upwards to find the sun in the hazy sky.

"Nothing of the kind, dear boy," Ned said. "Stay a while and entertain our house guest, while I read this document from one of the world's great women. You will find," he went on, reluctant to surrender the audience, "all great women are programmed to ruin a man's life to his great delight—usually under the banner of survival of the species. I am most anxious to find out what this particularly glorious one has in mind for me. Now then," he said, delaying the moment a bit longer, "I shall see to it you meet such ladies here, Cullen—Laura Warren you will meet tomorrow afternoon at our party. Susan Bates perhaps another time. However, I'm afraid Susan takes exception to something about the way I conduct my life, although that has not always been the case. However, she is another great woman, they are both of them great women. They will set out to ruin your life, and you will consider yourself fortunate. And now," he said, letting them go at last, "you boys will forgive me while I try to decipher this preposterous document."

They forgave him immediately. And watched him dutifully for a
moment longer, as he smoothed the tissue pages on his knee and began
to read. They leaned forward on their knees, speaking in easy and harmonious cadences about ambling through the days. "Last night, I had a
dream I was somewhere I have never been with people I never saw before,"
Brother said. "Do you have dreams like that sometimes, Jake . . ."

Via degli Scipioni, 32
Roma, Italia
12 June 1962

My dearest Trivett,

  *Oh darling friend from the days of my glorious and very early youth! This
is a most difficult letter. Since I have had not a word of condolence or comfort from
you in this time of tragedy when one tiny message of sympathy from an old and
trusted friend would have made life almost bearable, I must assume you haven't
heard the dreadful news, although it has been carried in the press and on the
radio and in ghastly pictures on the television everywhere in the known civilized
world. What kind of backwater do you live in, you poor old creature? Be that
as it may, if you haven't heard by now, it is my painful duty to inform you that
the Prince di Brabant is dead, God rest his soul, and I am once again a lone
and defenseless woman—albeit this time not a destitute one. At least, not for the
time being. Think of it, Trivett! Only six short and blissful months since my
marriage to Gianni di Brabant, the most charming and generous prince on the
face of the earth, and I must find the strength and courage to begin all over again.
Alas! it seems I am not to know any reasonable span of joy in this lifetime. And
let me tell you right now, here in Rome it has been dog eat dog since the moment
Gianni breathed his last but more of that later, if I can stand the strain. I am
still in deep mourning—you really should have seen me in my veils, Trivett, I
had no idea en deuil could be so becoming—so I feel sure you will understand
the tear blots on these pages knowing me as you do, Ned dear. I have never been
one to suppress my emotions, tragic or otherwise, as you may recall. As a matter*

of fact you may recall, I am physically and psychologically incapable of suppressing my emotions which is probably my good luck because, as you no doubt remember   Well never mind that for now, we can go into all that when I see you next which is going to be a lot sooner than you expected.

What happened is—and this is excruciatingly painful for me—what happened is the Prince drove his Bugatti off a cliff on his way back through the Alps from the races at Le Mans where he had come in second and was killed instantly. I do think God could have let him come in first in view of the circumstances, I mean certainly God must have known what was going to happen later even as the race was in progress. In case you don't already know, let me tell you a Bugatti is one of those little cars about the size of a coffin you have to lie down in—why on earth couldn't he have been satisfied with something more comfortable to run around in like a chicken with its head off like for instance a taxi? I mean to my way of thinking the automobile was invented to get a person from one place to another looking fairly presentable like an airplane or an ocean liner. It escapes me why some men are obsessed with running around in those little bathtubs trying to get ahead of each other at risk of life and limb and, I might add, at incredible expense. I have to admit there is something dead wrong with men but not much. And I ask you, what does it get you for heaven sake? I'll tell you what it gets you, it gets you a hideous silver trophy and an embarrassing picture in the newspapers and dead before your prime, that's what it gets you. In addition to which, it gets you a grief-stricken widow at the mercy of greed-driven in-laws and ex-friends and parasites all over the Italian peninsula who are under the impression that the fortune she has inherited should have been theirs and will go to any length to wrest it from her or at least a good size chunk of it.

Over my dead body.

I ask you, Trivett, have you ever seen an Italian enraged by the suspicion that he has been done out of a fortune that might have been his? Well, let me tell you it's enough to freeze the blood in your veins. And the women are worse than the men, they don't have those glittery black eyes for nothing. Oh, Trivett, I pray to God I have seen the last of these court cases. Everybody known to man down to *and including the damn maids has contested the Prince's will. I am exhausted with crying in lawyers' offices and my widow's weeds have seen their best days. Italians are bad losers, to say the very least. They haven't the faintest notion of good sportsmanship. They go straight from defeat to revenge and they consider death by violence a God-given convenience. I can tell you from personal experience, the Borgias are alive and well. Oh, Ned, Ned, I live my days in the grip of terror. I am a rich woman, Trivett, as the result of the tragic death of my late husband the Prince, but I am not so rich and certainly not such a fool as to give up what is rightfully mine.*

    Over my dead body.

    As a result of all this I find myself in grave peril. I can see the vultures circling. Aiuto! aiuto! as we used to cry in Venice. Oh God, I am fit to be tied.

    I think you will recall from long familiarity it's against my nature to run for help when the chips are down. All my life, I have either picked up my own chips or let them fall where they might, depending on the situation. But this is different. I realized just before dawn this morning when I received my fourth or fifth heavy-breathing telephone call, it was time for me to run for cover. I am on the brink of madness. My resistance is low and my friends ha! ha! have abandoned me. I keep my house in town as dark as Egypt and my villa in the hills is under siege. I am told the peasants are rioting and probably have put the torch to the barns. I haven't closed my eyes for weeks. The hounds of hell are snapping at my heels. Au secours! au secours! as we used to cry in Paris.

    Ah, Paris! Paris! Oh, Trivett, do you remember our rooms with the flowery wallpaper at the top of the tower of the little hotel on the Left Bank where Ezra Pound once lived? And the maids gasping up the stairs with trays of coffee and cognac for breakfast. Oh my, yes, and do you remember the charming young worker in blue overalls we found in Montmartre at three in the morning who promised to fix my trunk and who   Well never mind that for now, we can go into all that when I see you next which is going to be sooner than you expected, if you are still the generous and gallant gentleman you always were.

Be that as it may, as you can see I am in a desperate state and must at last bow to circumstances and run for cover. And since I am unwelcome in my own hometown of Mobile Alabama because of sins long past, yours is the only cover I can think of to run for. I promise not to be any trouble, dear Trivett. I don't need much these days. Just a corner of the couch in the library to curl up in and rest and try to regain a little peace of mind. Ah! Trivett, peace of mind, peace of mind! Did it ever strike you either of us would be praying for peace of mind when we were cutting a swath across the continent of Europe? Well, honey, tout ça change, as we used to cry in Paris. Or help! help! as we used to cry in London. Or once you've stepped in camel shit you're in the circus for life, as we used to cry in the Blue Parrot—on Fifty-Second Street, wasn't it?

Ah, Trivett, Fifty-Second Street! Fifty-Second Street! That was when everybody we knew started writing plays and books and we had to be the people they wrote about—or at least that's what we told ourselves. Do you suppose the time has come at last for us to write about the writers? And, oh, Trivett, do you remember Mrs. Lawson's rooming house where Mrs. Lawson with her poor stricken mouth—what was her name? Nettie, yes—Nettie gave the rooms a "lick and a promise" or rather "a wick and a pwomise" once a week and the johns in the halls smelled like cat boxes? And, oh my, yes, do you remember the prize fighter we found at the San Remo who took exception to my lady of quality ways and broke my   But never mind that for now, we can go into all that when I see you next which is going to be much sooner than you expected.

Yes, well anyway unless I receive word from you to the contrary, I shall arrive in your town—Milford, is it?—the first Saturday in July. You will meet me, won't you, dear Trivett? I shall be traveling with considerable luggage since there are some furs and jewels and flat silver I want to get out of Italy before the axe falls—my dear, we are being overrun by Communists, who could have imagined it? And you must bring along one of those charming young men you used to know so many of, you know the kind I mean, one of those who is lost and needs finding. I must confess I find myself in the flux of a kind of crise d'amour as a *direct result of my recent bereavement. Passion is the enemy of death, as they say. Actually, they say nothing of the kind—I thought that up just this minute, isn't it lovely?*

The entire import of this letter could have been put into one word: HELP!

Graziella, Principessa di Brabant
(alias Grace Jamison)

P.S. Ha! ha! Of course, Trivett, you do know we will continue to use my chosen name rather than the one imposed on me at birth. And of course, you do know you and one or more of your charming companions are always welcome to stay with me in my house in town or at the villa in the Umbrian hills.

Ned fell back in the settee and let the lavender sheets flutter to the floor like so many birds settling into a tree. The young man and the younger man looked up from their talk, reminded again of his presence.

"I don't know whether to laugh or cry," Ned gasped. "We are to have the company of a princess beginning the first Saturday in July. She is coming to ruin our lives bringing her furs and jewelry and silver like Sheba to Solomon," he proclaimed and decided to laugh. "She is at the moment putting down a peasant rebellion; however, we must prepare to run up the flag."

There was no immediate sign of astonishment from the two stunning accomplices except for an insincere look of rapt attention they considered sufficient to suit the moment. Brother Reeves had had no associations with princesses nor had projected any, since fairy tales are seldom read to the sons of tobacco farmers. Jake Cullen had no way of knowing whether or not he had kissed the hand of a princess, but he could assume he had, if he chose, due to the lost mystery of his life.

"Cullen, dear boy, you will have to surrender the royal suite," Ned went on in high good humor now. "You will have to do your sleepwalking from another couch for a while, now let me see—"

"I'm sorry," Jake said apologetically. "I'm afraid sleepwalking is something I have to live with."

"Oh!" Brother hollered, touched once again by this morning of recognition, of discovery of himself in a man much like himself. "Do you walk in your sleep, Jake? Do you wake up standing in the middle of the field, Jake?"

"Don't worry, Ned," Jake said and delayed Brother's persistence with a glance of his narrow blue eyes. "There is plenty of time yet before she is to arrive, and something will have turned up by then."

"Ah! I have no doubt," Ned said, dimpling.

"No, nothing so romantic as that, Brother," Jake said, turning his square-jawed, northern face back to the younger man. "I wake up peeing in a place not meant for the purpose, I'm afraid."

"Too true," Ned acknowledged, dimpling further. "Your palace obviously had indoor plumbing. We must fumigate the hall closet to house the princess's furs."

"Oh," Brother said and sat silent for a moment. "Well," he said, "I reckon I better go on and clip the hedge." He stood up and stretched with an arm over his head and surveyed the lawn the size of a pocket handkerchief, considering the pleasure of the work to be done. He slipped his shirt from his shoulders and hung it over the porch bannister, seeming almost to have forgotten the men who had shared the morning with him. "See you, Jake," he said, "see you later, Ned," and stepped down from the porch into the familiar and predictable round.

"You will note his back as he clips the higher branches," Ned instructed. "And you will see how man once could fly. He is the grandson of Icarus."

CHAPTER TWO

Pushing towards the shore against the return of the surf, Mrs. Skinner Bates, lonelier than lonely for many days now, made a picture in her mind of how she must look coming up onto the beach after a morning swim. She hoped it might make her feel more like a member of the convivial and lively race she had observed pleasuring itself along the strand. However, it did no such thing, as it wasn't at all the kind of picture she had hoped for. She seemed to herself ordinary and forlorn and felt nobody, man nor woman, would bother to turn and look at her a second time. There was nothing of the voluptuous birth from vast and silent depths she had been foolish enough to expect—nothing whatsoever of the placid and self-satisfied Venus standing naked on a shell in the famous painting she had seen in Florence Italy. Well then, she decided, something more disgraceful. "A Disgraceful Woman," she said to herself over the rush of the waters but rejected that as somehow absurd.

"Woman Emerging from the Sea," she suggested and was taken with the title, although there was no lust in it and even less sin. And so, face the truth, it was after all only Susan Bates, thin and growing thinner, coming out of the ocean in the hard light of noon, as she had done yesterday and the day before yesterday and the day before that. She could cer—*certainly* understand why the people sunning themselves on striped towels and under the umbrellas would not be amazed at her ascent onto the beach and turn to ask each other who she might be and where she came from. If they took any notice of her at all, they would probably assume she was on her way home to make a light lunch, which was exactly the case.

Well anyhow, she had done the best she could to conform the picture to a title, but she had to admit she was too much a prisoner of things as they really are to delude herself. What's more, she reminded herself, it was high time she gave up making pictures and titles. They always turned out to be disappointing, and cer—and *certainly* any damn fool could see there were enough disappointments already without inventing more.

Nevertheless, in spite of the excellent advice, she reconsidered the picture of herself as she might appear to the people gathering their towels and chairs to withdraw into their cool houses and concluded it was the sun directly overhead making sockets of her eyes that ruined everything. But then again, probably not. "I need to become another woman entirely," she concluded. "Another Woman," she announced and realized immediately that she was expecting far too much. Things as they really are had never come up to expectation.

Not even with Skinner Bates. With Skinner Bates, she had expected ecstasy twenty-four hours a day which, she realized now, was perfectly ridiculous. "The Foolish Virgin," she suggested further and was relieved that at last she had hit on a title that matched the picture, and she began to laugh. But she cut off laughing when a picture of Skinner stood facing her grinning like a cruel and lawless boy, afflicting her senses. Even the aroma of sweet grasses which was his lingered in her nostrils.

"Oh, my God, Skin, come home," she murmured as she walked up onto the beach and the last wave withdrew from under her feet.

"I'm sorry, what did you say?" a pleasant voice at her shoulder wanted to know. She stood quite still until she had adjusted to an unexpected and unwanted presence.

"Nothing," she said sharply and turned to find a man's dark form standing quite near against the sun. There was something in his easy stance that reassured her. "I didn't hear you, I didn't know you were there," she laughed and shaded her eyes to look up into his face. "I was talking to myself," she went on with the pleasure of sharing a secret she had never meant to keep.

"Why not?" the man asked, approving of her eccentricity. She could see then his even white teeth and blond hair, which she thought was certainly blonder than it should have been.

"People say I'm crazy," she explained further and thought she had no business whatsoever saying that kind of thing to an utter stranger.

"You mustn't let that worry you, people are always saying that. You probably are crazy, we are all crazy," he said in a voice that had not been used that morning or perhaps had been used too much. She thought she should take offense at this curious statement and shifted her gaze from his face to the back of her hand against the sun.

She saw immediately it was gone and was seized with alarm. "Oh, my *God!*" she cried out, "oh, my *God!*" and crouched suddenly as if she had fallen. She combed her fingers frantically through the sand.

"What is it?" the stranger asked and sat on his heels beside her. "What is it, are you all right?" Even in her distress, and even in this heat and against her principles, she felt the radiance of his proximity. She noticed the small black elastic bathing suit and knew immediately he was not from Milford.

"My ring," she said, "my ring. It's gone." Still crouching, she turned her head to look out at the ocean, and the man knew she had given up hope.

"Are you quite sure you had it on?" he asked. She turned quickly to look at him with what seemed to him to be contempt he did not deserve. "Are you quite sure you had it on?" he asked again, thinking perhaps she had misunderstood.

"Well, cer—*certainly* I had it on!" she said, and tears began to spill over her cheekbones and down the hollows of her cheeks. He stood up and thought he might try to lift her to her feet but decided, given her hostility towards him, that might be the wrong move.

"Is there anything at all I can do? I'm Jake Cullen," he said, trying to explain himself.

"I don't give a damn who you are," she said, "just go away and leave me alone." Her body shook and she seemed to him completely alone in the world. He studied the back of her head with the wet hair separated in a white line along her skull and the ridge of her spine curving over the sunburned back.

"I really don't know what to do," Jake said, actually to himself.

"I to—I *told* you what to do. I *told* you to go away and leave me alone," she said. It appeared to Jake this woman had determined to stay crouching like this indefinitely and there was nothing more he could do, no matter how much he would have liked to comfort her.

He stood for a moment longer looking down at her, undecided, and then, without further hesitation, walked away. Susan wondered how he could have abandoned her so easily. She peered around her shoulder at the tall, almost awkward figure striding away from her and got to her feet, regretting she had been insolent again. "Wait! Wait just a minute!" she called out after him.

He turned back halfway and hesitated briefly and then walked back towards her swiftly, as if he were returning to comfort her again. However, he stopped short, keeping a distance between them, and stood with his weight on one leg and his hands on his hips. He smiled, as she had expected he might, but she hadn't known the smile would be like that. He bared his even white teeth like a dog which has been trained to smile for a biscuit. And that was all there was to it. It was hardly a smile at all.

"Please, forgive me," she said to him, as if they had known each other for a long time, and she had been unreasonable in an argument.

"It's quite all right," he said, "but what was it? What could be so important as all that?"

The tears burned on her cheeks in the sun, and she felt the man must be thinking she had a face like a horse, all bone and nose. "My engagement ring," she explained, "I have never taken it off since the day— and he, and my husband is away." She couldn't think why she had volunteered this last or why it should make any difference at all to this strange man, but then, she realized she had said it in her own defense as an explanation for her sudden desperation.

"I do see, I'm sorry," he said, apologizing as if he had become another character in the drama of her life, which he definitely had not. "Is there anything at all I can do? Won't you let me help you look for it?"

She held out an arm, as if she were introducing him to the sea, another character in the drama. "No, don't do that. Just go away. There's nothing anybody can do—nothing," and she thought she might begin to weep again but did not.

Jake felt a sudden surge of tenderness for this odd woman and wanted to give her the ring, if that was what she really wanted. However, he doubted it was the loss of the ring that had disturbed her, it was something more than just the ring. And he discovered her presence had become an obstruction for him like a lost word that has left its echo in the mind and, because it cannot be recalled, takes on a significance beyond its true value. Her happiness, for whatever reason, had become his responsibility, and it made him uneasy, as though she were the ghost of a lover from some forgotten life.

"Won't you let me help you look for it?" he asked once more. "I think you came out of the water about here," and he began to approach her again.

"No!—no, don't do that," she said and put out her hand as though she were warding off a blow, and he noticed how pale the palm was compared to the rest of her body. "No, please. Just go away." She made him a smile not unlike the smile he had made for her and let her arm fall. "I'm being rude again. Insolent. I'm being insolent again. My husband says I'm insolent. I don't mean to be."

"I know that," he said and put his back to her suddenly and walked swiftly away. She faced the fact that she regretted his departure and decided, somewhat dishonestly, she had rejected her last hope of rescue.

"A Woman Abandoned," she whispered, falling back into vicious habits, and watched his form diminishing and wondered why she thought he was handsome when he really was not. Possibly, it was his strong, awkward frame; possibly, it was the way he walked—slightly bowlegged, stalking forward swiftly towards an urgent and indefinite destination. Perhaps, it was that he really wanted to help her, but she felt it was far too late.

She stood sideways to it, gazing out to sea. Her hair had dried to a salty blond, and the tear tracks stung her cheeks. She listened to the hiss of the heat on the lacey water and saw an occasional flash of the sun on the surface, as it sank and humped and fell forward indolently on the shore. She saw a picture of the damn ring on the ocean floor. The sand was drifting over it, and the diamond and the tiny diamonds flashed and were lost to sight. "I believe in omens, but I have no idea whatsoever of believing in this one," she said. And you're talking to yourself again, she reminded herself and recalled the tall blond man whose name she had either not heard or could not remember and turned to find his figure growing smaller and disappearing into the distance. And soon, the black bathing suit was the only thing she could discern and soon nothing.

"Well, he cer—he most *certainly* was blonder than any man has a right to be," she said, taking exception as usual. "Well, to hell with Skinner's ring," she said. "I don't really care," and she was immediately reprimanded by guilt, as if she had been rude to God. Insolent. As if she had been *insolent* to God.

Well then, let me ask you this. Why isn't he at home? Why doesn't Skinner just come home? she argued, probably with God. Give me one good reason why my husband should be permanently attached to my first cousin Julian Warren. Because I remember when I was seven or eight years old, Julian came back from World War Two looking like some kind of heroic hawk, so everybody in Milford and surrounding counties decided he had won the war by himself, and he took off the uniform and kept right on telling everybody how to be and what to do. And because when I was twenty-six, he found Skinner Bates somewhere and stood him up in front of me radiating lust in the middle of my father's living room. And because now he has attached Skinner to himself on a permanent basis like a beloved younger brother, bought and paid for. Why is that? she asked her adversary. And while you're at it, you can give me another good reason why my husband should have to accompany and assist Julian Warren to rescue Julian Warren's actual beloved younger brother who is crazier than everybody else in Milford put together, a fully grown man who fell out of a window in Rome Italy day before yesterday and disappeared off the face of the earth. Probably drunk. Probably all three of them drunk right now somewhere unacceptable in Rome Italy. Explain that, explain why that is while you're—

"Oh, God, I think I'm going crazy," she said aloud, looking over her shoulder to make sure there was no intruder lurking. "I'll tell you the truth," she declared. "I think that blond man was right, I think I'm crazy already."

She regarded her cathedral house in the middle distance, its angular peaks pointing upwards and reflecting the sea and its colors day after day and its phosphorescent restlessness night after night. She wanted to be safe inside it without neglecting her sworn duty to the damn ring. She turned to watch the rising and falling sea, trying to discover how she had managed to lose it there.

"Well, for godsake, that's simple enough. It fell off," she said, "because you are too thin. I'll do nothing but eat ice cream until he gets back, I'll be flesh like that Venus in Florence instead of bones when he leads me up the stairs. I have definitely gone crazy on a permanent basis," she said and glared at the sea.

When she stepped, still wet from the shower, from the deck into her cathedral house, she let her robe fall from her shoulders to the floor and stood naked in sanctuary. She arose from it like a wraith, slender and dark-skinned except where the sun had not touched her. She lay her hands lightly on her small pale breasts and then, after a moment's consideration, repositioned them, so that one hovered gracefully at her breast and the other hovered gracefully at the other place, so that she was as nearly as possible like the woman standing on a shell in Florence. Her green eyes, still stunned from the sun, scanned the sanctuary.

How could he forsake me? she wondered. "How can you forsake—how can you *abandon* your lovely bride of not even a year yet?" A Woman Abandoned.

Skinner.

"If it's like a cathedral, why is it you don't spend more time on your knees?" Skinner had asked her. Skinner was funny. Skinner was too impressed with the trappings of success—to the extent of being tacky to tell you the truth—but he was still funny. That was one of the things that rescued their being together. The other thing was his secret, as he called it—those feverish and intense hours in bed with her when she was the only woman in the world, The Only Woman in the World. She stared wide-eyed in the direction of the hall door, projecting the speechless and consuming culmination with which he had taken her by surprise. It was entirely possible that his secret and being funny sometimes were one and the same thing. Skinner was funny and Skinner was full of original ideas. Sometimes she had thought he might be even more impressed with his secret than he was with the trappings of success and her cousin Julian Warren. But she doubted it seriously. Skinner didn't understand about sin, she decided. She had never heard or even read about anybody else in human history laughing at a time like that. And on top of that, Skinner didn't know the difference between being stark naked and being dressed, he could walk around without a stitch on and not even think who was looking. "I've gone crazy as a bat," she said.

Leaving her robe where it had fallen, she mounted the stairs to the balcony that joined the sides of the roof angle, and walked with ceremony to her bedroom. She lay down softly on the unmade bed. The breath of Skinner's flesh had escaped over time, but a certain weight remained, as though he had left an invisible substitute which would not abandon her.

Later in the afternoon, still touched with sleep, she went out onto the deck in a blue kaftan with a drink in her hand. The beach was deserted as if there had been an announcement on the radio that only she had not heard. In close, the sea was a milky green dissolving into the air, while far out it had darkened to a menacing purple. The sun was brilliant but without the weight of noon.

Her spirit lifted with the light wind that moved in across the water but fell back in dismay when the tall blond man appeared as though he were an apparition out of nowhere near the spot where she had first seen him. He wandered about looking down and crouched occasionally to examine something at his feet. I wish he wouldn't do that, she thought, he knows as well as I do it is gone forever, and he knows as well as I do it makes no difference to me whatsoever.

Then the man stood straight up in the haze, looking out to sea as though he were expecting something or had gone into trance, and after a time, turned his regard in her direction and found her watching him. She understood the sea had betrayed her again, and she grew apprehensive as she did before an approaching summer storm.

"You are a fraud," she said to him, as if the two of them were standing in close proximity, to disguise her anxiety. "You are a liar," she added and went back into the house with her drink, stepping high and fast, deprived of standing alone on her deck so that the rising breeze fluttered the kaftan about her body.

She fell back against the door feeling something had gone terribly wrong, although she couldn't think what that might be. It occurred to her as it never had before in her life that she was alone and defenseless. A Woman Alone. "I am a woman alone," she responded sharply to some adversary that had appeared standing near the glass wall. "I am a woman alone, because I did exactly what Julian decided I would do, because I gave up everything and everybody for Skinner Bates at any instant he might want me, because he was perfect in every detail and smelled like a field of sweet grass. Now wasn't that stupid? Wasn't that stupid, Skinner? God knows who you're fucking now."

That word spoken aloud offended her so grievously, she hurried over to the bar to deny the company of the common woman who had said it. She poured more vodka in her drink, as the adversary and the common woman vanished without a trace.

And drifted back towards the glass wall where she made a picture of herself for the benefit of some fascinating person happening along the beach—for example, possibly even the tall blond person. A tragic figure in blue facing out. Beautiful as Venus, but tragic at the same time.

"Well, at any rate, thank God *he* has gone," she said, looking this way and that along the shore to make sure, and had to admit again she was disappointed. He is mysterious, she explained, and a mystery is always interesting, until some damn fool solves it. She considered for a moment and thought it was perfectly astonishing what came out of her mind sometimes. She decided she would continue talking to herself no matter what people said.

CHAPTER THREE

Laura Warren and her beloved son Jubie were the first to arrive at Ned Trivett's Sunday afternoon party. It didn't occur to Ned to take exception to the child's presence. He was, after all, Julian Warren's child as well as Laura's and Ned recalled some sweet Milford visionary had thought to say the boy had been possessed by an unhappy angel.

"Here come two will take your heart," Ned said to Jake, and rose, dimpling, from the wicker settee on his front porch to receive the guests.

Laura was laughing with her hand over her mouth like a schoolgirl who has heard an unsuitable joke, as she came along the shady sidewalk and through the picket gate.

"We came early on purpose," she sang out in a voice like crystal. "I wanted us to be in our places when the curtain went up. Come along now, Jube."

"Yes'm," the child said, wandering along in the wake of his mother's flowered dress and breathless laughter. He had stopped for a moment to

29

gaze about the landscape with great incurious eyes, as if to try and identify
his location.

"My actress, my divine little Duse!" Ned exclaimed, catching up
her laughter, and stepped down from the porch to embrace her. She
was smiling at Jake over Ned's shoulder, and he was struck by the
fragility of her pale face with its intense blue eyes and the cropped red
hair.

"And this tall person would be the honor guest," she said. "Jubie,
speak to Ned and tell him why you have crashed his party."

"I hate Annie," the child explained looking up at Ned, his face
clouding. "I don't want to stay with Annie no more."

"You can come to see me any time you want to, Jubie," Ned told
him, "morning noon or night, you know that."

"Yessuh," Jubie said and strayed off the walk and stood looking
towards something visible only to himself.

"I'm Laura Warren, one of Ned's inventions," she announced to Jake,
laughing again, and walked up to him with her chin raised as if to give
herself to him. "I would have been dead as a doornail long ago but for
him."

"That makes two of us," the man said without laughing. "I'm Jake
Cullen," he said and took her hand in his. It was trembling slightly, and
he thought possibly he had come upon someone who needed him.

"Come speak to Mister Cullen, Jube," she said.

"Jake," he said, "it's Jake," but she didn't hear him.

"It's a party, and I want a scotch, Ned, where's the bar?" she said.

There was a sudden hesitation in the air, and Ned's amused eyes
darkened. "Asa will bring you one," he told her.

"Oh, Asa!" she exclaimed joyously. "I'll go in and see Asa and get
it myself." She went through the screen door exactly as if it were her own,
flinging an arm behind her as if to say good-by. Ned raised his eyebrows
almost imperceptibly.

Jubie took a slow and deliberate step up onto the porch and stood watching the door as if his mother had walked off the face of the earth.

"She gonna get drunk," he said and turned his face to gaze into Jake's eyes.

"Come here, Jubie," Jake said and sat down again in his wicker chair. "We haven't met yet."

"Nossuh," Jubie said.

"Please, come here, Jubie," Jake said. "I need somebody to talk to." The child drifted towards him and stood just beyond his reach.

"Mislark gonna get drunk," he informed Jake.

"And who is that?" Jake asked and put his hand out flat.

"Miss Lark," Ned explained, observing from the lawn. "He calls his mother Miss Lark."

"She gonna get drunk, I'm gonna pour it all down the drain like Annie," the boy said. "I hate Annie."

"Give me your hand," Jake said.

"Yessuh," the child said and put his opened out hand on Jake's as light as a dried leaf.

"I'm Jake Cullen," Jake said.

"Yessuh."

"Would you call me Jake?" Jake asked.

"Yessuh," the child answered.

"I mean now," he said. "Would you call me Jake now?"

"Yessuh," Jubie said.

Men and women of all ages in cool summer clothes had begun to straggle along the sidewalks under the trees on Hooper Street and through Ned's open gate in twos and threes and indefinite clusters. They had appeared talking to each other and seemed never to have been not talking to each other.

Jubie moved in closer to Jake, resting a hand on his knee, and turned his attention with slight curiosity towards the front gate, where a short florid round-faced woman, daft with delight, was getting down with some difficulty from the back seat of an ancient and upright motor car. Her prominent eyes cast off in opposite directions, possibly due to her reluctance to miss what might be going on at either side. Her head was wreathed with henna-stained curls.

"Here comes Lyla Finch," said the arriving guests.

"Ned, honey, I'm an heiress," she hollered towards Ned, who went to greet her with delight equal to her own. "Don't park too far away, Pudding," she shouted at the sedate and elderly man at the wheel of the vehicle. He rolled away down the street, deaf with great dignity. "Pudding is my property, you know," she announced to the neighborhood.

"I've been aware of that for some time," Ned told her.

"Married forty years yesterday, and Uncle Virgil had the grace to die late in the afternoon. I'm an heiress, honey, and devoted to romance."

"Would you listen to Lyla," guests murmured to each other, smiling and shaking their heads.

"Miss Lyla crazy," Jubie explained, turning his face up to Jake, nodding and nodding and released himself to Jake's protection at that very instant. "Mislark inside getting drunk," he confided.

Jake beheld the boy's beautiful face with profound emotion and beholding him, loved him. He felt desperate to give him some ease but had no idea where ease lay for this sweet creature. He enclosed the fragile little body in his arms and found he had embraced the bones of a bird. "Let's don't worry about Miss Lark, Jubie, I'm sure she'll be all right," he said.

"Nossuh," Jubie said shaking his head in wise denial and shaking his head and shaking his head, still regarding steadily the light and ebullient advance of Ned and the heiress along the walk.

"Tell me something, Ned, honey," she said as she stepped up onto the porch. "Where is the princess, has the princess arrived yet? We'll recognize each other right off the bat, it takes one to know one, you know."

"The princess' arrival is imminent and has been for some years now,"

Ned told her. "However, I do expect her any day, having heard from her only yesterday morning. I have an idea you'd like something to drink pending her arrival."

"Oh, I've got my Hadacol in my purse," she said. "I don't drink anything but Hadacol these days, it keeps me young and snappy, and I don't tear down in one evening everything it took me twenty years to build up. Hello, Jubie child, my Lord, who's that boy you're with?"

"This is my friend Jake Cullen," Ned said, having the time of his life. "He has come from California."

"I can see that," she said. "California always did turn out the best in men and vegetables. I'm Lyla Finch and I'm an heiress and a firm believer in romance. Do you believe in romance, Mr. Cullen?"

"Jake," Jake said in his worn voice and made a smile. "Of course I do, I would be a fool not to." He stood up to greet her, and Jubie clung to his hand.

"Well, honey, I haven't seen anything like you since I left the Mississippi delta," she carried on at top volume. "I'm a Mississippi princess, you know, but that's all gone now—burned to the ground, gone with the wind like that little Georgia woman said. My daddy was in cotton, Pudding is in leaf tobacco. Jubie child, where is your mother?" she asked rummaging through a purse with fringe dancing on it.

"She inside getting drunk," Jubie said, regarding her with misgiving.

"My Lord, I've gone off and left my Hadacol," Lyla shouted, having exhausted the purse. "Here comes Pudding now, maybe he thought to bring it. Pudding is my property," she explained to Jake.

"So I heard," Jake said. Pudding was making his way through the company along the walk at the moment. He looked to be a lovely silver-haired gentleman resigned to life's variations.

"Come look at this stunning young man Ned found in California, Pudding honey," Lyla hollered at him. "Did you bring my Hadacol?"

"What's that you say, Lyla?" Pudding said, not even looking up.

"Deaf as a post," Lyla explained.

Laura came out through the screen door laughing with her head thrown back on her long white neck. She carried a drink in her hand as if it didn't matter. Jubie observed her without emotion. He took Jake's hand in both of his. Jake was his property. Jake pretended he was accustomed to being somebody's property.

"Well, at last, here she is!" Lyla announced to all present. "Here's our very own Maude Adams right here in Milford North Carolina—"

"Lyla—" Laura went on laughing and curtsied almost to the floor of Ned's porch, acknowledging the acclaim.

"Tell me something, Lark," Lyla said. "Is Asa serving inside?"

"He is," Laura said, taking in quick little breaths.

"In that case, I'll bid you a-dew for the time being," Lyla said. "Maybe Asa knows the formula for Hadacol. You come on along with me, Pudding honey."

"Oh, look! Here is my handsome son with the guest of honor," Laura exulted, holding out her arms in wonder, "the two handsomest men in the world." She thrust herself into the white wicker chair next to them, so that she extended into one long line from her perfect nose down to the points of her shoes. "I wonder would you be good enough to adopt me and my son, Mister Cullen?" she asked, looking misty-eyed and blissful into his face.

"It's Jake," he said. "Yes," he said. "Yes, I would."

People were still arriving along the front walk, exclaiming and sounding surprised at almost anything and even amazed when as a matter of fact they were not. Ned appeared to have achieved Nirvana. They filled his tiny house with babble and the heat of joyful congregation and spread out over the lawn in the pools of afternoon sunlight, speaking of what had happened and what would probably happen next within the circumference of their world.

At a certain pitch of high conviviality, Ernie Dexter pulled up at the front gate in a red truck with Bladens Beach Playhouse painted on the door. It was loaded down with an astonishing number of young and heedless summer theater apprentices who had ridden in a high wind all the way from Bladens Beach arguing about sex and fame about which they knew next to nothing. They unloaded out of the back of the truck and dispersed among the guests like an invasion of barbarians.

"Here come Laura Warren's rag, tag, and bobtail," Rose Medallion said to Ellen Grissom, "what do you suppose she sees in them?"

The rag, tag, and bobtail kissed Laura, each in turn, and called everybody else darling and said shit out loud when the occasion presented itself or even when it didn't. They devastated the hors d'oeuvre trays and confounded Asa among the liquor bottles. Ernie Dexter in his mattress-ticking shirt floated high behind his stomach among the company, speaking in the affected theater voice his apprentices detested. He became the celebrity of the afternoon and so was utterly content. "Oh, yes, of course," he said, pitching his voice from the diaphragm, "I'll be directing a number of fine actors coming to star this season. However, our best production will be *Summer and Smoke* with your very own Laura Warren in the lead."

"If the jackass knows what's good for him, he'll put that show on first," Rose murmured to Ellen. "You know how Laura can fall by the wayside."

"And she has brought that unfortunate child with her again," Ellen sighed.

"Well, as you know, she does as she pleases," Rose went on. "And I must say she seems very comfortable with the blond man Ned found in California. The three of them make a regular little family portrait sitting out there on the porch like that."

"He is probably a stage actor of some kind," Ellen concluded. "You know how Laura and Ned are wild on the subject of stage people. I don't understand it, it's like some terrible disease."

A trio of robust young men was holding close conference in the

corner of the picket fence, engaged in fantastic speculation over their bourbons with water. "Which one do you suppose this guy Jake belongs to?"
Walter Strain wanted to know.

"Maybe both of them," Rabbit Kendrick suggested and they burst
into raucous laughter, depending on it that such might be the case. They
set up a golf game for the next day and dispersed feeling somehow things
had gone far enough for the time being.

"I'm so glad you and my child like each other," Laura crooned to
Jake, putting her chin nearly onto his shoulder. "It means you are a man
of exceptional perception and special imagination, doesn't it, Jubie?"

"Yes'm," Jubie murmured, gazing off into the gathering and leaning
against Jake's other shoulder.

"Do you give him vitamins?" Jake wanted to know. "I have some
quite wonderful ones I brought with me from California."

"Vitamins?" Laura said and withdrew her chin from his shoulder,
possibly offended. "Of course, I give him vitamins, don't I, Jube?"

"No'm," Jubie said.

"These are really rather wonderful," Jake went on. "I'll read you the
label."

"I can hardly wait," Laura said. "And could you get me a scotch at
the same time—oh, dear Mister Cullen, would you be kind enough to
adopt me and my son? We are both orphans."

"Yes," Jake said. "I told you I would. We are put here to take care
of each other—I have concluded that is what life is all about."

"Have you now?" Laura said, rearing back and widening her blue
eyes. "I have always wanted to know what life is all about, and there's
my answer, plain as day. Now then, what about that scotch?"

Jubie withdrew from Jake's knee and regarded the two of them with
grave uncertainty. "Where Mister Jukes, Mislark?" he asked. "When Mister Jukes coming home, Mislark?"

"His father, Julian Warren," Laura explained, "whose life has seen enough of mine and vice versa. Soon, Jube," she said, "he'll be back soon."

"You and me gotta go home and wait for Mister Jukes, Mislark," the child insisted and separated himself at a lonely distance from the other two members.

"Oh, Jube, don't make me go home," she said. "Maybe you could have supper with Missook, I think Missook would love to have you for supper, would you like that?"

"We can all go see Missook," Jubie confided in them and nodded and nodded.

"I'll go call Susan," Laura said and stepped off into the crowd unhesitating, flinging out an arm, not even speaking to friends who smiled after her.

"Please, come talk to me again, Jubie," Jake said.

The guests began to scatter. Some drifted still chattering out the gate and along the sidewalks to their suppers. However, the three Street sisters still slouched about at the end of the porch in their lawn frocks and haircuts from another era. As was the custom, they had left their diminutive husbands at home to stand guard over the two daughters the three couples seemed to have produced communally. The husbands were grateful for this pleasant duty, since it seemed, in small part, to justify living on their wives' considerable fortunes and since their wives found connubial rites unsatisfactory payment in kind.

"There goes Laura Warren, still perfectly beautiful and falling by the wayside again, if I'm not mistaken," Ashley informed her sisters. "And Julian off with that Bates boy rambling all over Rome Italy trying to lasso his beloved brother John Thomas to come back home again. I wish somebody would tell me why he don't leave him alone."

"I understand she pitched Julian out, bag and baggage," Diana said, thin as a stick and longing to go home. "Apparently, the tragedy of that child and Julian watching her like a hawk day and night is more than her nerves can stand."

"Well, honestly! The Warrens are the most peculiar people I ever heard of," Lucy joined in, picking up the melody.

"The most curious people on the face of the earth," Ashley exclaimed, reaching up with her arms to anchor her hair with combs and tortoise-shell hairpins.

"Constance Warren, poor creature, sat down in her chair after breakfast one morning and went mad as a hatter before nightfall," Diana reminded everybody.

"Crazy as bats, every last one of them," Lucy concluded.

"Come on," Diana said, "let's say good-by to Ned. If there's a princess here, I wish somebody would point her out to me."

"Why doesn't he invite somebody sensible like Lady Bird Johnson?" Lucy complained. "At least she has a head on her shoulders."

"What are you talking about, Lucy?" Diana said. "The woman's from Texas. She's probably wild as a buck."

"And rich as cream," Lucy said.

"Rich as cream," Diana added. "My God, look at Lyla, she's left her Hadacol at home again."

"If you didn't know who she was, you'd think you were out with the wrong people," Ashley said.

Lyla Finch with a Bladens Beach Playhouse apprentice on either arm had catapulted out through the screen door. Her eyes seemed to have splayed out even more wildly in opposite directions, and several henna-stained curls had come uncoiled. The two stalwart young men eased her down the porch step and supported her along the walk towards the curb where Pudding waited beside the rear door of the upright car. "I haven't seen anything like you two since I left the Mississippi delta," Lyla let fly. "Do you boys believe in romance?"

They said, yes ma'am, they did.

CHAPTER FOUR

When Susan opened the door to her living room again, it was cold and the telephone was ringing and seemed to her to have been ringing for some time. However, she was so spent, she didn't care whether she answered it or not. Except the damn thing continued to ring for such a long time that, oh my God, it could be Skinner, and she rushed across the room, her kaftan clinging wet dark blue to the knees. When she put the receiver to her ear, a woman was laughing, nervous and spasmodic, and she could hear the chatter of voices in the background.

"Laura?" she said. "Is that you, Laura?"

"Oh, Missook," the woman's voice said, still laughing in a high and fragile register. "Susan? Is that you, Sue?"

"It's me, Laura, where in the world are you?" Susan asked. "Who are all those people?"

"You don't sound like yourself, Sue, what has happened to your voice?" the woman asked, forgetting to laugh.

39

"I've been throwing a fit down by the ocean—crying and running into the water and hollering I don't care," Susan said and saw how funny that was really.

"Oh, *dear*," Laura said. "He'll be back in a few days, Susan. Along with the one I was married to."

"Oh, *dear*," Susan came back. "I'm sure I don't know when they'll be coming back and, to tell the truth, I don't think I care. I don't think I like Skinner anymore. Maybe I never did." They paused to let the agitation caused by this statement dissipate on its own. "Where in the world are you, Laura, and who are all those others?"

"At Ned's. I'm at Ned Trivett's house with a lot of other people. We are waiting for the princess as usual, and Lyla Finch has left her Hadacol at home again. We're all going to have dinner at—"

"Oh, *dear*," Susan said.

"Now, Susan, don't say 'oh dear' like that," she said. "There's this man here. I think he's come from California to save us all," and she began laughing again in quick little gasps. "I wonder if Jesus was tall and blond and good-looking."

"And blond? Don't tell me he's blond—Mislark, you're drinking."

"Shut up, Susan. He's explaining to me what life is all about, and I've wanted to know what life is all about for as long as I can remember. All you have to do is read the directions on the bottle and take your vitamins and help people who seem to need help. I can't think why I hadn't figured that out for myself." She went off into another run of laughter.

"Oh, *dear*," Susan said. "I think I know the one, is his hair blonder than nature intended it to be?"

"Well, yes, I think you could say that."

"Oh, *dear*. And has he got small, blue eyes?"

"That's the one, that's the one all right," Laura said. "I don't know how he sees through them. Where on earth did you—"

"Wait till you get a good look at the bathing suit. That'll show you a thing or two," and they went off into harmonious, two-voiced laughter, practiced over years of agreeable intimacy. "Oh, Laurie, I wish you," Susan started out, going serious again. "I've lost my." She stopped short and turned her head to stare green-eyed at the white wall behind her.

"What, Sue? You've lost what?"

"That person was at the beach today in front of my house. Laura, what in the world are you doing at Ned Trivett's house? Laura, are you drinking?"

"Shut up, Susan. Listen, Sue. Sue, could you—wait a minute." A boisterous voice in the background was saying something to her. "I don't know, just wait a minute," she said to the voice. "Listen, Sue. Would you do me a favor?"

"Probably," Susan said. "What is it?"

"Sue, I don't know, I had to bring my child here with me, and he's not particularly happy—"

"Small wonder, poor old Jubie. What possessed you to do that, Laura?"

"Oh, Sue, you know—he decided he hated Annie, and I just couldn't—anyhow, Sue, we all want to go out and have dinner and be saved by this good-looking man from California, and I was wondering if you could give Jubie his supper and put him up for the night. Could you do that for me, Sook? I *do* so want to be saved—just a *minute!*" she said to voices in the background.

"You're drinking, Lark."

"Shut up, Susan. I'm going to be an actress again, Sue," she said, and they considered the history of regret that lay between them over the years. "It's all right, Sue, it really is. Could you do that for me, Sue?"

"It's always all right, Laura," Susan said, standing in her father's image, unpleasantly wise. "Oh, Lark, what do you need with all those left-over people? You've *always* been an actress for as long as anybody can remember."

"It's different this time, it can be different. I belong to myself now," Laura said. There was another pause, and they both sighed (sigh) into the telephone, so that the other could understand the sacrifice. And then, they laughed again, understanding very well.

"Well, all right, Lark, bring Jubie on over," Susan said. "I've wanted to see him anyhow, but don't bring any of those people."

"The savior from California is going to bring him over," Laura said. "I'll tell him where you live. Ned insists I shouldn't drive, oh, Ned, *do* shut up!"

"Oh, *dear*, what have you gotten me into, Laura? The damn fool already knows where I live, I'm afraid. Well (sigh), what's his name?"

"Jake, I think. Yes, Jake. And he's really very nice, and he's good-looking, and Jubie will be so happy. He's always happy with you, Missook."

"I'm doing this for Jubie. I wouldn't do it for anybody else—not even you, Lark. So all right, send him on over, and look here now, Lark, don't drink too much. You know how you—"

"Shut up, Susan. You sound like Julian. I'll pick him up in the morning, and thank you, Missook," and turning away from the telephone, she began laughing at something one of the left-over people was saying. Probably Ned Trivett.

Susan hung up and regarded the telephone for a long time as if to find out whether or not it was an adversary, and then, she went upstairs to change.

Trying to think of herself as imperious, Susan stood with another vodka in her hand in the doorway at the top of the steps which rose from under the house. She wasn't absolutely sure what imperious was like, but she did know she had to hold her head high and forget about standing around looking like Venus—at least for the time being. She had pulled her hair straight back into a knot at the crown of her head, which did nothing to soften the arch of her nose or the narrow temples. However, she wore slacks and an old shirt of Skinner's which disguised to some degree how thin she had become.

"You didn't find it," the blond man informed her, as if the ring had been his only concern since he had seen her last. Jubie was mounting one step at a time, incapable of haste, stepping up with one leg and bringing the other beside it and stepping up again. He glanced up at Susan with eyes which, had they not been so wide and crystal blue, could have been those of a very old man.

"Neither did you," Susan responded. "You wasted a lot of time for nothing," and she thought that was as imperious as she could be without being simply disagreeable.

"Not entirely wasted," he said, turning back with some impatience to help Jubie. "Come on, Jubie, you're old enough now to walk up steps like everybody else."

"He has always walked up steps that way, I *like* the way he walks up steps," she said. "Hello, Jube."

"Yes'm," Jubie said, nodding his head several times without looking up again.

"I'm Jake Cullen," the man said.

"So I've heard," she said. "Come on, Jubie, Mister Cullen is in a hurry to get back to the party. I understand there are a number of people there waiting to be saved. And we are going to have a private party of our own, we're going to have supper on the deck and spend the night together. Won't that be fun?"

"No'm," Jubie said, maneuvering the last step. She realized suddenly how tall the man was as he stood beside her, and she felt he was looking down at her with too much curiosity and thought it was time for him to go now.

"Sure it'll be fun, Jubie," he said above her head.

"He can speak for himself," Susan said.

"Sorry," he said, sounding tired and hoarse. "I just thought that—"

"Jesus loves me 'cause the Bible tells me so," Jubie chanted tunelessly as he walked away from them without curiosity. His curly hair seemed to have been blown forward once and to have remained that way, as though there were always a soft wind at his back—Laura's hair, Julian's colors— and his eyes were so completely guileless and candid they appeared to be observing what was within their range for no particular reason.

"Jubie happens to be a friend of mine," the man said. "I just thought that . . . sorry about the ring, I'll look for it again tomorrow."

"No, please, God, don't do that," she said. "Thank you very much for everything, but I think you can just forget that. I have."

"What we going to have for supper, Missook?" Jubie asked her.

"I haven't thought about that yet, Jubie—"

"Tomato sandwich," Jubie announced and went to the glass wall and looked out, standing quite still, as if he were hearing something, and whispered a mist on the glass.

"How old is he?" the man asked, frowning slightly.

"I don't think that's—"

"Eight," Jubie said with conviction and looked back at them over his shoulder, his cherubic lips parted so that his front teeth were visible. "Eight, going on nine. You going to have supper with me and Missook, Jake?"

"No, Mister Cullen is going back to have dinner with your mother," Susan said firmly, "and she must be starving by now."

"She getting drunk," Jubie said. "You can have supper with me and Missook, Jake—"

"No, he cer—no, he can *not*, Jubie," Susan said, wishing the man would go on and leave.

"Look here, where have I gone wrong?" he asked. "My name is Jake, and I'm a visitor here in this town for a while. Aren't you going to ask me in for a drink?"

"No," Susan said.

"No," Jubie said, shaking his head from side to side, "I'm gonna pour it all down the drain like Annie. I hate Annie."

"No," Susan confirmed. "I think they must be waiting for you at the restaurant."

"Do you now? Very well then," the man said, shrugging his shoulders. "I'll come back for him later."

"No, you won't," Susan said. "His mother will come get him tomorrow morning."

"I'll come check on the two of you later," he said.

"No, you won't—you won't do that either. My husband has been in Rome for well over a week now, and I have been perfectly all right without anybody checking," she said, looking at him for the first time and enforcing her statement with intolerant green eyes.

"I'll be back to check on the two of you later," he repeated and went down the steps so swiftly, in two or three long strides, she was startled. It was almost as fast as a fall.

"No—no, don't. Don't do that," she called after him, realizing that the man had taken the trophy in the imperious race without even trying.

"Jake coming back to check, Jake coming back to check," Jubie chanted.

"Oh, Jubie, for god*sake,*" she said. "Come on then, let's make supper together and eat out on the deck before it gets too dark."

"Tomatoes is terrible now, Missook," he told her. "You can't find no good tomatoes now."

"That's not entirely true, Jube. Mrs. Bender is beginning to get some good ones," she said, taking up the assumption that the two of them were normal and familiar adults, as she always did without knowing it when they were alone together.

"Tomatoes is terrible now, Missook," he insisted, looking up at her and shaking his head. "Annie say tomatoes is terrible now."

"Annie Davison knows a lot, but she doesn't know half as much as she thinks she knows," she said.

"Yes'm," Jubie said.

They ate supper on the deck in the declining light. The sky and the sea had lost rose and orange and lavender, and only silver and mauve and green remained, running horizontal. The waves followed one another in ragged, disconsolate parallels and hump-humped comfortably on the shore. Time hesitated, withholding the last of the day. Two boisterous young men in red bathing trunks leapt in the surf like dolphins, as though they had to expend surplus energy in order to survive the night, and an occasional joyous and witless shout would reach as far as the strange and apparently alienated pair on the deck.

Susan felt at peace for the first time that day. She loved the child and thought him very beautiful with his cap of hair and tall forehead and the swollen lips of a cherub, and, suddenly, she thought of herself as beautiful too. The two of them shared the difficult necessity of constraining their emotional natures, and neither questioned the behavior of the other. She ate very little, sipping vodka and watching the wide blue eyes of the boy gazing at first one part of the seascape and then another, recording information that would never be communicated. Laura's eyes, Julian's color, some evidence given by each partner at that ecstatic instant lying together; funny how it works, she considered. If I should ever have a son, I hope he would be lucky enough to get Skinner's. . . . She perished that thought, glancing about to make sure no adversary had seen it, and shifted emphasis. "Do you want to watch television later, Jube?" she asked him after a while.

"What else I got to do, Missook?" he said. "I got to do something to keep from being crazy. I ain't got no other children."

"You don't need other children, Jube. You're too smart for other children. God made you too smart."

"God made me too smart for other children," he explained to her nodding and nodding and nodding and put his napkin on his plate.

"Sit down and finish your sandwich," she said. "We have to gain some weight before Mister Jukes and Skinner get home. We're too skinny."

"Then, how come you don't eat yours?" he asked her. "How come you just drink likker, Missook?"

"I've been upset today, Jube. I'm sorry."

"You been upset today, Missook," he informed her. "Is Mislark upset, Missook?"

"No, I think Mislark is having a good time for a change."

"Mislark getting drunk," he said, observing the young men leaping about in the water as if they were a projection on a screen. "She falling down on me again."

"She's going to be all right this time, Jube," Susan said.

"No, she ain't," he said shaking his head and shaking his head, as he walked away from the table and went into the house and appeared at the glass wall looking out at her with enormous, joyless eyes.

"Oh, my God," she said softly and gathered the dishes and followed him into the house.

CHAPTER FIVE

After undressing Jubie and listening to his prayers and getting him into the bed farthest from the window overlooking the ocean, she stood outside his door for a while gathering her strength again. She was glad she had elected to sit on the bed during the prayer, as it had become a long and taxing ritual since she had last attended. He had God-blessed everybody in his acquaintance, which was extensive, if casual. So far as she could determine he had left at least half of the Milford telephone directory in a state of grace. And she realized how painful Laura's life must be in spite of her protestations that the child was a gift beyond value.

And so, she went out onto the deck again and lay down in a deck chair in the moonlight, curving her arm over the back of it, facing away from the restless, phosphorescent sea, shunning it for what it had done to her. She was reminded of the ring buried in the sand on the ocean floor, and she was reminded of sleeping for so many nights in a bed without Skinner swaddled in sheets, swimming in oblivion next to her, and she was reminded of Laura, drunk somewhere and laughing for air. And she was reminded of the possible arrival of the tall, blond man for whom, as far as she could tell, she had no feeling whatsoever one way or another. Except that he didn't belong here. Except that it was as if—she remembered Laurie telling her how it was—as if she were in a play and the cue for her entrance was coming up, and she had to be prepared for it, whether she wanted to or not. The world was waiting in the dark to watch and listen and pass judgment that could condemn you to a life like any other or project it upwards into a superior realm.

"I'll tell you what life is," she said, looking up at the countless and indifferent stars and the pale, insubstantial moon which was wearing away on one side. "I'll tell you what life is," she said to them, said to anybody listening including mostly herself probably. "Life is an arrest warrant." She laughed and enjoyed thoroughly having settled *that* problem once and for all, and she reached for her drink which was as translucent and cool as the moon.

When she had finished her drink, she considered seriously being sensible and respectable and doing the right thing, Julian, and going to bed and not answering anything but the telephone in case Skinner should call, and maybe not even that. But why—why should I reduce myself to mediocrity? she asked. "Don't let them reduce you to mediocrity—that's what father said to me once, thank you father," she said and on the strength of the recall, she decided to get herself another drink. She was glad she had thought of that, glad she remembered that again.

But, oh my God, then the beams of automobile headlights lanced along the distant highway and then turned into her drive and lanced up and then down again, as the car went over the hump at the entrance. She sat up alert and erect and half rose to her feet and sat back down again and checked the buttons on Skinner's shirt and lay down again and curved her arm over the back of the chair, as it had been before. *I have not moved.* The car pulled up behind the house where she couldn't see it, crunching the gravel, and stopped, and the lights were extinguished as though the car had vanished off the face of the earth.

He appeared without a sound where the deck rounded the corner of the house, as if he had been there all along and had known all along where to find her. He stood motionless, the moon high behind him, and she was uneasy at the apparent stealth, until she saw he was barefoot. It could have been no other man in the world. He was unmistakable.

"What are you doing?" he asked after some time had passed, still not moving.

"I'm getting drunk and wondering whether or not to tell you to get your pushy California ass off my property," she said, going way beyond imperious.

"When am I going to meet a Southern lady, I wonder," he said, and she was aware again of his worn-away voice.

"You're talking to one right now," she told him. "If you were expecting the sweet, prissy type that doesn't acknowledge bodily functions, you have been misled along with a lot of other people, including the sweet, prissy type. They are the ones with no brains or no humor or who haven't made the grade yet."

"I see," he said. "I'm glad to find that out. I guess I've seen too many movies."

"Everybody has seen too many movies. What do they know?" She shook the ice in her glass and watched him closely, freezing the moment. "What are *you* doing?" she asked, keeping him at bay with some pleasure. "I am told you are here to save us all. Have you saved anybody yet?"

"I've saved Laura Warren for the time being. I delivered her to that gray tomb she lives in. It's really quite wonderful, but it seems to be sinking into. . . ." The unsure light and the rush of the surf submerged him briefly, but he recovered. "Where is the booze?" he asked, strengthening his voice.

She considered a moment, looking at him with her long, hollow-eyed face, and then released him. "Inside on the bar, and take my glass with you. It's full of nothing but the moon, and that is not enough." God, that was beautiful, she thought.

He broke the spell that imprisoned him in the shadows and moved swiftly, his bare feet sounding on the deck now, and took her glass and went into the house for what seemed to her to be no time at all and was back with the drinks and pulled a canvas chair up to the table and sat down and lit a cigarette and said nothing. And it appeared to her that was all there was going to be to it, and so she tried to think of something insolent and provocative to say but decided against it.

"How is she, is she bad?" she asked.

"If you're asking me if she's drunk, yes. Quite drunk. She says her name is Miss Lark, and if it weren't for that man she was married to, she could be flying."

"The only flying she can do, she's doing right now. Poor, poor little Mislark. That's Jubie's private name for her, Jubie has private names for us all."

"Yes, I know," he said. "I found that out. It wasn't easy. Where is Jubie?"

"Where in hell do you think he would be at this hour? He's upstairs in bed where he belongs."

"What's wrong with that boy?"

"Nothing," she said, going hoarse, and looked at him with a kind of ferocity. "Nothing."

There was a long, constrained silence between them during which he finished his cigarette and most of his drink. "I wonder if you could say Jake," he said.

"Certainly," she said. "Jake."

"That wasn't exactly what I had in mind," he said. "However. And at the risk of another rebuff, I would like to ask you what went wrong with Miss Lark——"

"Her name is Laura."

"—Laura and her husband. She's very attractive when she's—"

"*Yes*," she said firmly. "Laura and Julian. Poor Mislark. Poor Mister Jukes too. They were driving each other crazy because of being two people. You'll find that to be the case in most marriages."

"But not in yours."

"But not in mine."

"Then, why is he in Rome?"

"My God, you *are* doing research, aren't you? I wonder for what reason. My husband is in Rome helping Julian Warren rescue his brother who doesn't need rescuing. Julian's brother fell out of a window and lost his memory, but he'll survive. He's a fairy."

"Whatever that is," the man said.

"Visiting with Ned Trivett, you of all people should certainly know what a fairy is."

"Ned Trivett is a good man," he said.

"Ned Trivett is a good fairy," she said and laughed, but he did not. "He says he's a nonpracticing poet," she said, trying to make up for disappointing him, but that was funny too, and she laughed again. There was another period of constrained silence, and she considered saying, Now then, you go on back to Ned Trivett's where you belong and I'm going upstairs to bed where I belong, but, "You have finished your drink, and I'm finishing mine, and would you be kind enough to get us another one, vodka and tonic," she said instead. She considered repeating the beautiful phrase about her glass being full of nothing but the moon but decided once was enough for one evening. He got up in that sudden way, as though he had come to a decision, and went into the living room and was back with a tray with the vodka bottle and ice and glasses in what she thought must be world record time. "God, you're fast," she said.

"Why waste time?" he said.

"Waste whose time?" she asked and looked at him with her head tilted on one side. "You probably think we're going to fuck, but we're not." Imperious was long gone.

"Southern ladies say that word too, do they?" he asked.

"Southern ladies—*any* lady says what she feels the situation calls for. Anyhow, we're not going to."

"Truth be told, I hadn't given that any serious thought until this very moment when you brought it up."

"I don't know how to do it with anybody but my husband anyway," she said, resenting his not having given it any serious thought.

"It works about the same whoever it is," he said, lighting another cigarette.

"I don't believe that, I refuse to believe that," she said and sat up halfway, putting her hands to her bosom, as if they held a cover, and stared at him hollow-eyed in the dark and lay back down again.

"You're probably right," he said. "I mean, you're probably right not to believe it. I take that back. It's just that I've been around too long."

The dark and probably unacceptable history hidden in this statement interested her enormously, and she thought he probably meant it to. She resisted for a moment being seduced by it but found it irresistible. "I think I've earned the right to a little research of my own, since you seem to have decided to make your headquarters here for the evening. What are *you* doing? What are you doing in Milford? *And* at Ned Trivett's?"

"I hustle," he said.

This one galvanized her attention completely, and she paused in her investigation, trying her best not to betray her curiosity. "What on—what on *earth* does that mean?" she asked. "Hustle. I believe that can mean a number of things."

"In my case, it means I use whatever personal resources I have at my disposal to get what I feel I deserve. It means that, like Miss Lark—

excuse me, like Laura, I was born to fly. However, at the moment, I find myself with no limb to rest on, and so, I have come to rest on whatever limb is available."

"Until a better limb presents itself," she suggested.

"Until a better limb presents itself."

"Well then, it behooves you to seek out the rich and lonely," she suggested further.

"The rich and lonely seek me out. It's a kind of unspoken contract," he said. "And I feel it's usually to their advantage."

"*Do* you now?" she said. "Well, Ned Trivett is neither rich nor lonely, he—"

"Nonpracticing poets rarely are."

"—and let me inform you that you have flown to the wrong tree this time. Some of us are lonely, but none of us is what you could call rich. We think of ourselves as having been rich some generations back, but we weren't even that. So you've struck out."

"Not really. That doesn't matter," he said. "I know when I'm needed."

"At what point in your life did you experience this revelation that you are capable of rescue?" she asked and laughed lightly.

"On the day of my birth, four years ago in a motel room in a little town in Mexico," he said easily, and she saw that he had set another trap, but she'd be damned if she'd step into this one. It took willpower.

He fixed the drinks again, as if he hadn't said anything of any unusual import, and sat back to smoke some more, apparently content and assured that what he had said had been accepted and a contract drawn. She wanted to let him know his assurance was unfounded, and she thought of several more things she wanted to ask him but couldn't formulate the questions she thought would get her the right answers without betraying her intense interest.

"I'm drunk," he said and got up and went to the deck railing back of her chair, she supposed to look at the ocean and rearrange his thoughts, as she was rearranging hers. However, there was a splattering in the sand some ten feet below the deck which startled her, and she took in a quick breath and lay quite still. The splattering went on for a long time and stopped. And splattered several short times after that. And stopped. There was a pause, and neither of them moved for some seconds, until there was a zipping sound and he returned to his chair and lit another cigarette and leaned back to look at the night sky and was content again.

Susan did not look at the night sky. She looked straight ahead without seeing anything at all. "What—what*ever* possessed you to do that?" she asked after examining several possible versions of her unusual situation.

"Do what? Oh," he said. "Why do you ask? It's one of those bodily functions Southern ladies don't mind acknowledging."

"Why do I *ask*?" she said, astounded. "Well for one—for *one* thing, I would say there are better places to pee. Just for example, my husband goes into the bathroom and closes the door."

"I don't happen to be your husband, and—"

"You cer— you most *certainly* are not—"

"I most certainly am not—and that happened to be the most convenient spot at the moment. Why waste time? And I hadn't finished what I was saying."

"You *never* finish what you are saying, and I'm not—"

"It seems to me that you have done most of the talking so far," he said.

"You pee *very* loud," she rebuked him in such a way that suggested he could have played *pianissimo* if he had so chosen. "Thank God, it's late, and the neighbors are probably in deep alcoholic sleep by now. Don't do that again. I don't like it, and I won't have it."

"I'll try to remember not to do it again."

"It doesn't seem to occur to you that I'm a woman—"

"A Southern lady," he corrected her.

"—woman, and you will definitely not do it again," she said and put her drink down on the metal table with considerable emphasis. "I think at this point we had better go our separate ways, so good night. Good *night*. Go pee off the porch at Ned Trivett's house. Go save Ned Trivett. He should be accustomed to being saved by now. God knows, everybody in Milford has tried to save him without success."

"I wonder if you could say Jake," he said.

"Jake," she said. "Good *night*. Go home. Go to Ned Trivett's. Go somewhere. Go anywhere."

"I'm too drunk to drive," he said.

"Well, for godsake," she gasped, sitting up in her deck chair facing him straight on. "That's *your* problem. You certainly—you *certainly* can't stay here."

"Why not?" he asked as easy as that. "I can sleep in Jubie's room. After all, I'm a visitor."

"You're what? Visitor? Well, let me just (gasp), let me just tell you you're not the kind of visitor I'm used to. Or want. And you're definitely uninvited. Now. If you'll just walk up the beach *that* way—" she pointed dramatically, sitting very erect, holding the imaginary cover to her breast with the other hand "—for about a mile and a half and then take a sharp right—" she changed the direction of her gesture "—for about three miles, you'll find Ned Trivett's house where I assume you are invited. That's where you belong. Hustling at Ned Trivett's house."

"That's nonsense, and you know it," he said, unperturbed. "I expected more than that from you." She was stunned by offense and was organizing her resentment to take final and angry action, when he sprang from his chair and, taking his glass with him, went into the house before she had found breath to utter a word.

"My God, what have you gotten me into?" she asked somebody. She stood up to discover that she was drunker than she had thought, but she managed to put the glass and the bottle and the ice bucket on the tray and take them inside to the bar and lock the house doors. It came to her that she was locking herself in with him, instead of locking him out. And there was something wrong with that.

She mounted the stairs self-consciously and with unsteady but determined dignity, feeling that she was being watched, and sat on her bed, not knowing what to do. She contemplated the dark, cavernous bedroom door at the far end of the balcony where she hoped Jubie was sleeping peacefully and where the stranger had taken the other bed against her wishes. Her express wishes. She couldn't think, then, how to manage this, and there was something wrong with that too.

Then, the light blinked on in the bedroom, and, my God, there he was—stark naked with his glass in his hand and a half-smoked cigarette stuck in his mouth. And as she watched, her world slanted and went out of control. Looking neither one way nor the other, bent on his mission, he made it down the stairs and back in about five, at the most six, strides and an absolute minimum of wasted time, and the light blinked off in the bedroom, and she thought perhaps it hadn't happened, but, oh yes, it had. And another world record, but something has got to be done about this. Now.

She went unsteadily and with outraged decision along the balcony to the guest room door and switched on the light. He was already looking up at her from the pillow with his small, blue eyes, smoking and insolently comfortable. Jubie was fast asleep. "You will get up and get dressed and get out of my house immediately," she announced.

"Why?" he asked, getting up onto his elbow and reaching for his drink on the bedtable. The sheet fell away from his body.

"Lie back down, lie back down," she said. "How *dare* you parade around this house like that, without a stitch on. Don't you know you are in the house with a child and a married woman—"

"A Southern lady," he amended.

"—whose husband is away? What in hell is wrong with you? Something is wrong with you. What is wrong with you? Now. Now, then. I'm going back to my room, and you will get up quietly and dress and get out, or I'll call somebody. I'll call Ned Trivett."

"Why do you always call him Ned Trivett, instead of just Ned?" he asked.

"Because he—oh, *God!*" she said. "How has this happened? What have I done to deserve this?"

"Where did you go wrong?" he suggested.

"Then, you could at least put on your underwear."

"I don't have any underwear," he said.

"I should have known," she said, finding herself lost at last.

"In spite of which, I'm an honorable person," he went on. "And you might like to know I have a great deal to offer."

"I know nothing of the kind. I know all I want to know about you and a great deal more. And what's more, I don't care. I don't *care!* Oh Lord, I'm being punished for some reason," she said. The ring in the sand on the ocean floor flashed into her mind, glittered, and, as suddenly, the sweet grassy aroma of Skinner's flesh drifted past her. "We have both had a great deal too much to drink," she tried to explain. And not knowing what else to do, she switched off the light and started back to her empty bedroom.

"Good night, Missook," he called after her in his dessicated voice.

"Don't you—don't you *dare* call me that!" she shouted and went into her bedroom and slammed the door and locked it and fell across the bed with all her clothes on.

Early the next morning, she came warily out of her bedroom in the slacks and Skinner's shirt, feeling dazzled and crazed and desolate, and the first thing she saw, looking downward from the balcony through the glass wall, were yellow bed sheets hung over the deck railing waving gaily like banners of residence. The next thing she saw was that both beds in the guest bedroom were empty, and it was *his* bed which had been stripped down, not Jubie's as she thought it might be. He hasn't gone, she thought. Oh Lord, he hasn't gone. Make him go away, Lord.

She made her way carefully down the stair and out onto the deck, where she found the remains of two breakfasts on the table under the umbrella, still floating, the fringe fingering listlessly in the morning haze. The tide had come in, and the sea had turned a milky gray-green, flashing white and copper from an invisible sun. In the distance, at exactly the spot where she had discovered the loss of her ring, two antic figures were making aimless circles in the sand, performing a kind of disorganized dance, stooping and bending their heads down and occasionally wandering into the lumbering surf. "Now, who the hell does he think he's fooling?" she asked. "I mean, he knows goddam well—but at least, he's got his clothes on." Jubie was wearing his undershorts, which his delicate frame could scarcely support, and he would fly into the water on his thin legs like a startled bird and fly out again, escaping an incoming wave.

"That damn ring has caused me more trouble in the last twenty-four hours than anything else in my whole twenty-six years," she declared. "I wish I had nev— I wish I had *never* in my life sworn never to take it off. If Skinner could only know how it has been, he would forgive me." Forgive me for what? She began to gather up the sheets to take them inside, and the ammoniac odor of urine assailed her nostrils. She left them as they were, lifting in the humid air. "Something terrible is wrong with him," she said. "What in the world could be wrong with him?"

She was brushing out her hair and examining the shadows under her eyes in the dressing table mirror when she heard them come in. Jubie was giggling hysterically, possibly even happy, at something the man had said or done out of the simple joy of close company, and they were as familiar as brothers. A shock of jealousy ran through her, and she stopped brushing her hair to find out why she should be jealous and of whom, holding the brush away from her head, as though she were about to strike the image in the mirror. But there it was, incontrovertible. If you have to be jealous, you ought to know at least what it is you are jealous of.

She went out onto the balcony, still holding the brush up like a stave, and looked down at them. Perhaps imperiously. He was making a vodka and orange juice at the bar, and Jubie was still giggling, his wet shorts clinging to his thin flanks. "It's eight-thirty in the morning for godsake," she told the man reprovingly and noticing how tired his face was, was reproved herself. "Jubie, stop that damn giggling and come up here immediately and get out of those wet shorts. Your mother will be coming for you any minute now."

"She dead drunk," Jubie said, looking up at her, shaking his head slowly from side to side. "Jake pee-peed in the bed," he said and went off into another fit of giggling.

"*Jubie!* That's not funny, Jubie," she reprimanded him. "Come on now and let me dry you off and help you on with your clothes."

"I ain't got no drawers," Jubie said and found this extremely delightful.

"Jubie, calm down this *minute.* You sound like a damn billy goat," she said. "You can do without shorts. Like Jake."

"Ah," the man said in his worn voice. "You said my name at last."

"Come on, Jubie, goddam it!" she shouted, and she had ruined his delight. Jubie came up the steps one at a time looking down at his feet, and she regretted bitterly what she had done. "I'm sorry, Jube. I'm upset," she told him.

"You always upset, Missook," he said as he reached the top of the stair.

"Now, that's not fair, Jube," she said.

"Yes'm," Jubie said.

She dressed him, studying his frail body, like a bundle of sticks, she thought, and brushed his hair forward the way the wind had blown it, and left him sitting halfway down the stair and descended—she thought rather imperiously—into the living room and isolated herself in a chair with a glass of orange juice, without vodka, opposite the man on the sofa. She didn't look in his direction. She watched the sea through the glass wall, denying his presence.

"I'm sorry about the bed-wetting," he said. "It happens."

"Jake pee-peed in the bed," Jubie proclaimed from the stair.

"Not usually. Not to people of your age," she responded. "You have some kind of terrible problem with pee. You also have a problem keeping your clothes on. You do a lot of research, I think it might be worth your while to look into those things."

"It's something I have learned to live with," he said.

"Well, thank God in heaven I don't have to live with it," she said, and he looked down into his drink. Again, she regretted what she had done. She knew she looked tired and thin in spite of having brushed her hair to soften her face.

"Say Jake again," he said, still studying his drink.

"Jake," she said to make up for her cruelty.

At which moment, silent and unheralded, an enormous and commanding woman with an apron wrapped about her waist surged into the room, as if she were being moved into place by some kind of theatrical contraption. The contraption halted abruptly, and she stood with her hands on her hips, looking at them with dark and undisguised contempt, as though she had happened on a situation through no choice of her own which she had expected but of which she disapproved in the extreme. Seeing the man looking over her head with an expression of astonished revelation in his eyes, Susan turned quickly, sitting erect in her chair. "Oh, Annie," she said. "I didn't hear you come in, you scared me."

"Where Jubie, Susan?" the woman demanded. Susan pointed to the forlorn figure sitting halfway up the stairs, peering at them through the balusters. "Come on here, Jubie," the woman said.

"This is Mister Cullen, Annie," Susan said pleasantly, as if she were hostess at an early party. "He's from California."

"I can see he is," Annie said. "Come on here, Jubie. Your mama wants you back home now."

"Jake pee-peed in the bed," Jubie said through the railing and began to giggle again.

"I said come on here, Jubie," she said. "I ain't got the heart for no aggravation from you this morning. Sweet Jesus knows I got enough with your mama."

"She dead drunk," Jubie said.

"All right now, Jubie, that's enough," Susan said sharply, standing with her hands on her hips in hopeless duplication of Annie's powerful posture. "If you want to spend the night with me again, get down here and go on with Annie this minute. This minute!"

"I ain't going with Annie. I hate Annie," Jubie said. "I'm going to stay with Jake. We going to look for something on the beach."

"I been in this family too long now," Annie said. "I can't take it no more. They breaking my heart, divorcing each other and throwing theyselves out windows and wandering off like they ain't got a place. One laid up in the bed with a bottle hollering at me and a eight-year-old child can't even tie his own shoes."

"I can so," Jubie said querulously, his voice veering downward.

"When you did it then? I ain't seed it yet."

"I hate you!" Jubie shouted. "Get out of this house!"

"Please, Mister," Annie said to Jake. "Would you get him out to the car for me. He got too big for me to handle old as I am."

"NO!" Jubie screamed and turned over onto his knees, clambering up the steps, faltering and falling back, and crying out, "NO!" again, lost and beyond recall, like a small animal escaping unreasonable and violent death.

In three incredible, soundless, weightless strides, Jake was halfway up the stair and had pitched him high and into his arms with such effortless invention that it was like some kind of rehearsed acrobatic performance. Jubie threw back his head and howled, thrashing his legs and pushing the man's face and shoulders, struggling frantically to free himself. They descended the stair slowly, locked in combat, as though it were still a part of the act. As they crossed the living room, Jake slapped Jubie smartly on the buttocks, and Jubie gasped harshly, making a scraping noise in his throat, and he became rigid, arching back like a bow in Jake's arms, his expression one of incredulous and inexpressible alarm. For an instant, no sound came from his open mouth, but then he released a hopeless, wild shriek of despair. As the contraption reversed, moving the three disparate figures in tableau out through the hall door, he collapsed forward over Jake's shoulder and extended his arms towards Susan in a desperate plea for salvation. She folded downward into the chair and put her face in her hands.

When Jake returned, he found her in that timeless woman's posture, and he watched her steadily as he sat down and took up his drink again, trying to regain his breath. "It had to be done," he said hoarsely.

"*Never,*" Susan said through her fingers and lifted her face back like a mask from her hands. "Don't ever. Don't *ever* touch that child again. He had to come this far to be struck by an utter stranger."

"Utter stranger," Jake said. "I'm no stranger to Jubie. I love him more than I love myself, which isn't saying much. However, I had no choice, I couldn't have managed him otherwise. He will understand that later." He lit a cigarette, having almost regulated his breathing, and they remained as they were without speaking. "What is it?" he asked at length. "Please, can't you tell me what is wrong with him."

Susan stared at him for a long time with eyes that had turned the color of steel. "Nothing," she whispered. "Nothing," she said in a voice as cold as the steel of her eyes. "Try to remember that now. Nothing." She stood and continued staring at him, as though she were trying to relieve herself of the contempt she felt for him. "And now. Once more and finally, you will put that drink down and return to Ned Trivett or go back to wherever it is you came from, so that I can go back to the life I had before you arrived. You have destroyed something here. I don't know what it is, but perhaps, if you will leave, I can find it again."

"What is it with you people?" he asked, his voice hardly audible. "I have been all over the world, but this is the damnedest place I was ever in." He put down his drink and snubbed out the cigarette and stood up and looked her in the eyes. "I'll be going then," he told her, and he left her suddenly and silently and without hesitation, and she stood listening to the car start up and then depart along the gravel drive.

CHAPTER SIX

The plane was late of course. Leaning on the guardrail separating her from the floodlit runway, Susan watched the planes arriving and departing like a disorganized school of silver whales, moving comfortably and ponderously in the warm, humid night air, as if it were their element, as if they didn't contain human life, blinking red and green lights signaling their intentions, whistling unbearably high and sighing down to silence.

She considered returning to her cathedral house on the beach several times, going so far as to walk halfway to the parking lot once and then changing her mind and returning to the guardrail, pretending to anyone who might have noticed that she had gone to check the schedule again. The people waiting with her at the gate were as much at home as they would have been drinking together in their light-bulb and fly-paper kitchens, imposing their presence by loud and mirthless laughter at unfunny jokes in the half dark, full of the public importance of themselves and the journey one of their number was about to make or, for some obscure reason, proud of having been chosen to receive some friend or kinsman from somewhere that didn't matter to anybody else.

She found herself unsympathetic with the pale, stunned infants with their enormous, vacant blue eyes and cornsilk hair. Raised on cornflakes and Pepsi and frozen pizza, she had no doubt and tried to find pity for them but couldn't manage even that. Why don't they stay in their little houses along the highway with all the trees cut down and a dusty yard full of new automobiles with dented fenders? And why should she care so much? Had they no right to fly?

"Hazeleen," the man with a sharp face called out louder than was necessary, "you better look out for them city boys," and snickered through his nose making a snort sound, glancing from face to face for appreciation. "I ain't studying them city boys," Hazeleen declared, unamused. Hazeleen was as pale and as blond as the wide-eyed baby she carried in her arms and had wound her hair on metal rollers and camouflaged the result in a blue, gauzy scarf as a concession to the world beyond the fluorescent supermarkets of Milford. She jiggled the baby up and down and the baby didn't care one way or another. It stared steadily and incuriously at Susan, until she was forced to move some distance along the guardrail out of its range.

Hazeleen is convinced the big city boys are going to faint with desire at the sight of her, Susan thought, and Hazeleen is in for a rude awakening. It worried her that she should take the trouble to dislike Hazeleen and that she should be pleased that Hazeleen was in for a rude awakening. She thought perhaps it was because of the smug, self-satisfied expression on Hazeleen's face, and then, she realized it was the same expression she had seen on Venus's face in the famous painting in Florence Italy.

When the plane swam up out of the dark into the floodlight, she knew immediately it was their plane. It just looked as if they were inside it; it harbored that threat. Her heart beat and the dread increased as they rolled the steps up and the little door opened like a gill to disgorge the passengers. The first few emerged looking as if they had been held captive for some days, dishevelled and dazed and lost, carrying strangely shaped packages in their arms and wrestling with the zippered cases slung over their shoulders. They stared wild into the lights, expecting something, or were indifferent and contained, pretending to expect nothing. And then, it seemed to her a spotlight was thrown on the door, and there they were. Drunk.

Julian made a nonchalant and precipitous descent, missing most of the steps, managing by sheer, courageous, drunken heedlessness not to fall, his fists thrust deep into his trouser pockets and his shoulders pushed up, as though he had forgotten to remove the wire hanger when he put the jacket on. Skinner followed, pausing in the door, and waited for a brass band to strike up, grinning serenely at some invisible reception committee, taking his own sweet time to the annoyance of the tired world travelers behind him. On the tarmac, Julian set off in one direction and looked about, thinking perhaps he had arrived at the wrong airport, and went off in another direction, until an attendant took him by the arm and pointed towards the gate, smiling, and Julian smiled back and shook hands with him and stumbled towards her. "Oh, shit," Susan said, and several of the graduating lint-heads, including the dazed baby, looked at her with curiosity but without censure.

However, their interest intensified considerably when Julian flung up his arms at the sight of her and enveloped her in a dank, alcoholic embrace, bleating, "Missook, Missook, my little Missook," and seemed to be on the verge of tears. The onlookers thought there must have been some terrible tragedy and waited round-eyed in the half dark to discover what it might have been. "Milford!" Julian yodeled, throwing his head back, "ah, Milford!" and his knees buckled under him as he began to fold down, taking her with him. The slat of a man with the sharp face came quickly to her aid, grinning broadly in spite of a missing front tooth, and took Julian by the arm. "It's all right, take your hands off of him," Susan said sharply, and the man retired into the shadows offended, muttering something about them rich sumbitches to his companions, who lost sympathy but not their intense interest in the tragedy. Rich, Susan thought, they think that's the difference. "Thank you so much, anyhow," she called to the man over Julian's head, making a smile, "he's all right now."

Then, Skinner was there and lifted Julian to his feet and separated them. He pressed himself against her suddenly, taking a breath as if he were going under water. He put his mouth on hers, so that she felt his teeth on her lips. "Oh, my God!" she gasped and pulled away from him, startled, and found him smiling at her in some new way that didn't make any sense, an utter stranger. "Skin?" she said, as if she were asking a question. "Oh. Skin. Welcome to Milford," as though she were the representative of the reception committee who had made arrangements for the brass band.

"Let's get the bags and go home," Skinner said.

"Yes," she said. "Welcome home. Welcome to Milford." She looked back at the preparations to get Hazeleen and the baby and her powder blue suitcases on the plane and withdrew the animosity towards them. She longed to turn back and explain to them how wonderful they really were or some such thing, but, "I wonder why she didn't check her bags," she said instead.

"What?" Skinner said in a loud voice.

"Welcome to Milford," she said, offering it to him with her arms out like a damn fool. She didn't like him very much, but she thought she might like him again when they got back home.

She drove towards the beach in silence through the hot, bug-flown night in the instrument-panel glow, air-cooled insulation of the automobile. Skinner sat next to her, and Julian sprawled in the rear, laughing sardonically to himself and snorting, muttering incomprehensibly, kicking the back of the seat from time to time. She felt a constraint between them, a rigidity that had never been there before, not since she had decided to fall in love with Skinner because of his open being and because he had become more brother than friend to her cousin. Something had happened, what had happened? But she knew she would be told nothing, that it was a difference that perhaps they could not define and which she would have to find out through indirection and guile. She tried to think of something funny to say to string them all back together again into the strange trio they had been, an insolent woman and her lover and the older, demanding cousin who loved them for no reason and protected their union as if it were his possession. But she could think of nothing, and so they remained silent, pretending to watch the flat, arid landscape roll backwards past them, the floodlit filling stations and the fast food restaurants and the desultory motels with tropical names written in neon tubing that had been there, exactly the same, when they had left ten days or so before. She took note again of the cinderblock whorehouse with her favorite sign—SOCIETY LOUNGE—and under that in only slightly smaller letters—TRUCKERS WELCOME—humped low in a gulch, pretending to hide its lights, denying the amiable welcome posted at the head of the dirt road leading to it. She was going to laugh about that with them as a release but decided it would do no good.

"You're driving too fast, have you had a drink?" Skinner said, and she felt comforted suddenly that he was with her again. He was back again telling her she drove too fast when she had the courage of a drink.

"Well, yes," she said and glanced at him with her long face. "Is that not all right? I'm sorry, I'll slow down. I forget."

"Well, don't," Skinner said.

"She can't drive fast enough for me," Julian said and bumped against the back of the seat. "Oh, I'm sorry," he said. "I'm drink—uh—drunk."

"That's all right, Mister Jukes," she said. "There's just too much of you for the conveniences designed for the rest of us." Skinner took his glasses out of his breast pocket and put them on and stared stolidly at the road ahead.

"There's too much of me for just about everything," Julian told her. "I'm naive, did you know that? They say I'm naive. I don't understand anything anymore."

"What a funny thing to say, Jukes," she said and looked at him curiously in the rearview mirror. She could see only the ghost of his face, but what she could see was unutterably woeful.

"Oh, that's all right," he said. "That's all right, it's true. I am naive." She knew there was significance in this statement and again she knew she would have to explore it on another occasion. "How are Laura and Jubie?" Julian asked her.

"Just fine, Julian," she said.

"Uh-oh. Just fine Julian. I don't like the sound of that. Just fine Julian," he said. "I guess I'll have to wait till tomorrow to find out what just fine Julian means."

"It means they're just fine," she said. "Jubie spent the night with me night before last."

"Ah!" he said. "Comes the dawn. I'm not so naive I don't recognize the dawn when I see it." And Susan left it at that, wanting to comfort Julian and protect Laura as well. "I wonder if you would be kind enough to drop me off at my bachelor quarters, Missook," he said. "I want to walk down to the beach and watch the old ocean ride in and ride out and ride in and ride out. That way I'll know I'm back home again. And I wonder why," and he laughed to himself.

"I think you had better spend the night with us, Jukes," she suggested, "and watch the old ocean ride in and ride out tomorrow."

"No," he said. "I don't want to spend the night with you. I've seen enough of your husband to hold me for a while."

There it was. She looked quickly at Skinner, who continued staring through the windshield. She felt responsible for the situation and that she must keep up some kind of communication to put a face on the estrangement. "Tell me about John Thomas," she said, not really caring.

"Ha! John Thomas," he snorted. "Lost. Vanished. I don't think we'll see my little brother again, and I don't much care. He don't suit me now, nobody suits me anymore."

"Don't I suit you anymore, Julian?" she asked and thought, my God, if his beloved John Thomas doesn't suit him, nobody can.

"Always and forever, Missook. You suit me always and forever," he said, kicking the back of the seat. "Excuse me, well, maybe not forever. That can depend on what happens, almost anything can happen, you know."

"You need a new car," Skinner said. "Slow down."

Skinner had seen Julian into his cheerless little duplex apartment—it doesn't know how to get dirty, Julian had said about it—helping with his packages and luggage, and as far as she could tell, watching them against the ineffectual, rectangular light of the door, Skinner studious and severe with his glasses, Julian something between a derelict and a scarecrow in his loose suit, they had not exchanged a word. There was something dead wrong with that. Skinner, still peering through his glasses and without so much as a glance in her direction, had begun to stare through the windshield again, even before she had started the motor. She decided she had a better chance of being The Other Woman than she did of being A Voluptuous Woman. A lot better. "Take me home, please," Skinner had said, knowing her only as his driver. And there was something dead wrong with that too.

"I have something terrible to tell you," she had begun. "I lost my— I lost your—" But then, she had seen that he wasn't listening to her, but she had been absolutely sure he was listening to something and perhaps was seeing something through the windshield. "Skin," she said, "is anything wrong?" Again, he hadn't heard her, wasn't listening to what the driver had to say, and so, she had started the car, hoping the trip to the beach would dispel the voices in his head. Eerie light blinked two or three times on the menacing black skies gathering above them, and thunder, muffled and stentorian, had rolled along the horizon moments after. She felt the guttering of her courage, which never responded to her will. Not when a storm threatened. "Oh, Lord, let's not have a storm tonight, I don't think I could take a storm tonight," she said, her voice rising to a quaver.

"Don't tell me you're still afraid of storms," he had said, seeming almost indifferent. But he had heard her—at least, there was that.

"My God, Skinner, you can't have forgotten that, you can't have forgotten what they do to me—not in ten days. You cer—you *certainly* can't think I've changed that much in ten days," she had said, beginning to lose patience with his mysterious behavior. "I'm afraid you'll find I haven't changed at all. The question is, have you?"

"Take the next right," he had said, insisting on the short cut as usual, and had let his hand come to rest on her thigh. It was an accustomed gesture of possession in an unaccustomed manner, and she had been so uneasy with the weight of his hand on her leg, she could give her attention to nothing else and had forgotten to resent the short cut, bumpy and black as it was. However, she had thought she ought to be relieved he still thought of her as his.

That was the way that had been.

So that when she pulled up under the house and turned off the headlights, she wasn't surprised when he drew her to him with such urgency and pressed his mouth to hers, hurting her lips with his teeth again. She didn't mind so much the smell of cigarettes and the sour taste of scotch he had been drinking nor the way he began to breathe deep right away, almost as if he were frightened. "Oh, Sue," he gasped. "Leaving home can be such a mistake sometimes."

"What on earth has happened, Skinner?" she asked him. "You and Julian—"

"Give me the damn keys," he said and took them from her and was out of the car and up the back steps fighting with the door, as though he desperately needed to escape through it, until finally he managed to open it and disappeared into the house.

"What on earth?" she said, sitting alone in the dark in the automobile, apparently forgotten. "This is more than drunk," she decided. "Where has he been he can't come back from? What has he lost?" After all, it was only Rome Italy, and we have all been there. But we came back the same as we went away—not even any more cultured. She sat for a while longer trying to match him to the picture of the man she thought she had known so completely only ten days ago. "I'll have to fix this," she said, A Married Woman. "That is supposed to be my job. I have to fix this, so at least I won't talk to myself so much and think I—and make people think I've gone crazy."

She got out of the car and went up the steps and into the house, closing the door that he had flung behind him, and went down the hall into the living room. She stood looking up at the balcony, wondering what he could be doing in the bedroom and why they had left the luggage in the car. She stood like that, a member of the reception committee again, until he came out of the bedroom in nothing but his undershorts. He looked down at her and smiled at the surprised reception committee, showing his sweet little white teeth. What is it about this house that inspires men to take their clothes off? "Ah—would you like a drink, Skin?" she asked, not knowing the protocol at receptions.

"Why, yes," he said, as though this were a brilliant, new idea, and she saw suddenly he wasn't even a grown man yet, only a boy pretending to be a man, although he was pushing towards thirty years old. "I think I'll have a cognac," he said.

"You think what?" she said. "Skinner, it's almost ten o'clock and you must be tired, what do you really want?"

"A cognac," he said. "It's not ten o'clock for me. Not by my watch.

By my watch, it's time for one more cognac before going on to somewhere else. Maybe to another party somewhere."

"Another party somewhere," she said. "Well, you'll play hell finding another party somewhere in Milford North Carolina, who have you been running around with? I'll get the suitcases."

"Fix me a cognac," he said and crossed the balcony and started down the stair. A spatter of rain struck the glass wall with such force that it was as if it had come from a long way out of space.

"Oh, Skinner, it's beginning to rain," she said as an appeal to him and went to the bar feeling far too obedient. "Aren't you going to put your pants on?"

"No, I'm not," he said. "Why should I?"

"It's just that—" and a second, more violent spatter struck the glass wall, and becoming suddenly apprehensive, she turned for reassurance to her husband and was stunned to discover another man entirely, sprawled nearly naked on the sofa. There was a slow, lazy half-smile on his face. His body was open as a hand is opened to show the palm, his arms extended along the back of the sofa and his knees falling out wide. She felt she was a strange woman being seduced in the most vulgar and possibly dangerous way by a strange man. "Truckers welcome," she murmured and was relieved at the small joke she shared with herself. "What was that?" Skinner said. It wasn't Skinner, but she smiled at him as best she could anyhow. "Oh, nothing," she said, "just—" anxious to lower the roman shades to protect him from the adversaries but not daring to for fear of offending him. She put the cognac on the table next to the sofa and sat in the chair opposite with her vodka in which she had no interest whatsoever and recalled on the instant the last time she had sat here opposite a stranger. "That's more like it," he said but didn't change his position, rather seemed to extend it, although he hadn't moved except to follow her with his eyes. Nor did he change the indolent smile. She returned the smile and took it back when he began to sip his cognac, so that his face was turned away from her and his attention inward on something inside his head.

Lightning flickered fitfully bright and less bright and brighter and paused and flickered again like a giant blinker transmitting a dreadful message. A thunderbolt rocketed across the sky over their heads and diminished. Several scatterings of rain rattled like stones on the glass wall, and she felt she was in grave peril and there was nowhere to go for help. "I think we're in for a storm," she said feebly, refusing to smile back at him any longer, feeling false and foolish and powerless.

"We're going swimming," he said and smiled and looked away so quickly she wasn't sure he had smiled at all. If he had, it wasn't the kind she was used to.

"We're what, Skinner? We most cer—we're doing no such thing. We can swim tomorrow, and Julian can watch the ocean ride in and ride out tomorrow. Tomorrow, everything will be fine again."

"Fuck Julian," Skinner said. He finished the cognac and put the glass on the table and stood up, looking at her steadily from under his brows and didn't stop looking at her as he stepped out of his shorts and stood there facing her with some kind of cruel challenge. There was no way she could tell how long he stood like that, but she saw he was more beautiful than she had remembered, and she saw he had strayed beyond her reach. He rested a hand lightly on his chest. It was then she saw the strange gold ring on his finger. *I lost one and he found one* came to her as if she weren't in profound difficulty. He held out his hand to her like a command and waited. She couldn't move. "Let's go, Susan, we're going swimming," he said quietly.

"I cer—I most *certainly* am not going swimming," she said. "*You* go swim—" He began to approach her, and she got up quickly and took the extended hand, overpowered by his flesh. "For God's sake, Skinner," she pleaded but went out with him onto the deck. She felt herself seized by a great, threatening movement and heard the door slam behind her.

In stammering flashes of lightning, she could see the ocean rise, mounting very slowly like a wall of granite, pitching forward and backward and downward at the same time, and in the darkness between the flashes, saw that it was lit from underneath, as though light were leaking into it from somewhere else on earth. A drop of rain struck her, hard and cold, on the forehead, as if it had been fired from a pistol and she was the chosen target. "Please, please, Skin!" she shouted above the tumult of the surf and against the force of wind which had begun to blow veils of spray along the surface of the sea. A barrage of rain pelted like scattershot and let up for a moment, gathering strength, and then blew against their bodies in horizontal torrents. She could no longer see the ocean for the rain, which had turned everything milky gray, obscuring the definition of land and sky. In the sickly yellow light through the glass wall, she could see only as far as the back of a naked man in front of her, leading her by the hand along the deck. *"Please,* Skin, I can't do this!" she shouted against the wind. He turned his face to her, and she knew she would never see anything so wild and so beautiful ever again. It was the head of a sea creature, its hair plastered along the temples and the hollow cheeks, with eyes of clear crystal and a mouth opened to fill the chest with breath. His head fell back in inaudible laughter, and she saw that his body shone like wet stone in the absurd, moribund light from the house. Then suddenly, still laughing, he released her hand and vanished into the white night, enveloped by the rain sweeping in successive curtains and by the thunder and the churning of the sea.

"Skinner!" she screamed. "Come back, come back here this minute!" She half fell down the steps after him, her hair whipping across her face and her shirt bellying from her, forcing her backwards. She drove herself to follow him, convinced that if she didn't find him, she would have lost him. Stumbling and falling in the sand, she lost herself in the relentless downpour that washed over her as though it were the sea itself. She had no idea where she was, sensing only that there was an immense, undulant mass ahead of her, uncontrolled and limitless, and she could only be sure it was there by the crash of the tides. She staggered towards it, calling for him, until she was seized by it and engulfed and hurled to the ground, fighting to keep from being dragged into oblivion.

And then, as she struggled to her feet once more, a blinding explosion of light and sound split the sky, turning her head to stone, and struck a brilliant arctic image on the back of her brain. It lingered in her eyes for seconds afterwards and in her memory forever. Motion had arrested, and she saw the sea and sky and the long curve of the shore in exact, grainy, colorless detail, as though time had been shut off on the instant. High in the center of the picture, she saw Skinner, frozen in midflight at the crest of a towering wave, his arms flung out lifting wings of spray, spiraling, no longer earthbound.

"What is that damn fool doing?" she said at the pitch of saving her own life, and it came to her that if, my God, she never saw him again, this would have been enough.

Time and motion and darkness took up again, but she managed to crawl away from the nightmare that could have killed her. I think I'll go home now, she decided and got to her feet. The wind at her back pushed her into the wet sand again and again, until at last she saw the triangle of feeble, yellow light she knew to be her house. She made her way to it and up the steps and along the deck, until she stumbled through the door into the house as though she had been rescued onto an unsinkable ship, not even pitching in the storm.

She decided she had come to the end of her strength and began to weep with a sound like laughing but thought that would be like some other damn fool woman and calmed herself with disapproval. *Call somebody, you idiot. Well then, tell me who,* but the telephone was stone dead, and she flung it from her against the white wall. Which brought her considerable relief, amounting almost to pleasure.

That, then, was as much as she knew to do, and so she drew the

wet shirt about her body and stood looking out through the glass wall,
so that when he returned, which he most certainly would, she knew that
definitely, he would find her waiting. Because, after all, that is supposed
to be my job, she reminded herself. And so she made a picture of herself
exactly as he should see it when he chose to return. A sad—no, not sad,
anything but sad—a *noble* figure looking out into the night. *Very* noble,
but on the other hand as desirable as Venus. More desirable. Much more.

The curtains of driving rain let up, swept across to another part of
the world, leaving in their wake soft-falling rain, no longer milky white,
no longer striking the glass, merely trickling down it as though it were
an amiable summer shower from some other time.

She had no way of knowing how long she stood there like that, time
having changed its character, but she wanted Skinner back. She wanted
him back for a number of reasons, one of them being so that she could
find out and fix what had gone wrong with him, if she possibly could.
But mostly she wanted him back so that—

But then, there he was coming out of the dark and into the light
of the window like something you could only imagine, not wild, not
frightening, a stark naked boy born out of the sea. She thought he might
have sea vines in his hair, but that's silly, of course he didn't. He came
in close to the wall and looked into her eyes, possibly preparing an explanation, but then he stepped back, unsteady with fatigue.

She left off making the picture of herself and ran to the door and
threw it open and went out onto the deck. She stood with her hands on
her hips and thought she was going to laugh. "Skinner," she said, "get
in this house immediately, you damn fool. Where the hell have you been?"
It was something of a reprimand, and she thought that was by far the
best thing. As if it had all been nothing, as if the frozen image of his
levitation were not still on the back of her eyes.

He followed her into the house, the fragrance of his flesh washed
away, and she lowered the canvas panels over the wall to protect him and

to shut out the other creature. She regarded him standing in the middle of her living room, exposed and vulnerable, and began to laugh. Skinner didn't laugh. Skinner was dead serious. Susan felt very beautiful now in her sodden clothes. She put her arms about his shoulders and held him close to her. He let his head fall forward, and they stood there for as long as they wanted to. At least, she thought, there's this much.

After a time, she put a hand against his face and kissed his mouth without passion. "Come on, Skin," she said, "come upstairs this minute." The sound of that and the sureness of it delighted her and she was convinced she was perfectly beautiful.

She led him up the stairs by the hand, as he had led her into the storm, and there was peace, or at least a truce, in the cathedral house.

"Oh, my God, Sue," he said.

"What is it, Skin?" she asked him.

"Oh, my God, Sue," he said again.

"Come on, Skinner," she said. "You're the second nakedest man I've ever seen."

And that was the way that was.

CHAPTER SEVEN

Something frightful struck up fitfully—coughing and wheez-ing and expiring and coughing and expiring and coughing and expiring and—finally—exploding into full vengeance right under the princess's bedroom window, rousing her from deep and, for a change, dreamless sleep. It took her some time to determine what the frightening uproar was—a lawn mower, it was a damn lawn mower—and even more time to establish where she was. It was a fearful adjustment she had made many times in her life, waking up to strange walls and strange closed doors and strange windows and beds with, sometimes, a stranger sleeping beside her and having to fit them into the sequence of her life, as if a stretch of it had dropped out and had to be fastened in again. And then, after all that, to find herself in that enormous bed alone in that tiny room with a lawn mower, sick unto death, coughing under her window at eight o'clock in the morning for godsake and after that exhausting trip by plane and train only yesterday. "I'll kill Ned Trivett with my bare hands and laugh at the blood," she muttered and got out of bed to put on a robe and make herself presentable.

As it turned out, the princess Graziella had arrived sooner than expected, which suited nobody, but nobody let on, as instructed. She had explained that all her clocks had slowed, some to a complete and final stop, and she had thought it was later than it actually was and so had sent the cablegram and taken flight for New York and then booked a drawing room on the Miami Champion with her trunks of silver and furs and jewelry like Sheba for—Milford, is it?—yes, Milford. Well, well, Milford, isn't it *clean?* she had said observing the landscape from the window of Ned's funny old car on the way from the railway station, and in view of his rather grand manner, she was disappointed in this charming but simple little town from which he had sprung. And further, she was angered, even now, that he had betrayed her and the riotous years they had spent making fun of living.

"Isn't it just like old times being together again?" she had cried out to Ned. However, they both had known it wasn't. Not at all and not ever again. And Ned had seen that she looked tired and nervous and had detected the edge of contempt in her voice and realized the final silk thread connection to youth had frayed and parted. "I had hoped it might be in a tree," she had said to him on their arrival at the gate of Ned's tiny salmon-colored house on Hooper Street.

"I couldn't arrange it," Ned had said, "something to do with the treehouse zoning laws. Do try to forgive me."

A tall, handsome man with hair blonder than it should have been had come out to take her luggage in, and she detested him on sight. He was much too sure of himself, and yet, on the other hand, he wasn't. He had the look of one of those second-rate American movie stars who had invaded Rome in a steady stream dressed up as cowboys to make third-rate films for the maids and juvenile delinquents. Women—and, of course, others, she was sure—went mad for the distant, mysterious look in this man's eyes, which the princess recognized instantly as severe astigmatism. Too vain to wear glasses, she was sure of that also, it takes one to know one.

And then, she and Ned had stood silent and alone on the tiny front porch, and she had had the feeling suddenly that she had been released from a prison cell. She had understood she could sit on this porch whenever she pleased as anybody she pleased—as Princess Graziella di Brabant or Grace Jamison or Disgrace Jamison from Mobile, as she had sometimes been called. Or even as Gray, if she chose.

However, what had transpired this morning wasn't at all what she had had in mind at the time. She sat now, scarcely past dawn, on the tiny front porch overlooking the postage-stamp lawn. Mad as fire. "You could mow the damn thing with a pair of scissors," she muttered to herself for want of a more agreeable audience. "Why would any moron with two house guests and any brains at all have the lawn mowed at eight o'clock in the morning? I demand an explanation," the princess said, coming into full voice.

It occurred to her as she was regaining her composure that there was a slow caravan of automobiles moving along the narrow, shade-dappled street, so slow Graziella had thought the first two or three of them had run out of gas or that the driver had fallen into some kind of trance. However, she observed that in almost every car there was a face with round, curious eyes looking straight out the front window and in a number the rear window framed the bright and inconsiderate faces of children and dogs. The faces had the flushed, expectant expression of pilgrims to a shrine, as if the tiny house had been written up in the morning newspaper as the site of an imminent and miraculous event.

Word had got out somehow that there was a princess staying with Ned Trivett at his house on Hooper Street, and very few residents of Milford could have recognized a princess, unless she was leaning out of a castle tower with her hair hanging down and some man in tights climbing up it. This princess, if that is what she was, sitting in a white wicker rocking chair on the front porch with what appeared to be a glass of orange juice didn't come up to expectation, although she definitely wasn't from Milford. She had black paint on her eyes at eight-thirty in the morning and was wearing some kind of a pale blue, silky-looking robe and no opening down the front, and she glared back in a very rude manner at the children and the dog and whatever offended face was framed in whatever car happened to be passing by Ned Trivett's house at the time. And she certainly was mad at somebody. Mad as fire.

As a matter of actual fact, the angry woman with the lion's hair and silver bracelets on her arms even in her bathrobe was a real princess. But just barely. She was a princess without a prince, which would have confused and maybe even saddened the citizens of Milford, although it neither confused nor saddened the many amused and amusing friends of the princess in Rome Italy. Who knew full well that the Bugatti in which the prince had plunged to his death had been closer to his heart than Graziella could ever hope to have been. Be that as it may, she had ended up with what was left of the Bugatti and the title and a sack full of money and the house in Rome and the villa in the Umbrian hills and a determined grip on her third identity.

The many friends in Rome had found it easier and less perilous adjusting to this third identity than it had been to live with the second. "Come se dice in Inglese?—practice makes perfect," Iliana Pianzola had suggested, smiling green.

It was no secret that Graziella, according to record at the courthouse in Mobile Alabama, had come into the world as Grace Lanier Jamison and had been moving up fast on middle age for almost a decade now. However, God protect any friend who said as much, since Grace, after many years on the European continent and an alarming weight loss, had transformed suddenly into Graziella by her own decree. She had even

convinced Italian law, which was no mean achievement. It appeared she
had concluded that women named Grace were usually retired schoolteach-
ers with angry glasses and nothing to fall back on but a room on the
wrong side of town and church services every Sunday. The transformation
had been extremely trying for her many friends, but then nothing about
Grace—ah—Graziella had ever been easy—and for many not worth the
candle—with the exception, of course, of Ned Trivett. Ned had taken to
the new name and then to the title with the effortless conviction of a child
playing children's games.

And so, it was understandable that Graziella was vastly relieved to
be in his company once more, away from the glancing basilisk eyes of the
Romans. In spite of which, it was all but impossible to understand why
anybody with two house guests and any brains at all would permit some
inconsiderate yard man to fire up a lawn mower at eight o'clock in the
morning. Right under the bedroom window, for godsake. She had worked
herself up to the point of springing out of her rocking chair and going
to the back of the house to set the situation straight, when Ned eased
out through the screen door in a black Japanese kimono. Slow passing
cars began to slam on brakes.

"Why would anybody with two house guests and any brains at all
permit some inconsiderate yard man to fire up the lawn mower at eight
o'clock in the morning?" the principessa wanted to know with raised
eyebrows and was a little overimpressed herself by the Japanese kimono,
scoring it from top to bottom and back up again with the black-mascaraed
lashes. It turned out that the pilgrim vehicles had begun circling the
block and were passing the house for the second and even the third time
now. "And what are those people staring at? Are they holding a parade
in my honor, or what?"

"They are hoping for a revelation," Ned said, sinking back comfortably into the white wicker settee. "They have so little excitement in

their lives. However, the only available revelation happens to be mowing the back yard at the moment."

"Well, you can just damn well tell the revelation to mow somewhere else while I'm in residence," she announced.

"I think the princess will feel differently when he rounds the corner," Ned said.

"And what the hell are we supposed to do then? Go shut ourselves up in that hall closet that reeks to high heaven of cat boxes?" she demanded, becoming shrill.

"I shouldn't think that would be the appropriate response to the appearance of a revelation—my! we *are* cross this morning," Ned remarked.

"We are," she said, "and when the revelation gets out from under our bedroom window, we are going back to bed."

"I think not," Ned said and dimpled benignly.

"And where is the California messiah this morning?" Graziella asked, not really giving a damn. "He seems to have cut a wide swath through rural society."

"He is no longer with us—he is watching over an unfortunate prince of the realm—and he cuts a wide swath wherever he goes."

"I don't want to hear about it," Graziella snapped. "Are those peasants going to cruise by here staring at us all day?"

"Patience, princess, calm down, calm down," he said. "They will have to go to the office and the supermarket any minute now. Would you like another orange juice? It's full of vitamin C, you know."

Brother Reeves, shirtless and shoeless, appeared around the corner of the house behind the uproarious lawn mower, and there was a small but resounding automobile accident at the front gate. "Get me another orange juice exactly like that one," Graziella instructed over the din, not having noticed the accident at all.

"I thought as much," Ned said, rising in a flow of sleeves. The
peasants being inconvenienced by the accident started blowing their horns
fervently. "Shall I send him home?"

"What?" Graziella asked, inclining an ear in Ned's direction without unglueing her gaze from the inconsiderate yard man.

"I said I guess I'll send him home," Ned hollered.

"You'll do nothing of the kind," Graziella shouted in a voice which
could just barely be heard above the coughing of the lawn mower and the
blowing horns and the frantic and embarrassed efforts of the unfortunate
pilgrims to uncouple their cars.

"What?" Ned yelled, canting towards her about an inch with his
hand cupped at his ear.

"I said, tell—" she took in a harsh breath "—tell him to cut the
damn thing off. And get me another orange juice and make it snappy."

"Things are moving along more swiftly than I had anticipated,"
Ned said, more or less to himself, and went into the house, slamming
the screen door to top the confusion.

Graziella rose up out of her rocking chair and waved her arms in
the air, as if she were flagging down a train. Brother kept right on mowing
a strip down one side of the lawn. When he reached the fence, he reversed
his direction to discover a tall woman in some kind of a blue bathrobe
waving her arms in the shade of the porch. She put her hands on her ears
and made her eyes wild at him like somebody was in bad trouble. The
cars at the front gate unlocked bumpers with a shriek and slunk off, bent-
fendered, down Hooper Street. The detained peasants stopped blowing
their horns, and Brother choked the lawn mower down to silence and stood
up straight and robust in a ray of brilliant morning sun.

"Yes, ma'am?" he inquired—standing right front on to her, his dark
eyes soft and serious and concerned.

"Oh, thank you, thank you, thank you, young man, whatever your
name is," she said and fell back into the rocker which rocked backwards

a lot farther than she had anticipated. "Could you—" she said, righting herself with a wild kicking maneuver and then rearranging the folds of the robe around her knees. She smiled graciously. "Could you just—"

Ned shouldered out through the screen door with two glasses of orange juice. He had on some kind of a bathrobe too, only it was black. "Brother, dear boy, could you just trim the hedge for a while? We can finish the lawn later. The princess here has a headache which she is taking steps to cure."

"In the front yard," the princess commanded. "Trim the hedge in the front yard."

"In the front yard, Brother," Ned concurred, standing massive black with an orange glass in each hand. There was a dragon on the back of his bathrobe, and the sleeves hung way down. Brother was used to Ned, he always had on something different, and nobody had ever called him dear boy except Ned, not even the ladies he found under him from time to time.

"Okay, Ned," Brother said and pushed the discountenanced lawn mower towards the back of the house, spreading his back broader.

"In the front yard, in the front yard," the princess repeated in a stronger voice in case Brother had a hearing problem, leaning way too far forward in her rocking chair.

"Yes, ma'am," Brother said and disappeared around the corner of the house. The shadow of a cloud swept across the lawn where he had stood.

The princess eased back up into her chair. "I don't like him calling me ma'am," she complained to Ned.

"You mustn't expect too much of love at first sight," Ned said, settling back onto the settee. "After all, you're his first princess. My!— this *is* marvelous orange juice, you always have known how to get the day off to a good start."

"He could call me Graziella, you put too much vodka in this," she allowed. "After all, I notice he calls you Ned."

"Ours is a case of long acquaintance and mutual admiration," Ned explained. "Brother and I are old friends. And I doubt very much his native tongue could make the effort it takes to form your chosen name. He has never had the privilege of a visit to Rome, although I don't expect it will be too long before he does."

"Oh, very well then—Grace," she relented, breaking her own hard and fast rule. "He can call me Grace. I'll make an exception in his case."

"Very gracious of you, indeed, princess," Ned said. "Remarkable boy. I see his magic has had its way with you, as it has had its way with half the gentry of the town. The husbands of Milford owe him a great debt, although they don't know that. Brother has calmed the nerves of many a matron and debutante daughter, although he is entirely unaware of his healing powers. He has simply done what nature expected of him, gallantly and agreeably."

"Well, for heaven sake," the princess exclaimed, "I had no such ridiculous idea in my mind. He and I come from vastly different worlds as you should know. Besides, I am never nervous."

Brother reappeared with the hedge clippers, not giving the costume party in the shade of the porch so much as a glance or a thought. Graziella realized she was getting nervous.

"Do take note of the effect the hedge-clipping has on his arms and back," Ned suggested. "It makes him look as if he's preparing to fly. But I see you *have* taken note. Now, finish your orange juice, and I'll fetch you another, I wouldn't want you getting nervous."

"I am *not* nervous, I am *never* nervous," Graziella insisted. She turned the rings on her fingers and rearranged the robe around her knees again with fussy care. "I must say," she mused, resting her cheek on two fingertips. "It's the golden head, the curls on the back of his neck. Like an angel in a painting."

"With wings," Ned reminded. "Don't forget the wings."

"Yes, but it's the head, how very odd," she said, studying Brother as if he were a greater distance from where she sat than he actually was. "That's the thing, it's the golden head," she said again. "The nose straight down from the forehead and the soft and gentle eyes, although they are not violet blue eyes. They should have been violet blue."

Ned observed her closely. He could see she was scanning her past and remembering a revelation of her own she had never shared. "Why violet blue, Graziella?" he asked. "Where did you last see a golden head with violet blue eyes, my dear?"

"I was wearing a green evening dress, I wish you could have seen it," she said. "Silk and pale green, I think it was silk, it had lights like silk, it went out full from my waist and it whispered when I moved." And that was all she said.

Ned understood then that she was not seeing Brother Reeves but was looking at a definite time and place beyond him. "You were wearing a green dress," he reminded her, arranging himself majestically on the settee in preparation.

"Yes," she said. "And William," she said. "Old Billy, my beautiful young brother."

"His was the golden head with the violet blue eyes?" Ned asked.

"In my lap, on the green silk, saying good-by."

"Would you tell me about him, Grace? I would so like to know," Ned said.

"Oh my, that Billy," she said. "He thought I was a princess—a real one and a wild one, doing as she pleased. And he judged nothing and protected me from everything and everybody, including Mother and Father." She paused again, projecting the past on the screen of the present. "It was four o'clock in the morning, and I had been out all night with a boy nobody approved of, he smiled the wrong way and had been to all the wrong places, and there was blood on the green silk dress. Father had been waiting for me in the hall, and I knew then it was time to leave home. Billy had heard us, Billy heard me when I said it was time for me to go, and Father agreed and went back upstairs and maybe even back to sleep."

"Why have you never told me?" Ned asked, feeling she had deceived him in some way all these years. She looked at him with the face of a faded and sad girl and turned back to look at Brother and the dappled street beyond the gate. The black lashes and the lion's hair were all wrong for this sweet and vulnerable face.

"I thought of him as if he were with me last night when that storm struck to drown us all——"

"Oh, Grace, I wondered if I should come to see if you were all right."

"——oh, no, it was a comfort, it was like the storms in old Mobile when I used to leave my bed and go to Billy's room. We would sit together in his windowseat and watch and pretend it was the end of the world and there was nobody left on earth but the two of us." She paused and smiled at him. "Oh, no, Ned, I welcome storms, I am in the best of company when there is a storm. Look, Ned," she said, half laughing. "They aren't staring at us anymore. They have all gone to the offices and the supermarkets. Do you suppose that is where we should have been going all this time?"

"Where is he now, where is Billy now?" Ned asked, choosing not to think about where he should have been going.

"Where is Billy now," she repeated after him, giving a title to the next chapter. "I don't know," the next chapter began. "His bones are mixed with all the other young bones under the wooden crosses in Épinal France. But his head is still in profile in my lap at the foot of the stairs in the front hall of a great dark house in Mobile Alabama. Saying goodby. He knew all the days of telling each other terrible secrets in the treehouse and climbing out of windows at midnight were over and done with that very morning. With the sound of my father's voice. 'I thought it was going to be this way for us forever, Gray,' he said to me. 'You won't like it without me,' he said. 'They will do you in and they will do me in, Gray,' he said. That's what he said, and he was half right. They did him in with his permission. That was the last time I saw him, but I pretend he sees me still. Surviving. He sees me surviving brave as hell and making it look like the trapeze act at the circus. Flying above all the upturned faces waiting for me to fall."

She put her glass on the floor beside the chair and pressed her hands flat on her temples, as if she were holding on a mask, and closed her eyes so tight the lids trembled. She picked up her glass again and rocked back and decided to go on and finish with the whole thing. "I went to his grave once against my better judgment, graves mean very little to me. Mother and I drove in the rain from Paris in a chauffeured limousine. She fell to her knees and tore her stockings in the mud and wept as only Latin and Jewish women can weep. It was the first time I knew she cared anything at all about either of us. Another gift from Billy."

"I grieve for you that you had to lose a brother like that," Ned said.

"Yes," she said, "they throw themselves away, those brothers, they are so generous with their lives. But!" she said suddenly, interrupting herself. She sat straight up in her chair, recovering her accustomed presence. "You will forgive a disgraceful princess her recollections—"

"Forgive them," Ned said. "My dear, I have made them my own."

"And now, there is his ghost again, a stunning reflection of him, clipping your hedge," she said, "while we sit maundering on this tacky little porch, and I must say, oh, I do say—that golden head—"

"Before we go back to reviewing the troops," Ned said, fiddling impatiently with the sleeves of his kimono, "—well, never mind. Perhaps we have had enough history for one day."

"Come now, Trivett. Ask on," Graziella said and leaned her head against the back of the chair with her eyes half closed, as though she had already heard the question.

"Well then," Ned said, protesting delicate hesitation. "Whatever possessed you to marry Gianni di Brabant? I mean, poor boy, he took it all so seriously, while you—"

"Look at me, Ned," she said and did some sleeve rearranging of her own, bringing confusion among the bracelets. "Don't you remember what it was like? After all, I have spent my life running scales and playing little pieces, and then, came time to play the concert and suddenly I had been abandoned by everybody, most of all you. You packed your bags and departed to come back to—*this*," she said, putting up her eyebrows, and swept her arm in a circle, confusing the bracelets even further, "and I suppose to the blond matinee idol from over the rainbow—"

"Now, now, Grace."

"Graziella," she said. "—but, *regardez!* as we used to holler in Paris. I have survived again, and I shall try not to dwell on all that."

She leaned forward to put her glass on the floor again and sat back up, rearranging herself, lifting her arms to see that the lion's hair was as it should be, leaning forward again for her glass, and began to review the troops again with renewed interest. She had changed the key from minor to major by a decision of the will. The troops was clipping the branches of a tall bush. "You are absolutely right as usual," she conceded. "It's a wonder the boy doesn't take off and fly away. We've got to think of some way to get the poor troops out of the hot sun and into the shade of this tacky little porch."

Ned recognized her again but was not entirely relieved of the presence of an unexpected guest. "Brother!" he called out, and the boy turned, surprised to find them on the porch still.

"Yeah, Ned?" he said, straining on the axis, letting the clippers down in one hand and pushing back damp hair with the other.

"Oh, my God," Graziella murmured.

"Put those clippers down, dear boy," Ned said as casually as if he weren't addressing a god descended. "I want you to meet a friend of mine."

"Oh," Brother said. "Okay, Ned," and didn't put the clippers down as he approached them, striding free and easy through a field of lespedeza, moving upward from the chest.

"This," Ned proclaimed, "is the Princess Graziella di Brabant. She wanted to meet you, you remind her of somebody she once knew."

"Oh," Brother said and grasped her extended hand, which waited to be kissed from long habit, and enclosed it briefly and firmly in his own. The princess was shaken by an electrical charge which ran through her body as a result of having caught her hand inside this hardened, over-heated, muscular contraction.

"Do sit down and cool off a minute, Brother—is that right? Brother?" she said, recovering slowly from the momentary weakness. "I'm sure the sun must be getting terribly hot out there." She inhaled the aroma of cut grass and young labor and felt faint again. Brother put the hedge clippers down on the step and sat back on the scrollwork railing and crossed his legs at the ankle, wiping his forehead with the back of his arm.

"Oh, my God," the princess murmured again, resting her chin on the heel of her hand.

"Oh, don't worry, ma'am," Brother reassured her. "It'll hold. This house is built strong."

"It most certainly is," Graziella agreed. "And you can call me Gray. Call me Gray."

"Yes, ma'am," Brother said and let it go at that.

"Gray," Graziella stressed, and Brother recognized a sudden enforcement in her eyes.

"Gray," he said, not without discomfort. "Where's old Jake?" he asked Ned to relieve his difficulty with informality.

"He is staying with Jubie, while his mother pursues the calling so dear to her heart," Ned said. "The pieces of the puzzle have a way of falling into place when he is concerned."

"That's Jake, all right," Brother said.

"Mister Cullen has a sharp eye for advantage in spite of defective vision," Graziella interjected.

"Now, now, Grace," Ned said, treading on thin ice. She shot a look at him, however it missed target as he had begun to levitate, floating some half-inch above the floor. "Let me get you some orange juice, Brother. The princess—Gray and I are having the least little splash of vodka in ours."

"Just some ice water, Ned, I got to finish up the yard."

"Oh, *nonsense!*" Gray exclaimed. "You've got to do nothing of the kind." Ned floated through the screen door, having levitated another half-inch.

The princess and the reflection sat in silence, each considering the other somewhat askance but without embarrassment.

"My! you *are* young," the princess declared and could have bitten her tongue off. However, it was the only thing she could think of to say, and she felt, if the silence had extended, it might have become overburdened with significance. "But then, I'm not all that old," she prompted and paused to laugh lightly and leave space for the confirmation.

"No, ma'am," the confirmation came, "you ain't all that old."

"No," she agreed, "you're absolutely right," and forgot to be even slightly put off by his reservation, as the inspiration of her next thought heightened her color and impelled her onward. "I am a collapsing star," she said, smiling with her lids almost closed. "Do you know what a collapsing star is, Brother?"

"No," Brother said flatly, at a loss for any form of address, habitual or respectful.

"Well," Graziella crooned, "according to astronomers, in our universe—or any universe for that matter—the closer you get to a collapsing star, the slower time goes by, until one day, it stops completely. And you see," she went on, putting out an arm jingling with bracelets, "I can't even wear a watch."

"That would be a nice kind of a star to get close to," Brother said, and Graziella computed instantaneously the range of possibilities veiled in the innocence of this statement. Ned eased back out through the door at exactly the wrong moment, just as she was formulating a provocative response.

"Here you are, Brother," he said. "Cool off with that and go home and put on your coat and tie. We are taking the princess to the club for luncheon. We must bend every effort to keep the natives restless."

"But, Ned, I got to finish the yard," Brother demurred.

"You've got to do nothing of the kind!" Gray exclaimed. "Not while I am in residence."

"Run up the flag," Ned said, dimpling.

CHAPTER EIGHT

Susan lay sunning in the deck chair, wearing a bathing suit which looked like a little girl's dress. It had a ruffley kind of a skirt, and she felt like a damn fool every time she put it on, but the woman at the department store had told her she looked precious in it. The woman had shaved off her eyebrows and made new ones with a lead pencil. "It fills you out, honey," she had said, and Susan did want to look precious and filled out this of all mornings.

She lay like a cat with her eyes almost closed, listening to the half-hearted waves stumble onto the shore and recede apologetically, giving the impression they had had no part in the violence of the night before. The day was crystal clear, nothing softened or obscured, making it difficult for Susan to believe she had been a part of the way it had been. It was a picture she wouldn't have thought to make in her wildest dreams, and she thought maybe it *was* only a wild dream. But, no, there it was: Skinner crazy as hell, shooting up out of the top of a wave, not caring about what could happen or what had ever happened before. And then, after that.

There certainly was no reason for her to lie in the sun. She had lived in the sun all her years, but she felt it might burn away the anxiety of the nerves left over from the emotional extremes she had survived the night before. She thought she was like some delicate musical instrument which had been played beyond its capacity and all the strings out of tune and maybe one string broken.

Skinner was sleeping swaddled in sheets, lost in oblivion, cloistered in the cool bedroom upstairs where she had imprisoned him with her will. From where she lay, she could open her eyes a little and observe the upper third of the bedroom door through the glass wall whenever she felt like it. She should lock the door and keep him there for good against his will. Lock Julian out. Lock Julian out, so he couldn't drag him off anywhere ever again and bring him back crazy. Drunk was one thing, drunk and crazy was quite another.

Well, that was silly, but, anyway, my Lord, she had learned a lot from it all. She owed the storm a great debt, she would try never to be afraid of storms again. It had come over her like the moon up there. Showing him what she was sure neither of them had ever suspected before. A Wanton Woman and more than glad to be. She understood now why Eve accepted that apple from the snake, any woman worth her salt would have done the same. She had new respect for Eve and was happier than she could say that Eve had made the wrong decision. Women all over the world should be advised.

Yes, well, she had heard about and read about and seen some pictures once about the way she had behaved up there in that bedroom last night, but to tell you the truth, she had never really believed it. Not until last night. After last night, it could be she could cure herself of making pictures and devote herself to actuality.

Yes, well, she had dried him off like that, stronger than he was, but realizing he was at once a boy and a rapist, understanding at last the vulnerability and the danger, which in some strange way came to the same thing. She had kissed the boy's face and hair and had dried the rapist's body, protecting it as if it were something precious she had always wanted and so had stolen, not even considering the risk. And then, after that.

"Boy, I was something else again," she murmured. "My God, I have wasted so much time." She smiled and began to purr.

She let her head fall on one side and studied the round, metal table through half-closed eyes. It had overturned, the umbrella still open, broken now, a victim of the storm. She let her head fall in the other direction towards the sea and was surprised to see Julian passing along the shore. His attitude, strolling without destination, head down, Susan found the very picture of dejection. He didn't lift his head to look in her direction, but at a certain moment, he put up an arm and held it there briefly, and she took that to be an acknowledgment of her presence on the deck. Forty-something and still so young, she thought, why is it Laura can't—

She sighed and directed her attention upwards through the glass wall towards the top third of the bedroom door and made a picture of Skinner, wound in sheets there, and she thought she must go to see him as soon as possible. There was something which hung in the air like a threat, so that she didn't want to approach it. "Skinner," she said and decided to leave the deck and the sun and the thrashing surf and the aimless people on the beach who were as indifferent to her as she was to them.

When she stepped into the living room, she found she had been blinded by the light again and stood in her precious bathing suit waiting for the shadows to thin. She looked upwards to find the white apex of the ceiling to discover Skinner leaning on the balcony rail looking down at her. She hadn't considered that he might escape from the bedroom, and so said nothing for a moment, taken aback, as if the substitute, leaning with his hands on the railing, were watching her with suspicion and possibly even disapproval. He was fully dressed with his coat and tie and his hair too carefully combed across his forehead.

"Oh, Skin," she said, trying not to betray her surprise. "I thought you were still sleeping."

"Something has happened here, Susan, what has happened here?" Skinner asked and she wondered how long he had been standing there like that. Suddenly, she felt herself in grave danger and said nothing, not knowing what the question meant and afraid of committing herself. "What has been going on here, Susan?" Skinner asked.

"What on earth are you talking about, Skinner, and why are you dressed for Sunday school?" she asked and waited for the smile, but there wasn't any.

"Who has been here, who has been sleeping in the guest room?" Skinner persisted.

"Jubie," she said. "I told you that, Skinner, I told you Laura had sent Jubie over to spend the night. Why are you dressed up like that?" she asked, foregoing the old joke about Sunday school.

"Since when has Jubie taken up smoking cigarettes?" he said.

"Cigarettes?" Susan said, as if it were a word she was not sure of.

"Cigarettes, Susan," Skinner said, his voice turning hard and severe. "There are cigarette butts in the ashtray in the bedroom, and as I recall, you didn't smoke when I left this house to go to Rome."

"Oh, yes, of course," Susan said and was frozen with fear, as though she had been apprehended in the commission of a crime. "Jake Cullen— a Mister Cullen, a guest of Ned Trivett's from California. He brought Jubie. He spent the night to keep him company. He is staying with Jubie now, while Laura—"

"Ned Trivett," Skinner said, his voice rising as if he had found the evidence he had been seeking, not even bothering to ask why an utter stranger had spent the night in his house with his wife in it. "Don't tell me Ned Trivett has been here, don't tell me you let him come here—"

"Why, no, Skin—"

"—since when have you become so intimate with Ned Trivett, and what does he want from you?"

"Skinner, why are you doing this?" she asked. "Why are you starting the day off like this? Ned Trivett has not been here, this man from California is a friend of his—"

"You haven't told me what he wants," he said. "You haven't told me what that kind of a man wants from you, Susan."

"Skinner, this is ridiculous, I think I've gone crazy. What kind of man? You mean he's a fairy?" she said and began to be amused but arrested the impulse. "Lots of people are fairies, I know that now."

"What do you mean, now? What has happened here that you say, now, like that?"

"My God, Skinner, it wasn't Ned Trivett, I don't even *like* Ned Trivett, it was this man from—Are you afraid of him, Skinner? You were never afraid of him before, what has made you afraid of him all of a sudden?" she said, feeling she had become entangled in a net from which there was no escape. "It doesn't rub off on you, you know, Skinner, it isn't catching like mumps or something."

"What the hell are you talking about?" he asked, gripping the balcony rail. "Afraid of that ass? I don't want him here, Susan. I don't want his friends here. You never know what people might say. I don't want people like that in this house," he said. "Remember that."

"*You* remember that. *You* tell him that," she said, growing tired of entrapment. "I don't understand this conversation, and I'm not going to put up with it a minute longer. Where are you going, Skinner? You've got your hair combed for Sunday school," she tried again and failed.

"What was your business with Ned Trivett?" he asked again, as if this were an official investigation, and he had never heard the joke about Sunday school before in his life.

"I can't believe this is happening," she said. "Ned Trivett hasn't been near this—My God, what happened to last night?" she asked nobody in particular, putting her hands on her hips and then realizing how foolish she must look in the damn bathing suit. "My God, Bates," she said to him, "are we the same two people we were last night up there in that bedroom?" She pointed towards the location under discussion and held the question like that for two or three seconds and then let her arm fall. "What did I do? Did I carry on like that with some stranger? If I did I want his telephone number."

"That's not funny," Skinner said, and she thought she had had him there for a minute, but he stood up straight and frowned down on her. "Last night," he said and regarded her as if he were trying to solve a puzzle to which she might have the answer, but an answer he was not anxious to hear. "What's been going on here?" he said instead. "What has gone on in this house in my absence?"

"Well, turnabout is fair play, what went—what went on in Rome for ten days, Skinner? What went on between you and Julian that has turned you into strangers? Can you tell me that?" She green-eyed him with all the intensity she could muster, but he remained impenetrable. "To tell the truth," she went on, "I'm getting tired of this long-distance discussion. Either you come down here, or I'll come up there, and we can get this thing settled on the same floor."

He frowned down at her for a moment longer, as though he hadn't quite heard the question, and crossed the balcony and came down the stair and walked right past her, as if she weren't standing there waiting for him, and went down the hallway into the kitchen. "Oh, I couldn't be better, thank you, and hope you are the same," she said and followed him into the kitchen. "Good morning, Skinner," she said heartily and sat down at the table with the feeling she had cornered him at last.

"Where is the orange juice?" he asked, peering into the refrigerator as though he were making a survey.

"It's where it always is," she said. "Good morning, Skinner."

"Nothing is where it always is," he said.

"Oh, you get that feeling too," she said. "On the top shelf, good morning, Skinner."

"Oh," Skinner said. He poured himself a glass of orange juice and walked out of the kitchen, leaving her in the damn bathing suit to stare at the refrigerator and an empty chair, her chin in her hand and her long brown legs crossed under the kitchen table. How long can I take this? she asked the empty chair. What do I do now, do I just sit here invisible until he decides to leave? "No," she said, "I don't," and followed him into the living room. He was standing with his glass of orange juice looking out through the glass wall, and she doubted that he was seeing anything. She felt if he was seeing the deck and the beach and the sea, they had lost all meaning for him. She leaned against the doorway watching him and found his back meant very little to her at this moment. "Good morning, Skinner," she said one last time.

"Good morning, Missook," he said without turning away from the glass wall, and his back meant more to her than she could possibly have said.

"Oh, well, dear Lord, thank you for that at least," she said, and she sat in the chair opposite the sofa and recalled the man she had seen sprawled in it the night before. "Can't we just sit down and talk for a minute, Skin? We haven't really had a chance to talk yet, we've just got to talk, Skin."

"I have to see Julian," he said. "I have to talk to Julian."

"You'll have a hell of a time talking to Julian," she told him. "He's out watching the old ocean roll in and roll out and roll in and roll out. You'll have a hell of a time talking to him this morning."

He turned to look at her at last, and she thought he looked very tired, and she thought she must look thin again. She was sorry it hadn't changed after all, she was sorry she had to worry still about being too thin, she was sorry Venus had gone out of her life so suddenly. "How do you know that?" he asked her.

"I saw him walking down the beach while I was sitting on the deck. He looked so lonely, I—When can we talk, Skinner?" she asked him. "There are some things I have to tell you."

"I thought as much," he said, and he smiled without any reason to smile. "I know there is something, but it will have to wait. I have to see Julian. We left several important deals hanging when we left here ten days ago. My business with him can't wait."

"But I can, is that it?" she said. "Susan can wait, after all she is only a wife." He put his glass on the table by the chair, and she remembered his hand on his chest the night before, "Where is that ring?" she asked him.

"I don't know," he said, and it seemed to Susan he didn't.

"That's funny, Skinner, isn't that funny?" she said. "Look." She thrust out her hand with the pale band of skin around the finger for him to see, but he didn't bother to look at it.

"I've got to go," he said. "I have to find Julian, no matter where he is. There are things that can't wait any longer."

"Is that the way it is now, Skin?" she asked him. "When do we talk, when do we find out what is happening to us—what has happened to us?"

"Nothing has happened to me, Susan. However, something happened here while I was gone, I can feel it."

"Well now, let me see. I decided not to go back to hustling," she said and suppressed her amusement, again finding none in him, only a quickening in his eyes at her easy use of an uneasy word. "All right then," she said. "Sit down and look at me, I've got this feeling you haven't seen me yet. Sit down and look at me, Skinner."

"There will be time for that," he said and smiled without trying. She put great faith in that smile, but, "Where are the keys?" he asked.

"Now, Skinner. Right now," she said. "It has to be now, we have to talk now."

"We'll talk when I get back," he said.

"I don't think it can wait. I don't know why I think that, but I do," she said. "I have the feeling we have lost something somewhere, and I don't think I can feel lost like this for a whole day. I might die or fly away or something."

"I'm sorry," he said and picked up the keys from the bar. "This is the future I'm concerned with, this is a matter of my place in the world. You and Julian—"

"What is happening this very minute between you and me in this house is my place in the world, and my future is in grave peril," she said, standing up so he could see how she was, and remembering the damn bathing suit, sat down again. "I beg you to take off your coat and sit with me and tell me who I am to you," she pleaded. "I beg you to be with me for a little while, Skinner."

"I don't understand you, Susan," he said. "You have to realize my position in Milford demands my time, and I have let too much time slip by me." He paused and looked at her, wondering what move to make next and came forward to kiss her.

"No, don't do that," she said, turning her face away. "Don't ever do me favors, don't ever do anything for me you don't feel."

"All right, goddam it," Skinner said. "Have it your way. You always do."

"And the same to you," she said. And he left suddenly and without hesitation and she sat listening to the car start and then depart along the gravel drive.

CHAPTER NINE

Skinner went down the back steps to his car under the house, and his heart turned in his breast. He thought he was going to cry. It came to him like a sudden rush of lust that has no object, a movement of memory without images. He saw his suitcase in the back of Susan's station wagon, and it seemed to him it belonged to somebody with whom he was only vaguely acquainted. He tried to explain to himself why neither of them had bothered to take it in last night—that was strange—and the sense of some terrible loss ran through him like a shudder. It was as if the suitcase belonged to another life or awaited another departure or had no final destination at all. He took his glasses out of his breast pocket and put them on, and the chill subsided, as though he had put the immediate present into focus.

As he backed his car into the driveway, he decided, well, he'd been drunk, and it was unreasonable to think Susan should carry a heavy suitcase up all those steps, although she had always insisted on doing that kind of thing. "African natives do it," she had explained to him once, and he thought she had probably made that up to accommodate her determination of the moment. The picture of an African woman, bare-breasted and with a ring in her nose, carrying her husband's suitcase stuffed with Brooks Brothers shirts almost amused him, but not quite.

Driving along the highway, he took his glasses off and put them back in his pocket. Nonetheless, it was clear to him there had been no real reason for him to have dressed and left the house—except that he didn't want to be with Susan. Her insolence and her approach to the events of the night before would have demanded a response he didn't feel he could make so soon. She would make it funny or sad or both, and there was nothing he could do with that now.

He had nowhere to go. He didn't want to be with Julian either. He could see exactly how Julian would look and he was tired of that. Julian would look like a blue-eyed Indian chieftain whose warrior son had violated the ancient and honorable tribal code. He had looked like that for some days now, hurt and offended at the same time and nothing spoken.

Skinner was almost amused again at having an African native wife sitting bare-breasted in his kitchen and an Indian chieftain ranging the shore considering his fall from grace. He could almost determine the exact moment of his fall, and a fall, he knew, there had been. He considered it himself and wanted to stop considering it as soon as possible. Well, fuck Julian and his code, he concluded, and knew he didn't mean it.

Oh, God, all right then. He would just drive around for a while and see if any of the properties he and Julian managed had changed hands in their absence. Fuck Rome Italy too, he thought, and he knew he meant that. There should be a way to get things moving again. There should be a way to pick up the rhythm of his days, so that tomorrow might be something like the days he had lived before. Those days, easy in retrospect, that followed one after another in comfortable progression with the same small approved retards and advances everybody had. Moving up in the world.

He passed Mrs. Bender strutting and pecking in her vegetable garden like an enormous hen, wearing a large, insouciant straw sombrero tied under her chin, as if she had exchanged head-gear with some kept woman in Acapulco, say. The kind of woman who wore jewelry on the beach. Mrs. Bender's highway property was very valuable, that he knew for a fact, and its value increased daily with no effort or concern on her part. Mrs. Bender, Skinner realized, was not interested in moving up in the world. She was interested in keeping the bugs off her tomato plants and enhancing the reputation of her table among a lot of people who didn't count for much. And in talk; she was interested in any kind of talk. He was relieved she had not caught sight of his car, because he knew she would have summoned him for consultation, pointing sternly—"You! Skinner Bates!"—and throwing back a heavy arm like a basketball coach signaling a substitution. And when Mrs. Bender summoned you, you went. Especially if she had known you since you were a boy and still instructed your mother on the telephone as to cuisine and manure at least once a week. He couldn't think of a worse fate than having to check in with Mrs. Bender with a terrific hangover. She had no traffic with drink, Mr. Bender having fallen to his death under a train in questionable condition some years back. Dorothy Bender is a remarkable woman, people always said. And she was.

He was stopped by the red light—bleached an ineffectual pink by countless summer suns—at the Casino corner and was assailed by mindless music and the smell of beer and frying food, and he was aroused by the incendiary atmosphere of youthful promiscuity. This aimless crossroad, where they wore only enough clothing to stay within the law and sometimes not even that, had always troubled him. He had seen them laughing with each other in the knowledge of secrets he could only guess at, and when the laughs had played out, he thought he could see in their throw-away attitudes secrets yet to be revealed. These were people indifferent to approval or disapproval of any kind, and yet, as always, he found himself excited by the promise that hung in the air, and despite any effort, his body seceded from his will, making promises of its own. He knew then that the Casino corner was the real reason—on this as on many other days—for his not raising the window of the car and turning on the air-conditioning, even though he had always told himself he thought air-conditioning in automobiles was ridiculous except on long trips. He recalled having come here on feverish nights during the early days of his marriage, sitting by the hour in his car, observing the circuitous rituals of pursuit, aroused and avid, until it became urgent that he go home to Susan. It was a deadly memory.

But the memory resolved suddenly when he realized that a stranger was watching him from the shadow of an awning, leaning in one of the arched doorways to a malodorous place where cold drinks and hot dogs were sold. Although the place was crowded with young people turning in circles among themselves as always, this man—this stranger with side-burns sliced down his cheeks—stood apart. He seemed not to feel the heat that caused the others to frown and pant and push damp hair back from their foreheads. He stood somehow in a cool shadow of his own. It appeared to Skinner that the man had recognized him from sometime in the past, and it troubled him unduly that perhaps he recognized the man. But that was not possible. He was trash, one of those who spend the summer naked in and out of the sun during the day and sleeping in any available bed with any available person at night, satisfying themselves without regret. He smiled at Skinner from under the brim of a worn, bandless panama hat and arched his shoulders back so that his bare chest thrust forward in the buttonless vest he wore as if it were a mark of superiority. He raised his dark eyebrows slightly and made a summoning gesture with his head.

Against his will, as if his own will had been dispossessed by another more decisive will, Skinner pulled the car over to the curb and waited. "Goddam!" he said and his heart turned in his breast again. The man drifted over to the car, looking without curiosity first one way and then the other, and leaned his arms into the open window smiling with swollen lips as if he had just been sipping from a cup. It was more the remains of a smile.

"Yeah?" he said.

"Yes, what is it?" Skinner asked sharply and thought he would have pulled away had the man not been leaning in at the window.

"You tell me," the man said in an almost inaudible, dragging voice that seemed muffled by drowsiness or ennui. "You're here, ain't you, man?" He withdrew his dark gaze from Skinner's eyes and looked over his shoulder down the busy street as though he were watching for somebody he had promised to meet but didn't care whether he met him or not. In profile, silhouetted against the blazing sun on the cement block building behind him, he was extraordinarily handsome and more than that. He was a black promise of anything you could think of.

"What the hell is this all about?" Skinner asked, realizing he was trapped, and it tormented him that he had trapped himself.

The stranger returned his contemptuous and amused gaze to Skinner's face. "I believe you were looking for me, right? This is the place, I'm your man. I'm Dick," he said and waited for this information to predict the way things were to go. "What can I do for you, man?"

"Not a goddam thing," Skinner said. "Get your goddam arms out of my window, I'm in a hurry."

"Oh?" the man said easily, not in a hurry ever, anywhere. "Well, don't his mama dress him cute? You need a party, man?" he went on with no intention of releasing his prisoner. "You look like you could use some good company, man, and you've found your boy. Crazy Dick is good company and Crazy Dick needs some bread bad, man. Maybe you heard about Crazy Dick. Here it is, man, nothing like it anywhere. The best, man," he said, "the very best." He loomed farther into the car, emanating a kind of vicious decision. Skinner began to panic and tried to remember how he had come to get himself into this situation. It struck him suddenly that he was at the most visible crossroad possible and that probably two or three people who knew who he was had already seen him in this humiliating circumstance and would be curious enough to ask other friends what he could have been up to with such riff-raff. "Come on, man, make up your mind, let's get it on," the man said and the smile had vanished. "You got something on your mind and I got something on my mind. I got what you want and I can tell from your set-up you got plenty of what I need. You didn't look me over for nothing, you didn't pull over here for nothing, man."

"Now listen here, goddam it, I didn't—*please,*" Skinner said and fell back against the door to avoid the promise. "Please, I've got to—" he said.

"Mama's little boy lost his nerve all of a sudden," the man announced and the swollen smile crept back like a cut. He extended his arm well into the car and opened out his hand, palm up. Skinner stared at it. It was a beautiful hand, strong and muscular. "We can't let Dick get too thin, now can we, man?" he droned on. "Crazy Dick needs a fix."

"Oh!" Skinner said. "Oh, I see. Here," he said, searching the pockets of his coat desperately. "Here," he said and took a strange gold object from his pocket and put it in the hand which remained flat open.

"Jesus," the man said, betraying surprise for the first time, and closed the hand into a fist. He withdrew from the window. Skinner took off fast from the curb, skidding his tires, but to his dismay, found himself stopped dead in traffic a few yards distant at the turn onto the bridge. He couldn't understand his desperation, he couldn't recall how he had come to be talking to a stranger nor the certain threat the stranger must have made to frighten him into paying for his release with a ring which, he realized now, had been a threat in itself. When had he put the ring into his pocket and had he brought it along as a bribe? And really, where had the ring come from? He would try not to remember that. He thought perhaps he could live out the rest of his life without remembering that. But he knew in his heart he would not forget that he had betrayed in a moment of cowardice the sweet promise of his being.

He glanced into his rearview mirror. The stranger stood there regarding him, his arms thrust into his trouser pockets, pitching his shoulders forward, so that the vest hung open exposing his smooth bare chest. He was laughing, insolent and corrupt, a cigarette clamped in his white teeth. Suddenly, he turned and disappeared into the shadows of the arch from which he had appeared and just as suddenly disappeared into the shadows of Skinner's mind forever.

Susan did the best she could with the rest of the day. She didn't die and she didn't fly away. She pushed the vacuum cleaner around knowing that it really wasn't necessary, and she changed the sheets on all the beds. "We might as well start out with a clean slate," she said and gave in to amusement and laughed a little. She was glad to know serious things were still funny to her. She even opened a drawer to Skinner's dresser, thinking she might see the ring, but felt furtive and dishonest and unhappy that she could do such a thing behind his back. So.

She sat down at the kitchen table and tried to smoke one of Skinner's cigarette butts with a cup of coffee but found the cigarette unsatisfactory as she always had, regretting it was a gesture she couldn't make. Other girls—other women she knew sat down and had a cup of coffee and a cigarette when they wanted to think or wanted not to think, but, she thought, I think too much doing anything, I think too much standing up or lying down. She decided it would be wonderful to be one of those girls—one of those women who never seem to think, and she decided you couldn't think things out anyhow, you have to live things out, you have to be standing in the door to meet them. Even when you're not looking all that well.

In the middle of the afternoon, she made herself a tomato sandwich whether she wanted it or not. A tomato sandwich. "Jubie," she said. "I wish Jubie were here." Oh Lord, she thought, just at that moment, I understood Laurie. A gift beyond value. You look in his eyes and you see yourself just as you are, whether you are a girl—a woman who drinks likker or one who thinks too much and finds everything wanting. "Love," she said, her eyes filling with tears. "Or distress, like the rest of us. Only he doesn't understand cruelty, the rest of us expect it. We meet it at the door. It takes him by the throat every time, my Jubie." And he goes right on wanting life.

She wandered back into the living room and stopped to stare at the telephone. "No," she said, "I have begged him once, I won't beg him again. I am about to conclude Skinner Bates is just one of those good-looking, get-ahead boys." She hadn't thought that out, it had just come to her, not standing in the door but by the telephone. She watched the ocean collapse and then billow like a great silk scarf. "I'm tired of this fucking house," she said and resented again the woman who had dared speak that word in her presence. But she was tired of this house. Yesterday, her life had been in this house, but everything had changed since yesterday. "Well, I'll take the only available means of transportation and go to the supermarket." She laughed and was glad, once more, that she laughed about serious things. "Maybe, I can be beautiful again tonight," she said. "There's still that hope. There's always that hope." Thank God for sin.

She painted her eyes in the dressing table mirror, whether her father and Julian and Skinner like it or not, and she parted her hair in the middle and brushed it out straight like the girls who pretended to fight with the golden boys in the surf and weren't fighting at all. She put on a blue shirt and a pair of white slacks and her sandals. "Who the hell am I getting ready for?" she asked the girl—the woman in the mirror.

Riding along the highway, she passed Mrs. Bender's place and saw Mrs. Bender marching, like a stout, displeased admiral on the way to inspect his troops, towards her garden to pick vegetables for the evening mess. Mrs. Bender ran a tight ship and took in boarders and everybody said, "Isn't Dorothy Bender a remarkable woman?" However, Susan knew Mrs. Bender had more to say than anybody could possibly listen to, and so a tight ship and an obedient crew were a necessary discipline. Some members of the crew had gone deaf over the years, but Mrs. Bender never knew the difference. It isn't always a sacrifice to be a remarkable woman.

In my own way, I'm a remarkable woman, Susan concluded. It is, to give you an example, remarkable what comes into my mind sometimes, and she felt the excitement she had always felt as she approached the Casino corner. The corner had always been for her a kind of carnival with people who hadn't come from anywhere in particular and hadn't anywhere in particular to go but came together as if by instinct to desire and be desired. It was there the young and indifferent and abandoned gave a performance she felt put sensual life to the test and which intrigued her more than she cared to admit. Even as a child, she had been attracted by the fantasy of the dress and the near nudity and the sense of urgency, of defiance, of rising heat.

She had seen once, riding in the car with her father, a man carrying a woman in his tattooed arms, and the man and the woman were naked from the waist up. They were laughing in a way she hadn't known before and that she could not put out of her mind. She had never stopped wondering what their secret might have been, and she had never stopped hoping someday she might know the secret herself. The people she knew, the grown people she saw every day, didn't seem to have this secret, and they didn't seem to miss it. "Don't look at that white trash, Susan," her father had said. But then she had seen them, and they had changed the way she thought about life.

As she approached the corner, she saw from a distance the indolent figure of a man who seemed to her, for some reason, to have been waiting for her to pass. He had come from nowhere, wearing a faded vest hanging open exposing his bare chest and a stained, bandless panama hat pulled down over one eye. His bronzed arms were thrust into his trouser pockets pitching his shoulders forward. She drew abreast of him in the slow summer traffic, and he smiled at her through the open window of the car, a half-smoked cigarette clamped in his teeth. The smile was insolent and intimate and malignant, and he did no more than raise his dark brows under the brim of the hat. But that was enough. In the rearview mirror, she watched him blow cigarette smoke upwards, still smiling, as if their encounter had not ended.

My God, I am beautiful, she thought. My God, I have been a faithful wife to my husband, white trash, but in your case, if you will take off your hat and your vest, I'll make an exception. She drove on with the traffic, but she longed to turn back and pass him again, to light his cigarette, perhaps, even just return his smile. To be beautiful again.

Sin. She decided he must know about sin. Only sin can be so careless, only sin can make you feel beautiful in that malignant and cruel way. "I wish I had been born somewhere else," she said. I wish I had been born another woman, I would gladly have given my life to sin. I would always be beautiful to somebody who had nowhere to go and all the time in the world to get there.

But she did not turn back. She went to the supermarket, and she stopped by Mrs. Bender's place on the way home for some of her beautiful tomatoes. Mrs. Bender had set the table for ten. Dorothy Bender was a remarkable woman.

CHAPTER TEN

Skinner waited, scarcely able to catch his breath, impatient to desperation in the broiling traffic, held up under the ineffectual pink stoplight. It seemed essential to his sanity that he turn his car onto the bridge over the sound and escape the Casino corner forever, although he couldn't comprehend why this might be, except that he had contracted a terrible fever of the mind.

He took his glasses out of his breast pocket and put them on hoping to see something more clearly. A girl with lustrous hair down her back, her brown skin slick with oil, passed in front of his car in the embrace of two young men, one dark, one light. They were laughing, leaning in to each other. Skinner decided they were telling unspeakable secrets. The girl turned her laugh towards him through the windshield almost as if he had called her name. He was subjected to her indifference and her brilliant white teeth. "I could show you secrets," he murmured and turned against himself for having said it and was transported against his will to certain clandestine places he had visited with John Thomas in Rome where

careless young bodies were on display, more seductive and naked than had
they actually been naked, as he felt he was naked now, idling under the
pink stoplight.

His heart turned in his breast once again, and he was frightened by
his loneliness in an unrecognizable world. He could not face his wife, he
couldn't face Julian, he couldn't face Mrs. Bender even. And he couldn't
possibly remain alone in his own company. He was a divided spirit, and
he found he hadn't the strength to lead more than one life at a time. He
thought he might be able to talk Dorothy Bender into selling her property.
Possibly even tomorrow.

But, no.

Automobile horns were blaring like angry, electronic trumpets, having no connection whatsoever with human breath. The open car in front
of him full of blond girls drinking from beer cans under the blazing sun
moved off at last. And Skinner escaped onto the bridge that spanned the
broad sound. Sailboats flew on midday water like kites. It surprised him
that he was headed towards the country club, and he decided it would be
pleasant to sit and exchange small talk with Asa, who had tended bar in
the grill there, unhurried and contained, for as long as anybody could
remember. It would be getting on towards lunch time in the rambling
old plantation house where rutted fields had long since become golf course
and tennis courts, and he thought it might not be too difficult hailing
the early-drink golfers and the lunching wives in summer dresses. They
might wonder why he was there without Julian or Susan and ask each
other, leaning over the shrimp salad and iced tea, why he was there alone
and drinking in the middle of the day. But what was that? That was
morbid curiosity—diversion from not enough money or a marriage growing tedious in long unhappy nights.

Asa was glad to see him again or made gentle sounds and faces that
indicated as much and shook his hand with his worn brown hand with

white nails, a gesture bestowed in a remote manner upon a chosen few. In this tiny region, it was a sign of acceptance and recognition, and Skinner knew that Julian, without thinking about it, had obtained this favor for him.

"You back, Mister Skinner," Asa informed him. "You see anything over yonder you ain't seed right here?"

"More than I wanted to see," Skinner told him.

"Uh-oh," Asa said, understanding everything. "Where Julian? How Julian make out? He make out all right?"

And here was where the line was drawn; Julian's place was such that he could be called by his first name by an old colored man, who had known the father and the father's father and all their absurd triumphs and failures and who had hauled Julian home, staring stone-eyed through the windshield of the immaculate old car, many a Saturday night, so that he wouldn't drive when he had had too much to drink. Which he always had. Of course, everybody had too much to drink on Saturday night— that was the way it was done—but Julian was the one delivered buckle-kneed to his mother's front door. At least, Skinner mused, I have progressed from Mister Bates to Mister Skinner.

Moving up in the world.

"Julian doesn't change, no matter where he is. Julian is always Julian," Skinner said, and the turn of his voice betrayed an edge of disparagement he had not intended.

"He is," said Asa, letting it go at that, knowing how it was already for a long time. "And look the same he always did. You want a scotch?"

"I think I'll have a martini, I got used to martinis," Skinner apologized.

"Uh-oh," Asa said.

"Oil to ease the ride," Skinner quoted and looked about him, feeling in a shock the difference between this dim, cloistered room and the joyous stone squares of Rome, thrown open to the sky, sharp-pointed obelisks spiring upwards and great marble gods disposed magnificently naked in fountain spray.

"That oughta ease it," Asa said, putting the martini on the bar. He had put aside the mask he wore for occasion and exposed the inscrutable and guarded face which was his own, although there was no noticeable change in his features.

Skinner sipped the martini and came back to himself at last, having been located to some degree. The bite of the martini and the paneled room with the prints of English racing horses and no windows, so that there was no time of day, removed him from the present to no particular time at all, although he could see familiar figures moving about under the awnings of the verandah at the far end of a narrow entrance hall and although the light from the adjacent, many-windowed dining room flooded through the double doors. From time to time, some member or other peered in, balanced halfway in at the doors, looking for a companion or checking out the action, and retired again, leaving Skinner to himself, except for Asa who had withdrawn into an interior landscape more mysterious even than his countenance. Waitresses in peach-colored aprons turned up at the end of the bar, speaking a language of their own, and gave orders and wrote on pads and hurried out on rubber soles carrying trays of drinks without having bothered to notice him. He had another martini. He could make a bundle on Dorothy Bender's place.

But, no.

Suddenly, he found himself returned to the delirium of the night before and could scarcely believe that he, Skinner, had been that person. And God knows the woman bore little resemblance to Susan, but it had been Susan all right, not insolent but something else inconceivable. It appalled him he had known his wife so little. She had taken him as he remembered his uncle's wife had taken him for the first time when he had been not long captive to the constant and overwhelming suggestions of his body. It had come about in a derelict shack among the grassy dunes of Cobbs Island—he meant to go back there someday now and verify the spot to make sure it had not been a dream; he could recall the fragrance of the sun on rotting wood and the stripes of light that fell across their moist, striving bodies from the cracks between the weatherworn planks and her frenzied, mindless instruction and then, afterwards, falling back in consternation. She had been astonished at his maturity, comparing him to his uncle David, his father's younger brother, as if she saw them standing there together, side by side, almost touching. What was her name? Did she remember or had it been nothing to her?

Did Susan remember and what had it been to her? She had taken her advantage and given instruction like the other woman, his aunt, wasn't she? speaking in a low, harsh voice, not her own, almost like a man's voice in the darkness of the bedroom, as if he wouldn't have known what to do with her. He knew very well now she had consumed him in some way and would have consumed him, even if it had been against his will. She had compared him to some other man who had gone before, even though the man who had gone before had been himself, as if she saw him standing there, two men at the same time, side by side, almost touching. There had been the same urgency and even the fragrance of the sun on rotting wood. Could it be possible he had given away too much of himself, had they revealed too much of themselves and (suddenly!) what would Julian have thought of them?

He laughed out loud, delighted at the look (suddenly!) on Julian's face and glanced up, startled, to find himself where he was. And (suddenly!) it fell upon him with tremendous weight why he had been so sad, why he had wanted to weep when he was leaving the house. It had overwhelmed him. He had been desolate that his father—so handsome, so young he must have been then, so like himself, Skinner, now, standing laughing before the mirror with lather on his face—had been killed by a spurt of shot from a foreign sky when he had been still only a boy, and

there was nobody left to call him son. Not the way a father can say son.
Julian might have done it, had even tried, but Julian had resigned and
didn't call him anything at all anymore, because he. . . . Vividly now,
Julian's face came to him as it might have been had he come upon the
two of them tangled in the sheets of the disordered bed. He laughed like
the boy he had been, showing his little white teeth, enjoying the shock
that the angels were ordinary sinners.

"What you laughing at, Mister Skinner?" Asa asked and took up
a corner of the laugh, catching the spirit of rebellion, neglecting to put
up the mask. "That ain't no back home in Milford laugh. That laugh
come from somewhere you ain't telling nobody."

"I couldn't tell it, even if I wanted to," Skinner said and flushed red
and half drunk, feeling the secrets his body knew had been exposed. "Give
me another one, Asa," he said and reduced their exchange to the usual
wary smiles.

"Uh-oh," Asa said, recognizing the rejection.

A foursome of paunched and balding boys, purple from the sun and
pocket flasks and middle age, wearing colorful open shirts and Madras
trousers, rambled down the polished hall from the verandah, laughing in
wheezy spasms at a joke Skinner knew would be malicious and not funny
—not even to the foursome. "Princess, he calls her, some kind of back
door blue blood, I guess," one of them said, keeping the joke on the rise.

"And with Brother Reeves in tow, I wonder which one of them he's
for," another said, and they wheezed another round of mirthless laughter
and pulled back chairs around a table in the middle of the room.

"Funny kind of a princess, if you ask me. Did you see her fixing
Brother's tie, like he ought to be out here in the first place?" the first one
wanted to know.

"I got an idea what else she's fixing," the other said, and they were
overcome with a small storm of rasping, turning a deeper purple as they

sat down and pushed away the water glasses and struck up a round of cigarette lighters.

"Brother Reeves," Skinner commented to Asa.

"Mister Reeves' boy, I know who brung him, onliest one got the nerve. Uh-oh," Asa said, giving Skinner his martini on a paper napkin, and for a moment, they shared a certain bemused understanding.

"Ace! can you get a waitress in here, we're dying of thirst," shouted the one with the mud-colored eyes and frail plumes of ginger hair. A shiver of a frown touched Asa's face—his name was Asa, a great king out of the Holy Bible. "Well now, Skinner!" the man hollered on, loud enough to be heard as far away as the first tee and slid back his chair, as though he might get up to speak, but thought better of it for reasons of his own. "You back, are you?"

"Back at the old stand," Skinner said, feeling foolish.

"How'd you like them Eye-talian girls?" he asked, and there followed a quartet of aspirate expulsion around the table.

"None better," Skinner said and smiled obligingly.

Another chorus of wheezing. "Where's old Julian? How'd old Julian make out over there?"

"Never better," Skinner said on a closing cadence, making the smile thin to insure there would be no mention of John Thomas Warren, and the man turned back to the table, realizing suddenly that further hearty investigation might lead to trespass. "Wait till you see what's coming in here," he threw over his shoulder to close the exchange on a harmonious note. The four balding heads sank in towards each other, and the voices turned confidential, as they waited for the waitress to bring them their bourbons and branch.

Without any kind of warning or announcement whatsoever, the Princess Graziella di Brabant flowed in through the doors from the sun-flooded dining room, and the four men watched over their hunched shoulders, lying low and furtive, as if they were in some way suspect and could be called to testify on a later occasion. "In here," she called out, without having taken notice of the suspicious quartet, her voice pitched for a much larger hall. "Let's sit in here—that *light!* Who can stand that much light this time of day?" she demanded of someone following in her train. Her presence was as arresting as her entrance had promised. She was tall and slender, not beautiful nor young but something else quite definite, and she moved in a flutter of beige silk pajamas, unaware of the dim and subdued surroundings, obviously indifferent to the sanctum she had invaded. Skinner turned from the bar and his martini and recognized some superior world she represented and regretted the distance between them. He found himself envious of her company and felt she was an emissary from the unattainable, and this caused him great anxiety.

"We can take lunch anywhere you please, princess," a man said from beyond the door, "but it's so dark in that cave you can't see what you're eating."

"Oh, God, don't tell me it's Ned Trivett," Skinner said, turning back to the bar. He was disappointed and dismayed.

"Mister Ned Trivett, I knowed it," Asa said. "He always got something different going on."

"I do want to look my best for your many friends and acquaintances," the woman said. "But that blinding light! Not in there, I prefer the cave, we all started out in caves anyhow." The princess was fully aware she looked to have come from anywhere but a cave. She lifted back her mane of sun-struck hair—or what had been made to *look* like sun-struck hair—with ringed hands, and Arabian bracelets rang on her wrists. "Quel' tavola là, nel angolo," she said, pointing dramatically, and a silk sleeve fell from her long, thin arm. The foursome at the center table, following the command of her gesture, directed their baleful surveillance towards the far end of the room. "E voglio un vino, subito, subito," she announced.

"Si, si, subito, principessa. Pazienza, ti prego," Ned Trivett said, surging into the cave, diminishing the brilliant light momentarily, supported by supreme and amused confidence. "We'll take the table in the corner, Sue Ann," he said, leaning aside to the waitress.

"Okay, Ned, honey," Sue Ann said and set about pouring ice water into the glasses and distributing menus.

"You see, Graziella, you've managed to get it all arranged exactly as you please, as you always have," he said.

"Indeed!" the princess trumpeted, as she sailed past the conspiracy of balding suspects who had been stunned by an unjust verdict. Their morning of hilarious condescension had been ruined.

Brother Reeves followed in Ned Trivett's wake, dark-eyed and observant. He appeared to be a guest at a celebration, without knowing exactly what was being celebrated but nonetheless pleased with the festivity of the occasion. In Brother's wake, spectators in golfing clothes, doing their best to look disinterested, gathered in clusters to hang by an elbow at the bar, and there was an unusual and chattery tide of pastel dresses demanding tables in the grill, although everybody knew the dining room was the place to lunch if you had gone to the trouble to wear a dress. The waitresses began to look harried and stuck pencils in their hair and ran about soundlessly on their rubber soles.

"He done got 'em going again," Asa said. "Mister Ned the onliest one can do it and nobody say boo."

"Not so far, anyway," Skinner said. "Make me another one when you get a chance, Asa."

"Now, here," Asa said. "This ain't Saturday."

"It's Saturday to me," Skinner told him.

"Uh-oh," Asa said.

"Come sit here by me, Brother," the princess sang out from her corner seat, "and, Ned darling, you sit over there. Now, tell me," she went on, bringing her full attention to bear on the young man as he took

his chair. "How many brothers have you got, and are there any more at
home like you?" She settled her chin on the heel of her hand but thought
better of it and let the hand fall gracefully to his arm without changing
the intensity of her concentration.

Brother was only momentarily startled. "I don't have any brothers,"
he told her, regarding her with soft, brown eyes which should have been
shy but were not.

"Graziella, leave Brother alone," Ned said.

"Shut up, Ned, and get me some wine," she said, her attention
unwavering on the target. "If you haven't got any brothers, then why do
they call you Brother?" she asked, paying no mind to anybody else anywhere. The general conversation in the room had reduced to an alert and
sibilant murmur.

"I don't know'm. They just named me Brother."

"How *interesting!* Perhaps they hoped there were more to come,"
she exclaimed, removing her long-nailed hand from his arm, put off by
the shortened form of ma'am she thought she had detected. "I have known
some people named Junior who weren't juniors, but you are my first
Brother who doesn't have any brothers."

"I reckon you'll get used to it," Brother said, wondering how long
it took the lady to put the colors on her eyes. "All the others did," he
said, meaning no offense.

The princess laughed airily, if not entirely sincerely, and the hushed
diners, making as little noise as possible with their knives and forks, tilted
towards the corner table as though the whole room had slanted off center.
She would have cut the young man dead for the rest of the day at least,
except that she found herself subject to a certain Emanation which she
recognized immediately from long research as rare and promising. "Oh!
all the others did, did they?" she asked archly—offense taken—main-
taining the airy laugh and clinking the silver bracelets to her elbow. "Well!

I don't expect I'll have the same intimate occasion (ha! ha! ha!) to adjust to it as the others had."

"I reckon not," Brother said, unaccustomed to following the devious trail the princess was blazing.

"Don't count on it," the princess snapped, putting the airy laugh to rest. Ned dimpled.

Brother Reeves had spent his boyhood working his father's tiny tobacco farm out on Radio Road. Except for his astonishing appearance, an unaccountable, almost miraculous genetic gift from a large, pale mother and a dark, wiry, irate father, his youth had been unremarkable. He had done as sons of farmers in Martinet County had always done. There had been no harbinger of his easy-riding and carnal future, save perhaps for a brief and awkward encounter with a curious and insistent cousin in the dust-flown hayloft.

Nevertheless, one misty dawn, he had emerged from the curing house in an aromatic cloud of smoke into the time of the Emanation. Barefoot and bare-chested, shining in an armor of sweat, he had stood in sweet wonder as the haze dispersed; his years of honest labor had forged a perfect knight, and the days of invulnerable innocence lay before him. He accepted the vague restlessness that had come over him as another unaccountable gift and went his way across the furrowed fields into the rising sun. From that time forward, he fell into seduction as lightly and guilelessly as he fell into sleep.

As fate would have it, the first witness to the Emanation came to be a forceful wire-haired woman from Ohio, whose Plymouth had conceded defeat in front of the Reeves farm. She had taken what she thought to be a short cut on her way to a veterinarians' convention in Miami, only to come upon Brother, standing in the dust of Radio Road offering succor. Under her vehement and superfluous instruction, the two of them had fogged the car windows into privacy and disordered the pantsuits hanging in close order over the back seat. Immediately thereafter, the Plymouth had recovered miraculously and, backing and forwarding violently, the woman had turned around and headed back towards Ohio.

The second manifestation had come about in the belfry of the First Presbyterian Church of Milford in the company of the wife of a state senator, a tiny, fervent lady obsessed with civic duty. The reasons for their having found themselves in such a place remained obscure to Brother. He did recall, however, that she had furnished him with detailed information under difficult circumstances about the unreasonable cost of casting bells.

And so it went, one manifestation following on the heels of another in pleasant and rhythmic succession. The roster of casual delight was extensive and various to the point of being haphazard. However, Brother took it all as a matter of course, unaware of his stunning good fortune and the poverty of requited passion in the lives around him.

"What's Brother Reeves doing here?" Skinner asked Asa, who was administering the fifth or sixth martini.

"The Reeves was on this land before this club started up," Asa said with the slightest hint of reproach. "Besides, Mister Ned Trivett brung him, ain't that all right?"

"Caesar's wife," Skinner mumbled.

"Come again," Asa said, making a shell of his hand at his ear.

"Oh, nothing, I just—" Skinner said, giving his full attention now to the threesome in the corner.

"Uh-oh," Asa said, returning to his work, knowing more than anybody else could know.

"Who is—*who* is the lovely looking young man who keeps watching us from the bar?" Graziella asked, pitching her voice above the chatter which had taken up again in the room.

"That's old Skinner," Brother informed her.

Ned picked up his glasses from the table and strained around in his chair, scanning the bar. "Oh," he said, turning back and putting his glasses down by his plate again. "Yes. Skinner Bates. A young man who married himself halfway to success and is charming himself the rest of the way. . . . I must say, princess, your eyesight is remarkable for a girl who has seen as much road as you have."

"Don't fuck with me, Ned," Graziella shot, and a spark of amusement startled Brother's eyes. He had never heard such a woman say such a word in such a place, and it took his fancy. "And what, may I ask, does old Skinner do when he's not drinking martinis and cruising the bar?" she asked, leaning so close to Brother he could feel her breath on his cheek. He colored.

"Pretend you are looking for somebody and turn around so you can see what she's up to now," Rose Medallion said to Ellen Grissom who, unhappily, had been seated with her back to the performance.

"The woman is shameless and a disgrace to her class," Ellen pronounced, turning back. "Poor Brother Reeves, trapped with that creature, I must say he is such a fine young man."

"He is, he really is," Rose definitely agreed. They colored.

"In real estate," Brother announced, and was relieved the lady had gone back to peering across the room at old Skinner. "Julian took him into his real estate business. He and Julian sell houses all over Milford but mainly on the beach."

"*Real estate!*" Graziella exclaimed, alarming several diners in her immediate vicinity. "Oh, Brother, it's destiny! Mother Destiny has come to my rescue once again. Perhaps old Skinner would help me find a little villa by the sea—"

"Graziella," Ned said as a father cautions his unruly child, looking at her over the top of the menu. Sue Ann, standing there with the pencil point ready on the pad, couldn't believe what she was hearing.

"—where I can find peace at last and recover from the misfortunes of my—"

"Graziella."

"—life, oh Brother, the sooner the better. A villa by the sea, not too grand but not too simple either, away from the wolves and vultures of this—"

"Graziella, let me remind you that Mother Destiny has done very well thus far without any interference from you—"

"—world, is exactly what I need to rest and contemplate the loneliness of my existence. And I must say, I must say," she went on, beginning to contemplate her existence in advance and paying no heed whatsoever to Ned's admonition, "there, just across the room, is another golden head. Two golden heads in one morning, it's almost more than I can bear," she explained to anybody listening and everybody was, "one with dark eyes, one with blue eyes—"

"The one with blue eyes is taken, I must ask you to keep that firmly in mind," Ned reminded in a voice like flint, and there came a retard in the celebration. Ned gave Sue Ann the order for shrimp salad and two bottles of wine.

Brother realized the lady had stopped talking suddenly and that she was looking down at the knives and forks, biting her lip and blinking her eyes without looking up again. He had sat for some time now, unassuming and seraphic, listening to the constant, intemperate talk which he had recognized almost from the beginning as a desperate plea for deliverance. It had not occurred to him, however, that he and the princess were, in a way, a matched pair, that Mother Destiny for her own ironic amusement had crossed their paths in this sparse and sentineled seashore forest, where the crossing of paths was supposed to be determined by rigid and unsympathetic protocol. In spite of or possibly even because of which, here they sat, the almost princess from Mobile and the perfect knight from a small tobacco farm out on Radio Road and no elegant past to account for his gallant and chivalrous nature. He was moved to compassion for this excitable lady who had discovered only recently that she was losing her way. And the mantle of responsibility for lonely and disappointed women fell about his shoulders once again. He sat straight up and was serious for a time, as if he were waiting for a signal.

"I'll be back in just a minute," Brother said, having received the signal, and put down his napkin and pushed back his chair and left the table.

For the first time in their long and talkative history, the two old friends sitting at the table in the corner found they had nothing to say to each other and so remained silent, waiting for the return of the perfect knight.

CHAPTER ELEVEN

Asa, you making out all right?" Brother asked.

"Always did, reckon I always will, the good Lord willing. You making all right, Brother?" Asa responded, looking off over Skinner's shoulder as he poured a line of drinks on the bar without spilling a drop.

"Fine as wine," Brother said over Skinner's head.

"That the way it look from back here," Asa said and laughed with the book of knowledge in his head.

"Well, now, if it isn't Brother Reeves," Skinner said looking around from his martini to find him standing solemn and at ease at his elbow.

"In person," Brother said. "What say, Skinner?"

"Not much," Skinner said. "You?"

"Fine as wine," Brother said.

"What can I do for you?" Skinner asked, still leaning on the bar over the martini as if he were protecting it.

"This lady wants you to help her buy a house," Brother said, slanting his head and shoulders ever so gently towards the table in the corner.

"What lady is that?" Skinner asked, seeming annoyed, and picking up his drink, he faced Brother, accepting his presence with a suggestion of impatience.

"Gray. Miss Gray, that lady with Ned," Brother said, not having conquered the complicated forms of address enjoyed by his luncheon companions. "She wants you to help her find a house to buy on the beach. She says the sooner the better."

Skinner squinted his eyes towards the table in the corner, focusing with difficulty. Graziella and Ned Trivett were sitting quite still as if they were posing for a portrait. She had rested her chin on the heel of her hand again and was gazing vaguely in his direction. Ned Trivett, on the other hand, seemed to be expecting somebody to appear at the far end of the room. Skinner was puzzled to find them so constrained, so that they were no longer the center of speculation. He still didn't like Ned Trivett at all, but he liked the woman unreasonably. He stood divided.

"I don't want to get mixed up with that pair," he said and blurred his eyes back to Brother's open face.

"I don't know why not," Brother said. "She's good-looking and she's rich and she's some kind of royalty. She's already got two houses somewhere, she might as well get another one here, and she might as well get it from you." He knew Skinner better than he knew he did.

"That Ned Trivett," Skinner said with distaste.

"What's wrong with Ned Trivett?" Brother wanted to know. "Nothing wrong with Ned Trivett," he answered himself. "Come on, Skinner, before you get too drunk."

"Who's drunk?" Skinner asked.

"You, that's who," Brother said.

The rumble of conversation in the grill room had found its level, idling easy, shot through with an occasional laugh or greeting. Washed

in on a swell of recognition, Miss Lilly Atkins, with her cane and her
daughter and her granddaughter in tow, maneuvered in through the sun-
bright dining room doors, inching forward one foot at a time as though
she had been wound up too early and was beginning to run down. The
faltering mechanism automated her legs and cane only. Miss Lilly was
upwards of a hundred years old and was not deterred or distracted by the
flurry of attention her arrival inspired. Ramrod erect and beyond recall,
she moved in heartbreaking slow motion to the table next to Ned Trivett's.
They broke her in the middle to conform to her chair. She had not been
known to speak for some ten or twelve years now, apparently exercising
her right to remain silent. She could point, however. She pointed her
staunch and graying descendants into their places with a crooked finger
and a waitress into action with her cane. Everybody got the message.

Boyd Wilson, the best-looking get-ahead boy in town, leapt up
from his table like an enraptured porpoise and made a beeline to Miss
Lilly's side. It never hurt to be seen cozying up to Miss Lilly, since she
was the oldest living member of the oldest family in Milford. She had
been born and bred in the very plantation house she sat in at the moment,
although she probably didn't recognize it in its present incarnation.

"Well now, how's my sweetheart?" Boyd Wilson hollered, and Miss
Lilly looked up through her thick lenses as if she had heard the last trump
but couldn't locate its source. "You the purtiest thang I've ever seen in
all my born days," Boyd hollered on, sitting on his haunches beside her
chair and putting an arm about her skeletal shoulders. "When you going
to give me a break, Miss Lilly, honey?"

Miss Lilly, stolid and remote, tilted to one side and broke wind at
length. There was no immediate response, except that Boyd Wilson was
reduced to silence. Either Miss Lilly didn't know what she had done or
didn't care, and the strained faces around the table froze their smiles long
enough for Boyd Wilson to get back to his feet, still grinning but with
a trace of pain.

"I guess that answers that," Graziella said, as Boyd stumbled backwards to his table, stricken but game, accepting with a grin his dismissal from the presence.

"Here's Skinner Bates in person, Miss Gray," Brother said, standing easy on one leg by his chair. Graziella started a smile at what she found to be Skinner's back, and Ned rose, touching his mouth with a pink napkin.

"How are you Miss Lilly, honey?" Skinner was yelling and stretched a smile. Miss Lilly glared up at him through her glasses with enormous vacant eyes. She had heard the last trump again but didn't care. "Oh, to hell with it," Skinner mumbled and turned to Graziella who let fly a dazzling smile. He reestablished his balance and put out a tentative hand. "How do—"

"Blue eyes!" Graziella gasped, "oh, my God, violet blue eyes!"

"This," Ned announced, "is the Princess Graziella di Brabant. Mister Skinner Bates, our most stunning real estate agent, stunning in every way, I'm told."

Skinner shot a glance halfway between annoyed and puzzled at Ned's beaming face. "How—"

"*Violet* blue eyes," Graziella persisted, as though she were dictating to a deaf secretary. "Do sit down, Mister Bates—"

"How do you—"

"—right here next to me," she went on, putting a languid hand on the back of the only other chair at the table. "Get him a drink, Trivett, what are you drinking, Mister Bates?" Ned submerged behind the glasses and plates, as though he were standing in quicksand, and flung up a hand with a pink napkin in it for rescue. His expression betrayed an unaccustomed loss of control.

"I'd like a martini," Skinner said. "How do you do—princess? is that right? Do I say princess?"

"Oh, for heavensake, *do* call me Graziella," she cried out graciously, waving the title aside as nothing at all really, and Skinner gave way into the chair, so that it was more like falling than sitting. "Oh my!" Graziella cried, "are you all right, Mister—did I hear you say martini? Now, now, that won't do at all, we've got to talk a little business. Order more wine, Trivett."

"I call her Gray," Brother declared in a loud voice.

"*Gray!*" the princess exclaimed, as if Brother had just come up with an inspiration. "That's *perfect,* Brother! Call me Gray, and I'll call you Skinner, Mister Bates. *Violet* blue eyes," she insisted to the deaf secretary.

"Are they really?" Skinner said. "I didn't know that."

"God knows you do now," Ned said, and Skinner still didn't like him.

"Wine, Trivett," Graziella commanded. "Now."

"I got everything she likes but blue eyes," Brother said, bright and happy to be included at court, spraddled out in his chair with his tie coming loose. It was not Brother's custom to take wine with lunch.

"Wrong, Brother, darling," she chanted. "There's nothing about you I don't find absolutely delicious—"

"Delicious," Brother said, trying the word.

"—now then, Mister Skinner Bates, let's you and me get down to cases before the wine comes," she said, casting a glare at Ned and leaning in closer to Skinner on her elbow, so that she could be heard more easily. The rumor of amazement and shock at the strange conference around the corner table had reached almost the same decibel peak as had the lawn mower and the parade of pilgrims at Ned's house.

"Get a load of Skinner Bates and the princess, I wonder who he's for," the purple man with ginger plumes and mud-colored eyes said to his companions.

"Wait'll Julian hears about this," another said, and they wheezed a round of brown-toothed laughter and struck up a camp fire of cigarette lighters.

"Oh, El, I do wish you could see what she's doing now, I think she's going to—I *do* hope nobody is idiot enough to say anything to Susan about who Skinner is having lunch with," Rose Medallion said to Ellen Grissom, and they hurried through what was left of the shrimp salad, making mental notes of the friends they must telephone immediately to warn them against saying a word. You wouldn't want to hurt Susan, you know how strange she is already.

"What I want, Mister Real Estate Agent, is a simple little villa by the sea," Graziella began to explain. "Well, not *too* simple—"

"What you want is difficult to put into words in polite society," Ned said and poured wine all round against his better judgment.

"Don't fu—ah—don't mess with me, Trivett, and what would you of all people know about polite society?" she snapped. She and Skinner glared at Ned in almost identical ways. Ned paid no mind to either glare. Brother tilted his chair back and stuck his thumbs in his belt and gazed dreamily across the room, never considering that violet blue eyes—or rather eyes which had become violet blue by dictation—were doing him out of a trip to Rome Italy nor that he had joined the ranks of the questionable.

"I simply can't understand it," Ellen Grissom declared. "That Brother Reeves used to be such a fine young man."

"Extremely," Rose Medallion agreed again. They colored once again and cleared their throats before continuing their chat.

"I must find somewhere I can get away from the world to do my writing," Graziella got back down to cases, locked eye to eye with her real estate agent.

"Oh, I didn't know you were a writer," Skinner said.

"Her best work is done on checks," Ned said. "You owe it to yourself to read some of it."

"Well, not yet, I can't write yet, not until I've found the right place to write *in*," she explained, giving no sign she had heard Ned's remark except for a slight quiver of the black-encrusted eyelashes.

"I know just the place," Skinner said, brightening at the mention of checks and the pressure of the princess's hand on his knee. "The Duncan house. It's isolated—"

"The Duncan house," Brother said and rejoined the table from his reverie. "They got divorced. A lot of people in Milford have started getting divorced."

"I ran into your darling wife at the bank just last week, Skinner," Ned interjected. "She gave me short shrift as usual, however, I'm happy to say that she, unlike a lot of people, seemed more blissful than usual. Although far too thin, probably due to your abs—"

"*Isolated!*" Graziella exclaimed, crying him down, as if isolation had been the one unachieved goal of her life. The word rustled through the grill room like a light breeze through a canebrake. "I want the kind of house I can see out of, but nobody can see into."

"A wise decision considering your uninhibited enthusiasms, Graziella. I found Susan lovelier than ever, however, far too thin, have you noticed, Skinner?" Ned pressed on, and Graziella saw herself putting the torch to a tiny salmon-colored house on Hooper Street.

"This is the place all right, all right, all right," Skinner said, shining like the moon into the princess's face. "Yes sirree bob, this is the place all right, all right, all right."

"Oh, Skinner, Skinner, Skinner, when can we go see it?" she exulted, clasping her ringed hands at her throat, as though her ultimate prayer had just been answered.

"I can take you to see it anytime you want to, Miss Gray," Brother offered. "I know where the Duncan house is, I been there many a time. You go past Mizz Bender's place about a mile and a half—"

"Don't you agree, Skinner, our beautiful Susan is far, far too thin? I'm really quite worried—" Ned pleaded with the look of a man who has found he can't bail enough water to stay afloat.

"She's just fine, Ned," Brother volunteered. "I saw her at the hardware store yesterday. She looked just fine. She was trying to find a—"

"Oh, Skinner, Skinner, Skinner, when can we go see it?" the princess exulted all over again, duplicating the phrase exactly, deleting the intervening lines as not essential to the script.

"Grace—" Ned began, using whatever weapon was at hand.

"As soon as you get me a martini," Skinner said.

"*Martini!*" she exclaimed. "I'll get you a whole pitcher of martinis."

"Grace!" Ned attempted one more time.

"Order a pitcher of martinis, Trivett," the princess commanded.

"I love you," Skinner declared, overcome by the sweet joy of arrival.

"That was quick," Ned said, accepting defeat. "A pitcher of martinis to go, before it's too late. This will keep the native drums throbbing for some time to come." He waved the pink napkin back and forth like a flag of surrender at Sue Ann, who shot her eyes up to heaven, having had about enough of all this, more than enough to tell the truth. Ned felt this particular children's game had gone further than ever it should have; Graziella had abandoned the long observed rules, tacit though they were. "Grace, dear," he said, making one last desperate appeal.

"Stay out of this, Trivett," she said. She rose to her feet and wrestled with Skinner until such time as he could rise to his. His chair fell over backwards making considerable clatter. Miss Lilly Atkins looked up at them, her great automatic eyes swimming about in the fishbowl of her lenses. Her stalwart kinswomen sat spellbound, their forks poised in midair.

"If you continue with this performance, Grace, I'll have no choice but to have your trunks removed from my house and sent to the hotel," Ned said, every trace of delight having vanished from his face.

Graziella arrested action on the instant and turned on him in disbelief. "What was that?" she demanded.

"I said if you continue this farce, I'll have your trunks sent to the hotel," he repeated, looking her full in the face.

"Farce!" she said, her voice having become hoarse. "Don't you understand, you old fool? I am sick of being alone, I am frightened of being alone."

"And for that I am sorry, Grace. However, you are not the only lonely woman in the world. God knows most people are lonely, but very few are so indifferent to the lives of others as to behave as you are behaving now. We can't pretend to be naughty children any longer, Grace, not even *old* naughty children. It is far too late," he said. "Now then, the two of you sit back down, and the three of us who came here to have luncheon together will leave this place in reasonable time in an orderly and seemly fashion."

"Not with me, you won't," she said, rearing backwards into the posture and tension and widened eyes of a serpent about to strike.

"Look here now, Grace—" Ned warned, recognizing the menace.

"You have betrayed me again," she said. "You have become a tedious old man leading a tedious and boring life—I was a fool to come to you for help. Be good enough to have my things sent to the best hotel in town. I won't say good-by, I said good-by to you years ago. Come along, Skinner."

"Your trunks will be at the Seacoast Hotel," Ned said quietly. "Skinner will know where it is."

"But, Ned—" she began and looked at him with the face of a faded and sad girl, severely stricken. However, she stiffened her spine immediately and turned away. "Follow me," she said to Skinner.

Brother had observed the proceedings with intense concentration, sitting erect and secure in a private silence. He continued to watch, not even puzzled, as Graziella and Skinner made their way on a groundswell of mumbling through the grill room of the Milford Country Club. She swept among the tables in the silk pajamas, never more the princess, with a gracious smile for those citizens who might need it, yet at the same time letting it be understood they were obstacles to her swifter flight. It was a trick she had learned over many years of disguising expulsion for departure. It worked beautifully. Except for Skinner, who wandered into the corners of tables and turned over another chair. He had put on his glasses as a kind of badge of office and carried the thermos of martinis in both hands, as though it contained an important document the princess was to read before the populace later on. She paused in the doorway, impatient with his faltering progress. "Come along now, Skinner, darling," she said. "Darling," Ellen Grissom repeated to Rose Medallion, happy to be in the observer's seat for a change. The word went bounding around the room for some minutes like a great rubber ball thrown with enormous force.

"I could have showed Miss Gray the Duncan house, if Skinner would let me have the key," Brother said, stepping out of his privacy. He finished his wine with relish.

"I'm afraid, in this case, the key is not transferable, dear boy. Sometimes, Mother Destiny's logic is impossible to follow," Ned sighed, signing the bill witnessed by the exhausted waitress.

"You'll pardon me for asking, Ned, honey," she said, "but what is that woman's problem?"

"Not to worry, Sue Ann," he reassured her. "The poor girl has stayed on too long with the circus."

"Oh, my Lord, I get the picture," Sue Ann sighed wearily. "You're talking to Mizz Noah about the flood." She stuck the pencil in her hair and with a tiny shriek from her rubber soles, she bounded away.

"Miss Gray must have heard about old Skinner," Brother remarked.

Ned looked at him quickly with the thought that perhaps Brother's innocence was not the simple gift it had seemed. "Heard what about old Skinner?"

"Oh, nothing," Brother said. "Just heard about old Skinner." He was neither guarded nor abashed and so confirmed his innocence as genuine, so far as Ned was concerned.

"And now, Brother Reeves," he said, "the time has come to prepare for our departure. Straighten your tie and pray we are not stoned. We must follow in the wake of reprehensible behavior and disgrace for which I am responsible, I am sorry to say. I shall return to Hooper Street and prime myself for the tar and feathers."

"And while you're doing that, I can finish the yard," Brother suggested, never having been threatened with exile.

"Nothing of the kind. You'll sit on the porch and get primed along with me. The best is yet to be. I have no idea of getting tarred and feathered without the best of company. You may very well be my last remaining friend, dear boy, and so I must keep you at my side as long as possible," Ned said and rose, dimpling, from his chair.

"Okay, Ned," Brother said.

PART TWO

THE MOON WANING

Whatever can see wants to be seen, whatever can hear calls out to be heard, whatever can touch presents itself to be touched.

—Adolph Portmann

CHAPTER TWELVE

Madelyn Haskins had called a special rehearsal. Madelyn Haskins was the Star of the Week at the Bladens Beach Playhouse, and she was well aware that the Star of the Week was what packed the house—certainly not the raffish little resident company with the Actors Studio mannerisms and the shabby hopes and the eight-by-ten glossies in turtleneck sweaters and intense expressions on their faces. Madelyn Haskins had not been getting her laughs, and she had not been getting a hand on her exits, and she damn well knew why. "I could play this show under water and get my laughs," she said to Ernie Dexter. "I have done this play two hundred or so performances but never to such deadly response. Call a rehearsal for tomorrow morning at ten. If you can't direct it, I can. These—ah—actors haven't the vaguest idea of timing, and the next one to step on one of my lines will be replaced— even if it has to be by one of the bellboys." Ernie Dexter sighed.

She still had the pale blue eyes that seemed to be stretched back at the temples with the long eyelashes which, it appeared, were no longer her own, and she still had the husky, undulant voice that had attracted her fans in the thirties and forties. However, the rest of her had let down to a considerable degree, although she either was not aware of the effects of time's passage or refused to admit to them—even to herself. She played every performance with exactly the same steely will and exactly the same sweet electricity as she had the last or the first. When the lights went up, Miss Haskins turned on, and she was a force to be reckoned with. "Indomitable," Ernie had admitted with reluctant condescension.

"All right, now then, ladies and gentlemen," she said, standing under the rehearsal light center stage. She inclined her head to study them over the half glasses and looked reproving and stern in spite of the narrow ribbon, exactly the color of her eyes, with which she had tied up her blond curls. The ladies and gentlemen remained motionless and wide-eyed under her gaze. "Now then," she said, taking resolve and releasing them from inspection. "We have six more performances to go before I depart, and I have no idea of leaving without having done this play as it is written—slight though you may consider it. It was written for amusement and laughter and has absolutely no social or psychological significance, no matter how hard you work at it. I ask you to keep that firmly in mind, and I ask you to forget for the moment your arduous training in whatever method you happen to have embraced and simply read your lines as they are written and make your moves on cue with the lightness of heart that the playwright intended. All right, now then, ladies and gentlemen, if you would just take your positions for the beginning of the second act."

The ladies and gentlemen mumbled to each other and smiled behind their fans, as it were, and shuffled about finding their places and resented being English upper class, when they had prepared for the tension of the highly nervous drama they were to perform the following week. To great critical acclaim, they had no doubt, and without the encumbrance of a Star of the Week.

"You, young man," she said pointing through the French doors into the garden. "You are the stage manager, I believe, Mister—ah—"

"Blake. Gordon Blake," the young man said, stepping lightly in from the garden. "And you are absolutely right, Miss Haskins. I *am* the stage manager, just as I was during your week of rehearsals. What's your pleasure, darling?"

She hesitated at this familiarity and tilted her ribboned head forward and regarded him significantly over the glasses for a moment, trying to decide whether or not to overlook this unexpected presumption. After brief consideration and under pressure of time, she decided to forget what may or may not have been a small lapse of respect. "Well—ah—Mister Blake, if you could just bring the lights up a little on the sofa. After all, that *is* where the action is, now isn't it?"

"Done," the stage manager said and smiled winningly and retired again to the garden. The Star of the Week paused, still disconcerted, and cleared her throat and went back to the business at hand, filing the possible breach of faith behind her famous eyes.

"Now then, you, young lady, you with the red hair. Miss—" She lifted her brows.

"Warren," Laura said.

"—Warren," Miss Haskins repeated and lowered her brows. "Miss Warren, you are on the landing there, and you are not to move a muscle until your cue to come down the stair. And, please, no characterization, none of those quick little nervous movements you are so taken with."

"I—I'm sorry," Laurie said, almost inaudibly, and was amazed the woman had been aware of her on the landing at all, since she had never once looked in that direction.

"Don't be sorry," Miss Haskins said. "There's no time for sorrow, just do as I say. Don't even blink."

"Yes, ma'am," Laurie said and realized instantly she had been too

respectful, as the pale blue, stretched-back eyes rested on her for too long
for any reason other than hostility. With Madelyn Haskins, the balance
between respect and disrespect was delicate and perilous.

"I think I'm about here," David Worth said, standing at a point
midway between the star and the stair. Miss Haskins directed the eyes
towards the actor with a mixture of contempt and admiration. He was
indeed handsome, she conceded, and did some further filing for future
reference.

"You are no such thing—" she started.

"No, Dave," Ernie Dexter spoke up from the dark of the house.
"You should be—"

"Shut up, Mister Dexter," Miss Haskins said lightly. "You, Mister—
ah—"

"Worth."

"—Worth, are standing next to me here by the sofa. That's it exactly. Bravo, Mister—ah—I *do* hope those are not the trousers you wear
for the performance."

"No, they—"

"Good!" she said firmly. "Now then. You say—just as clearly as you
can possibly manage—'I think Lavinia has run away with Cyril,' and sit
right down. Don't think about it. Just sit down. And you there at the
French doors, Mister—"

"Don," the actor said looking intense.

"—Mister Don, go right off. No fancy turns. Just go right off
through those doors."

"What's my motivation?" the actor asked with his hand in a closed
fist on his forehead. "Nobody has given me any motivation for this move."

"Your motivation," Miss Haskins said, double-stopping the undulant voice, "is the words in the script which happen to be: Exit Richard.
And so you damn well exit right through those doors, just as Mister—
ah—Dave here sits down. And then—"

"Ernie told me to take a beat here," the intense actor said, pounding his forehead gently with his fist.

"Did he indeed?" she asked. "Well, Mister Dexter has slowed this show down to a near stop. Your artistic little pause has killed the longest laugh in the play. You just go right off. And then—"

The doors at the back of the theater opened admitting momentarily a flood of brilliant sunshine, and a tall man in a rumpled seersucker suit strolled deliberately and without haste down the aisle and took a seat beside Ernie Dexter, obviously unaware that he had ruptured the obscurity of creation. Laurie put her hand over her mouth, and Miss Haskins in her movie star beach pajamas sighed with exasperation and waited extremely patiently for him to take his seat, saying nothing, since it seemed to her the man had an air of some kind of official inspector or had come, perhaps, to rectify an injustice. However, nothing daunted, she took heart and began again where she had left off. "Now then. Sit. Exit Richard—"

Laurie gasped and caught her breath, staring in dismay at the interloper in the front seat of the auditorium.

"Oh, for God*sake!*" Miss Haskins said, turning to the stair landing, and took her glasses off and put them back on again. "Please, Miss—ah—*please,* no nervous little characterizations. You have had a hand in killing my laugh as well as Mister—ah—"

"Don," he said and looked put-upon.

"—Mister Don," she said.

"I'm sorry," Laurie said tremulously, her hand still at her mouth.

"I *told* you we haven't the time for you to be sorry," she said, nearing the end of her tether. "Don't even breathe. Can you remember that? Freeze. All right now. Once more. Sit. Exit Richard. And then, I fall back on the sofa and say, 'God, I wish somebody would play something beautiful on the piano.' And there is a thirty to forty-five second laugh, depending on the size of the house. Now, I ask you, isn't that simple?

It's as simple as that, you can take my word for it. All right, let's run it. Places."

"Who the hell is that woman?" came from the interloper in the front seat in a loud and casual and conversational voice. And another sound like a swallow or a gasp or a giggle came from Laura on the stair landing.

"Goddamit, Miss—ah—you with the red hair," Madelyn Haskins shouted, turning in fury on Laura, having reached the end of her tether. "Who the hell ever told you you could act? You can't even follow direction. No wonder you are still playing second lead in stock companies at your age." Laura put her face in her hands and folded in on herself and froze, as she had been told to do.

The tall man in the rumpled suit stood up slowly, towering like a ghost in the dusk of the theater. "Who the hell do you think you are, lady?" he asked easily. "I will not permit you to speak to my wife in that manner."

"Oh, my God, Julian, please!" Laura cried out and took her hands from her face and gripped the stair railing, still bent over, as though she had been struck in the stomach.

Madelyn Haskins' eyes glared into eyes even paler than her own, and she was taken aback in spite of herself by their intensity and by the easy, slack manner of the man who dared ask her who the hell she thought she was. Had the eyes not been so blue, she would have thought she was speaking to an Indian of some kind, so defined was the bone structure of the man's face. She put all her will into staring him down, a talent she had depended upon throughout her career, but her anger would not allow her the time she saw it was going to take.

"Just who is this gentleman?" she demanded, turning on Ernie Dexter, whom she had stared down on several occasions. "Is he a member of this company?"

"He's—"

"And if he is not, what is he doing here? How many times have I told you, Mister Dexter, there are to be no outsiders at my rehearsals? And how dare you, sir, interrupt me in my work, whoever you are?" she went on, turning her eyes back to the calm and careless face of the enemy. "Just get out of here, and get out of here right—"

"I will not permit you to be rude to my wife, whoever *you* are, lady," the man said, as though he were arguing a case in civil court. "You will apologize to—"

"Oh, my God, Julian, please," Laura whispered, still gripping the stair rail, and, letting her head fall forward, began to weep. "Miss Haskins, he is not my hus—"

"Get OUT of here! Get out of here, both of you," Miss Haskins screamed, the undulant voice leveling to a straight, shrill line toward the back of the theater. "Dear God, have I come to this?" she asked all her admirers from the past. "Have I been reduced to playing for a crowd of yokels with a bunch of amateurs? Oh, my God!" And she put her face in her hands, in her turn, and stood there a tragic figure to show how it was done, and she could do it to perfection.

"Come on, Laura," the man said, extending his arm to her from the dark.

"Julian, why—" She wept and came slowly down the stair from the landing and passed among the guests of the house party, all in their places on the stage, and followed the man up the aisle.

"Now then. Once more. Sit, Mister—ah—Dave. Exit Richard. And then, I fall back on the—" Laura heard the voice, undulating once more, as Julian opened the doors and flooded the theater with midday sun. Madelyn Haskins had healed quick and had released the tragic muse with ease when she found her no longer useful. Miss Haskins, as Ernie said, was indomitable.

Julian preceded Laura onto the broad, tiled terrace of the Ocean Manor Hotel and stood in the stark, late morning sun with his hands in his pockets, looking intently out to the horizon. It seemed to him that the elements had fused into a haze of sound and sight; the crashing of the surf was the same for him as the white bowl of the sky which was indistinguishable from the steaming sea, flashing pale fire here and there. He waited for his eyes to adjust to the light and assumed Laura's presence behind him. However, he turned to find that she had drifted past him, as if he weren't there, and continued along the terrace with her head down and the forlorn shoulders of an older woman. He watched her slow and uneven progress, frowning and confused, apparently surprised that she had forgotten him, and put out an arm, as though he were near enough to deter her. "Laura," he called after her, letting the arm fall. "Laura," he called out again, more insistently, and started after her. "Mislark!" he shouted, and she stopped dead in her tracks and stood that way for a moment and then turned back to him. The expression on her face alarmed him so that he found it impossible to continue pursuing her. Her red hair blazed like a helmet in the sun, and her skin was whiter than the light she stood in.

"Mislark," she said in the nervous, crystal voice, contemptuous of the name. "Don't call me that again, Julian. That name is for the people who love me. I wonder, Julian, if you ever loved me. How could you have loved me, when you never knew me? Not ever." She put her perfect chin up and dried the tears on her face in the sun. "How can you love me, when you come along now and ruin my last hope? How can you have done that?"

"Good God, Laura," he said, astounded at her reaction, and it seemed to him that he had more difficulty than she did making himself heard above the rushing of the surf. "Good God, Laura," he repeated, raising his voice. "Of course, I loved you, you know that. Everybody knows that. And of course, I love you still, right this minute. But you can't—"

"Can't what, Julian?" she demanded of him and wondered at the force of her voice and wondered that she did not gasp or cry or stammer.

"Go away, Julian. Leave me alone, Julian. I have asked you again and again to do that for me. Why do you deny me the very breath of my life?"

"This, Laura?" he asked, amazed, moving his arm in a half circle which embraced the Ocean Manor Hotel and all it contained. "This is the breath of your life?"

"It is now," she said.

He turned his back on her to consult with somebody invisible behind him and stared straight out for a while and then faced her again. "So what you're saying is, there's nothing for me but to go back to my bachelor apartment," he said.

"There are a lot of places you could go," she said.

"It don't even know how to get dirty, that apartment," he said. "That's the kind of place it is."

"I know," she said. "You told me that before, it's very funny." And they waited for something to lift between them, but nothing did.

"And your son?" he asked quietly with his head back, looking down at her as if he wore bifocals, which he didn't.

"My Jubie," she said. "Tell him to keep all the clocks wound, so that we'll know exactly what time it is when I get home."

"Oh, he does that all right," he said and looked down at his feet and then out to the horizon and back again. "You have forgotten who we are, Laura," he said, overcoming a feeling that nothing was much use. "You seem to have forgotten that we are people who have to do the right thing, it is expected of us, Laura. We are people of place. Whether we want to or not, we have to do the right thing. Why is it you can't manage that, Mislark?"

"I told you not to call me that," she said. "And are you telling me what the right thing is, Julian? Or should I listen to my soul for that advice? 'My name is Alma, and Alma is Spanish for soul,'" she said, and her face changed to another person and changed back again.

"I don't understand that remark," Julian said. "What does it mean?"

"There's a lot you don't understand, Julian," she said. "I sometimes wonder if you try, but then I know you do, poor old Julian. You can't understand what I want or what I am trying to do. And there's no way to explain to you that I am trying to free myself of confinement, a confinement you have lived in so long, it is the only place you know as home."

"You can explain that to me sometime, but for right now, I'm afraid for you, Laura," he said, wanting to approach her but finding it impossible to traverse the space between them. "I will not let you go like this. I will not let you go, I want you to know that," and it frightened him that for the first time, he had begun to realize that she may have discarded him and was moving to a place beyond his reach or comprehension. "You belong to me and you always will. That's the way of it. I will not let you go, you had better understand that, Laura."

"Oh, my poor old Mister Jukes," she said, tilting her head to the side and smiling. "You don't even know that you can never find me again, do you?"

"It is my sworn duty to take care of you," he said.

She laughed hysterically, taking great gulps of air, feeling she had lost ground again, and left him standing alone on the terrace.

CHAPTER THIRTEEN

t had not turned out to be the light-hearted seduction scene Graziella had had in mind. It had gone far beyond—oh, far, far beyond anything she had known in the past, and had she not been slightly drunk, she could not have gone through with it as she had. As if it had *been* light-hearted. It had been frightening actually. As if she had come upon evidence of past violence and so was privy to the secrets of a savage spirit. She felt she had been plundered of her identity and left utterly on her own. The words whispered or shouted in the heat of generation had not been whispered or shouted to her but rather through her to some forbidden god. She comforted herself, however, that she was an adventuress who had made an important if dangerous discovery which must now be her responsibility as well as her addiction. And too late for regret.

They lay separated by silence in the least unpleasant of several unmade beds in the Duncan house. Graziella had draped herself skillfully in a faded and stained, blue sheet which she felt might bear the marks of blood, but, of course, it didn't. Skinner wasn't draped in anything. The impulse to modesty had not returned to him, he wasn't even smoking. He seemed becalmed but still intense, lying flat out on the bed with his golden boy's head cradled in his arms on the pillow, so that it was like the winged head of a cherub at the bottom of a painting. She observed him like this and was as amazed now as she had been that first moment when his clothes had fallen away from his body like an unnatural skin. He had laughed waiting for the shock on her face and, oh my God, who could have guessed?

He was studying intently the ceiling of Miriam and Charlie Duncan's bedroom which one or the other or both of them must have looked at hundreds of times before the time came to divorce, silenced and confounded by misunderstanding. Consequently, it was a sad ceiling. Miriam had never been good-looking enough or in the same class with Charlie, Skinner had explained. Charlie was a good-looking man and a Deke at the university and played the best game of golf in town, he had said. Well, let's hear it for Charlie, Graziella thought. And where is Charlie now with his fraternity pin and his golf clubs? Class, indeed.

Graziella propped up on one elbow and stared out the salt-rimed picture window at a bead-eyed sea gull perched on the deck railing. The sea gull stared back at Graziella. It seemed to know she didn't belong there in that bed, and she was almost convinced the stare was one of disapproval. Her lion hair was in disarray, and her bracelets had proven to be something of a distraction during the last hour or hour and a half or however long it had been—somebody ought to time this boy sometime when he runs the marathon again, she thought. The bracelets hadn't been *that* much of a distraction, however, once things got rolling. She didn't like the damn sea gull's presumption, and she didn't like Charlie and Miriam's bedroom. It *smelled* of dissatisfaction and failure. Nonetheless, she had to admit. She had been overwhelmed by the last hour or hour and a half or however long it had been, and really, I mean it, somebody ought to time him sometime and put him on record. He was a record-breaker in more ways than one. After all, champion runners deserved due credit no matter where the race was run. And also, she recognized—she had seen it before—a heedless perversity amounting to a kind of departure in Skinner's performance. It was entirely possible that at a certain moment they had become weightless with frenzy and risen some distance from the bed, until he had shouted a word from some barbarian tongue, and they had settled by convulsive degrees down into the washed-out blue sheets again. She had never experienced such a thing before.

She was astonished now by Skinner's radiant and unmarred flesh and the turn of his limbs in the sockets, in spite of which she had set herself the task of staring down the sea gull. She failed. Most of all, she was astonished by the perversity. She knew very well that perversity runs with deep disturbance under undisturbed surfaces. It had frightened her, that perversity.

Yes, well then, it was time, she decided, to return to the world as it is from day to day and to get down to cases. Right or wrong, she had taken resolve. She began to tell Skinner in her most violincello voice and in an accent compounded from all the shades of all the accents she had encountered in her travels that she was a collapsing star. Do you know what a collapsing star is? she asked him. The sea gull chose the moment to turn its back and fly away, well so much the better, and Skinner chose not to respond. He lay there losing heat, exposed and removed. Well then, according to astronomers, she went ahead and told Skinner anyhow, the closer you get to a collapsing star, the slower time goes by, until one day time stops completely. She extended a thin arm rattling with bracelets to show him she couldn't even wear a watch, a watch on the arm of a collapsing star slows down and eventually stops.

She waited. A tremor of envy and contempt ran through her at his youth and his lack of shame, his body thrown out on the bed like that. How dare he be so careless of her eyes?

Skinner, still looking upward at the ceiling, was almost smiling. "Don't hand me that line of bullshit," he suggested in a soft, indifferent voice. "You're an old bag and you know it," he said. She waited again and took resolve again. Well, she said, however that may be, she was a rich old bag and a highly connected old bag in certain international circles where money was no object. And he was a real Southern Charmer as well as a son of a bitch among a lot of other things she wouldn't go into for the time being. Think about that, she said.

He left off studying the ceiling and looked at her and smiled at her, showing his little even white teeth, and she realized, my God, he's not even a man yet in spite of all the physical evidence to the contrary. Not even a man yet and bound headlong for disaster—a disaster she could avert, what with her years of experience averting disaster for herself and her disaster-prone friends. Separate the boy from the man, she had always cried. Once the boy has become a man, there's no return, she had always declared to anybody who cared to listen. He has also become a bore— even with a golden head and violet blue eyes, they lose their luster—and it's an easy thing to convince a boring man he has hung around too long wasting his time with her and must leave her to go out and fascinate and seduce the rest of the world. And make his way. And get ahead. Whatever.

This one, this Skinner, she knew had more problems than retarded manhood. She had recognized the full weight of his perversity, even if he had not or would protest he had not.

Suddenly, she could see herself in tears on her terrace in Rome some nine months to a year hence, saying good-by again to a boring man who had used her with her complete approval and enchanted her while he was still only a boy. How can you leave me after all we have been to each other? she had always said on such occasions. And then, after closing the door on whomever forever, she wondered how she got by with saying such a tacky thing. And had laughed, not unkindly, and dressed to go out to a party somewhere.

She regarded the boy in the sheets alongside her from underneath the black-encrusted eyelashes, slightly smudged. He was young and sweet-breathed and unhappy in this house, where there was still half-eaten breakfast toast on the kitchen table and all the beds left hanging open without explanation, and even the sun through the windows was stale. His flesh was lubricous and anxious and there was an exhalation of this desperate—this sinister infection.

"You know, of course, I wouldn't be caught dead living in this house," she said at length.

"I know," he said.

"You know, of course, I wouldn't be caught dead living in this town," she said.

"I know," he said.

"Very well then, why don't you save two lives at a stroke, yours and your wife's, and come back to Rome with me and try to find whatever it is you left there, whatever it is you are looking for?" she said.

"It's something to think about," Skinner said, and he felt a surge of sweet relief.

"Listen, boy," Graziella added, "once you've stepped in camel shit, you're in the circus for life. Remember that."

CHAPTER FOURTEEN

The trespassers had taken over the old house among the pines suddenly and with an offensive indifference. It was not only the laughter and the raised voices in the night that dismayed the residents and the summer people, it was the way the play people seemed not to care about anything or anybody except themselves and the words they memorized and spoke and the thing they were making. It was as if these displaced persons felt they were a superior breed from a distant and magical place and were pausing in transit only long enough to present themselves in splendor to Bladens Beach while waiting to be summoned to another more civilized locale. Consequently, the residents and the summer people watched them from their screened and awninged houses with curiosity and misgiving as they straggled like so many glorious derelicts to the theater at the Ocean Manor Hotel at eight o'clock every morning of the world, including Sundays.

"If they're so damn good, why do they have to practice so much?" Dr. Fred Bartlett had asked his wife, standing comfortably on the screen porch in his pajamas and terrycloth bathrobe. "It looks like a crowd of New York riff-raff and not a movie star among them, if you ask me. I wonder where Laura Warren rounded them up."

"Laura went to acting school in New York for two years, as you well know," Lib Bartlett said from the living room, "and she should know good play actors when she sees them. She almost didn't marry Julian on account of being invited to take a part in a Broadway play. And, in my opinion, the shows they give at the hotel are perfectly wonderful."

"And, in my opinion, it would have been better for all concerned if she had gone on and been on the stage instead of marrying Julian," the doctor said, running his fingers through his thick, white, disordered hair, which always had the look of having just left the pillow. "Now, look here, here they are unmarried again, or trying to be, and here she is, back with the riff-raff and standing in the stage lights every night with paint on her face, talking and laughing in that short-of-breath way of hers, as if she didn't have a perfectly good house and a perfectly fine husband who still loves her over in Milford. I don't understand that girl. What makes her—for that matter, what makes any damn fool want to stand up in the middle of a stage and have people look at her for? And kissing that young actor—if that is what he is—in front of everybody as easy as she should be kissing Julian Warren in the privacy of their bedroom."

"You don't understand artists," Lib said and looked at herself critically in the mirror over the mantelpiece.

"I'll certainly agree with you on that," he said. "But I take it you do. I take it you think it's just fine for her to leave her husband and her home and her retarded child—"

"Jubie is *not* retarded, how many times do I have to tell you that? He is just a little slower than—"

"—and move in with that crowd in the old Lowe house, falling to pieces as it is."

"It's a nice roomy old house," she said, and she put her coffee cup on a table and tightened the sash of her robe, glancing at the mirror again and pushing at her stray, gray-blond hair. "And Laura has her own room to rest in and learn her lines."

"She damn well ought to have her own room, since I understand she's footing the bill for this thing. Her father would turn over in his grave, if he knew how the money he worked for delivering every baby in Milford was being wasted. I don't know what I'd do, I don't know what I *wouldn't* do, if I were Julian. Why, Elizabeth, the Warrens are fine, upstanding, well-thought-of people in Milford and, for that matter, all over the state—and now, look here; here she is with this crowd of strays up hollering and laughing till all hours of the night."

"They're probably practicing for the next show," Lib explained.

"And a lot more than that, I'll vow. Sitting out in the yard for all to see, drinking likker and not enough clothes on and saying words I haven't heard since I left the United States Navy."

"You don't understand artists," Lib said again, returning to her most successful defense.

"That may well be," the doctor conceded, coming in from the porch and wondering why his wife was looking at herself in her grandmother's mirror over the mantelpiece. "But I do understand that Laura Warren is a pretty little thing and nervous as a cat and can't drink normal like other people, and I do know that young actor—if that is what he is—doesn't wear those tight pants and leave his shirt unbuttoned for no good reason, and I do know that you can practice kissing just so long until it gets to be something else, and I do know that it hasn't been all that long since she left Julian Warren's bed where she was used to—"

"That young man happens to be in love with the telephone operator at the hotel," Lib interrupted, feeling that her husband was on the verge of improper speculation. "I don't like this mirror anymore," she said, regarding it as she would a person who has just made an unpleasant remark. "I don't like the way things look in this mirror."

"Who pays him no mind whatsoever, tight pants and all," he said. "What's wrong with that mirror? We've always had that mirror."

"It's—bent or something," she said, looking into it and putting her head first on one side and then on the other, pushing at her hair. "And besides, Laura is giving all her time and energy to becoming a great actress, and she wouldn't—"

"And you know as well as I do, this is as far as she'll go in that direction. She's too high-strung to do anything, she's too nervous to go more than a month without getting drunk for relief."

"Well, maybe this play-acting will help her," Lib said, making things come out all right. Maybe this is what she was meant to do and just put it off too long like a lot of other women."

"You women always stand up for each other until you can get together and start tearing each other down. What are you looking at in that mirror, Elizabeth? And you watch my word, she's going to have one too many one of these first nights, and we won't hear the end of it. Julian Warren will—"

"Julian Warren will do absolutely nothing," Lib said, still resenting her grandmother's mirror. "After all, they are separated, Laura is free to—"

"There she goes now," the doctor said, standing in the front door, so big he almost blocked her view. "Pretty little thing with that red hair. Thin as a rail and white as a sheet. You'd never guess she was born by the ocean. And now then, just guess who she's with."

"Oh my, he *is* handsome indeed," she said over his shoulder.

"He's chronically hoarse," the doctor said. "I'll stake my reputation there's a polyp on his vocal cords somewhere."

"Polyp," she said. "Why do you take all the fun out of everything? There's such a thing as being too practical. That's not hoarse, that's the way he talks, and in my personal opinion . . ." Her voice drifted off, and they watched the young actor with the profile as definite as an axe blade and with eyes the color of slate set under down-slanted brows which be-trayed, Lib felt, a wound from the past and the determination—or per-haps the hope—not to be wounded again. At the same time, Dr. Bartlett thought he recognized the quick step of a man who has covered a lot of ground and plans to cover a great deal more. A tremor from lost youth turned his heart. "That telephone girl had better not play games with that boy too much longer," Lib mused. "You see there now, Fred. They're saying their lines, they've got their parts in their hands."

"I only wish we didn't have to live spang across the street from them," he said, conceding something about the young actor.

"Well, we wouldn't have to," she responded, "if you had bought that piece of ocean front property before you retired, the way I told you to."

"I wish I knew as much about life as you do," Fred said.

"Lord knows, so do I," Lib said and laughed the coy, girlish laugh which had annoyed him even in the days when she was coy and girlish.

The evening performance was over, and Madelyn Haskins had got all her laughs and a hand on her exits, as well as three curtain calls, as she had predicted she would. Miss Warren—reinstated—had stood stock still on the landing of the stair, as she had been instructed to do—except perhaps for her hands trembling a little in the folds of her skirt.

David Worth and Gordie Blake were sitting on the curb just beyond the reach of the street lamp, smoking and waiting for something in the dark. There was a furtive and expectant anxiety in their attitude, as though they were keeping watch on the dun-colored dormitory building among the scrub pines across the road, which housed the staff and service of the Ocean Manor Hotel.

"It's the third window from the left," David said.

"I'm well aware of that," Gordie said. "It was the third window from the left last night and the night before that. I'm getting tired of this."

"Tomorrow, you've got to go and ask her to marry me," the handsome actor indeed said.

Gordie regarded him sideways for what seemed to be a long time. "I came here as stage manager to learn how to direct plays, not to act as procurer," he said. "How can I tell a girl who won't even look your way that you want to marry her? Besides, I think that should be your job. I think that's the way it has been done for some time now."

"She might say no," David said.

"There's not the shadow of a doubt in my mind that she would say no," Gordie said. "Either that or she'd say, marry who? I'm not entirely convinced she's seen you yet, and it appears to me——"

"I don't like that," David said, as though Sancho Panza had suddenly turned on Don Quixote. "I don't like that at all. I wish you hadn't said that, why did you say that?"

"I'm a realist when it comes to other people falling in love. When it comes to me falling in love, I'm a romantic," Sancho Panza said. "It's easier to delude yourself that way. Now, it's past midnight and I'm dead tired and I'm going back to the——"

"Wait a minute, wait a minute," David said, putting a restraining hand on Gordie's arm. "Sit back down. Here comes——"

From the darkness beyond the reach of the street light, a tall, ghostly, shambling figure was making his way towards the stakeout. Whoever it was made his way not directly but veering first one way and then the other but, in spite of that, gave the impression he had a definite destination in mind.

"Drunk," Gordon said.

As he came nearer, they recognized the man in the rumpled seersucker suit who had dared not know who Miss Madelyn Haskins was. He had his hands thrust deep in his pockets and his shoulders pushed up and the air of a man defeated who did not accept defeat. He passed at an unsteady but determined pace without a word and without looking their way, but he put up an arm and held it there for a moment, vastly elongating his shadow, which elongated even further the other way as he went beyond the street light. He thrust his hand back in his pocket and continued towards the house with the lighted windows and the music and the raised voices.

"Laurie's husband," Gordie said. "Drunk."

"It takes trying hard to get that drunk," David said.

"Laurie's *ex*-husband," Gordie corrected himself. "Love never gives up."

They sat in silence on the curb, possibly thinking about love, possibly not, and after a while, the light went on in the third window from the left. "There she is, thank God. Welcome home, honey," Gordie said. "It's twelve forty-three. We had better go home, so you can enter that in the log and have a drink and protect Laurie from her ex-husband."

"I wonder if she's thinking about me," David mused, taking a long last look at the third window from the left. And it went dark.

Eleanor Bacon and Doris Ann Hawkins were sitting, silent and oracular, in the white board chairs among the pines in the front yard, when David and Gordon returned from the stakeout. They were two of the apprentices, so-called, that returned to the playhouse like swallows every year to haul furniture and drive trucks and clean up the theater after performances in exchange for board and lodging and the hope of a part of some kind and to get to know movie stars in person. Eleanor was tall and thin and spinsterish and painfully ladylike with the tips of her fingers to her lips a good deal of the time, as if she might be missing a front tooth and must cover her smile.

Doris Ann, on the other hand, was all flesh and chuckles and busy little hands, with the round curly head of a cherub, and didn't seem to care whether or not she got a part so long as she could kiss the boy apprentices and call everybody darling and say shit when she pleased. Her father had hauled her in out of the country two seasons previous in his dusty truck. So she was into her third year of cheerful and unsuccessful seduction.

"He's locked in there with Laurie, and she's crying and carrying on. You better go see," Eleanor said through her fingertips, her large, white-shod feet glowing like radium in the dark. She considered it improper to suggest that any male and female, other than husband and wife, might seclude themselves in a bedroom.

"Shit, Eleanor," Doris Ann said. "There ain't no harm in it. He did use to be her husband, so it ain't like it was the first time."

"Doris Ann, she's crying and carrying on, and she's got to get up in her part," Eleanor said, stifling disapproval.

"Well, that is right," Doris Ann admitted but gave the impression that, as far as she was concerned, there were more important things sometimes than getting up in your part.

In the living room, the accountant, who dodged about constantly as if he were on the other side of a tennis net anticipating a difficult serve, and the production assistant, a frazzle-haired woman with what looked to be a broken jaw but wasn't, were sharing a bottle of bourbon and making pronouncements of impending doom. The character man and wife, known in the company as the Lunts, were about to retire. On the side porch, the pretty blond apprentice and the juvenile were doing something, or rather the juvenile was doing something, and the pretty blond apprentice was saying, Quit it, Tom, every thirty seconds or so. The balance of the apprentices were in the dining room drinking beer and wearing dark glasses and declaring, I've had just about enough of this shit, thrilled with the bravado of the phrase.

The sounds from Laurie's bedroom at the end of the hall were grievous. From time to time she could be heard weeping, soft and then not so soft, crying out that she wanted to be left alone. His voice droned underneath constantly, rising and falling melodiously and argumentatively. The words were indistinguishable.

"Something has got to be done about that, but I don't know what," Gordie said, pouring two straight vodkas at the table with ten thousand interlocking, glass-bottom circles on its surface.

"She'll never do this show, if this keeps up," David said.

"Leave them alone," the woman with the jaw that wasn't broken instructed. "She hasn't got the stamina to play this part anyhow, even if she *is* perfect casting." She leapt up suddenly and loped across the room to the table, seized the bottle of bourbon and loped back to put it on the floor between her chair and the accountant's.

"Tomorrow, we rehearse the anatomy scene, and she's got to do two performances with that bitch. She'll never make it. Go do something, Gord," David said.

"Go do what, David? You tell me what to do," Gordie said. "There's nothing I can do, not even for you. I mean, who can tell me which one locked the door?"

"Without a guest star, this production won't make a dime anyhow," the accountant said and cringed to one side, avoiding a powerful serve from the production assistant.

The stage manager had taken the tiny room with the inadequate, cement bathroom stuck onto the back of the house, to insure some privacy and to have a place to hide. He decided that it had been the cook's room in grander days, and it occurred to him that the cook may have had *her* privacy, but the employers certainly didn't have theirs. The little room shared a wall with the master bedroom, which Laurie had taken, and since his cot was on one side of the wall and the double bed Laurie slept in was on the other, the cook, he discovered, had not wanted for late night entertainment—depending on the liveliness of the owners.

And so, after everybody had said good night darling and shrugged shoulders at each other because of what was going on in Laurie's room, he had put out the lights in the windows and checked the side porch to make sure the pretty apprentice and the horny juvenile were not still at it. And turned off the light on the front stoop and was not surprised that Eleanor and Doris Ann had left the white board chairs and retired to their attic rollaways. "Once a stage manager, always a stage manager," he whispered and had gone to his cot in the cook's room.

But not to sleep.

The unhappiness on the other side of the wall next to his cot made sleep impossible. He longed to hold Laura in his arms to comfort her. And yet, he could understand the consternation of her once-husband at her determination to abandon him for this insubstantial world, when he had a world of substance to offer her. He had seen in the man's strange, bleached eyes his love for this slight, tremulous woman with red hair and china-white skin and knew that her intransigence threatened the very foundation of the man's life and conviction.

Through the long night, he listened to the voices and the clink of bottle and glasses. It was like the exchange between a violin and a cello and was very sad and beautiful and final music. Julian, he heard her cry, and the violin would take up a pleading and piteous phrase with the cello running under everything, insistent and gentle. At first light through the pines outside his window, the stage manager slept at last. However, the music played on in his dreams with distressing visions of Laura looking into the face of the tall, unhappy man who had no violent intent and asked for nothing but the reasonable contentment of approved existence.

The closing of a door somewhere, in or out of his dreams, awakened Gordon an hour or so later, and he dragged himself from his cot to prepare

for another day trying to bring some order into this life of fantasy and
reproduced emotion that he had been put in charge of. He asked himself
if the members of the audience in the darkened theaters around the world
could ever guess what pain it took to give them what they saw when the
lights went up. And did they understand its value?

In the living room, he found the tall man in the red leatherette chair
with his head in his hands and still wearing the seersucker suit, still with
the coat and tie. He could see that the man was exhausted and at the far
end of unhappiness and he stood in the doorway not knowing how best
to make his presence known. The living room looked as if it had been
the temporary headquarters for a drunken and victorious horde. He
thought he must get Doris Ann up. Doris Ann could eradicate the traces
of barbaric victory and the half-empty glasses and butt-filled ash trays in
no time at all.

"Good morning," he said from the doorway.

The man lifted his face from his hands and focused the pale blue
eyes, dislocated and in some alarm, as though someone had shouted incomprehensible commands from a distant place. It took him some time
to adjust to his condition, to determine where he was and why, and he
sat up wild-eyed and looked about at the disaster and ran his fingers
through his hair and cleared his throat several times.

"*Oh!*" he said. "Good morning," and he tried to think of something
to explain the situation he found himself in. "I—"

"How about a cup of coffee?" Gordie asked him.

"Oh, yes. Oh, yes, please. That would be . . . I am Julian Warren,"
he said and put out his hand and took it back again. "Laura Warren's
husband. I mean—"

"Yes, I know," Gordie said easily. "Is she all right?"

"What?" the man asked and put up his eyebrows, offended slightly
by the question. "Oh. Yes. Fine, she's fine," he said and searched through
his coat pockets for a cigarette and found nothing.

"Here. Here's one," Gordon said, taking a pack from his bathrobe pocket.

"What? Oh. Oh, thank you," he said, taking the cigarette, and looked into Gordie's face with the long-distance eyes, thinking perhaps he had found an ally, and Gordie saw that he was extraordinarily handsome with the high cheekbones and bleached-out eyes with tiny pupils.

"I'm Gordon Blake," he said. "She is my special friend."

"Who?" the man asked, looking directly up into Gordon's eyes again.

"Laura. She is my special friend and I love her."

"Oh, Laura," the man said and passed his hand downward over his face as if to erase something. "Yes, she is my wife," he said. "She was my wife," he corrected himself.

"Yes, I know," Gordon said.

"I had better go," the man said, struggling to get out of the broken-down, red leatherette armchair.

"Oh, no, please," Gordon said. "Let me get you some coffee."

"No, thank you, I don't believe so, I had better—" He looked into Gordie's face again and came to a momentous decision, widening the intense eyes at him. "Will you take care of her?" he asked.

"I can try," Gordon said.

"No. I mean, take care of her. Take care of her for me," and he gave himself entirely away. "She is all I want, but she doesn't understand. I don't understand."

"I understand," Gordon said.

"I don't know why I'm saying this, but I think you do," Julian said and managed to struggle to his feet. "She needs something I can't give her, because I don't know what it is."

"I understand."

"I don't know why, but I think you do," he said. "I have to go," he said.

"Let me get some coffee," the stage manager urged.

"No. I have to go. But I do thank you." He opened the screen door and stood for a moment looking out at the early light and then turned back to Gordie. "Please," he said. And left without slamming the screen door.

CHAPTER FIFTEEN

Well as I live and breathe, look who's tippy-toeing around the corner of the house. You always seem to turn up when my—ah—when Skinner's away. Well, let me tell you, this time you can go ahead and pee off the deck or run around stark naked or anything else that comes to mind without fear of unpleasant consequences. He's gone and he's gone for good and good riddance, if you ask me."

"I know. I'm sorry."

"Oh, are you now?"

"Yes, I am, I'm very sorry, although I feel sure you won't accept that with any kind of grace. May I just—are you going to keep me at bay like this again, Susan? I was hoping we—"

"How is it you always know where to find me and why is it you always sneak around that corner barefoot like that—"

"Oh, for godsake, Susan, is it going to be like this again? I was not sneaking, I don't sneak. I don't know how to sneak, and you—"

"Well it cer—it most certainly *looks* like sneaking to me when you—when a person comes tippy-toeing around a corner barefoot like that without making a sound and knows exactly where the other person is going to be, I call it sneak—"

"I was just wondering if I could fix myself a drink without fear of unpleasant consequences."

"I don't know why not. You certainly should know where the likker is by now, and the orange juice is in the refrigerator. As I recall, you drink what you people from California call an Orange Blossom and what we here in Milford call a vodka and orange. You have such lovely names for things in Calif—"

"And I was just wondering if I could fix you a drink without fear of unpleasant consequences."

"I don't know why not. Vodka and tonic, heavy on the vodka. If you're here to do research again, you might as well get me good and drunk—"

"I wonder if you could let up on me long enough to say Jake."

"I don't know why not. Jake."

"That hasn't changed much, has it? I had hoped it might have."

"Well, God knows everything else has. I suppose it's the talk of the international set over at Ned Trivett's. I suppose Ned Trivett is being witty in two or three languages about me and my house and my father and my hus—my *ex*-husband for whom I have little feeling one way or the other, let me assure you in case you are in any doubt."

"Ned is devastated, Susan. He asked me to tell you he—"

"He'll recover, he always does. He wounds and heals at his convenience according to which way he can get the most attention."

"That isn't fair and you know it. Ned is devastated. He feels what has happened is his fault, and he is devastated. You should accept that, Susan. I expected more than that of you."

"Did you now? Why is it you are always expecting things from me that aren't a part of my character, I wonder why that is, can you explain to me why that is? Is it because you are under the impression you were sent all the way from California to save us all? Well, now. Let me just tell you, if you think you are going to do any life-saving during the cocktail hour on this deck, you are sadly mistaken. For your information and probably according to an old and dear friend of yours across town, I am beyond saving. I don't want—"

"Not really. I have never heard him mention your need for salvation. I believe you said heavy on the vodka."

"I did. Very heavy."

"Well, my God, that's one thing that hasn't changed. You're still the world's fastest long distance bartender. I must try to remember to clock you next time you make the run for drinks. I'm convinced it's a world record."

"Why waste time."

"Waste whose time? We've both got plenty of time now. You're still visiting and I have become single and unprotected on a permanent basis. However, if you think you're going to set up headquarters here for the evening and pee off the deck and run around without a stitch on, you're in for a rude awakening. I won't have it. I said heavy on the vodka, I didn't say straight."

"You're an unforgiving woman, Susan."

"Am I? I guess I am. I guess it's part of my character."

"I wonder if you could say Jake?"

"Jake."

"Ah, well. . . . You know, it's really quite wonderful sitting here in this late afternoon light. Right out there is where I saw you for the first time, when you had lost the ring, and it was from there around this time of day when I saw you here on the deck wearing that same blue robe—"

"Kaftan. It's a kaftan."

"Kaftan. Wearing that same blue kaftan."

"It's from India."

"I see. Yes, well, it's very pretty whatever it is."

"It is, isn't it? . . . You knew perfectly well you'd never find that ring, didn't you?"

"Of course, and you knew perfectly well I knew. It was a pretext, truth be told. I had a feeling it was important to keep pretending."

"To save another life, I take it. Well, you wasted your time."

"Not really. Here I am."

"Yes, here you are big as life. At least, here you are for the time being."

"You needn't worry the time being will go on for too long. I have to relieve Annie. I'm staying nights with Jubie while Laura is in Bladens Beach."

"I see. I didn't know that, Lark didn't tell me that. Why didn't she tell me that? What's wrong with Julian, what's wrong with the child's very own father staying with him?"

"Well, Julian . . . Laura didn't want that at this point."

"Drinking too much."

"That too."

"I see. So you're sleeping in Laura's house."

"Yes."

"Every night."

"Almost."

"Without any underwear on as usual, I suppose."

"Yes."

"Still traveling light, still resting on the nearest available limb. I see."

"No, I don't think you do. It so happens I love Jubie, I love being with Jubie. In a way, Jubie belongs to me."

"Does he now? Well, I should hope you realize that is one life that does not need saving."

"I'm aware it's a life misplaced on this planet. Truth be told, I'd say Jubie is saving my life."

"Would you now? I don't know what it is, what is it? Ever since you appeared on the scene, everybody seems to be running around saving lives. It occurs to me none of us was aware our lives needed saving until you drifted in from California. Everything was all right, until you—until that damn ring. Losing it was an omen, whether good or bad remains to be seen. I never did like it anyway, it was always a burden to me for some reason I don't fully understand yet."

"I think you do. It's my feeling a person like you should never settle for less than the impossible."

"Oh, my! Did Ned Trivett say that? That sounds like Ned Trivett."

"No, I said it. It just came out like that."

"Then, I must say, for that I'm glad you're here. I like that. That's on a par with never let them reduce you to mediocrity, thank you father. On the other hand, that may be what went wrong. I *expected* the impossible. I expected ecstasy twenty-four hours a day. As it turns out, it was only about an hour and a half of ecstasy in just under a year. Possibly two hours. And then, he walked out to find some more ecstasy with an utter stranger."

"That's not quite the way it was."

"Isn't it? I wish I knew how it was. I wish I knew whether I was glad or sorry, I don't even know that. I have been lying out here at night thinking about how it was. I have been thinking about this play I saw half of by mistake in New York once. About a damn fool kind of a woman buried up to her waist in a mound of dirt that took up practically the whole stage. Her husband lived behind this mound in some kind of a hole and spoke to her only when it suited him, which wasn't often and even then he didn't say anything worth listening to. But she was grateful for whatever he said. She could lean way back and see him, but he couldn't see her—or didn't choose to see her, I don't know which. Every now and then, this woman would feel the pull of gravity cut off and the earth release her, so that she felt she could rise upward free. I left at intermission. I thought it was just intellectual foolishness everybody in New York had to pretend they understood for fear of being considered nonintellectual— they're terrified of being considered nonintellectual in New York, you know. It's exactly the opposite of California. Anyway, I'm sorry I left now, because I think that play was about me and Skinner Bates. I would like to know what became of that woman. I think the thing was she was too cheerful for the wrong reasons. I think she was cheerful for her husband's sake, but, no, maybe even worse than that. Maybe because being cheerful about her dreadful existence was what was expected of her, poor fool. I wonder now if she ever rose up out of the earth even for a minute to relieve herself of what was expected of her and what she had come to expect of herself. Or if she kept on being cheerful as expected until she sank down into the earth over her head and died. I do worry about that woman. I was never buried in the earth, thank God, but I've got good reason to believe I am trapped in a picture without a title somewhere, which is not nearly so . . . what *am* I carrying on about? you made that drink *much* too strong. I said heavy on the vodka, not straight."

"Forgive me, I'll try to do better next time."

"Oh, that's all right. I probably needed it, I probably needed to be cut off from gravity and rise upward a little. I've been much too nervous since Skin—as a matter of fact, as far as I'm concerned, now is as good a time as any to try to do better."

"Yes, you're right. I agree, let me try again. Now, Susan, you did say heavy on the vodka, didn't you?"

"Light. This time make it light, *very* light on the vodka this time, practically no vodka at all. I don't want to get too . . ."

◇

"Well, as I live and breathe, look who's back again and another world record. How *do* you do it? Oh, thank you, thank you. I had forgotten how nice it could be having somebody bring you drinks. Oh dear, now *this* one—I don't think you put any vodka at all in this one."

"Shall I—"

"Oh no, that's all right, it's probably just as well, I don't want to get completely . . . I was just lying here thinking during the forty-five seconds it took you to make that last trip to the spring. Would you—ah—could you . . . I don't know just how to put this, so that it doesn't sound like doing research. What is she like? Is she beautiful?"

"Is who—oh, you mean Graziella. Well, she's—"

"Oh Lord! Graziella. Is that her name? Word has it she's a princess as well. I didn't know there were any of those left, but if there is one still around, you can bet your ass Skinner Bates will find her. He—"

"She's a princess in a way. Princess Graziella di Brabant by right of marriage. Her real name is Grace and she's from Mobile Alabama."

"Oh, I do see, I really do. That's the way it is, is it? That makes them a matched pair, birds of a feather, don't it? She's not a real princess and my hus—my ex-husband ain't a real prince. It's really terribly sad, isn't it? Two full-grown people running around trying to be princesses and princes, knowing all the time they are not but hoping everybody else will think they are, which everybody else knows perfectly well they are not. She must be rich. You'd have to be very rich or very beautiful or both to get by with that."

"She's rich. She's very rich to hear her tell it. Truth be told, she's really quite wonderful. But, no, she's not beautiful. It's hard to explain. Not young and not beautiful but something else."

"Well, any old port in a storm (oh, ha, ha, ha) you don't know how funny that is. Any old port in a storm. It comes to me now I was myself any old port in a storm only a few days ago. It was a terrifying storm, and—oh, never mind all that. Rich but not young and not beautiful but something else. Comes the light. It all begins to fall into place. As it turns out, Skinner Bates is the one who seeks out the rich and lonely. It may be he's the best hustler of us all."

"I am supposed to tell you. Ned put her out of the house, he wanted you to know that. She had to go to a motel, the hotel was full of conventions. She said she didn't even know what a motel was."

"Good for old Ned (ha! ha! ha!). Oh! good for old Ned! I've always liked Ned, although we've had our differences. I've always liked old Ned. I really have always liked Ned, even if he is a fairy."

"Whatever that is."

"What do you *mean* whatever that is? You of all people should know what a fairy—"

"Let's not go into that again. I think that's what got us off on the wrong foot—"

"*Indeed* it is not. What got us off on the wrong foot was when you got up out of that chair you're sitting in right this minute and went to the railing right there at that exact spot I'm pointing at and took it out and—"

"Let's not go into that either. I had hoped I might have been forgiven for that by now. You're an unforgiv—"

"Well, for heaven sake, Jake, there's nothing to forgive. You of all people should know that. We were both drunk and lonely and you were hus—ah—visiting."

"Oh my. . . . Oh my, there it was. Did you hear it? You called me by my name. Just like that. You said Jake, just like that, as easy as it should have been to say it all along. I can't believe—"

"Let's not carry on too much over things that don't amount to a hill of beans for goodness sake. Although I dare say, as a result of that famous evening alone together I know more about you than I know about any other man in the world with the possible exception of Skinner Bates who kept the door shut and the lights off when—oh, but never mind all that,

I've seen the last of that and good riddance, if you ask me. *Well.* I don't know about you, Jake, but . . . *would* you be kind enough to take my glass, it's—"

"—it's full of nothing but the moon, and that's not enough."

"Oh lordy, ain't that lovely! Oh, Jake, how did you remember that? You must have loved me to remember that."

"I did love you. I love you now. You're ruining my life."

"Ruining your *life!* Isn't that *wonderful!* Every woman ought to ruin at least one man's life."

"While I'm at it, why don't I get the tray—"

"Ruining your *life!* Isn't that *wonderful!* I'm a part of world history like Venus at last! You know what, Jake, while you're at it, why don't you get the tray, and while you're at it, Jake, make it snappy. Maybe you can break your own world record (hee, hee, hee, sigh)."

"You know what, Jake. Put it right there on the table under the umbrella. *Light,* I said *light* on the vodka, make it *light,* you're getting me drunk. You know what, Jake. Well, not really drunk. Cheerful. You're getting me cheerful like that woman sunk in the dirt. What happened, you didn't establish a new world record this time? You must be slipping—"

"I stopped off in the john to pee like a Southern gentleman."

"Well, chalk one up for onrushing civilization, although I don't know why you bothered. It's getting dark and all the neighbors are in an advanced state of intoxication fighting over the supper table. And I mean, why waste time?"

"Waste whose time? I'm still a visitor—"

"Hustler. You're still a hustler, I like hustler better—"

"—still a hustler, and you have become a single and unprotected woman on a permanent basis."

"Oh, true. Oh, too true (sigh). Ruining your life, isn't that wonderful? Oh, Jake, don't the moon look lonesome sliced in half like that? Well, for a change, you made this one just about right."

"Chalk another one up for onrushing civilization."

"Look here now, don't you get smart-ass with me, you son of—You know what, Jake?"

"What, Susan?"

"You know what, Jake? He walked right into this house and walked right past me and walked right up the stairs to that bedroom where we've been doing it for the past not even a year yet. Oh Lord, the Foolish Virgin and the Good-Looking, Get-Ahead Boy, ain't that a laugh? And you know what, Jake?"

"What, Susan?"

"He didn't even stop packing his shirts and all those little rolled up socks and he didn't even look at me, and he made the announcement of the big news. Big News (ha, ha). I had a hard time understanding him he was so busy packing his little socks. 'I find my position in this house and in this community untenable,' he told me. Untenable, for godsake, where did he come up with that word, untenable? He must have gotten that word from Miss Princess. Untenable was never one of his words, but he could pick up new words the way he picked up anything else along his upward path. 'Untenable,' he said. 'I'm going to save both our lives at a stroke,' he said, walking back and forth to the closet packing his favorite clothes not looking at me. Save both our lives at a stroke. You see what I mean, Jake? You see how you've got us all running around saving each other's lives—"

"Now look here, I had nothing whatsoever to do—"

"*Untenable!* for godsake. In what way untenable? I'd like to know. Here, we've been doing it in this house for just under a year now, and he told me I did it well, he really did, Skinner Bates in person told me that. Oh, my God! and now he's gone off to do it with somebody else, I wonder why that is. I wonder if that's why she's a princess and I'm not. Maybe they make you a princess when you can do it better than other people. Ain't that a laugh (ha, ha, ha, ha). Or maybe it's because she's rich, maybe you can do it better when you're rich—"

"They say money is an aphrodisiac for some people."

"Where did you hear that? Did Ned Trivett tell you that? That sounds like something Ned Trivett would say. Why is it fairies think they know everything, can you tell me that?"

"Susan, I'm not going to sit here and listen to you saying such—"

"Shut up. Where was I?"

"Untenable, I think."

"The hell you say, you're not listening to me. I had gone way past untenable, and I had gone way past saving both our lives at a stroke. *Way* past. 'I'm leaving you, Susan,' he said, just like that. 'I'm going away to find something I lost or something I have been looking for all my life,' is what he said. Another quote from Miss Princess, I have no doubt. And closed his fine suitcases with all his favorite suits and all the little rolled up socks and walked right out without looking back once and drove off down the driveway. And it was like he had never been here at all, oh, my God, oh, my God, oh, my . . ."

"Don't cry, Missook, please don't cry. It's not your style."

"Oh, shut up, you son of a—not my style, what on earth does that mean? Did you expect more than that of me again? Goddam it, I'm a person too, you know. . . . I'm sorry, Jake, I'm sorry for everything, Jake, I can't help it. I think I've been through an amputation. It's not easy, not even for a woman of my character."

"I know it isn't. I'm sorry."

"Are you now?"

"I am. I really am. Can't you see you're ruining my life?"

"That's not funny anymore, we've worn that one out. It's late. I want to be by myself out here with the lonesome sliced in half moon and the likker tray. Annie'll be waiting for you. Jubie will be waiting for you.

Everybody will be waiting for you. Go somewhere else and be sorry. Go anywhere."

"You're going to make it, Missook."

"Do you think so, Jake? Do you know that, Jake? Will you promise me that, Jake?

"I promise you that, Missook."

"You know what, Jake?"

"What, Missook?"

"You know what? You're a good-looking life-saver, even if you do blondine your hair and wear a little black bathing suit to show off your— to show off. Oh, Jake, I would ask you to hold me, I would so love you to hold me close to you. But I would be listening for the phone to ring from Rome Italy and I would be waiting to hear Skinner Bates' voice from somewhere. You can't hold anybody close the right way, if she's listening for the sound of somebody else's voice, can you, Jake?"

"No. That would be untenable."

"Oh, *Jake!* Untenable (ha, ha, ha, ha, ha). God, we're a funny pair! How has it all happened like this? Oh, Jake, be careful for my sake. The life you save could be your own."

"You're going to make it, Missook. Good night, Missook."

"Good night, good night, good night. You know what, Jake? I know what it is, Jake, you're full of light, Jake. I just this minute realized what it is, you're full of light, Jake. Good night, good night, good night."

CHAPTER SIXTEEN

T here they go, right on time anyhow," Dr. Fred Bartlett said, standing like a bear after hibernation on the screened-in front porch with a cup of coffee in one hand and the *Bladens Beach Bugle* in the other. "Up all night, in the house and out in the yard and parading from room to room with all the lights on and all the windows wide open."

"I told you before, Fred, and I'll tell you again. You just don't understand artists," his wife said in the doorway, trying to see around her husband standing in her way in his bathrobe, as he had done the forty years they had been married. "And there's Laura Warren with that nice young man that makes the scenes and pulls the curtains. There's certainly no harm in him. My, she looks bad, that child."

"Don't any of them look too good this morning and no wonder," the doctor said. "I saw him leave the house at before six this morning."

"Who? You saw who leave the house this morning?" Lib Bartlett asked, rising to curiosity.

"Why, Julian Warren," the doctor said, a little impatient with his life's companion. "I told you that."

"You no such thing," Lib said, annoyed that she had missed a news flash. "Ever since you retired, you forget what you have told me and what you haven't."

"Or could it be you're the one who forgets? I told you I saw Julian come stumbling out the front door, looking like he'd been in a wrestling match all night in his suit."

"Well, I certainly wouldn't forget a thing like that," she said. "Do you want another cup of coffee, Fred? Maybe they're going to get back together, wouldn't that be perfectly wonderful? You see, I told you this play acting might be the best thing for Laura."

"No," he said. "You're wrong about this, as you are about a number of things. From the look of him, he had been given the worst kind of news and a long time getting to it. Yes, get me another cup."

"He was probably just worn out from talking things over all night, as we have done on many an occasion."

"Not dead drunk, we didn't," the doctor said. "Look at that poor little red-headed thing. Looks to me like she can hardly make it to the hotel. Thinner and whiter than ever. She's not strong enough for this thing she's doing. It won't be long now, till they have to carry her off. Watch my word."

"Oh, you know so much. Give me your cup."

Ernie Dexter stood in the middle of the aisle studying the stage with his pale, pawlike hands on his hips and his stomach sitting out under the mattress-ticking shirt. "Gordon, where are you?" he called out in the artificial, half-strangled voice which so exasperated his charges and which had no resemblance whatsoever to the voice he used in ordinary daily communication.

"Here he is," Gordie said, smiling his way through the French doors of Miss Haskins' English country house. "Radiant and ready. What's your pleasure, honey?"

"Gordon," Ernie went on, projecting from his diaphragm and the back of his throat, disapproving of such levity under his authority. "Would you show me the door to the doctor's office?"

"Why certainly. Right here, honey," Gordon said, indicating two chairs. The members of the company kept their scripts close to their faces, being accustomed to this daily ritual of challenge and riposte.

"And the anatomy chart?" Ernie asked, choking down. "Where is that?"

"Oh!" Gordie said, caught out. "Oh, it's right back here, I'll get it."

"Do that, honey," Ernie said. "There isn't enough time to get this show into shape as it is, without you forgetting little details such as the anatomy chart, which is the heart of this scene."

"Sorry, Ernie," Gordon said and disappeared again through the French doors and reappeared instantly with the anatomy chart, rolled up like a window shade, and hung it carefully, checking out the positions of the chairs representing a door here or a sofa there. "Now," he said. "What else?"

"What else is where is our star this morning?"

"She—she's resting back stage. She's not—I'll get her," he said and hesitated as though he doubted he would find her.

Laura materialized in the French doors like a specter, her white face projecting like a mask from the black handkerchief with which she bound her head. "Here she is, honey," she said in the crystal voice. "Here is the star," and her eyes were misty and half-closed. "Radiant and ready and indomitable," she laughed. But her presence in the doorway seemed so impermanent and insubstantial that Ernie took alarm.

"Are you all right, Laura?" he asked in his natural, charming voice. "You don't look . . . are you sure you're all right, darling?"

"Perfectly," she said. "I told you. Radiant and ready and indomitable." She laughed again, swallowing air, and walked on stage, having summoned strength from somewhere.

"She hasn't slept, Ernie," Gordie said.

"Shut up, honey, and bring the lights up on the sofa. I never sleep," she said.

"And now, all we need is our young Doctor John. Where is Mister Worth?" Ernie said, returning to the voice placement.

"Mister—ah—Dave, here, is preparing," David said, standing up in the rear of the auditorium. "Mister Worth is radiant and ready and indomitable and could run a mile."

"What we've got to do this morning," Ernie pronounced, "is much more difficult than running a mile. What we've got this morning is a meeting between body and soul. Let's take it from the top."

David Worth strode down the aisle and sprang onto the stage as if he were leaping a fence.

The members of the company took their folded-back books away from their eyes and sat up in their seats, reflecting in their earnest faces the glow of the light from the stage. It seemed to Gordon Blake at his stage manager's desk as he watched the rehearsal that there had grown between Laura and David, or between the two characters—he couldn't decide which—a new, more intimate communication that suggested a closer relationship than was indicated in the script. Laura was playing the scene with a kind of tremulousness, an increase in tension, and the parabola of her light voice cut through the air of the theater with more conviction than was reasonable. When she made her exit, and when David had made his later, Gordie felt the emotion he usually experienced following a love scene.

"I want to speak to you both," Ernie Dexter ordered from the front of the house, and they wandered on stage and stood easily and, the stage manager felt, a little defiantly. "What the hell happened to that scene?"

Ernie asked. "What have you done to it? I can't figure it out. Where was the rejection? You seem all the way through to be agreeing with each other, which is hardly the point."

Laura sat down in one of the entrance door chairs and cupped her hands in her lap. "I think it must be me," she said. "I think my feeling has changed here. I feel that John and Alma are prisoners in the same prison and are fighting for release in their own different ways. It came to me just that moment."

"It may have come to you, but that is not what came to Tennessee Williams when he took the trouble to write this play. You are doing the wrong play. I wonder if you would run it again from the beginning—as we rehearsed it originally. Laura do you think you could—"

A husky and undulant voice sounded from the back of the house, underlining the contention of the moment. "It's none of my business," it said, and the cast strained around in their seats, surprised to find its source standing in the semidarkness. "But it seems to me, it behooves you, Mister—ah—Ernie, to leave that scene alone. It plays. I had no idea Miss Warren had it in her," Madelyn Haskins said. "Right or wrong, I believed every minute of it. Besides, that girl looks ill, and she's got a performance to do with me tonight."

Ernie Dexter stood at the front of the theater and faced the woman standing alone at the back. "You direct your play, and I'll direct mine, Miss Haskins," he said in the unnatural voice.

Laurie shaded her eyes, searching out her admirer in the obscurity. "Thank you for that, Miss Haskins," she said. "But I'll run it again, and I'll be ready tonight."

"I'm sure you will," Miss Haskins said and left, permitting the brilliant sunshine to shatter the magic through the doors as she departed.

"Where the shit did *she* come from?" Doris Ann Hawkins wanted to know.

◊

Through the week, Miss Haskins continued to get her laughs and a hand on her exits, and she spoke no more about the performance of the play for the week to come. For that matter, she spoke no more to anybody, and as far as Gordie could tell, she had forgotten her words to Laura. She kept her counsel.

And through the week, Gordon kept his counsel. He closed the theater and set up for rehearsal for the next day and sat hunched on the curb with David Worth beyond the reach of the street light and turned out the lights in the windows of the old house after all the good night darlings had been called out. And then, sleepless, through the wall of his little room, he listened to the seemingly endless clinking of a bottle and glasses and the sorrowful argumentative and piteous exchange between the out-of-tune violin and the pleading, repetitive cello in the next room.

Laura seemed paler and weaker and more oblivious to what was going on around her every day in her black rehearsal clothes with the black kerchief binding down her red hair around her face. However, when she began to perform, the tension seemed to sustain her, and she charged the lines with a perilous, nervous vitality. Gordon followed her music with wonder from his script on the stage manager's desk.

On Saturday night, Madelyn Haskins fell back on the sofa and asked for something beautiful on the piano for the last time and got her thirty to forty-five second laugh. And when the last member of the audience left the theater, she held sway, standing in the French doors, where the light was best, at the obligatory party of appreciation given by every Star of the Week after the last performance. However, Miss Haskins managed to give it a more exciting quality with a combination of charm and hostility in her stretched back eyes and a brilliant smile, seen infrequently since the days of glory on the silver screen. The drinks flowed and the supper was consumed almost before it had been laid out on the folding tables.

The apprentices got drunk immediately. Eleanor Bacon burst into tears in the middle of her second glass of wine as usual, and Doris Ann Hawkins surprised David Worth with a sudden quick fondle of her buttery little hand. The Lunts were gracious beyond all reason, and Ernie Dexter clung to his mattress-ticking shirt and his stage voice and his drink. And then, everybody was drunk, and the excitement over the coming production exceeded all bounds, its success, both critical and financial, as sure as sunrise. The accountant and the production assistant played a violent game of tennis across Miss Haskins' sofa, disparaging the world of fantasy between volleys. "*I* should be playing Alma," the pretty apprentice was overheard saying to the horny juvenile, who agreed with her adoringly for the rest of the evening.

Sometime after midnight, the entire company kissed Madelyn Haskins good-by, and the party moved en masse to the white house among the pines, and the lights went on in the windows and were on all night long—even after the raised voices had stumbled and stopped.

Once again, there was no sleep for Gordon Blake. The plaintive, downward curve of Laura's voice and the melodious reason of Julian's took up again over the clink of the glasses and the running of water in the bathroom. It seemed to him that they were speaking simultaneously through the hours, as if the words were so old that they need not pause for response but sounded on in a kind of hell of searching for something they had lost and could not find again ever.

At a certain point, the wind from the sea lifted, and the sighing of the pines matched the sighing of the voices through the wall. He thought Laura was weeping and he thought Julian was weeping. The voices had that sweet, descending movement of despair. He turned on his side, cradling his head on his arm, and watched the window for the first light.

He thought he could see the shadowing of the pines against the paling end of night, and he thought he did not sleep.

But suddenly, out of oblivion, David was bending over him saying something in a harsh, rasping voice, something he couldn't understand at first. He was sure then, for a moment, that it was a dream, since David was wearing nothing but his trousers with the belt hanging unbuckled.

"Quick, Gord! Come on!" David said again, emerging from the dream, shouting, "Hurry! It's Laurie! She has . . ." as he disappeared swiftly through the door. The stage manager sat for a moment on his bed, finding his way, realizing the first light had come and gone, and the pines stood against some later hour outside his window. The pounding of his heart warned him that he must move and that the gray light was thin with disaster. He ran from his room and past Laura's door which had been left open, and he wondered at the bed which was neatly made, not having been slept in or even sat on. And he heard the water running in the bathroom.

Julian was standing in the entrance hall with Laurie in his arms like a sleeping child. Her head was thrown back. Her eyes were closed and her mouth open, and the helmet of red hair was all that seemed to have retained life. And then, he saw the white towel that bound her arm with a spot of red-brown that increased as he watched it. She could have been stone, except that she seemed weightless in Julian's arms.

"Help her for me," Julian said to him, and Gordon felt she was beyond help. He heard David's voice barking something into the telephone in the living room and was not surprised when Doris Ann appeared on the stair in her pajamas.

"Over there," she said, pointing towards the front door, and he noticed that the light on the front stoop was still burning. "Over there," Doris Ann said again. "That old man across the road is a doctor."

Gordon looked into Julian's face and was committed to him. The bleached eyes were confounded and had lost their long-distance power. "Doctor Bartlett," he said. "Fred."

"Put her on the bed," David shouted from the telephone in the living room.

"Over there across the road," Doris Ann said, still pointing from the stair.

"Put her in the car," Gordon said and ran barefoot out the front door and crossed the street to the neat, yellow house with the screened-in front porch and onto the porch and ringing the bell and pounding with the shiny brass knocker on the door. He won't come, he decided and was about to turn back, when a light came on in the panels of the window-panes on either side of the door. It was a long time before the great bear of a man with tousled white hair in his pajamas and bathrobe and slippers opened the door.

"What is it, young man?" he asked and then saw the expression on Gordon's face and, raising his shaggy brows, seemed to know everything. "Let's go," the old man said and pulled the door shut carefully and quietly behind him, recalling in a flood the early days of his practice.

"She has cut her wrist—" Gordon began.

"Laura Warren," the doctor said and crossed the road, still not hurrying, and leaned on his elbows into the window of the car, filling it completely. He glanced at Laura in Julian's arms and David Worth at the wheel and ducked back out of the window and got into the back seat with difficulty, slamming the door shut. "Go to the emergency room at the hospital right this minute!" he shouted at David as though in anger. "*Now,* boy!"

The stage manager and Doris Ann stood like victims of a disaster in the front yard among the black pines and watched the car turn onto the highway, casting its headlights into the thin, gray light. Anybody seeing it would have known that it carried tragedy.

"Just goddam the son of a bitch," Doris Ann said. "He's gone and kilt her."

"No," Gordon said. "He couldn't help it and she couldn't help it."

"She ain't dead," Doris Ann decided. "I can tell you that, she ain't dead." She went into the house in her pajamas, and Gordon was full of hope that she was right about that, as she was about most things. He sat down in one of the peeling, white board chairs and began to weep.

Monday morning early, Gordon walked into the front hall to discover the accountant dodging and bounding about, still apprehending the impossible serve, confronted by the woman with what looked to be a broken jaw but wasn't, as evidenced by its being in constant and critical use. She was once again the accountant's formidable opponent, and Gordon sympathized with his plight.

"I sup*pose*," she served vigorously, "we will have to cancel this week entirely. I *told* you she didn't have the stamina for this role."

The accountant cringed to the side. "If we cancel this week, we might as well count the entire season a loss. Can't one of the apprentices replace her? Can't—"

"Can't anybody tell me what the hell is going on around here?" the production assistant demanded, turning her attention to Gordon, permitting the accountant a brief rest between volleys. "You're supposed to be the stage manager. What the hell has been going on around here?"

"People have been killing themselves, why don't you join in the fun?" he returned and walked down the hall to find Ernie Dexter in the door of Laurie's room. "I just can't allow you to do it, Laura. I can't take the chance," he was saying in his own charming voice.

Laurie said something the stage manager didn't understand, and he stood on his toes and peered over Ernie's shoulder into the bedroom. Laurie was lying, pale and smiling vaguely, on the pillows, and Doris Ann sat at the end of the bed with a breakfast tray on her lap. "Oh, *there*

he is," Laura said. "Come in here. Where have you been? Come in here
this minute," she said to Gordie. "Oh, my God," she said laughing feebly,
covering her face with a hand, "you've never seen me without my eyes
on. Wait a minute. Doris Ann, put down that tray and get me my eye
pencil and a mirror."

Gordon laughed and saw that it was going to be all right. Ernie
Dexter stood to one side so that he could go in and stand by the bedside
looking down at her. "What have you found to do since I've been away?"
he asked.

"Oh, the same old thing," she said. "Acting in plays and killing
myself."

"I can't leave you alone a minute," he said. "What do I look like,
a nurse or something?"

"Yes," she said, trying to smile, and he saw that her eyes were filling
with tears. "Go away, Ernie," she said. "Go away, Doris Ann. I'm all
right."

"I ain't going nowhere," Doris Ann said, sitting like a stone. Ernie
left the doorway and went down the hall. They could hear him engaged
in contest with the accountant and the production assistant.

"Close the door," Laura said. "They'll have me dead before I've had
a chance to eat my breakfast." The tears spilled over and ran down her
face, but she paid them no heed. "Don't let them count me out, Gordie.
It's all over now, all that is over now. Don't let them cancel my last hope.
Promise me that."

"We've made you a beautiful set," he said. "I wouldn't want to miss
seeing you in it."

"It's a pisser," Doris Ann said. "You can see right through it."

"Count me in," Laura said.

"I never considered anything else," he said and kissed her on the
forehead and went to the door and opened it. "Eat your breakfast, you'll
need it," he said. "Now, listen to nursie."

"Oh, nursie," she said. "I'm so glad I didn't die," and the tears ran over again in spite of her.

"It didn't turn out to be that simple, did it?" he said and went off down the hall where the furious tennis match was still in progress, watched helplessly from the sidelines by Ernie Dexter.

"She's going to be just fine," Gordie said pleasantly as he passed by.

"Then, get somebody in the goddam box office," the production assistant fired off.

"Any way you look at it, this show's going to be a flop," the accountant declared, having found the courage to return the serve at last.

The accountant needn't have worried about packing the house for the opening on Tuesday night. All of Milford and Bladens Beach were on hand to see the results of Laura Warren's two years of acting lessons in New York City, and a lot of people were there who wanted to see the rich girl who had tried to kill herself. The devotees of the resident company were there to see the sofa or the lamp they had loaned for the week, and there was a contingent of the married women David Worth had seduced during his lunch hour. You couldn't have asked for a more expectant and apprehensive audience. The hum of anticipatory excitement filled the little auditorium and penetrated to the dressing rooms. Programs fluttered and fanned and wives leaned in and whispered to their husbands, that's the husband, when Julian lumbered in and slumped down in the seat Gordon had held for him on the aisle in the last row. There was general admiration for the skeletal set and some consternation.

"You can see right through everything but that statue at the back," Fred Bartlett said.

"That's imagination!" Lib said. "You don't understand imagination."

"And I take it you do," he responded, looking down at her through his bifocals.

The cyclorama glowed serenely blue behind the tracery of the Victorian houses, and the Angel of Eternity brooded over all, her wings protecting the residents of the small, coastal town whose foibles she would witness and accept.

As the house lights dimmed and the lights began to come up on the little park in front of the fountain with the angel, the audience murmured down to a hush, preparing for what was to come. Gordon Blake at the light board felt his heart pounding as he watched Laura standing like an apparition in the wings. The play began, and the house was absolutely silent. Doris Ann Hawkins at the prop table put her face in her hands.

When Laura—when Alma made her entrance into the little park, the hush in the theater changed quality, as if a page had been turned or a door opened somewhere. She irradiated a kind of glow in her pale yellow dress and with a chiffon scarf of the same color tied loosely about her wrist. There was a shimmer to her image, as if she were being seen through water, but the pure, white voice cut clear through the dusk of times past. She was no longer Laura Warren from Milford nor the rich girl who had tried to kill herself. She was Alma, and Alma is Spanish for soul. Julian at the back of the theater, his face supported in his hands, tried to remember that this frail creature had been his wife and had thrown her head back on the pillow beneath him.

The members of the audience enforced her will, as she suffered the disappointments and attempted to contain her spirit in the constricted circumstances that had been imposed on her by birthright, and longed for her to throw off the constraints that separated her from flying free and from the realization of the love she had for the young doctor. They followed her through the difficult and wounding summer and into the winter during which she was not well and made the discovery that it was no longer worth the pain it took to contain her spirit, surviving with the aid of her little pills and mysterious solitary walks at night. It occurred to them, without having to say it to themselves, that John and Alma were opposing forces that had to be consumed in vastly different ways.

Finally, they went with her back into the park and observed with understanding her chance meeting with the young salesman and were not dismayed at her decision to accompany him to the disreputable Moon Lake Casino. At one point in the lyrical exchange between the two lonely people, when Alma offered him one of her pills, saying to him that they were infinitely merciful and "the prescription number is 96814—I think of it as the telephone number of God," there was a shocked intake of breath in the house, and for an instant, Laura Warren and Alma Winemiller were simultaneous.

They watched, hushed and wary, as the young man left the park calling, "Taxi!" And they watched as Laura turned her back to them and approached the angel of the fountain and raised her arm in what seemed to them to be a leave-taking, and they thought that was the end of it. But she turned on them, with her arm still raised in farewell salute, and they saw that her slight smile was one of triumph, perhaps even of defiance, as she walked swiftly towards them, not meaning to stop, until the light that was on her face blinked off. And it was over.

They released a breath and were silent in the temporary blackout, until a murmur blew through the theater like a light wind, and there was the smell of candles just blown out. Somewhere in the darkness, a woman's voice cried out, oh!, as if she had come upon herself in what she had supposed to be an empty room. As Gordon brought up the lights, the applause scattered with the wind, replacing the murmur, and swelled in release and increased and swelled again. Laura Warren, standing alone, became their messenger, their representative. She lifted her pale, half-smiling face into the amber light, not seeming to realize that she was not alone.

Through his observation window, the stage manager saw Julian Warren leave his seat at the back of the house and disappear through the doors onto the terrace outside. "Doris Ann," he said, "do you think you could pull yourself together long enough to take care of the curtain calls?" Doris Ann was overcome, her round face streaked with tears, but she nodded, bouncing her curls, and took her stand courageously before the light board. The applause increased again, as the observers decided that it was actually only a show, not related in any way to their own lives.

Lib Bartlett leaned forward in the tumult. "Oh, Fred, it was perfectly wonderful," she said, beating her little hands together. "It took all the hope out of life."

"I don't know who wrote that show," the doctor said, "but in my personal opinion, he missed the point."

"Oh, Fred, for heaven sake," Lib said.

Gordon couldn't have said why he felt it necessary to find Julian Warren. After all, his allegiance and his affection were Laura's, and this man had caused her unbearable suffering, but, Gordon thought, perhaps the man suffered unbearably also and had no lights nor poetry nor applause to relieve him. Then again, there had been an instant of rare friendship and understanding between them, one of those instants that illuminate existence from time to time and are, more often than not, put away somewhere to fade in the archives of memory.

He found Julian leaning on the balustrade of the terrace with the sounds of the wash of the surf before him and the applause washing through the theater doors behind him. He leaned on the balustrade near him and lit a cigarette and saw that the prominent cheekbones and hollows beneath were wet. But no tears fell from the long-distance eyes, turned now out towards the sea, and there was no acknowledgment of Gordie's presence. Only an acceptance.

Their silence went on too long, as the applause was going on too

long, perhaps because it had become applause for the rich girl who had
tried to kill herself, rather than for the actress who had breathed the breath
of Alma Winemiller.

"Well, she did it," Gordie said at length over the waves of sound
which had become the same indistinguishable sound.

"Yes," Julian said. "Give me a cigarette."

"And?" Gordie asked, putting the damp package of cigarettes from
his pocket into Julian's hand.

"That about says it," Julian said. "And. It kills me that I can never
give her that. It kills me that I can't give her the strength to live with
that. It is beyond her strength."

"Maybe not," Gordie said. "Maybe that kind of strength, doing
what she can do, is what will get her through."

"I would like to believe that," the man said, becoming a stranger,
"but I know better. Anyhow, I thank you for what you tried to do." He
turned to go but turned back and leaned on the balustrade and became
a friend again. "I wish there were some way to take care of her, I wish I
could say to you, take care of her. But that is only a wish, and they are
about as dependable as that applause in there now. I must explain to you,
for some reason I don't understand myself, why I have done as I have done
with her. It is because I believe that she will end as she tried to end."

"That would be her choice," Gordie said.

"Yes," Julian said, standing and facing the theater doors from which
there came now the hum of general chatter and conversation and an occasional couple hurrying home to release the babysitter. "But at least, she
has had that for a while, whatever the hell it is," he said and thumped
his cigarette towards the rushing sea and walked away.

CHAPTER SEVENTEEN

H e has returned reluctantly to his bachelor quarters that don't even know how to get dirty. He is having his first scotch of the afternoon after a day of showing houses—or "homes" as they would have it—to people who have no business being in Milford in the first place. Bill and Jackie Goins. Nice to meet you, Mrs. Goins. Likewise. His father, certainly, and his mother, occasionally, would have said they were common as pig tracks. But you couldn't say that anymore. Because, Julian concludes, everybody is common now, or rather, everybody is *not* common, and no relief in sight. No further hope for the gentle and predictable life of recognizing your own kind. Your own kind: assumed to be unassuming and honest by election and courageous in the face of misfortune, articulate and funny in a horizontal and referential way, attentive to certain approved and sometimes even disapproved eccentricity and contemptuous of avarice, gallant in poverty, not acknowledging the terrible weight of its presence, suspicious of riches and amused by the display of riches. In a place where no woman of advanced years was never

not a famous beauty in her youth and no man was never not a pedigreed
seducer of grateful and nameless women—but not too nameless, mind
you.

That's funny, Julian thought. Missook would laugh, Laurie would
have once, the three of them being offspring of famous beauties and im-
modest seducers, no matter the evidence to the contrary. But don't you
see? It doesn't matter what you are, so long as you know who you are and
who everybody else is and are known in return by people who agree with
your estimation. Understand now, this exalted and gentle way of living
demands sacrifice, as everything of importance demands sacrifice, usually
the sacrifice of beautiful and aberrant dreams whose realization opens
doors which are better left closed against intrusion, gives away secrets
which could give comfort to the enemy, to the ambitious and intrusive.
However—and this is the puzzle—it's the fly-aways, the ones who defect
to pursue the reckless dreams who confirm the faith. Without the dazzling, rebellious apostate, the structure becomes nothing more than pre-
tentious sham. Take Ben Stone's son, Edward, who happened to learn to
play his mother's piano too well and was impelled into a life of playing
the piano for money all over the world, a great deal of money, they say.
And some of us flew to New York to hear him play with an orchestra but
didn't get to speak to Edward afterwards, because he had had to leave
immediately to catch a plane to London to play with another orchestra.
Ben lost his son to aberration. Ben said, My God, I always thought a
piano was just to strum on and play hymns, otherwise I wouldn't have
had one in the house, and everybody had laughed, knowing better but
not saying so.

But take these people today. To whom he had had to betray the once
gentle diocese parcel by parcel in exchange for the money it would take
to live out the time left in some proper fashion. Bill and Jackie Goins.
Nice to meet you, Mrs. Goins. Likewise. He had known what they were

the minute they had pulled up in the drive of the Duncan house in the white Cadillac with the HIS license plate. The only wonder that she hadn't brought along the HERS Cadillac—probably baby blue. With her pulled-back platinum hair and dark glasses stuck up on her head, putting on dark, slick lipstick every few minutes with a little mirror out of her pock-etbook, sucking a peppermint at the same time, and her skin tanned to the color of saddle leather with one of those silver reflectors, no doubt. Baby blue eyelids to match the HERS Cadillac. And, oh God, Bill—the same careful tan, wearing several gold chains tangled in the grizzled hair on his chest and a Honolulu-looking shirt.

"Papa's awful good to Mama, Junior. Papa's into cocktail lounges and used cars, and Mama stays home by the pool all day looking gor-geous." Loud laugh. Large teeth stained by the long, thin cigarettes and the gold flame-thrower.

"For godsake, Jackie, Junior don't want to hear all that garbage."

"It's Julian."

Another loud laugh, another peppermint to suck, tucking the stray strand of bleached hair back into the bun with a white-nailed finger, the heavy gold hoops stretching down her earlobes. "Oh hell, Mama's talking too much again. I'm sorry, Junior, Mama talks too much and gets Papa Bill all upset when he's doing some business."

"Julian. It's Julian."

"Godamighty! (louder laugh) this boy must of got a call about a raid and had to cut out fast. There's his socks by the bed, looks like he didn't get to finish the job he was working on at the time, don't it, Junior?"

"Why don't you just shut your goddam mouth for a minute, Jackie. Now let me ask you, Junior, you got a bigger home we can look at—"

"Julian. It's Julian."

"—this one ain't up-grade enough for our life-style."

"Papa and I entertain a lot, we want a classy summer home to entertain clients. We got a gorgeous home in Atlanta, ever get down to Atlanta, Junior?"

"Not if I can help it, Mrs. Goins."

A home. They call it a home, they want to buy a gorgeous home. They don't even know what you do is buy a house, but you have to live in it the right way with the right kind of people, before you can say "go home" and mean it—and even then, you avoid stating the fact it's A Home, particularly A Gorgeous Home. Or even A Lovely Home. The HIS and HERS Cadillacs are probably as near home as they can get, the CB radio being the fireplace and the bookshelves.

So he takes a long swallow from the scotch and sits forward in his chair as if he is about to get to his feet again. He stares at the wall, wide-eyed and unseeing, and thinks what walls are. People don't understand walls anymore. These walls, just for an example, enclose him, remind him he is indoors and not outdoors, but they don't *contain* him, don't you understand that? He has lived in houses with walls which contained him all his years. Even the parties he has gone to have been in houses with walls which contained as well as enclosed the parties and the unusual things that happened at some of them. The walls of the club, to take another example, contain its members and the children, include and exclude, and the membership protects the members from exposure to the curious and resentful. Asa now. The walls of Asa's immaculate and unpainted shack sitting under the shade of one great tree in the middle of a red field contain Asa and Asa's son, private and diffident and respectable. That is the right way of it, Julian considers. Why is it only he and Jews and the Colored understand that now?

For godsake, the world has turned into a motel with furniture anchored to the floor and pictures screwed to the walls which have never belonged to anybody and with air that has been breathed stale by God-knows-who or God-knows-what the night before, not by people who might know who you are or know what you must have come from just by looking at you or listening to you talk. Babies are conceived on the way to somewhere else in unaccustomed beds and taken out on the freeways in fine cars to be delivered in some enclosure somewhere on the road by a doctor who never looks up to see the faces.

Now, take this place again. Missook, thank God for Missook, has arranged familiar furniture and hung familiar pictures on the walls here, but the pictures and the furniture seem to be as ill at ease with this arrangement as he is. Annie dusts them with contempt, flicking her dust rag at them once a week, but it doesn't do any good, since there's no dust to dust. And the walls remain nothing more than partitions on a floor plan, marking off division of cubicles. Good God, even the walls of the Martinet County Orphanage contain the orphans. Even those homeless children are at home.

He gets up and fixes another drink in the kitchenette. *Kitchenette,* for godsake! And *dinette,* for godsake! And returns to his chair with a drink, stranded in a duplex, a *duplex,* for godsake, with a kitchenette and a dinette and nowhere else on earth to go that's yours and nothing to do about it but drink a little to ease the ride. Sometimes the only available means of transportation, as Ned Trivett says. He drags a hand down over his face to erase what he is thinking and leans forward with his elbows on his knees staring straight out. It may be it's his turn to go crazy now. Maybe he hasn't gone crazy yet because he hasn't had the time out from having to watch the others take their turns at it.

No stranger, God knows, to people going crazy, slow and fast. However, it is his long-considered opinion that, although going crazy is part and parcel of everyday life, it can be resisted if you stay on your guard—not only can be, *should* be. Oh, yes. Follow these few simple rules and delay the disintegration of things as they ought to have been. Oh, reinforce the walls! against the day you face oblivion.

Another drink. The ice in the refrigerator has remembered without being reminded to increase itself, remember the ice-box on the latticed back porch? The pupils of his salt-blue eyes are contracted to pinpoints as always—not that he is a hostile man, but that he must survey, close up and at a distance, the maintenance of sanity and eccentric propriety which are one and the same and insure the union of blood and faith. When was this exhausting vigil imposed and how much strength is left to keep it now?

There they are, take a look. Mother, Mrs. Constance Warren, sitting in her chair in the falling light in her falling-down house, slipping from voluntary insanity to involuntary insanity without the warning to recognize the difference. Why did she threaten him—defy him to watch her change worlds? so that she no longer knew the people or events of the world her body lived in (*What* war? she had asked him once)? Good-by. His wife. Oh, yes, I love you truly his wife, Mrs. Laura Warren, how could she deny him his existence? grow restless for a life beyond the limits of the life they had agreed upon together? and break the agreement and grow so restless she was willing to try to terminate her life finally? Good-by. All this falling away, falling away. His beloved brother, oh yes, man and boy his brother, John Thomas Warren, remembering a child of five or six waiting for him in the doorway of his bedroom one desperate hot summer night when he, Julian, was a boy of eleven or twelve. A little boy standing in the door in the hall light. Worried. Worried about his older brother even at that age, by God. That was the night he was sure mother loved John Thomas best, and that was the night he was sure he loved John Thomas best too. That was the night John Thomas had become his beloved brother instead of just another little boy around the house. But John Thomas had grown up without serving notice, asking more of one life than it could possibly deliver, and caught airplanes at airports all over the world, until at last he claimed to have become another person. Good-by. "Oh God, little brother, how could you break the promise too?" Julian cries out and is embarrassed at the sound of his voice in this solitary confinement. All those years, all those years.

And now then, this Skinner Bates. Not even blood kin but some way closer than that, sleeping in the bed with . . . but that's enough of that. He'll see to Skinner when the time comes or will it be just good-by again? Falling away, falling away.

Suddenly his body rouses without reason, responding to some mysterious and unremembered signal of the senses. From which of his shadowy images could his senses have taken the signal to rise? None that was acceptable, therefore—none. Never mind. Let it be like that, an insistent promise demanding to be kept, ever-present no matter what, a stout reminder living like that in the body. What could have been the signal? Certainly not Skinner sleeping in the bed with . . . no, certainly not, but he finds an image in reserve. Evelyn. Evelyn Black, not the true signal but never mind. Never mind. The two of them gasping for breath, moist and fevered in the broken grass under the low-hanging bough of a tree, the sweet perfume and taste of young bodies swelling and subsiding, vanquished by desire. "My Lord, Julian, look! Ain't it nice?" she had whispered. "I'll try, I'll try—ah! Let's do it till day breaks!"

Embarrassed again. He sips away the dusk into nightfall, not looking out the window by his chair, since there's nothing to see, turning on a lamp to find his way through the dinette to the kitchenette and another drink, choosing the voluntary insanity of too much to drink over the involuntary kind he has seen strike down his wards. It occurs to him that some degree of madness is a part of every important life.

And sips away another hour or two listening to the refrigerator eliminate ice cubes, as if it were some kind of shameful biological process essential to its survival.

And then, at last, all right, the riding is easier now, he begins to grieve for his son, Julian Johnson Warren, Junior, born into the insufferable misfortune of unchanging childhood in a body that will make the changes nature has ordained. Why does death hover? Why does the specter smile along with Jubie? If he could die. Perhaps as time goes by it might be better if he could manage to slip away. Good-by. But, oh, sweet Jesus, not for his father who would lose the only love on earth or in heaven he can be absolutely sure of.

"I'm drunk now," he assures himself and leaves the duplex apartment with the kitchenette and the dinette without turning off the lamp or closing the door—to go and touch the child of his loins who loves without question.

CHAPTER EIGHTEEN

Although the light was off on the front porch, Julian, even in his condition, put out his hand and found the key hanging on the nail beside the door right off and let himself into the cool, dank hallway of the great ghost of an old house sunk among the motionless black trees. He stood in the darkened hallway, his hand still on the doorknob for support, and breathed the familiar air with relief. The summer night outside, so still and airless, had stifled him, and he thought the house smelled of the tomb. Too much of the past had been left to molder here. The white shirt hung open halfway down his chest and bloused from his trousers, and he had run his fingers through his hair too many times that evening.

Uncertain light fell through the double doors of the living room at the far end of the hall, and he thought Annie must still be up and realized for the first time that it was late and that Jubie would be asleep upstairs in Laurie's room and that he had had too much to drink again. He made his way down the hall, again without faltering, towards the lighted room;

he had done it so many countless times, he could have done it blind. Standing in the door of the living room, he widened his eyes and put up his eyebrows in surprise. Not Annie. A man with blond hair had replaced her, as in a dream. He was reading under the lamp in Laurie's chair by the window that reached from the floor to the ceiling. It seemed to Julian the man had read in this chair many times before; he sat in it as if it were his own.

Sensing his presence, the man looked up from his book, not taken aback by Julian's dishevelled appearance, only reluctant to take time from his reading. "Yes?" he said with the indifference and contemptuous patience of a desk clerk in a late hotel.

"This is my house, and I have come to see Jubie Warren," Julian said, unintimidated, and, tilting his head back, looked down at the man with easy disdain. "Where's Annie?" he asked and shifted his weight from one leg to the other.

"Annie isn't here, and since it is past eleven o'clock at night, Jubie has been in bed asleep for some time," the man said, not rising from his chair, unintimidated in his turn, and Julian saw that his eyes were small and blue and his hair, in some way, too blond. There was a drink on the table by the chair, and an electric fan droned on the black marble hearth, turning one way and the other, and made no difference whatsoever. "And who might you be?" the man asked.

"Julian Warren. I am Julian Warren and this is my house," he announced, and, in spite of himself, he was embarrassed. "This *was* my house, I guess that's the way it is," he explained and regretted having done so. "And if it's all right with you, I will go up and see my son now."

"Oh, Julian," the man said, as though he had known him at some time in the past, which he certainly had not, and only half closed his book, keeping a finger in it. "Jake Cullen. I'm staying with Jubie tonight, and I don't think it's a good idea to wake him at this hour of the night, do you?" They regarded each other, reserving judgment across considerable distance without moving, and the air held them as they were, and neither could have said how long the silence between them lasted.

"I suppose you're right, Mister—ah," Julian said to move the air again and shifted his weight again and put his hands on his hips.

"Cullen. Jake Cullen."

"Cullen," Julian said. "Do you mind—" he began. "I think I'll have a drink," he said, and Jake pointed at the table in the corner with the bottles and glasses, as if Julian didn't know where it would be.

Julian hesitated and glanced at the table and changed his mind several times, before he resolved and went towards the chair, holding out his hand. "Pleasure to meet you, Mister Cullen," he said, taking care of the amenities.

"Jake," Mister Cullen said and stood up and shook hands and sat right back down again and took a sip of his drink.

"Jake," Julian consented. "I think I'll have that drink now." He withdrew to the table in the corner, feeling awkward, and fixed a drink in silence, wondering if the man had gone back to reading his book in Laura's chair and if he would have to sit drinking, becalmed in the dim recesses of his own living room. "And where are you from, Mister Cullen?" he asked to cover his uneasiness.

"Jake," Jake said. "California."

"Oh, I see," Julian said. Well, that explained the blond hair; they all had hair like that in California. "I met a beautiful woman from California when I was in Rome recently," he went on in an attempt to get things rolling. "She was with the embassy."

"Really," Jake said, and Julian thought he heard a page turn. "There are a lot of those in California." Julian saw that the man wasn't going to be any help at all in this unusual situation. He wasn't even trying, his voice was scarcely loud enough to be heard over the hum of the electric fan and the singing of the crickets outside the window.

He sat down in a small chair in the shadows with his drink, his
knees spread wide, leaning forward with his elbows on the chair arms,
not settled yet, as though he were considering it for purchase. The blond
man closed the book on his finger and looked up, becoming the interrupted hotel clerk again. So he *had* gone back to reading. "I hope I'm
not disturbing you—ah—Jake," he said, still taking care of the amenities. "It's just that I needed one more drink before . . . it's been a long
day."

"It's been a long life," Jake said, and Julian sat back in the chair,
having decided to buy it. He had been surprised again. Surprised that a
man from California with hair that was too blond would say such a thing
as that.

"Yes," he concurred and looked down into his drink, and the air
stilled them again, the man smoking in the pool of light from the lamp
and Julian feeling lonely in the dark. "And what are you doing in Milford,
so far from your home in California?" Julian asked.

"California isn't really my home," Jake said. "I am visiting Ned
Trivett for a while."

"Oh," Julian said. "Ned Trivett." This information caused him
some consternation and he sat forward in the chair to disguise it. "Yes.
Well. Ned Trivett is a very fine man," he said. "A *very* fine man."

"That he is," Jake agreed. "As a matter of fact, that's where I first
met Laura. At Ned's house."

Julian looked up, startled, with the pale, questioning, almost hostile
eyes and cleared his throat. "You met Laura at Ned Trivett's house?" he
asked.

"And your son."

"Laura and Jubie at Ned Trivett's house," he said, incredulous, his
voice rising uneasily and his pupils contracting to pinpoints, extending
his depth of field.

"Yes, at a party he gave for me—there were a lot of people there."

"Jubie? Jubie at a party at Ned Trivett's house?" Julian asked again. "I can't believe that, I find it hard to believe that Laurie would. . . ." He turned on the table lamp beside his chair to confirm his presence and emphasize his disbelief. It illuminated a photograph taken on a bright day—a grainy enlargement of a snapshot—of Laura and Jubie laughing with their heads together, thinking the moment captured in chemical emulsion was the way it was and the way it was going to be. Its brilliant and radiant joy obscured the room the two men sat in even further. "I just can't believe Laurie would . . ."

"There were a lot of people there," Jake repeated, as if that would make a difference. "They all seemed to be old friends. I drove Jubie over to spend the night with Susan," he explained, trying to give Julian some comfort. "That's when Jubie and I first became friends, on the drive to Susan's."

"My cousin," Julian stated. "You seem to have become friendly with my entire family. Susan is my first cousin on my mother's side. She understands Jubie, she loves Jubie, she really loves Jubie."

"So do I," Jake said. "It's easy to love Jubie. Too easy. We have spent a lot of time together in your absence. I take him to the beach. He is really quite wonderful."

"He is the light of my life, he is a gift beyond value," Julian quoted. He lay back in his chair and finished his drink to extinguish rising emotion and resisted returning silence. "I have had to be away in Rome Italy with my business partner," he said.

"Skinner," Jake said.

"Do you always call utter strangers by their first names?" Julian asked, raising his sketched-in eyebrows to indicate his disapproval of whatever the response to his question might be.

"I don't think I have ever known an utter stranger."

"You have never even been in the same room with Skinner Bates to know whether he was an utter stranger or not," Julian informed him.

"Oh, well. True. Sorry," Jake said. "It's my way."

"No. No, I'm sorry, I'm the one that's sorry," Julian said. "It's been a long day."

"So you said," Jake said. Julian took in an offended breath and crossed and uncrossed his legs and decided against further contention.

"I have had to be away in Rome Italy—"

"With your business partner, Mister Bates," Jake prompted.

"—Rome Italy," he went on. "My brother fell—ah—my brother had an unfortunate accident and . . ."

"So Susan said."

Julian took another offended breath and prepared to rise from the chair but then relented and looked at something invisible and distant to the left of Jake's head. "I think we could have another drink," he said. "Would you like another drink?"

"Why not?" Jake said. "Thank you," and he held out his glass and closed his book completely finally and put it on the table beside him. Julian stood up, tall and unsteady, and took the glasses and went to the table in the corner, feeling that at last he had recaptured the role of host in his own house, that he was no longer the intruder.

"I guess this is a funny situation for you," he said, putting ice in the glasses, and made an attempt at a light laugh but failed and cleared his throat instead. "I guess this is a funny situation for you," he said again, leaving the laugh aside. "Sleeping in a stranger's house."

"Not really. I have slept in many a stranger's house," Jake said. "However, this is not a stranger's house, I understood it was Laura's house."

"Oh. Of course, you're right. It is. I forget," Julian said and paused before he poured the whiskey into the glasses, adjusting once more to cruel rejection. "She was born here," he went on, pouring the whiskey, "upstairs in that bed Jubie's sleeping in right now. But I lived here with her so many years it got to be mine too," and he wondered why he was explaining himself so much to this outlander, who appeared to be at least as tall as he was and who already knew too much that was none of his business, as if he were planning to move in or, at least, to assume some kind of authority that was not his due. He decided to dislike the man but found he couldn't. Rather, he found he wanted to sit talking to him and tell him the terrible things Laurie had said to him and why he was drinking too much these days. But he didn't approve of this admission, considered it a weakness; you told men like this as little as possible; you shook hands with them and maybe had a drink and let them go on off to somewhere else. He gave Jake his drink and sat down again and took a damp pack of cigarettes out of his shirt pocket and put it on the table. "Still—" he continued and found his voice was in an unexpected falsetto register. "Still," he said, having adjusted the register, pretending he was at ease, "it is a funny situation, the two of us here together and Laura off acting in plays at Bladens Beach, you have to admit that."

"Not really," Jake said, and his voice was almost worn out. "Not for me anyhow. My life is one long situation. Mostly interesting. That's why I live the way I do."

"And how is that?" Julian asked, before he could stop himself. "I mean, what is it you do? What is your business?"

"I wish for your sake there was a respectable name for it," Jake said. "Visit. I visit. I am a visitor. Some people call it hustling, sometimes I call it hustling, but that isn't what it is. It . . ."

Julian put a bent cigarette in his mouth and was rummaging through his pants pockets for a match, rocking up on one hip and then the other in the chair. Jake got to his feet suddenly, and Julian saw he was younger than he had thought to begin with. He lit Julian's cigarette with unbending condescension and tossed the clip of matches onto the table with the pack of cigarettes. "Oh, thank you," Julian said and was relieved when Jake had sat down again. They sat facing each other and there was an unexplainable challenge between them. *Shoot-out at the O.K.*

Corral, Julian thought to himself and couldn't imagine where on earth that had come from. "There couldn't be much money in that. In visiting," Julian said and tried another light laugh. He didn't admit even to himself how curious he had become.

"I manage," Jake said in an off-hand way, and an insect thumped violently against the screen in the tall window beside his chair. He gave up his end of the challenge and watched a large, pale moth and a smaller, dark one flutter vainly against the screen to reach the light of the lamp and thought the summer night smelled like the torn wing of a moth must smell or like a couple making love in the grass.

"They never stop trying as long as the lamp is on," Julian commented and glanced up for Jake's response to find that he was looking into an uncertain and crazed mirror, cracked down the middle so that there was one and a half of everything, the room and the man and the lamp and an echo of the room and the man and the lamp. He drank halfway down his drink and leaned forward on his knees, holding it in both hands, as if it were a chalice. "Don't you have a house somewhere with people in it?" he asked.

"No," Jake said, and Julian thought there was going to be more, but there wasn't.

"Come to think of it, neither do I," Julian mused, as though he were singing softly to himself. "I visit too. I'm a visitor too. I try to visit my wife in Bladens Beach, and I try to visit my unfortunate little son, but nothing works. I guess we're two of a kind, we both visit." The song ended on a dying note, and his head fell forward, and he appeared to be looking between his knees at a spot on the carpet. His body heaved convulsively once. He released a breath he had been holding and took it in again and put his drink on the spot on the carpet and covered his face with his hands.

"Are you all right, Julian?" Jake asked, pushing his voice stronger with anxiety, and the two men got to their feet suddenly as if at a signal—perhaps the thump of another armored insect against the screen.

"No, I'm not all right," Julian said. "I'm drunk. I think I'll go on back home to my bachelor quarters," and he picked up his drink and finished it and put the glass on the table and made a ridiculous attempt to shove his shirttail back into his trousers. "Go home," he said, looking sideways at Jake. "That place don't even know how to get dirty," he said. "That's supposed to be a joke, but I notice we aren't laughing."

"I wish you wouldn't do that, I wish you wouldn't go yet," Jake said. "I think we could both do with company tonight."

"Sold! You've convinced me," Julian said heartily and grinned straight across his face, as if he had turned on another light. "Give me your glass, Jake."

Jake was taken aback by this unexpected and sociable flash of charm. "Thank you for that," he said. "Thank you for calling my name. People here have trouble calling me by my name." He gave Julian his glass, and they stood in the middle of the room waiting for something more, until Jake decided to sit down again and watch Julian make it to the table in the corner to fix the drinks.

"I wonder if I can tell you something," Julian said over the ice and glasses. "For the first time in my life, I have to tell somebody something that is more than I can stand by myself."

"Shoot," Jake said.

Julian faced into the room with a drink in each hand. It looked to Jake as if he were reciting from the darkened corner a list of grievances he had committed to memory. "I go to Rome to rescue my little brother, who doesn't want to be rescued, and my little brother and my best friend spend the nights together in the same bed. What do you think of that? And I go to Bladens Beach to rescue my wife, who doesn't want to be rescued, and she cuts her wrist trying to die. How do you like that? I come to touch my unfortunate child who lies sleeping in his mother's bed upstairs—oh, I know that without even going to look—and who will never be more than a child, and I can't rescue him. How do you like that? What the hell kind of a man am I?"

"Do you want me to tell you?" Jake asked, trying to think what the hell kind of man he was.

"No, I certainly don't," Julian said, still holding by the table in the corner. "I'm not sure I want to know, I'm afraid you might tell me more than I want to know. I don't understand this life, Jake. I have always done the right thing. Haven't I always done the right thing?" he asked, as though Jake could know.

"Sit down," Jake said.

"I'll sit down when I'm good and goddam ready," Julian said and came right out of the corner and gave Jake the drink. "I'm sorry," he said. "As you said earlier, it's been a long life," and his shirttail was almost out now.

"Sit down," Jake said. Julian sat down. The air stilled them again, and the moths kept fluttering against the screen, and the two men lit cigarettes, marbling the light under the lamps.

"This is nice," Julian said, crooning again. "I don't know why, Jake, but this is nice. It is keeping me from going crazy, Jake." He put his drink under the lamp on the table and looked for a long time at the picture of Laura and Jubie laughing together and, at a certain moment, took in an uneven breath and broke forward with his hands grasping his knees like claws and his shoulders pushed up, looking down at the spot on the carpet again. His body lurched in regular spasms, and he made a wounded sound that people make who are dreaming another, more honest reality. "Oh God, oh God," he said as best he could, blinking his eyes and containing the spasms by force of will. "Goddam, I'm sorry, Jake," he said, making an upside-down smile. "I swear I never do this kind of thing."

"Maybe it's time you did," Jake said. "It will keep you from going crazy."

"It's killing me," Julian said and sat up and found a handkerchief in his back pocket. He pressed his eyes with it and blew his nose vigorously two or three times and put it back in his pocket. He glanced at Jake, slightly abashed, and grinned straight across his face, turning on the light again. "I've been saying I'm sorry, and I won't say it again. Let's get drunk together, Jake, a little oil to ease the ride. And maybe, since there's just the two of us here, I can sleep in my own bed in the room with my unfortunate child."

There had occurred an atmospheric change in the tall room. Jake felt it just as Julian finished speaking. The air had become oppressive and vibrant, more difficult to breathe, as though a cloud had come in at the windows. Rising heat moistened the flesh and muffled the haze of night sound, dimming further the failing light of the lamps. Moths no longer fluttered at the screen, losing fragments of their wings. There was the sensual aroma of lush vegetation and of the effulgence of the sea and the bitter fragrance of suspicion. The two men sprawled in their chairs exhausted, gripping the arms, their legs thrust out onto the carpet like open scissors.

"It's hot in here," Julian said, letting his head fall back, and turned his hands over, palms up, on the chair arms. "This room was always cool, I don't understand it. The walls are two feet thick," he said. "At least, that's what Laurie always says. I wish she were here to say it now, and I wish you were visiting somewhere else." He paused and lifted his head and let it fall back again. "No, I don't wish that, I take it back," he said and, arching backwards, offered himself to the ceiling. The electric fan on the hearth droned on and turned its head from side to side but could not move the air. "Do you wish Laurie was here, Jake?" he asked quietly. He paused again and then sat up suddenly, as if he had been discovered doing something he should not have been doing.

"Mislark is doing what she has to do," Jake said.

"You don't know her well enough to call her that."

"So I've been told. Forgive me."

"*I* don't know her well enough to call her that. Not anymore, that's what she told me," Julian said. "That's a hell of a note, isn't it, Jake? Who gave you permission to call her that, did she give you permission to call her that?"

"Why don't you just go ahead and ask me what you want to ask me," Jake said, exposing himself.

"What do I want to ask you, since you know so much?"

"You want to ask me how well I know Laura," Jake said.

"You know what? Let's get drunk together, Jake," Julian suggested, coming up with a brilliant new idea.

"We *are* drunk," Jake said and got to his feet. "Only you are drunker than I am, a lot drunker than I am. However, finish your drink, it's my turn to be bartender." Julian drank off his drink dutifully, as if it were a glass of milk he had to finish before he could leave the table, and held the glass out to show he had done as he had been told.

Jake found himself at the table in the shadows, without remembering having left his chair, and Julian had grown pensive and peaceful, watching the idiot fan turn its head hopelessly from side to side on the hearth.

"How well do you know my wife?" he asked, and his voice veered upwards into a yodel. He cleared his throat. "How well do you know my wife?"

"She's my friend," the bartender said.

"Every—" He cleared his throat again. "Everybody is your friend, even Ned Trivett is your friend, for godsake. What I want to know." He stopped short.

"If you're asking me if I've laid your wife, I refuse to answer, you don't deserve an answer," Jake said, making it back into the lights and standing close over Julian. "Getting laid would be her choice, now wouldn't it?"

"Listen here, goddam it, don't you ever use that word in the same breath with my wife, you son of a bitch," Julian said, flushing blood red. He would have got to his feet, except that Jake was standing at his toes. His chest rose and fell in the opening of his shirt. "I think you had better get the hell out of this house, you son—"

"That's another thing you do here. You're always asking people to get the hell out of the house," Jake said, unintimidated and amused. "You have lots of do's and don't's, Julian. I have only said the word that was in your head. I wonder what else is in your head you don't say." Julian's excitement subsided, since he couldn't recall its cause. Jake held out the drink to him, but he wouldn't take it, having retained a sense of violated respect. Jake put it on the table and went back to his neutral corner. "Anyhow," he went on, "Laura was in trouble, and we became close friends—not close enough for me to call her Mislark, mind you, but very close friends. Trouble makes close friends, doesn't it, Julian? Also, Jubie and I became close friends. I feel in a way that he is mine."

"Well, he's not," Julian said. He took the drink from the table and settled into long, wide-eyed thinking, and the fan whirred, swaying its heavy head, denying everything, and an insect struck the screen with sufficient force to recall him from his reverie. He turned his drink up and did his best to finish it off. "Oh, God, I'm lonely, Jake," he said.

"That's the way it is," Jake said in a voice that wasn't much more than a humming in the ears. "Everybody's lonely, don't you know that yet?"

"That's all right for you to say," Julian sorrowed. "You choose to be lonely. Visiting has got to be a lonely way to live, and a person has to pay the bill one way or another. I have—I *had* a wife, and I *had* a brother, and I did all the right things. I took care of them according to my lights. But they don't want me, they want something else I can't understand.

They are like strange birds that left the nest, they got too big for the nest or it was the wrong kind." He looked up suddenly and flared his eyes, as if one of the strange birds had just flown through the room, and fell back in the chair, exhausted again, holding his drink in both hands. He stared intensely at Jake with the pale, salt-blue eyes, and tears ran down his weathered jaws and onto his chest. "I'll have you know I don't do this kind of thing," he said, considering the tears an offense against nature. "I don't cry. Except in Rome with John Thomas. I cried in Rome with John Thomas. But not with an utter stranger . . ."

"Let me take you up to bed, Julian. It's late," Jake said, tired of being an utter stranger.

"No," Julian said, reviving miraculously, and reached back and got his handkerchief and blotted his eyes and blew his nose some more. "No. I'll go to bed when I'm good and goddam ready. Besides, I don't want you to take me to bed, I can take myself to bed." He rocked himself up out of the chair with a series of awkward maneuvers which ended with his facing the wall with the portrait of Laurie's great aunt Sarah as a young girl. "Dead three years now," he grieved and thought about Aunt Sarah for a while, until he remembered to turn himself back around to face the living, standing uncertain, looking down on the utter stranger with triumphant disdain. He smiled brightly. "Rebecca is going back to the well," he announced.

"Excuse me?" Jake said.

"I said, Rebecca is going back to the well, that's what John Thomas always says. Rebecca is going back to the well, that's what he always says."

"I think Rebecca had better not make this trip," Jake suggested.

"I don't care what you think. Rebecca is going back to the well anyhow," he said petulantly and made his way through the furniture to the table in the corner. He leaned forward onto the table, as if to recover from a long, steep climb, and looked back over his shoulder at Jake, frowning, wondering who the blond man was and then remembering. "Why are you staying with Ned Trivett?" he asked.

"He invited me," Jake said.

"He invites a lot of people, all kinds of people. Do you stay there with him alone?"

"Why do you ask?" Jake said. "As a matter of fact, no. There was a Roman princess staying there too."

"There are some fine old families in Rome," Julian said, still peering suspiciously around his shoulder. "But not many."

"Actually, she's originally from Mobile Alabama."

"There are some fine old families in Mobile Alabama. A lot more than there are in Rome, I can tell you that from personal experience," Julian said and lurched upright, teetering backwards, and poured whiskey on the table and in his glass and let it go at that. He made his way back through the furniture, lifting his knees as though he were walking through tall grass, and positioned himself in front of his chair, his head on one side, and tried to put Jake into focus but realized he was looking into the crazed mirror again which had yet another break in it, so that there were several echoes of everything. "Are you a fairy?" he asked. "Ned Trivett is a fairy, John Thomas is a fairy, are you a fairy?"

"Why do you ask? What possible difference can it make to you? Sit down, Julian."

"It's just that . . . you know, there are fairies even in fine families," he warbled mournfully. "John Thomas is a fairy, and maybe old Skinner is a fairy and who knows who else, I don't know anymore. Why did they do that to me like that, Jake? Why did they sleep in the same bed, when all the time I was right there?" He took a swallow of his drink and gasped and collapsed into his chair, spilling whiskey down the front of his shirt. "Oh! You didn't put any water in this," he said, dazed and dismayed, and then sat up, bright-eyed and daft. "If you're a fairy, Jake, you could tell me why they did that like that, when all the time I was right there. . . ." The muscles and determination that impelled him ran down like a clock spring, and he flung up an arm in a final gesture of abdication and despair and gazed intently into a hypnotic void in the far corner of the room.

"It's time for Rebecca to go to bed," Jake said and got resolutely to his feet.

"Rebecca ain't going nowhere," Julian said. Jake took the drink from his hand and put it on the table and, gripping his arms, attempted to lift him out of the chair. Julian began to giggle. Jake straightened up and stepped back, considering the situation seriously. It struck him that this wasn't at all the way things were supposed to have been, and he couldn't remember when it had begun to go wrong.

"Rebecca, you're a very big woman," Jake said.

"Stop calling me Rebecca," Julian said.

"You started it," Jake said and crouched straddle-legged and worked his arms around Julian's chest, struggling to move him, and rolled forward, slowly and ineluctably, into the chair. Julian's giggling accelerated. A stranger passing the door at that moment might have thought he was witness to a fight to the death or a crime against nature between two tall men in a small chair, except that the hysterical giggling would have dispelled any threat of violence and replaced it with the happy impression that, perhaps, two middle-aged brothers were reliving a boisterous boyhood. Panting explosively and grappling against odds, they achieved somehow an upright posture, Julian's knees giving way, his shirttail completely out finally, and wrestled their way, sweating and muttering desperate instructions (Move your leg, move your damn leg!) to the foot of the stairs in the hall.

"The chair," Julian gasped, pointing behind him. "Aunt Sarah's chair," and he broke Jake's hammerlock and stumbled backwards into what looked to be a child's school desk attached to the stair wall. "The button," he breathed, "push the button, push the damn button." Jake pushed a button, and the chair began the ascent into the gloom at the top of the long flight of stairs. "Mister Jukes is going to heaven," Julian sang, supported on his elbow, looking wistfully down at Jake, as he rose throbbing and grinding into the shadows.

"Mister Jukes is a pain in the ass," Jake said, witnessing the ascent with tempered amazement.

They fought their way along the upstairs hall, perspiring profusely, and into Laura's bedroom. At the end of his strength, Jake released his burden onto the bed and turned on the lamp and stood between the beds, breathing heavily, to regain his composure. He pulled off Julian's abused shoes and determined to remove the whiskey-soaked shirt next. Julian began to giggle again, and Jubie sat straight up in his bed, fresh and velvety from sleep, and observed the two men without censure, as if it were a performance for his benefit.

"Mister Jukes dead drunk," he announced.

"Lie down and go back to sleep, Jubie," Jake said and began unbuttoning the buttons and determined not to remove the whiskey-soaked shirt. Julian cut off giggling suddenly and looked up with dazed, unfocused eyes, searching the face above him. "John Thomas," he said, unexpectedly and pleasantly surprised. He put his arms around Jake's shoulders and pulled him down onto his damp, malodorous chest. "John Thomas," he said, holding Jake close, as if he had found his beloved brother at last. "Johnny, please. Please, come home with me. Laurie's gone and I'm lonesome."

"That ain't John Thomas, that's Jake," Jubie said shrilly.

"Shut up and go back to sleep, Jubie," Jake said and freed himself from Julian's embrace.

"Oh, please, please, John Thomas," Julian said, his voice broken and wavering, and Jake thought he was going to cry again. But he didn't. He turned on his side and slept, holding the pillow as if it were a doll, or even a person who loved him.

"Mister Jukes don't smell too good," Jubie said, dewy-eyed and alert in the absurd nightshirt Jake had put on him earlier.

"Please, Jubie, I've had about enough for one night," Jake said. "I'm supposed to be a hustler not a mother, I wasn't cut out to be a mother."

"You ain't no mother, Jake. You a man," Jubie said and began to giggle, happy for this late-night diversion.

"Oh, God," Jake said and put him back on his pillow and pulled the sheet over the thin and beautiful little body, feeling unreasonable and powerful love. "Maybe I am a mother," he murmured. "Maybe I've been a failure at hustling. Maybe everybody is a mother."

"You ain't no mother, Jake," Jubie said soft in the pillow, falling slow.

"Shut up and go to sleep," the mother said. "We'll go to the beach tomorrow."

"With Mister Jukes," Jubie said.

"Shut up," Jake said and kissed the narrow, protuberant forehead, and Jubie shut up.

He turned off the lamp and stood in the door looking at the two of them for a long time. Which one is the child? he asked himself. Which suffers more? Which is caught in the crueler trap? I can't stand anymore, I've been in this family too long now, he said.

He went down the hall to the guest room—the visitor's room— and removed his shirt, damp with whiskey and the sweat of two men, and reminded himself in the dark that he was probably useless here. That he was probably useless everywhere.

There was a prolonged and desolate shout down the hall, and he knew that Julian had cried out from the terrible wilderness of nightmare. He hurried to the door of the bedroom, his shirt still in his hand. Julian was flung back on his pillow as if he had been pinioned there, and Jubie was sitting up straight among the covers, his eyes bright and black in their sockets, already looking at Jake, as though he had seen him before he had got there. "Jake," he said.

Jake lifted him in his arms and took him to the visitor's bed.

"Mister Jukes having a bad dream," Jubie explained, as Jake got into bed beside him.

"Shut up," Jake said and felt at home for the first time since he could remember.

CHAPTER NINETEEN

27 Hooper Street
Milford, N.C.
7 July

Dear Susan,

How do I start? How do I get a thing like this started, Susan? It has been a weight on my heart and mind for days now, what I have done, and I am weary of the weight. So let me try. And I am nothing if not honest, Susan, at least that hasn't changed.

To begin with, I try to tell myself I am not the worst kind of coward for deciding to write rather than come across the sound to see you face to face, but I'm not entirely convinced of that. Then again, I tell myself that you, like so many others these days, might prefer not to see me, and I'm not convinced of that either. But almost. Enough so that I don't feel too craven making this overture from my desk.

Of course, I am aware that I haven't been a great favorite of yours for some *years now—however, that has not always been the case, as I shall reveal to you in due course. But first, there are things I want to say to you to clear the air we breathe in common, to dispel the pollution of gossip and misunderstanding so far as is possible. It is my hope you will see this letter as an attempt to open channels between us, if only in the spirit. I hope also you will not mind too much that I feel our spirits are not too distantly related.*

Circumstances, yours and mine, have changed dramatically since we saw each other last, do you remember? We were waiting in the lobby of the Milford National Bank for the doors to open at nine o'clock in the morning. You green-eyed me with such—what shall I call it? disdain? yes—with such intense disdain the woman standing near me cried out, Oh, my goodness! *thinking you had aimed it at her, poor creature. Remember? And I said, "Where is Skinner Bates?" And you said, "With Julian, of course." "I see," I said, "and where might Julian be?" "Drunk as usual," you said. "Ah, well, sometimes that is the only available means of transportation," I said. Your expression of severe disapproval gave way instantly to one of surprised amusement, and the woman standing near me was so spellbound by the whole exchange she didn't wait for the bank to open but fled into the street, presumably to look for the nearest telephone booth or perhaps to summon the police. Be that as it may, you gave no sign that you might consider becoming friends again because of the remark. You are a stiff-necked people, indeed, Miss Susan. In spite of which, there was not a cloud in my sky, I was perfectly secure in my every step and statement. Fool!*

As it turns out, the crucial occasion of our lives, yours and mine, was the disastrous luncheon I gave at the Milford Country Club some days later for the Princess Graziella di Brabant, if you please. Everything began to turn dark as of that moment due to Mother Destiny and my unfortunate character which drives me to deride local custom and offend those who cling to it—actually, depend *on it for reassurance. Whatever made me think I had the right? I mean, who the hell did I think I was?*

But there it is, done and no way to rub it out now. I am sure you have heard by now that I am in disgrace with fortune and men's eyes—and women's eyes as well, God knows. As a matter of fact, I would find myself completely outcast were it not for Cullen, your devoted admirer, and Lyla Finch and Brother Reeves, who have not learned the rules of the game and are not likely to. When I walk the shady streets of old Milford, the same dear friends who pressed me to their bosoms when I returned from my far-flung but unheroic wartime service with the Armed Forces, now turn their backs on me or cross to the other side of the street, as if I were ringing a bell and crying leper. I confess this surprised me at first. However, I don't know why. Certainly, I should be aware by now with what delight perfectly ordinary people take up arms against what they perceive to be a corrupter of hallowed ground. It makes for such fine drama, and everybody but the goat gets to be courageous in the face of no danger whatsoever. An irresistible set of circumstances.

I don't know whether this change has been due to reactivated opposition to certain persuasions which, so far as I know, have been mine since birth or to the fact that I brought about, however indirectly, the abduction of your husband—if that is what it was. For the former, I make no apology whatsoever. For the latter, Susan, I am abject. I ask your forgiveness on my knees, a most painful posture at my age. As God is my witness, what transpired between Skinner and the princess has made me miserably unhappy with myself and the foolish life I live. You are sure to know by now—have you received your call from Rose Medallion?— Skinner and the princess met at the infamous luncheon at the club after far too much to drink for all parties present, including Brother Reeves, and the heat and the momentum of the encounter were so intense and increased at such a rate that no man could have stopped it. Least of all myself, since Graziella pays me no heed, having turned her back on me along with everybody else, although for vastly different reasons. Trying to recapture a careless past which is over and done with can have devastating and painful consequences. Some of us try to move forward into the present, and some of us prefer to remain fixed in time arrest.

You are sure to know also that I have been asked to resign from the club due to unacceptable behavior and the introduction of unsuitable company onto the prem-ises. This seems to be the equivalent of being drummed out of the corps. Well, it was never my kind of outfit anyhow—too much sniping and close order drill. And frankly, I will be glad to save that money. In addition to which, I do not play golf—I have never been that desperate—and I no longer dance, neither waltz nor foxtrot, which, only a few days ago, was said to be a great pity by the wives of loving husbands who can no longer remember who I am. I shall miss the shrimp salad, but not for long. Sue Ann Beasley tells me she can get the recipe for me without being shot at dawn.

Since the war, I have spent most of my time abroad and have lived a life of fantastic variety and more riotous living than I care to confess to. I regret not one moment of those days, they are the treasures of my memory. And there were other reasons for my voluntary exile. One was that I felt I deserved better, being who and what I was—well, my dear, haven't we all been young and arrogant? Another was that I wanted to avoid just the kind of unhappy confusion I have now caused, and most of all, I wanted not to wound friends and relatives who loved me and saw in me the whitest of sheep.

And yet, Susan—isn't it strange?—it was always my plan to come full circle back to Milford. I have often asked myself why that was, and I have thought perhaps it is like returning to the site of the wreck of an ancient and beautiful sailing ship which you know somehow to have been heavy with treasure. You hope one day to find it raised, or from time to time, to find a chest has surfaced. Something of inestimable value. Proof that the treasure is still there, and that makes it worth it, since you know it is partly yours and that you too are a survivor of the wreck. I have always considered you to be one of those chests, Susan. I pray you have not permitted the locks to have rusted shut.

My, wasn't that beautiful? I think you might find me invaluable com-pany—of inestimable value, so to speak. Consider that, Susan.

And so, Susan, I am here to stay. I am tarred and feathered, but they'll never get me even so far as the city limits. I shall go on living in my little house on Hooper Street which my father gave me when I graduated from the university. Hoping, I think, to anchor me to this curious little town. It didn't anchor me at that time, but it does so now—or something does. I suppose I shall have to try and play the concert, as Graziella has it, whatever that may be in my case, after all the years of practicing and running scales.

I must add further that I have had to forgive Graziella. She is her own masterwork. The life she lives is her concert, and playing it demands all her will and imagination and ferocity. Nothing nor nobody will stand in her way, it is all she has left. She has lost touch completely with the obligations and sensibilities of the world outside her performance. We are her audience, and God knows we are expected to applaud. I shall applaud always, recalling the days when the lights were brighter and the performance less frantic. . . . I am told she has not forgiven me. I understand that. If she forgave me, she could not forgive herself.

I have known you off and on all of your life, Susan. You liked me—more than that, you loved me when you were a little girl and I was a swell young man about town. I can see you now smiling at me from the door as I came up the walk to your father's house to dinner or a party. I have never since had a hostess greet me with such radiance. Perhaps, your mother was almost as glad to see me— yes, I'm sure she was. I am sorry you knew so little of that beautiful woman— how unfair she had to die when you were so young. If you can forgive me the sorrow I have caused you, perhaps someday you will let me tell you my memories of her. She would like us now, you and me, in spite of all. She said to me once, "What would we do without the night, you and I?" I think you will know what she meant by that question.

I pray for your forgiveness, if only from a distance. I pray for some word from you, comforting or otherwise. I hope you will let me know if there is anything at all I can do.

> With affection,
> Ned

1213 Ocean Front Drive
Milford, N.C.
July 10

Dear Ned Trivett,

I won't deny that there was a time when I would gladly have seen you dead. Except that I decided that was much too good for you, because I knew you would have made some kind of a grand opera or something out of the death scene and had the time of your life dying. And I would have had to listen to people tell about it for the rest of my days. As it is, time has passed and I have concluded after many nights spent talking to the moon on my deck that this community owes you a standing ovation instead of running you out of town on a rail, which is exactly what would happen if it were put to a vote. I mean, what on earth would we be doing without you? Go to work and hope for some more money and go to the damn supermarket and come home and play bridge and go to the club and play golf and get drunk with the same people saying the same drunken things and try to think up some way to get in bed with your heart's desire, approved or disapproved, without anybody finding out, particularly your beloved spouse or worse than that your beloved spouse's devoted friends. Nobody out of step with the regiment. It makes for a colorless and sneaky kind of a life, unless a person succeeds in the last named activity, which could lighten things up a great deal for an hour and a half or two hours at the outside. With you around town, things take on some kind of restlessness and maybe even some mystery.

Now then, I don't want you to think for one tiny moment that I don't still love Skinner Bates which was and is my big mistake. But it is a big mistake I would make all over again, given half a chance, and I keep waiting around for that in spite of knowing better. Poor old Skinner is in a lot of trouble and needs Julian, but Julian is still riding on the only available means of transportation and has put Skinner out of his life because of unsuitable behavior at home and abroad. You might let Miss Princess know that. The more true love you give Skinner Bates the more interested he gets in something else, namely close connections in high places. Or the more he wants something else he can't even put a name to.

I have found out with the help of one of your unusual friends that what Skinner is is a world champion hustler and God knows he's got what it takes to succeed in that profession. Except in his case, that profession is its own disaster and will end before it even gets started.

And so I fear for Skinner, and I know now that we would never have been the kind of perfectly wonderful married couple Julian Warren and I had in mind when Julian stood him up for inspection in the middle of my father's living room. What's more, I have decided that I am not the kind to be half of a perfectly wonderful married couple, which is a grave disappointment, maybe because I am insolent and disdainful and, God Knows, lustful. A Sinful Woman. However, I am trying to think up another way to work things out without having to pack up and leave home. You see, you are right. My circumstances have changed dramatically. The future for me and Miss Princess is uncertain, due to you and poor old Skinner Bates. Miss Princess probably don't know that yet.

My trouble was and is I have had all the wrong ideas about how life actually works. I expected the nonexistent, I expected ecstasy twenty-four hours a day and had to settle for an hour and a half, two hours at the outside, which was and is another grave disappointment. And so, it is entirely possible that people like you who talk about sad and serious things in a funny way and go away and come back home from unusual places with white trash and princesses nobody ever heard of must have the answer to something. Although, it seems to be the answer to a question nobody dares to ask.

Listen here, Ned, if you aren't blind as a bat and stone deaf, you are bound to know that everybody in Milford and surrounding counties says you are a fairy. Whatever that is, as Jake Cullen always says. Jake Cullen of all people should most certainly know what a fairy is. Well, I use to think I knew. I use to think they were left-over children making everything imaginary and exaggerated combined with men and women mixed up in varying proportions depending on the fairy. But recent experience has brought it to my attention that there is no firm definition having to do with who or what is a person's heart's desire on a permanent or temporary basis. It appears to drift. I also found out that some people are fairies who haven't found it out themselves yet. When the news gets to them, it is a terrible surprise. Their circumstances change dramatically overnight like yours and mine.

Anyhow, none of that makes the least bit of difference to me, except yes it does too. It is a good thing to keep in mind when you want to get even with somebody that you are not and wish you were. I always wanted to get even with you, Ned Trivett, because you thought you were such hot stuff and because your life seemed to be better than I could ever expect mine to turn out to be, particularly since I was a woman. If you happen to be a person restless in the soul, you usually want to just cut loose from gravity and sail out free and easy looking for whatever it is you are supposed to be doing instead of what you are doing now. I am a person restless in my soul, and I have never told that to another living soul but you. Not even to my father. Never let them reduce you to mediocrity, that's what my father told me once, thank you father.

And so, Ned Trivett, get off your knees. There is nothing to forgive you for. You made it possible for my husband to run away with a spurious princess and for me to spend time with a perfectly wonderful hustler. And Miss Princess has forced me into the untenable position of having to find out what I'm supposed to do next. One thing I do know, I know I have to stop listening for the phone to ring with Skinner Bates' voice from Rome Italy on the other end of the line.

I want you to come and sit on my deck with me under the moon and let me tell you what love is all about. I think I know that now, and it's the same for fairies as it is for everybody else. Mostly balancing on the tightwire without an umbrella and no net underneath to fall into.

I agree with my mother. My beautiful mother, thank you mother. What would we do without the night, you and I?

Yours truly,

Susan

P.S. Where the hell is Jake Cullen?

CHAPTER TWENTY

Jake Cullen sat through Laurie's performance as if he had seen it hundreds of times before. His face remained the same from beginning to end in the light reflected from the stage, and when it was over, he didn't applaud with the others but left his seat to smoke on the terrace and watch the ghosts of whitecaps chasing up onto the shore in the dark. He leaned on an elbow against the balustrade where he could see the company taking its calls in the rising and falling amber light of the theater, and when Laurie took the bouquet of roses from Doris Ann Hawkins into her arms and made a deep curtsey with her face lowered into the flowers, he might have been her manager planning the future, so unimpressed did he seem by the excitement of this last performance of her play.

He had left Brother Reeves and Jubie in their motel room on the highway discussing the matinee they had seen in the afternoon. Brother, Jake decided, is the eternal soldier, ever willing to stand guard at the tent door, and he had been deeply moved—again without a change in his features—sitting in his chair with a scotch as he watched Brother get Jubie into the absurd nightshirt, as if he had done such all his days.

"Brother, how come Mislark run off with that man in the park?" Jubie had asked. "She was out of her head," Brother had explained, "all them others had run her out of her head, so she just went on off with him." "Oh," Jubie had said and reviewed the moment from a distance with great serious eyes. "Everybody runs Mislark out of her head," he had concluded. "But she wasn't being Mislark, Jube, she was playing like she was somebody else," Brother had said. "Oh," Jubie said again. And Brother had swung him up under his arm, as if he were a calf or a lamb and put him onto his pillows, and Jubie had struck up with a giggle for a minute or two and then cut it off short. "Jake going to see Mislark in the show, you ain't leaving, is you, Brother?" he asked apprehensively.

"I ain't going nowhere," Brother said. "We going to watch us some TV."

No better soldier anywhere, Jake considered. At home wherever he finds himself. Soldiers, he decided, are essential to life, no matter what. Soldiers and whores. They would always be there for the homeless, no matter where, being homeless themselves. It doesn't take war to make a soldier. Nor a whore either, if it comes to that.

The amber lights had gone dark, and the house lights came up, killing the magic, and impatient with illusion now, members of the audience straggled out through the French doors onto the terrace on their way to a more comfortable reality. "That girl looks sick to me, I don't know how she does it," a woman said moving ahead of her husband in her haste to get back to her house with solid walls. "I don't know why Julian Warren puts up with it," the husband said, "I know I wouldn't."

Jake ambled back into the theater and took an aisle seat. There was the smell of candles just blown out. Laurie stepped out from behind the stone angel, putting cream on her face. "There you are," she called out.

"Here I am," he said.

"Did you put Jubie to bed?" she asked.

"He's in bed," Jake said. "Put there by one of God's soldiers."

"Oh, I see," Laurie said and laughed with the pleasure. "Brother. I'll be a minute." And she disappeared into the shadows to discard, so far as she was able, the traces of the woman she had been for two hours.

A harsh light bulb lowered on a cord into the middle of the stage, making the gulf coast town into so much muddy paint and lumber, tawdry and lifeless, and Jake could see that one of the angel's wings had been mended with tape and was about to fall off. A number of young people in various states of disrepair wandered out of the wings onto the stage with paper cups in their hands. They were shepherded by a young man with black-fringed blue eyes and a clipboard. They all slumped into the chairs and sofas except for the young man with the clipboard and a fat girl with bouncy curls.

"All right, you mothers, this set has got to be struck before you get drunk," he said without much conviction.

"Okay, you heard Gordie, you mothers," the fat girl said with considerable conviction. "We got to strike the set before we get drunk. Get off your dead ass and let's get going."

The mothers said something incomprehensible and reslumped on the chairs and sofas.

"Doris Ann, you are the light of my life," Gordie said.

The mothers got off their dead asses reluctantly and began to haul off the furnishings and the bones of the skeletal town, but without putting down the paper cups, except when absolutely necessary. Gordie went off through the doctor's house and the lights brightened. He returned almost immediately with the clipboard in one arm and Laurie in the other. They were laughing, as though they knew something nobody else could know. Laurie took his head in her hands and studied it thoughtfully, as she might study the photograph of somebody she remembered. "I never would have

made it without you," she told him. "You and your spirits of ammonia."
She put the photograph away and turned a bright face to Jake, letting the
memory go. "There you are," she called out. "Gordie, this is the man
who has come to save us all—he reads the instructions on vitamin bottles.
Ladies and gentlemen, Jake Cullen!" she announced and made a sweeping
gesture of presentation.

"Hello, Gordie," Jake said and unfolded from his seat. "Ladies and
gentlemen."

The ladies and gentlemen made another incomprehensible response,
which had to do.

The blue-green neon sign at the motel said VACANCY, but it wasn't
convinced. The C and the Y were fluttering down, about to give up,
signaling to passersby in the night that it was probably a vacancy that
nobody would want to fill. It was a withdrawn, rambling structure con-
structed of cement blocks which had been painted an uncertain pink some
years back. Even the kidney-shaped swimming pool, gathering distorted
stars and fragments of what was left of the moon, and the imported palm
trees leaning disconsolately this way and that at the corners of the build-
ings couldn't relieve it of the look of a forgotten barracks or a last resort
to which inmates were consigned when there was no place else for them
to go. The air-conditioners churned on and on, leaking condensed mois-
ture on the cement galleries, manufacturing breath for the rooms, oc-
cupied and unoccupied, like so many artificial lungs. However, when Jake
unlocked the door of number twenty-four, the ambiance of abandonment
was dispelled. The television was still on, and a man with hair parted in
the middle over a sincere face and an earnest voice was delivering his
cheerful version of why Jesus Christ had had to die for us all. The eerie
filtered light from the set revealed the swaddled forms of two of the re-
deemed sinners in twin beds, paying no heed at all to the news of their

Redeemer, wound fast in sleep among the sheets, locked in the mysterious reaches of dreams. It was a secure and protected retreat, beyond the thunder of violence and sin.

"No vacancy in number twenty-four," Laurie said and could have laughed from some strange exhilaration.

"Shhhh," Jake said.

She turned down the sound of the television, despite which the man with the sincere face continued pushing his message to the fallen. She sat on the foot of Jubie's bed and suppressed the compulsion to laugh again. She couldn't discover the source of this sudden and irrational wave of happiness.

"What!" Brother hollered out and sat up bare-chested in the bed, as if somebody had called his name from a distant meadow.

"Hush, Brother, it's me," Laura said. "I wanted to see Jubie."

"Oh, Miss Laura," Brother said as loud as the middle of the day. "Jubie's sleeping."

"I see he is," she said and gave way to a light laugh. "Go back to sleep, Brother." The sincere man on the television gave way to a picture of the Savior with a lamb on his shoulders, and He gave way to a picture of the American flag flying in a high wind.

"Hello, Jake," Brother shouted.

"Shhhh. Hello," Jake said from the door flooding with the warm, moist air. "Did you boys make out all right?"

"Fine as wine," Brother said in his middle of the day voice still. He pulled his knees up under the sheet and rested his arms on them, enjoying the visit, not bothering to cover his nakedness. "We watched TV, but Jube didn't like it too much and went to sleep." There was a long silence during which Brother and Jake watched Laurie watching Jubie with a look on her face that fell just short of being a smile. "You was good in your show, Miss Laura," Brother said at last, feeling that the silence had lasted long enough for a visit.

"Oh, Brother, thank you, that's the first unsolicited brava I've had tonight."

"You're welcome," Brother said.

"Shhhh," Jake said.

"And thank you, Brother, for taking care of Jubie," she said.

"You're welcome," Brother said. "We had a pretty good time, he don't quit talking even when the TV is on."

"I know," she said softly. "What did he talk about?"

"He wants Julian to come to Bladens Beach and be with everybody," Brother stated. "And he was worried about you running off with that man in the park, he says everybody is running off leaving him."

"Oh God," Laura said, and the unreasonable happiness turned quickly and sharply to take its revenge.

"Come on, Laura," Jake said, a shadow in the door. "Go back to sleep, Brother."

"I ain't sleepy," Brother said.

"Go to sleep anyway."

"Okay, Jake," Brother said agreeably and flattened his legs under the sheet in preparation. They watched Laura watching Jubie for a while longer, until she got up and kissed him and felt his forehead, pushing back the damp curls.

"What is it in the blood that turns love into insanity?" she asked anybody. "And why must this little creature suffer love?"

Neither the soldier nor the whore had a ready answer.

"Good night, my sweet soldier," she whispered.

"Ma'am?" Brother asked as loud as ever.

"Good night," she said. "Take care of my child."

"Oh, Jubie can just about take care of hisself," Brother announced, not quite finished with the visit. "He brung his clock with him, and he's a world champion talker."

"I know," she said. "Good night." She switched off the geometric test pattern on the television and went to Jake in the door, and Brother flung himself back on the pillows. Jake closed the door on the protected retreat.

"Oh, my God, Jake," Laura said and put her forehead against his chest. He enclosed her in his arms, and they stood very still. "I had thought to break my fast," she said from his embrace, "but this is not the time, is it?"

"No," Jake said.

"No," she said and put back her head and looked at him, almost as if to make sure who he was. "I should have kissed Brother too. I didn't kiss Brother."

"No," Jake said again. "I don't think Brother would know a mother's kiss. There are some of us who have never known one, or who can't remember one."

"You, Jake?" she asked and tried to see his face in the dark.

"We need new glasses and new drinks," he said and removed his arms from her shoulders, as though he had been reprimanded, and walked away from her to the door of number twenty-six.

They were lying back on the pillows of the twin beds, fully clothed, their legs crossed at the ankles, supporting cloudy plastic glasses on their stomachs with one hand and waving cigarettes in the other. She sat up suddenly and crossed her legs and put her cigarette in the ashtray, and her skirt opened out into a fan on the edge of the bed. Jake noticed the dress for the first time. It was green with a full skirt and a loose sash low on the waist, the kind of dress nobody has anymore, made for a particular person for a particular occasion.

"If we're in room twenty-six and Jubie is in number twenty-four, how is it we're next door to each other?" Laura pondered. "Whatever happened to number twenty-five?" Her manner suggested she was inquiring after the whereabouts of a long lost friend. She realized at that moment that her slow drinks were hitting home and that the long nights of Alma Winemiller were giving way at last to the easier nights of the silly and provocative young wife she was to play in the week to come. This girl was a lot of laughs.

"I would guess that the odd numbers are across the pool on the other side of the court," Jake said, lifting his head a little from the pillow and regarding her curiously with the narrow blue eyes.

"Then by all rights, we should be on the other side of the court," she said and giggled without having to catch her breath, "because Lord knows we're two rooms full of odd numbers. I mean, now, who would believe it? Here we are, a stunning man and a stunning woman stretched out in a motel on Highway Twenty-One without a lustful thought between us. And right next door, one of God's soldiers keeping watch over a child consigned to—"

"We need new glasses and new drinks," Jake interrupted.

"Oh, all right," she said, grateful for the interruption, and called Front Desk for ice and glasses and soda water, and almost immediately there was a tapping at the door so gentle as to be all but inaudible. When she opened the door, she gasped and put her fingers to her mouth. She had revealed what appeared to be a great, daft baby, smiling benignly, filling the door frame like a doll in its box, wearing a crisp white shirt with short sleeves pressed into tiny wings and a minute, black bow tie. "Front Desk, Miss Warren," he announced and paused briefly on the threshold, as if in preparation for a difficult acrobatic feat, and then swirled enormously into the room with incredible lightness, balancing the glittering tray in an arc through the air, as though some wiry, agile juggler had taken possession of his ungainly body by mistaken incarnation. Laurie thought perhaps she was supposed to laugh but decided against it because of his portly dignity.

"You are perfectly wonderful, Miss Warren," he said, as he spun the tray onto the desk, possibly on the end of one dimpled finger.

"Excuse me?" she said, not quite recovered from the brilliance of the performance.

"I saw your show, you are perfectly wonderful," he said and stood at attention so that he seemed to be leaning backwards and beamed down on her with the wreathed face of a happy child. "I was going to write you a note, you are a perfectly wonderful actor, you are a genius, Miss Warren," he informed her and turned pink. "I want to be an actor myself someday."

"Aha! You see," she explained triumphantly to Jake. "Another brava—unsolicited! You're to have an enormous tip for that," she said.

"On, no, Miss Warren," he demurred, turning a deeper pink, "there's no charge for you, Miss Warren." His deep-set, black eyes flicked for an instant in the direction of the man on the bed, as if there just might be a charge for him.

"You see there, now," she pointed out to Jake again. "A bouquet of roses for the star. Why aren't you working with us at the playhouse, young man?" He took an awkward step backwards, the juggler's spirit having forsaken him, and failed at reassuming his position at attention, abashed by the attention he was getting from the Star of the Week and the man regarding him from the bed with the small, sleepy eyes.

"I have to work the desk at night," he apologized and then decided, because of the bright and loving look on the star's face, he could tell the whole truth. "And my mamma don't take to actors too much. She says if they hadn't of been run off from somewhere else, they wouldn't be standing in the middle of the stage for all to see. She says it's God's punishment for the way they—" He brought himself to a sudden and alarmed halt and left his mouth still open, realizing he had gone too far in the face of present evidence, which confirmed his mother's most dire convictions against this breed. Confounded by embarrassment, he fumbled back of him for the knob of the door.

"Maybe next year," Laurie said.

"Yes, ma'am, maybe next year," he said and backed into the humid night with what might have been a tiny bow.

"Poor old imprisoned Front Desk," Laurie mused as she fixed drinks at the desk. "God's punishment. I guess Mamma's right. It's God's punishment. But what have I ever done to deserve punishment? And besides, what has God ever done for me? What has God ever done for my child?" she demanded and left off talking to face the wall separating her from room twenty-four. "I'll tell you what He's done," she took up again with new vehemence. "He has consigned my child to hell and consigned me to hell and consigned my poor old ex-husband to hell. And what was my sin?" She turned on him, as if he were responsible for what had been done to her. "What was it? Can you tell me that, since you have come to save us all?" Her voice broke and she glared at Jake, waiting for an answer, but he gave none.

"Lie down," he said. The iron lung pumped refrigerated breath into the room, and she sat on the bed and crossed her legs and the skirt opened out into a fan again.

"Why couldn't God have made him a little worse while He was at it? Why couldn't He have at least made it so his feelings didn't get hurt, so that he didn't miss the only thing in the world he really wants and can't have, which is people? My God, it takes that child the better part of a half hour saying his prayers, blessing all the people who don't want him around. Why couldn't God have punished us just that much more? Or is He just mean enough to know this was the cruelest punishment He could have inflicted?" She folded inward, crossing her arms across her breast, and shook her head and kept on shaking it, overwhelmed by hopelessness. Then, she sat still, fallen over.

"Lie down," Jake said.

"Lie down," she said sharply and stood up between the beds, rigid with resentment. "Who the hell are you to tell me to lie down? Who are you that you can walk into our lives and tell us what to do and walk right back out again? Man of mystery," she said contemptuously. "Just who the hell are you and where the hell did you come from?" She took a cigarette from the bed table and lit it and shook the match long after the flame had gone out, looking down at him with the ferocity that turned her china-blue eyes almost black.

"I don't know," Jake said.

"Oh, you don't know," she said and made a high, false laugh. "Answer me!" she shrieked, and the sinews in her slender neck stood out.

"That is the answer. I don't know," Jake said and turned his face to the wall and turned it back again. "As far as I know now, my first day on earth began on a morning four years ago when I woke up in a motel room much like this one in a little town in Mexico. All I had with me was a brown paper shopping bag containing four hundred and fifty dollars in travelers checks on a Los Angeles bank, an electric razor, a bottle of hydrogen peroxide, and a dog collar. That's it."

The rigidity forsook her and she fell back on the bed, as though something had given way inside her. "That's it?" she asked.

"That's it," he said and watched her with sleepy, smoke-blue eyes. "I had to start from there. It has been a long visit, except sometimes there are echoes. Here, there are echoes. I don't know why, and I don't like them very much."

"That's it," she repeated, astounded at the impossibility of it, and she laughed, gasping for air. "That's all you have to tell me?"

"I'm sorry," Jake said. "That's all there is."

"I wore this dress for you," she said in a new voice, as though she had taken leave of the present or as if she had just arrived.

"I know that," Jake said.

She stood up again and untied the sash and slipped the dress off over her head and lay beside him on the bed. "We're running out of cigarettes, I'll have to call Front Desk again in a little while," she said.

"You leave Front Desk alone," he said.

"Save us all, Jake," she said and put her face up to his and laughed. He turned and covered her with his arm and shoulder, so that nothing could fall upon her for a while.

Next morning, Brother thought to wind Jubie's clock. He and Jake had had to dress and pack and take a taxi with a philosophical driver to the house among the pines full of the sleeping condemned. However, they had made it alone together with extraordinary ease, being two extraordinary men. Neither considered sexual or romantic events satisfactory topics for conversation, and neither was surprised by any eccentricity of human behavior, understanding as aristocrats, that his eccentricity is the mark of a man.

Laura had left room twenty-six at some dim, indeterminate hour of the dawn and knocked on the door of number twenty-four until Brother opened it, draped in a bed sheet, looking like a legionnaire from ancient Rome who had stayed too long at the orgy. She had abducted Jubie—talking in a fresh morning voice—in his nightshirt to her double bed at the house in the pines, offering no explanation, and Brother expected none. He had fallen back into bed in his toga and rejoined the orgy. At breakfast, he and Jake wondered briefly how she had managed to urge Ned Trivett's antique automobile onto the highway without having been initiated into the rituals necessary to its operation, but neither had complained of her taking it, accustomed to the adversities of fortune.

"She looked right young and pretty," Brother had said, "but I think maybe she was drunk."

"Something of the kind," Jake had said.

They arrived, bag and baggage, at the house to find Jubie still in his nightshirt enjoying fortified cornflakes with Doris Ann Hawkins at the crippled table in the kitchen, asking each other why everybody didn't come on and get up. "They was all drunk last night," Doris Ann told Jubie. "I don't git drunk, I'm going to pour it all down the drain like Annie," Jubie said and shook his head endlessly.

When Brother Reeves turned up in the kitchen door, Doris Ann said, "My Lord," and dropped her spoon.

"Mislark still sleeping," Jubie told them right off. "Doris Ann say Mislark been sick, she still sleeping, Jake."

"That's good, Jube," Jake said, and he and Brother put the suitcases down by the refrigerator, side by side, in neat order, as though they had come on official business and might have to make a hurried departure.

"She need the rest, Jake," Jubie went on explaining.

"You want some coffee or something, honey?" Doris Ann asked Brother.

"We can all go on down to the beach, Jake," Jubie said. "Mislark don't care, she still sleeping. I don't want no more cornflakes."

"He already ate two of them little boxes anyhow," Doris Ann said. "You want some coffee, honey?" she asked Brother again.

"I reckon so," Brother said.

"Come on then, Jubie," Jake said. "Brother, why don't you have some coffee with Doris Ann."

"Okay, Jake," Brother said.

"That Jubie can talk up a storm," Doris Ann told Brother over the coffee cups. "He's been talking nonstop since I taken him off Laurie's bed this morning, he was sitting up right straight when I passed the door like he was ready to get started."

"He's the world champion talker," Brother confirmed.

"What ails him?" Doris Ann asked.

"He don't know how to grow up," Brother said.

"I don't see nothing wrong with that," Doris Ann declared. She had turned pink and creamy and attentive. "You want some more coffee, honey?" she asked Brother.

"I don't believe I do," Brother said. They pushed back their chairs and stood up, as if at a signal, and left the dirty dishes on the crippled table, which wasn't Doris Ann's way at all.

A muffled cry of alarm and a loud thump on the wall next to her bed roused Laurie from light, insignificant dreams at some point during the morning. She glanced at her alarm clock and wondered what Gordie was doing banging around in his room at this hour of the morning, when he should be building the new set and talking things over with the Star of the Week.

The days of Doris Ann Hawkins' apprenticeship had come to an end.

Along about noon, Laurie blew out through the French doors onto the terrace of Bladens Beach Manor in the same green dress she had worn the night before, even though it wasn't a daytime kind of a dress. She was flanked by Brother and Doris Ann like staunch soldier guards to a fragile queen. She shaded her eyes with one arm and flagged the green sash back and forth with the other. Her red hair shone like metal in the sun.

Jubie ran up from the surf breathing hard and sputtering water. Jake was the first friend of his life to permit him into the water unattended. "There Mislark, Jake," he piped above the rush of the waves and spraddled out on his thin legs like a sand crab, pointing straight with his arm, as though he had thrown a light spear and was following its flight. The three figures on the distant terrace leaned in together onto the balustrade, and Jake recalled it later as an echo of sweet, unthreatened peace.

The five of them had lunched in the dining room with the summer tourists, reflected in the panes of the mirrored doors which should have been in a grand hotel in the south of France. Doris Ann had assumed the air of a governess in order not to be excluded, and neither her presence

nor the reason for it was questioned. "You up in your part for dress rehearsal?" she asked Laura. "Letter perfect," Laura said. "How come you
got a bandage on your arm, Mislark?" Jubie asked. "She hurt it," Doris
Ann said and cut up the chicken on his plate. "Who you going to be this
week, Miss Laura?" Brother said. "A damn fool," Laura said. "She ain't
so much a damn fool she don't know what she wants," Doris Ann said
and quick-glanced at Brother. "We coming to see you be somebody else
next week," Jubie said. "We'll see," Laura told him. Only Jake said
nothing.

After lunch, they all stood by their chairs and were silent for a moment as if it were some kind of ritual. The tourists watched them with
interest, and some of the wives leaned forward to their husbands and
whispered that there was the girl with the show. "I see it is," the husbands
said.

"Now then," Laura said, after the moment of silence had been observed, "I think Jubie and I would like to be by ourselves for a while,
wouldn't we, Jube?"

"Yes'm," Jubie said.

"I got to get to work," Doris Ann said and her eyes flicked across
Brother's face again. "Gordie's going to be mad as a wet hen."

In the lobby, the party separated with reluctance, as though they
feared the end of something. Laurie and Jubie went to her cool room at
the house. Doris Ann to the dusk of the theater with a face that protested
she had been laggard in her duty and didn't give a damn.

Brother and Jake walked along the shore, looking down at the glassy
strip of sand, talking in fragments of statements when the spirit moved,
as the spent waves ran flat under their feet, until they were out of sight
and there were no more people. They became of an age. They were two
men.

"I don't know what she's going to do, Jake," Brother said.

"I don't know either," Jake said.

"I don't know what she's going to do about him," Brother went on.
"One of these days soon, it's going to happen to him, and she or nobody
else can handle him," he said.

"What's going to happen?" Jake had to ask and looked up at him
as if he had become the older man.

"It," Brother said.

"Yes," Jake said. "I don't know either."

Jake stopped in his tracks as if they might have lost their way, and
then they turned and walked back towards the white, wedding cake hotel
in the distance. They were locked in timeless, fraternal understanding.

As the night began to fall and the time for the dress rehearsal drew
near, Laurie and Jubie and Jake and Brother stood around Ned Trivett's
patient and contrary old car among the pines in the sand-swept yard of
the house. Doris Ann was halfway out of the screen door watching, more
like a farm woman seeing her husband off to the fields at dawn than what
she had in her head she was or was going to be.

"This has been the best visit a famous star ever had," Laurie said
in her light, tremulous stage voice as fragile as crystal.

"You coming too, Mislark," Jubie told her. "You come on home too,
why you ain't coming home too?"

"Hush, Jube," Laurie said. "You know I can't come this time."

"Yes, you can, you can if you want to," Jubie said and his voice
veered upwards towards distress.

"Hush, Jubie," Jake said and tried to take his hand, and Jubie jerked
it away from him and crouched and clamped his hands between his knees,
hunching his shoulders so nobody could touch him.

"I ain't going to hush," he wailed. "You shut up, shut up, Jake, I
hate you. You come on, Mislark."

"Oh God," Laura said and gave down so that the green dress hung
limp, as though it had lost its life.

"You, Jubie," Brother said. "Come on now. We're coming back sometime."

"We ain't coming back, we ain't coming back, shut up!" he cried out and threw his head back, looking up into Laura's face with his arms clasped around her waist. "Come on now, Mislark, we got to go home," he pleaded.

"Oh God," Laura said again and leaned down to him very slowly as if she were lowering her face through murky water and kissed his swollen lips. "Take that kiss to Mister Jukes for me," she said.

"He don't want no kiss!" Jubie screamed. Tears ran down his face and his mouth was opened downward like the mouth of a mask.

Brother took a long step forward suddenly and swung him up under his arm, as if he were a calf or a lamb and sat him in the front seat of the car, pushing in beside him. "Okay, Jube," he said. "We got to be men, ain't we men now?"

"No!" Jubie shouted and cut off crying and sat stock still.

"Brother," Laurie said and took his face in her hands and kissed his mouth. "Jake," she said and took his face in her hands and kissed his mouth exactly the same.

"Get in, Jake," Brother said. Jake looked to him as if he had got lost.

Jubie sat stone silent between the two men like a surrendered prisoner between two heartless guards. The lights from the dashboard lit their faces from underneath. They were all looking straight out through the windshield. Jubie's eyes looked like glass. Laura leaned in the window and smiled at the perfect profile of her son.

"This has been the best visit a famous star has ever had," she said. "Try to forgive me, Jube," she said.

"Yes'm," Jubie said under his breath, but he didn't look at her.

As they drove off, Jake watched her in the rearview mirror as she walked slowly towards the house without looking back at them. The green dress swayed from her shoulders and down her back, and she was pale and thin and evanescent in the looming dark. Doris Ann left the lighted doorway to meet her.

CHAPTER TWENTY-ONE

A Woman Abandoned went out onto her deck in the pearly light of dawn with a cup of coffee. It was early enough so that she still wore her nightgown and bathrobe, and would probably be wearing her nightgown and bathrobe when the day finished, for all she cared. The edge of the red ball of the sun hadn't come up yet, and the ocean was as flat as a plate, except for an occasional slow swell. There wasn't a breath. The cries of the seagulls could be heard up and down the beach for miles.

She turned a chair towards the sea and sat down with her coffee to watch the colors change and try not to think about what was to be done with the rest of her life. There wasn't a soul. After a while, the small, dirty dog trotted happily along the shore from left to right without even glancing in her direction. "Either jogging or going to work early," Susan said and made the beginning of a laugh. She was glad she could still laugh at the little things that turned up in her mind. She was glad she could laugh in spite of the empty room upstairs with the bed which looked as if it had been struck by a hurricane and a closet full of Skinner's suits, which seemed to have been struck by death. She felt she was recovering from some kind of amputation. Something essential which had supported her, far more than she had supposed, was gone, and she thought perhaps the handicap was more than she could overcome.

She was sorry she had devoted all that time to making titles and pictures and thought she had in some way made them come true, but in the wrong way, as if there was punishment from God for her indulgence. The Other Woman had turned out to be Another Woman, and she was neither of them. Nonetheless, at last, the picture had matched the title. She decided she would get another cup of coffee in a little while and take up smoking on a permanent basis whether she liked it or not. It fit the way she was now.

The rim of the sun pushed up and shot red light straight across the flat water and the beach and put the houses in sharp relief, so that they were cut out of cardboard and there was nobody inside them. At the same time, in the distance, it cast golden light upon a man stalking down to the surf supporting a scrawny-limbed child on his hip, the way a mother carries a baby on her hip so that one hand is free to stir the pot on the stove. But the child was far too old to be carried in this manner, and the man . . . oh, my God, was blond and tall and wearing a small black bathing suit. He let Jubie down and—standing straight up at rigid attention—stood watching him with what appeared to be intense concentration, as he scattered into the surf on his thin, coltish legs, flailing his arms about as if they were controlled by invisible wires. He squatted in the water facing Jake and flapped his arms like a wet bird trying to fly. Jake crouched on his heels, still watching him intensely, certainly not laughing.

Susan couldn't understand why her heart began to fill with dread at this perfectly ordinary and reasonable scene. There was no threat except for the red light, which was the same light as on every cloudless summer morning. She got up out of her chair and walked barefoot to the end of the deck and put up her arm and waved it back and forth, swaying from the waist, to get their attention, hoping for their attention, almost desperately. But, like a pair of lovers, they had no thought for anybody but each other. They seemed to exist for themselves only, as though they were the only people on the earth. The man sitting on his heels and the boy running out of the water to him, the two of them alone.

She decided they shouldn't be disturbed and went back to her chair and her cup of coffee on the deck rail, but she couldn't stop watching them, although she felt she was intruding on some private consummation. She didn't understand this feeling, but she could not deny it no matter how much she hoped she could.

Jubie walked up to Jake taking quick, silly little tightrope steps and put his arms around his neck, and they put their foreheads together for a very long time, saying something to each other probably. Jake stood up slowly with Jubie in his arms, their foreheads still touching, and then, walking swiftly forward towards the sea, swung Jubie in an antic, circular, swooping movement onto his back. Jubie clamped crablike to his shoulders, as he went into the shallow surf and out onto the flat, dark green water. Soon, she saw Jake push out to swim with strong arms. Soon, she could see only their heads struck by the red light, rising and falling on the gentle swells. They made an arrow pointing out.

There was something unbearable in this for her. She stood up again and put her arm up halfway and held it there for a moment but without hope and left the chair and the coffee cup and went into the house. Through the glass wall, she watched the two heads, like a sea monster diminished by great distance, moving slowly out and out and out onto the darker green water where the gentle swells were longer and lifted them easily.

Without thinking about anything, as if she had gone into a trance suddenly, she went up the stairs to her bedroom and sat in her bathrobe on the edge of the bed. Next to her on the bedtable there was an ashtray full of Skinner's cigarette butts which he had lit and put out as she stood in the door watching him pack his clothes to leave her. She picked one out without looking at it and struck a match and took up smoking on a permanent basis.

She smoked several, flicking the ashes on the carpet around her bare feet, and thought it was too bad she didn't have a cup of coffee to go with the cigarette the way other women did it when they were thinking or not thinking. She couldn't move. She thought probably she would never leave this bed with the tangled sheets from which the breath of Skinner's flesh was escaping now forever.

She sat there smoking until all the cigarette butts were nothing but filters and sat for a long time after that.

From the depths of profound entrancement, she heard somebody calling her, but she couldn't answer, as often in a dream she had not been able to remove herself from the path of some monstrous oncoming vehicle. Again and again, she heard her name, but she didn't move until she understood there was somebody standing in her bedroom door. She looked up with incurious eyes. It was Brother Reeves.

"I think you better come on downstairs, Susan," he said.

CHAPTER TWENTY-TWO

For Brother, there had been another long, dreamlike night of standing guard for Jubie in Laura Warren's living room, Annie Davison having been called to her church for the refreshment of her soul. Jake in Laura's chair again and Brother confined to the chair opposite, Julian's chair. He was too young and vigorous for it, leaning on one arm and then the other and shifting in the seat as though he were taking a sharp turn in his pickup. The same electric fan turned on the black marble hearth and the same two moths, a large one and a smaller one, fluttered at the screen and the same breathless summer night leaned in at the window, smelling of torn moth's wings or two people making love in the grass. The moon was the only cool thing, only a part of it and paper thin, luminous and serene, halfway behind a great black tree. Jubie, becalmed and fevered-sleeping in Laurie's birthbed upstairs. Brother had assumed the demeanor of manhood and innocent wisdom in Julian's chair, so that he and Jake Cullen were of the same and superior cast, sharing the adverse and inexplicable parabolas of life as they saw it, explaining

256

them to each other, adverse and inexplicable or not. Preferably inexplicable.

For example, Brother had never before spoken about where love was nor about what it was to leave home or not leave home or hang somewhere between leaving and not leaving. He had divined how such things were when he was working in the fields or in the curing house or lying flat out on the bed in his little room jammed like a lean-to onto the side of his father's house, but he had never considered the time would come when he could speak about them to another man. He had had to sow his love out onto the air over the furrowed fields. Love, he had concluded, was not necessarily where you lay with your left hand under a woman's head and your right hand embracing her waist, although it could show itself there on the breath and in the joining, if you knew to look for it, if two people looked for it at the same time, sometimes not even knowing at all that they had seen it there. So he hid his face in the curve of a woman's neck and tried to forget that he had seen it so clearly and wanted so profoundly to hold the sight of it in his eyes. He had wondered from time to time if he were the only person in the world to see it that way. He had wondered if the man and the woman, alien to him but his mother and father, had ever been transported and known they were bound to eternity, even though eternity was only an instant, and that that instant would have to be enough. He had hoped such an instant had been his creation, and then he had known, considering himself, that it would have had to have been.

Reconsidering aloud to Jake, his life turned in him with overwhelming relief that there were at least two of them that knew all of this. "It can come on you sudden," Brother had said, "like when you turn over a rock and find out what's under it you didn't expect," and glanced up quick at Jake under the lamp. "Yes," Jake said, "exactly." Brother had laughed like a boy running who had had to run, because there was too much going on inside him and no other way to dispel the violent exaltation except just by running. "I feel like that sometimes when I look at Jubie,"

Brother said, testing the accord. "Yes," Jake said, "exactly." Brother didn't laugh. "I feel like that now, just sitting here saying things," Brother said. "Yes," Jake said, "exactly." And then Brother laughed again, not from having to run but from the accurate pitch of the world.

The two men had spread out their lives for each other like tarot cards, telling their destinies aloud as clearly as they could be told with words and the broadcast of intimate feeling without fear of regret. Jake's birth or birth again, "delayed in a way like Jubie's," he had said, "but progressive, unlike Jubie's," had impressed Brother unreasonably. "Maybe you was somebody else once, Jake," he had insisted. "Maybe you will find out you was somebody else."

"We are all somebody else at one time or another," Jake had told him.

"That's true," Brother had said, not knowing exactly, but knowing exactly at the same time. That had been one of the times when they had both sat still for a rest, even Brother, too alive for the small chair, not speaking but still transmitting feelings and getting them back on a screen like radar, so they could be felt again and reexamined without haste. It had been about then that Brother understood that revealing did not necessarily betray the secret heart, and that was mysterious and satisfactory.

"Do you believe in God, Jake?" he spoke up suddenly, enveloping Jake with a look at the same time apprehensive and expectant.

"I would be a fool not to, wouldn't you agree?" Jake said and was moved as the trees of the wood are moved in the wind.

"You can't not believe, can you?" Brother went on. "If you believe in that other thing, you have to believe in something else. If there wouldn't be one, there wouldn't be the other. You can't not believe, ain't that right?"

"There has to be something of God in everybody, like it or not," Jake had said and felt he had taken a risk with Brother's life.

"Yes," Brother said, "exactly."

Jake had wanted to laugh, not like a boy having to run, but like a man who has come upon a formula unexpectedly that confirms a theory he has held for a long time which will change the direction of the history of mankind. "I'm sorry you know that," he had said. "I'm sorry you found that out. It will burden your days with more responsibility than you can bear. It will turn you into a visitor with terrifying obligations and no place to go to rest, which is against nature. Nature didn't make us strong enough for that. Nature made us just barely strong enough to live in a cave and leave it and look up once or twice, but only to return to the cave. A man that leaves a cave for good is an outcast, maybe even a crime against nature, having had the arrogance to take on himself more than he has the right or the strength to bear."

"Like you, Jake," Brother had said.

"Oh, I don't know," Jake said. "Possibly. But they will call you a hustler, since you will be held responsible for the awful weight of other people longing for love and nobody to talk to about your own."

"You can talk to me, Jake," Brother offered.

"I know. I have. It's too bad, isn't it?" Jake had said, glancing up at him with the narrow blue eyes. "You are a born soldier and a born hustler, or what people recognize as such."

Brother had accepted that, although in his existence, it had been permissible to call a man a soldier but never the other thing without risk of dire consequences. "They call me that already," he said. "They think I don't know that, but I do," he said.

"You see," Jake explained. "It has already started. You are being held responsible."

"Maybe I don't belong here, Jake. Maybe I belong somewhere else," Brother had said.

"Too late to turn back now," Jake said to himself. "Well, don't go looking for where you do belong," he had told Brother, "because you won't find it, it isn't anywhere. You'll see. People will want you and not want you, they will ask you to stay and tell you to leave. They won't let you in, they won't call your name, unless they are looking for a soldier or a whore as a diversion of the moment. Only now and then, you'll find a friend who loves you back for a while—not a lover, a friend. That's the only word I know for it. There should be a better word, but there isn't."

"When you leave here, I'm going with you," Brother said at last, sitting bolt upright in the little chair, staring at Jake with hollow eye-sockets.

"No, that won't do," Jake had said. "Two visitors is too many."

He had accepted that too. "That's right," he said. "One hustler is more than enough, ain't that right?" And finally, they had both laughed in delighted accord.

They had talked through the night, wearing the dark away into gray and paler gray, and the moths gave up fluttering at the screen, and the idiot and joyous birds took up outside, testing each other and the creeping dawn. Jake got up and cut off the electric fan which hadn't been doing anything anyhow but denying everything. He leaned with one elbow on the black marble mantel under the mirror with the gold pineapple and bananas around it.

"You'd better go now, Brother," he had said. "You've visited this cave long enough."

"I ain't through yet," Brother said.

"No, and you'll never be through from now on," the older man said to the younger man, and inequity and difference took up again where they hadn't been for some hours, but there was still the rag-end of the Great Accord which had left Brother permanently intoxicated. He wanted to know definitely why it was he had to go back to his room and go to sleep, if such a thing as sleep was possible ever again, as if nothing had happened, when everything had happened. More than that. He felt an obligation to stay on the watch, as a soldier might feel, not wanting to desert his post. "Go home, Brother," Jake had said.

"Am I dumb, Jake?" Brother had wanted to know, playing for time. Had he grown tiresome, he wanted to know, as he had grown tiresome in the past when it was over, and he had at last lifted his face from the curve of a woman's neck?

Jake laughed, still leaning on the mantel, baring his teeth but not making any laughing sound. "No," he said, "but I wish you were, you know all the things that will keep you dissatisfied with what is. Go home, Brother," he said again. "I promised Jubie we'd go to the beach early to make sure the sun comes up on time, and visitors have to keep promises."

Then, Brother understood it wasn't his being tiresome that was ending this night, but that Jake was relieving him of his post, or rather removing him from some danger. At the door, they stood looking at each other, and the younger man had thought there ought to be more to make the end come out right. He opened his mouth and drew in a breath to speak, but there was nothing to say without sitting back down in the chairs and facing each other again and starting all over. So Jake had said it. "Don't let them get you, Brother. It would be a terrible loss," was what he said. And then, he had put his hand on Brother's neck and kissed his mouth, if kiss was the right word for what he did.

And Brother had gone to his pickup truck, still reluctant, not even thinking about this unacceptable and imponderable act. He hadn't thought about it, until he had taken off his clothes and stretched out on his narrow bed in the rose light that crept in through the single square window at the head of his bed before the day could get started. Then, he remembered that a man had kissed his mouth for the first time in his life, and his heart flooded with terrible dread. He sprang up suddenly and pulled his clothes back on and ran out the kitchen door, letting the screen door slam behind him.

Mrs. Emma Bunce Reeves had been standing placidly over the stove frying ham. When the screen door slammed, she paused and put her hand with the fork sticking out on her massive hip and looked, broad-faced and incurious, after Brother, her son. She had gone back to turning the ham.

Susan remembered that morning and afternoon as if she had sent an entranced substitute to take her place.

"I think you better come on downstairs, Susan," Brother had said from the door of her bedroom, and she had smiled at him, relieved of some dreadful finality over which she had no control. It was at that instant that she had divided into two people, or rather, the insentient emissary had detached itself as a snake sheds its skin. "Come on right now, Susan," Brother had said. She thought how glad she was that whatever it was was now in his strong hands. The substitute rose, still smiling, and followed him like a child responding to a not unwelcome command but reluctant to appear too obedient, and left her real self, too vulnerable for what was to come, sitting on the side of the bed, perhaps to continue smoking Skinner's cigarettes—*Skinner*, she thought—perhaps to drowse, safe from unbearable suffering.

Brother had bounded along the balcony and down the steps two or three at a time and was standing, panting and agitated, in the middle of the living room looking up at her as she drifted, detached and bemused in her nightgown and bathrobe, activated by some remote obligation to-wards the top of the stair, where she paused. She had never seen Brother moved by revealed emotion before, so she stopped to consider how he was now. She had known him from the time she was a child in grade school and in high school and, like all the other girls, had loved him without hope of return, until later when some of the older and wilder girls had let it be known that . . .

"Please, Susan, come on," he said, and she realized he needed some kind of help. "I found Jake on the beach," he said, "and I was with him all night at Miss Laura's house, come on, Susan, I found him on the beach." He watched her steadily as she descended, still unhurried, even humming the fragment of a tune, to the living room where she stood facing him. She may even have been still smiling, a smile with the edge of a challenge. "I went home, he told me to go home, but something made me come back, they was going swimming early, I found Jake on the beach, Susan," he insisted, as if she doubted him. He thought he could not explain about the kiss. Probably not ever to anybody.

"I saw them," Susan said without knowing she was going to say it.

"Who? Saw who?" Brother asked in a voice loud enough to be coming from another room.

"Them," Susan said. "Jake and Jubie."

"Oh Lord, where? Doing what?" Brother shouted.

"Swimming," she answered. "Swimming out." She lifted her arm, standing like a statue, and pointed through the glass wall at the ocean which folded in on itself and slid up onto the beach. She smiled again and let her arm fall on its own. "He was swimming out with Jubie on his back," she said, "and I went upstairs to wait." She felt a great longing to go back to her bedroom and smoke and perhaps doze, but she knew that for some reason she could not. It was far too late for that now. "Have you got a cigarette?" she asked. *Skinner,* she thought.

"Cigarette?" Brother said, shocked and offended at the same time, as if he had found himself dealing with a stranger who had pretended to be a friend. "You don't smoke, Susan, you ain't listening to me, you got to wake up," he said in an even louder voice in the way of a man speaking to a foreigner who might understand if the volume is increased sufficiently. "Jake, Susan," he said. "I found Jake on the beach when I come back to see where they was. Jake couldn't talk, Susan, I had to . . ." He let up for a rest, finding the effort to explain the incredible too much for the moment.

Susan sat down leisurely in her chair opposite the sofa and gazed out at the ocean. "Where is Jake Cullen?" she asked casually, starting up a new conversation.

Brother exhaled. "At the hospital, Susan," he said, speaking low and exhausted. He moved to stand in front of her, looking at her with such intensity that she was distracted from the sea and shifted her gaze to his dark eyes. How beautiful he is, she thought. *Skinner,* she thought. "I had to call the ambulance. Susan, he's. Susan, you got to get up and telephone somebody. Jubie—"

"At the hospital," Susan said, showing mild interest for the first time. She looked up at him inquiringly with clear green eyes. "Have you got a cigarette?" she asked.

Brother gasped and turned his back on her, suffering an instant of defeat. "Susan," he spoke to the wall opposite. "I think you better try hard to understand me. Jake is, I think Jake is dead, and I can't find Jubie, I called the house but, Susan, I come here to, Susan, we got to do something quick, please, Susan. Please, Susan." He thought he was going to cry for the first time in his life but turned back to find she was no longer in the chair. She had gone to the telephone barefoot and picked it up and put it to her ear as if she were going to order groceries. He saw that she dialed one digit and waited.

"Operator, would you give me the police, this is an emergency," she said. "Yes," she said and stood waiting again for an interminable length of time. She leaned against the wall and put one bare foot on the other. "Yes," she said finally. "This is Mrs. Skinner Bates—" *Skinner,* she thought, "—there is an emergency, would you come immediately," still speaking calmly and waiting patiently for the grocery list to be read back to her. "Twelve-thirteen Ocean Front Drive, here at my house, yes," she said. "Immediately." Again she waited. Brother waited, watching her as if she held in her hands the promise of continued life. "Please, officer, this is an emergency," she said, and a sudden wrath possessed her, as though she had awakened for the first time since Brother's appearance in her bedroom door. "Goddamit, a child went swimming here, and we can't find him," she said, looking fiercely into the mouthpiece, as though she could see the over-bellied, heavy-hipped police officer sitting at his desk. "Yes," she said again. "Immediately," she said. "And you better inform the Coast Guard. Immediately," she said and put the receiver on the cradle and glared at Brother with clear green eyes. "I wish I didn't know you," she told him. "I wish I didn't know any human beings," she said still leaning against the wall with one foot on top of the other, her hand quiet on the telephone. "I could easily spend the rest of my life without the human race, have you got a cigarette?"

Brother regarded her seriously for some time, trying to see inside her head, and then said, "I don't smoke," and left her standing there in her bathrobe and went out onto the deck. He leaned forward on the deck railing, pushing up his shoulder blades like an eagle's wings when they are closed back, and looked down at the sand below him and did go ahead and cry for the first time in his life, or at least as far back as he could remember. But without a sound. It was more than he could stand that he had lost the two best friends, possibly the only real friends he had ever found, including his mother and father and his schoolmates, who had always made him restless, and the women who lay under him and then lit a cigarette right afterwards as soon as he could hand them their pocketbooks to find one and then got dressed and smiled bright and said good-by. The child who had forgotten how to grow up and the condemned visitor took him for who he was, whatever he was, nothing more than that and nothing less, maybe more than he was. Neither of them wanting anything beyond his company, even anxious for his company. The delight of being together for no other reason than that seemed to be the way it ought to be, was planned out to be.

Brother didn't know when he had stopped crying, not crying exactly, just letting the salt tears run out of his eyes and fall some ten feet into the sand below the deck. He thought the salt tears were the same water that is in the ocean, that somehow the salt water from the ocean had got into human beings, otherwise why would tears be salty? He was sorry he had stopped crying, because he wasn't through yet. But the years of not crying because there was really no reason to came back to him like a dog comes back home in the dusk. He looked out at the top edge of the ocean, sharp as a knife in the morning light, still leaning on the deck rail with his shoulder blades pushed up, and thought about how and why Jake had carried Jubie into all that and lost him. And he remembered running along the beach and finding Jake sprawled out on the wet sand in his black bathing suit, almost exactly where he had expected to find him, with the tail-end of the waves running up under him lifting his arm and hand. He had called out Jake's name and turned him on his stomach, still calling his name, and pushed salt water out of the mouth open in a last gasp like the mouth of a fish and turned him back again and returned the kiss he had understood and not understood, blowing breath into the bubbling lungs which didn't seem to need his breath. And running and falling down and running again up to the Holiday Inn where the pretty, sparkly-eyed girl behind the desk had smiled at him and not been surprised, but had dialed for the ambulance for him while he stood there trying to get enough breath back into his lungs and figure out what all was happening, or had happened, from the good-night kiss until now, or had happened from the first time he had seen Jake Cullen at Ned Trivett's house until now.

The Coast Guard patrol boat came up, low and dirty white, fuming and muttering, way off to the left, its blue light blinking cold and dreadful in the sun. At the same time, the door onto the deck slammed behind him, but he didn't even look around to see who it was. Early people were standing on the beach asking each other questions, and Rabbit Kendrick, with his small head like a fist and his barrel chest, who was getting older but didn't want to know it, ran along through the early people on his long legs that took up half his body and away towards the casino pier, as he did every morning of the world. Mrs. Stanley's little raggedy white dog passed Rabbit coming the other way, panting towards his breakfast and Mrs. Stanley laughing like a man and asking him where the hell he had been, as she did every morning of the world. Neither Rabbit Kendrick nor the dog looked up to see what the Coast Guard patrol boat was doing there. They had other things on their minds and could not know that an unthinkable end had come to something unimaginable. Unthinkable and unimaginable, unless you thought about how Jake Cullen was as a man. Brother knew now why he had had that feeling of deserting, he knew he should never have left Jake alone with Jubie in those big, dark rooms after all they had said and after Jake had put his mouth on his, hard and dry, for only one possible reason. Good-by.

He looked around his shoulder, and Susan was standing barefoot in her nightgown and bathrobe at the corner of the deck, staring out over the people gathering—there were a lot of them now—towards the Coast Guard boat moving slow and indolent among the swells as if it didn't care where it went or what happened, leaving a stink which disappeared into the air. She was a good-looking woman for a homely woman, he thought, with that nose and long face, and he wondered how Skinner could leave something like that for that other one with all the rings and bracelets and always talking hard. He couldn't help thinking about that, even now with what was happening. She was staring right straight out with her hands limp and helpless on the deck rail, as if she might never move again. Brother couldn't stand seeing her like that and looked back out to where the Coast Guard boat was sinking and rising, flashing its blue light.

"I'm sorry, Brother," she said, still looking out, so he could hardly hear her voice for the ocean. "I just don't know this is happening, and I don't think I can take it anymore. I didn't mean what I said. Was he dead?"

"Who?" Brother asked. "Oh, Jake," he answered. "He wouldn't answer when I called his name. They picked him up in the ambulance, and they covered up his face with that sheet so . . . I couldn't breathe no air into him, Susan." She kept staring out at the boat without changing the dreaming look on her face. Brother went and stood next to her, leaning forward on the rail again, so he could hear her when she spoke again, if she spoke again. They both looked out at the boat over the heads of the people on the beach who were pointing off in different directions and talking louder.

"What terrible mistake has that strange man made," she said. "That hustler."

"Visitor," Brother corrected her. "We don't know nothing yet, Susan."

"I do and you do," she said. "I can't find Julian," she said. "Some man, Blake—"

"Gordie Blake," Brother said and listened intently.

"—Blake," she went on. "I woke him up and he's coming with Laura, but, Brother, I can't find Julian."

"I'll find him, I can find him," Brother said.

"I guess so. I can't stand to see Julian," Susan said. "I can't stand to see him, but I can see Laura, I guess because she's a woman, but I can't stand to see Mister Jukes. Oh, God!" she said, the name said like that kicking in the air, "Mister Jukes, where is he?" Salt tears started running out of her eyes without changing the look on her face at all.

"I'll find him," Brother said. "We don't know nothing yet, Susan."

"I do and you do," she said. The tears stopped running.

"No, we don't," Brother said without meaning it. "And Ned. Did you call Ned?"

She flared around at him, as if he had gone crazy. "Ned? Ned who? Ned Trivett?" she asked wild-eyed and amazed, and the sudden wrath filled her again. "Why? He's responsible for this! He brought that man here—why, for godsake?" she asked in a loud argumentative voice.

"Susan, somebody's got to see about Jake," Brother said. "Ned's the one has to see—"

"Goddam Jake Cullen!" Susan screamed at Brother. Two or three of the early people on the beach looked over their shoulders to see who was screaming but were relieved of their curiosity when they saw only a man and a woman in her bathrobe still standing on the deck of their house, probably waiting to cook breakfast. "Just goddam that man to hell," Susan kept screaming. "God Almighty, how I hope he's dead! He didn't belong here, he never should have been here."

"He don't belong nowhere," Brother said and looked at her with soft brown eyes, sorry she could say such a thing but knowing why she did. "I'll go find Julian," he said and set off around the corner of the house.

"No, wait. Wait, Brother," Susan called after him, changing from angry to pitiful. "The rescue men are coming, don't go yet, Brother."

"I got to find Julian," he explained.

"That's right, you have," she agreed and gathered herself together, becoming taller, and closed her bathrobe around her thin body as though it were some kind of a royal robe. "I'll call Ned," she assured him, and Brother left without looking back at what she was about to do, since whatever it was, it would be the right thing. She took after Julian in some ways.

Chapter Twenty-Three

Julian punched the doorbell under the porch light and heard the peephole blink, and the door swung open on Evelyn Black's hoarse laugh.

"Well, damn if it ain't Julian Warren, where the hell you been keeping yourself, boy? Get in here and sit down and let me get you a drink." She put her fleshy arms, cool from the conditioned air, around his neck, and Julian could smell the rich perfume and feel the starch in her ink-black hair. She trailed before him in her long sparkly gown into the parlor, still laughing. In the soft, pink light from the lamps, Julian could see it was Evelyn's face under the powder, although it had a swollen look to it. The hands that had played the piano so many nights at Gene's Bide-a-While Bar and Grill were veined and glittered with rings. "Lord, come here let me look at you," she said, standing on a tilt with a hand on her hip, considering him from under the sapphire-blue eyelids. "Well, it's you all right," she said, coming up out of the tilt, "same as ever, you

270

ain't changed a bit, still thin and limber like you always was. Damn if I ain't glad to see you, Julian, why ain't you dropped by to see me before now?"

"I guess I miss the piano," Julian said.

"I guess so," Evelyn said and threw a sideways glance at him. "That's as good an answer as any, seeing the condition you're in, I bet you been sipping away by yourself in the dark somewhere. You're going to freeze to death in here in nothing but that shirt. You could of wore a fresh one on your first visit since I left Gene's place. Here, honey, let me get you a drink, although Lord knows you don't need one. Stick your shirttail in and take a seat, Julian, you're in a lady's parlor," she said and laughed again to make it easier for him.

"Oh," Julian said and did the best he could with his shirttail and looked about in a state of confusion, not knowing where to sit.

"On the settee," Evelyn said, pulling open the bottom drawer of Mama's old chest. "Scotch, ain't it?" she asked. "Sit down, Julian. I see I got to talk to you about yourself after all these years." She poured two drinks on the rocks and arranged herself at the other end of the settee. She lit a cigarette and crossed her knees under the sparkly gown and leaned in towards him. "Tell me now," she said.

"Laurie left me," Julian said and turned young and puzzled and ill at ease, as if he were confessing to a sin he had committed without knowing it was a sin.

"I heard," Evelyn said. "Show business. It's a curse, I ought to know. And all the way to Bladens Beach to get in it. I wonder why none of us with the itch ever leave home. We ought to of knowed nobody in Milford cottons to show business much, although there ain't one of them wouldn't give a mint to come down here and see how I made out."

"Well, to tell the truth, it wasn't all the show business," Julian said, settling back, crossing his legs and then crossing them the other way. "It was more—she always said she wanted to be free, she said she wanted to—" He hesitated and searched his shirt pocket and his trouser pockets and decided to go ahead with what he had to say. "—fly," he said.

"Here, Julian," Evelyn said and gave him her cigarette. "Show business is as near to flying as you can get without growing wings or taking a plane, which ain't what she meant. How the hell do you think I got as far as this set-up, ain't it nice?"

"It's nice," Julian said and looked around the room as if he had been surprised by it. "It's nice."

"Nicest place in town," Evelyn affirmed in case there was any doubt left in his mind.

"It is nice, Ev. But it was more than that, Ev," he went on, with the feeling that at last he had happened on somebody who understood what he was saying.

"That boy," Evelyn said. "Don't tell me she faulted you for that boy, that's God's business, nobody can understand about that child but God. We all got our cross."

"Jubie," Julian said. "No, it wasn't that so much. Jubie is a gift beyond value."

"I guess so, drink your drink," Evelyn said. "I ain't got any of my own, thank the Lord. All I know is I had four brothers that thought I hung the moon and they quit me the minute I went into show business. What would a kid of thought of me now, I wonder?"

"Everybody respects you, Ev," Julian said, "and so would a child."

"Don't horseshit me, Julian, we've known each other too long for that," she said. "For godsake, let me get you a pack of cigarettes, you're running me crazy rummaging through your pockets, why don't you get yourself some new pants?"

She got up and sauntered sparkling over to Mama's old chest which apparently housed all the human weaknesses and returned to the settee with the cigarettes and a pint of scotch. "Tell me, then," she said, pouring into the glasses, and reared back on the settee as though she could tell the number of the stars and call them by their names.

"I just don't suit," Julian said. "She wants more than I can understand. I've done all the right things, I've done everything I know how to do. But I just don't suit, it ain't enough."

"That's what it always comes down to," Evelyn said and thought about herself for a minute or two. "You can suit playing the piano and you can suit lying down in bed and you can suit drinking and having a good time, but you can't suit over the long haul, and it's the long haul we're all worried about now. Don't tell me. I know a whole lot about not suiting."

"I wish you had a piano you could play for me," Julian said.

Evelyn lifted her powdered shoulders and her ink-black eyebrows at the same time. "I gave up show business," she declared, "but maybe I'll take it up again someday. Right now I'm doing too good to think about it. I'm thinking about the long haul right now. I'd play the piano for you anytime, Julian. Anytime. And I'm the best damn piano player in the county or just about anywhere else, for that matter."

They sat making the ice ring in their glasses and blowing smoke, not looking at each other. It was as if there was a slide show on the wall they had been instructed to watch for a while.

"I always did like Laura, even if there was ten years between us and even if her people did think they was better than everybody else in that old falling-down house," Evelyn took up when enough time had passed for her to get bored with the slide show. "She had something extra, I felt kind of kin to her and was glad when she got you. I guess it was both of us always wanting to get into show business, no matter what anybody thought, and they thought plenty. I saw it in her way back when I was about to graduate from Milford High and she was still in grade school, red-headed and nervous as a cat."

"Why don't I suit, Ev?" Julian asked, pleading for some final answer.

"Lord, Julian, how the hell would I know?" she said. "As you may remember, you always suited me fine on a number of occasions, if you'll excuse me digging up the past. My brothers would of killed us both, but you was too good to let pass. And you're still set up like a boy. I don't understand it, you've got money in the bank, and you're one of the last ones knows how to treat a lady even when you're drunk. That's more than most of us girls get offered. But knowing what I know now in my position, I don't think many people suit each other for very long. They just get the habit of each other and put up with it for the look of it, and Laura and I ain't the kind to take on the usual habits or put up with anything just for the look of it. We need more air than most."

"That's right where I stop understanding," Julian said and took a long drink. "And, oh God, Evelyn, I'm so lonesome."

"And so you come to see old Evelyn Black at two in the morning, too bad I ain't the girl I used to be. Tell you the truth, I don't know when I stopped being the girl I used to be," she told him. "Well, for godsake, Julian, don't start crying on me. Do you want me to ring for one of the girls, is it that kind of lonesome?" Julian stood up suddenly and searched through his pockets again, looking up at the corner of the ceiling. "They're right down there on the table where you left them, Julian, sit down, why don't you get you some new pants? Do you want me to ring for one of the girls? I got a sweet one with red hair wants to be a marine biologist, whatever that is."

"Oh! Oh, Lord, no," Julian said. "Don't do that. Can't we just sit here and talk for a while longer? I wish you had that piano here, Ev."

"Sure we can, honey, sit down, Julian," Evelyn said, and Julian sat down and blew his nose on the handkerchief from his back pocket. "We owe each other that much," she crooned on. "I don't know why we do, but we do. And ain't it nice, ain't it nice, Julian? Maybe because you was about the first for me, and I got the feeling I was about the first for you. That counts for a whole lot, a lot more than these young ones coming along these days know about, poor little creatures. Besides, this is the afternoon for me, my day don't start till the sun sets. The eye of the adulterer waits for the twilight, like they used to say in church." She lit up two cigarettes, since Julian didn't seem to be able to keep up with his pack, and poured another round of drinks out of the pint bottle. They watched the oil painting of the sailing ship in a terrible storm at sea that hung on the wall before them and idled silent in a miasma of comfort and familiarity in the sweet, dazed, lambent, decaying glow of alcohol, as if the sun were always low and golden on the horizon. Evelyn smiled. "Church," she took up again. "I ain't been to church since I left Gene's place for good. Moral turpitude, I guess you call it. Ain't it funny the way things turn out, Julian? Here we are, the two of us old sinners, sitting here, abominations according to the book, abominations without even meaning to be. Me waiting here for the adulterers to ring my bell, and you ringing it. Ain't it funny, Julian? Who'd of thought of it in those days? A person can just slide into being an abomination without even knowing it. It don't seem fair to me. All them hard rules made up thousands of years ago when they didn't know how things was going to turn out, maybe that's why I ain't been to church for a while." She stopped talking suddenly, as if she had heard the groan of a pipe organ starting up a hymn.

They were closer than they had ever been, even closer than they had been lying together young and moist and confounded in a summer glade, although neither of them would have thought of that. They assumed the present was about all there was for a while, and that that was the way it was and, probably, had been. Mama's old chest got frequent attention for what seemed many hours, and in an easy overlap of low voices, they mused through the night counting the dead stars, interrupted from time to time by the distant ring of the doorbell. Not interrupted really, more like punctuated. Paragraphed.

He went so far as to tell her about Skinner's apostasy, and then, went

beyond that, not meaning to—still baffled about Skinner and John
Thomas in the same bed in Rome Italy.

"Good God, Julian, how old are you and where have you been?"
she asked him on a rising tide of amusement. "You can't tell me you ain't
run into that situation before, I'd of thought maybe you'd of been through
some of that yourself, loving certain things the way you did and drinking
the way you did. And do." Julian reared back in his corner of the settee
and flared his pale eyes at her, indicating offense, and was getting up the
breath to set her straight. But she paid no heed and went on: "I wouldn't
of chose them two together, though, I got to admit I didn't see that one
in the crystal ball. But that Skinner Bates, he's in for bad trouble one of
these days. My girls used to ask me not to put him with them, he took
it too serious and forgot who they was or what they was, and there was
another reason I won't go into. They got afraid when they was with him,
doing everybody a favor to be around. He's good-looking but he ain't that
good-looking."

Julian located his pack of cigarettes on the table at last and lit one
up and finished his drink and put it down, half turning his back on her,
as though he'd just as soon do without her company. "Skinner Bates is a
fine boy and a good husband to Su—" he started off, meaning to keep
going.

"Hah!" Evelyn interrupted. "Where is he then, and what's she doing
rambling around in that glass house by herself? Turn around here and
talk to me and don't get all puffed up like that. Why don't Skinner Bates
leave himself alone? He's always reminding himself he ain't you. He ain't.
He don't suit himself, think about that for a minute. In my personal
opinion, Susan Johnson is better off without him, the trouble would of
jumped up along the road somewhere."

"But *that*," Julian said, referring to the unthinkable. "The time
comes when you have to make up your mind and do the right thing in
this life—"

"And I take it you're going to tell me what the right thing is," she said, the tide of amusement rising in her again. "Come right down to it, it's all the same thing. Being with somebody, that's what it comes down to. He should of took some lessons on being himself from Ned Trivett." Julian started to puff up again and then decided to let it go. "I pity that poor left-over woman he run off with. Piss pot full of money or not, she's in for hard times, watch my word," she predicted and, having lost interest in the subject under discussion, went back to Mama's old chest to clear the air.

And so it ran along. Julian had the feeling they were answering many questions, and at length, the night lamps blurred dim for him, and the drone of their voices reduced to the hum of distant memory, a ponderous sound, remembered rather than heard. During one of the long pauses, he rested his head against a bunch of carved grapes on the back of the settee and closed his eyes and stayed that way. Evelyn, still talking along, looked at him and stopped talking along, realizing the easy time was over. She put her drink down and her cigarette out and leaned over him, heavy in her sparkly gown, watching his fine face for a long time, smiling slightly. "Lord, I do wish you could of been mine, Julian Warren," she said and laughed out loud at how it should have been. She rang for one of the girls. It was the marine biologist. "Help me with him to the little room at the end of the hall, honey, it ain't busy is it?"

"No'm." the girl said, "we ain't been too busy tonight."

"A blessing in disguise, I reckon. Mama Black had to nurse one of her old time babies," Evelyn said.

"Yes'm," the girl said, unquestioning. The threesome made it to the room at the end of the hall like exhausted and maimed pilgrims on the way to a shrine of miraculous cure. The women eased Julian onto the bed with serious and concerned faces. "Pull off his shoes and cover him up," Evelyn said.

"Yes'm," the young girl said. The two women stood together in the door, one in a sparkly gown and the other in a wrapper, and watched the sad man on the bed sleeping like a child with a kind of longing.

"Ain't he something?" Evelyn said.

"Sure is," the marine biologist agreed. They shut the door behind them.

Julian woke up in a midnight room, alarmed and in a state of desolation, not knowing where he was. Lamps with ruffled shades were burning and the heavy, flowered curtains had never been opened. The room had never seen the light of day. Brother Reeves was standing in the door, breathing hard, seeming to have brought the light of day in with him, and behind him in the hall was a woman with black hair stuck out like dead bird wings and paint from her eyes running down her cheeks. Julian realized it was Evelyn Black and recalled in waves of despair where he was, or rather where he had been and where he probably was.

"Oh!" Julian hollered, lifting his head off the pillow and making his eyes wild. "What time is it, Brother?"

"You got to get up, Julian," Brother said.

"You got to get up, Julian," Evelyn said over Brother's shoulder, and Julian thought she was crying or that the black paint had gotten in her eyes.

"What time is it?" Julian asked and put his head back on the pillow and turned his face towards the never-opened curtains.

"Late," Brother said, "maybe twelve o'clock noon, you got to get up now, Julian."

"Get up, Julian," Evelyn said and made a hoarse, down-turning noise as though something she treasured had been broken suddenly.

"Oh God, what time is it?" Julian said, still turned to the curtains.

"Take him to the bathroom and wash his face, Brother," Evelyn said. "He don't have time for a shower. Where's Laura."

"Laura!" Julian shouted and turned his back to them, seeing them through a prism which double-edged everything, even the voices, and drained everything of color and substance.

"She's on the way from Bladens Beach or she's at Susan's by now," Brother said.

"You all better get going," Evelyn said.

"I know it, come on, Julian, you got to get up," Brother insisted and stepped over to stand by the bed, looking down at Julian like a doctor watching his patient surface from anaesthesia following surgery.

"What's wrong," Julian asked and lifted his head, flare-eyed from the pillow again.

"Oh, dear God help us all," Evelyn croaked from the hall and made the hoarse noise again only worse this time.

"Something's wrong," Julian insisted, sounding angered, and sat up suddenly on the side of the bed and rammed his feet into his shoes which had been placed primly side by side, exactly where his feet hit the floor, as though he were going to run for the door. He was still seeing and hearing through eyes and ears that seemed to belong to somebody else, still hearing and seeing in a way that made no sense. He sat straight up and put his hands on his knees and blinked hard several times, trying to regain control of the core of his senses. "Something's gone wrong," he persisted, flaring his eyes again, "and I want to know what it is."

"Take him to the bathroom and put cold water on his face," Evelyn suggested. "I'll go fix him a drink."

"He ain't got time for that, Miss Evelyn, come on, Julian, get up. Let me get you to the bathroom," Brother said and took Julian by the arm. "It's Jubie, he's—"

"Jubie," Julian said and looked up into Brother's face with the strange eyes of a child confounded. "What's wrong with Jubie? I can get to the bathroom myself, goddamit, where is it, Evelyn?" he said and jerked his arm away from Brother and stood up suddenly and sat back down and stood up again immediately with his heart pounding in the cage of his ribs.

"That blue door yonder," Evelyn said, pointing at the pale blue door from the hall. "Put cold water on his face, I still think he ought to have a drink."

"What's wrong with Jubie?" he demanded, staring at Brother with what looked to be fury.

"We can't find him," Brother said.

"Can't find him?" Julian shouted, holding Brother responsible, and flung himself through the blue door like a man escaping capture and slammed it so that the house shook. It sounded to Brother as if Niagara Falls had started up in the bathroom.

Evelyn fell heavily against the doorjamb in her bathrobe and put her veined hands with the glittering rings over her face. She made the hoarse, broken noise in her throat, and her shoulders began to heave. "Sweet Jesus," she cried through her fingers, "what in the world happened, Brother?"

"Susan said they just swam on out, just kept on swimming out, and that was the last she could stand to watch."

"It don't make no sense," Evelyn said, letting her hands fall helplessly.

"It makes sense if you knowed Jake," Brother said.

"Well, I don't and I don't want to," she said. "How did you know he was here, Brother?" she asked.

"I looked everywhere else," he said, "and I just felt like it was time he might be here."

"I see," Evelyn said. "The last stop."

Julian burst out through the blue door looking as if something had caught fire and he had to get away from it. "You want me to fix you a quick drink, Julian?" Evelyn asked, her face blotted with dirty tears.

"He don't have time for that," Brother said.

"Wait a minute, wait a minute, Julian," Evelyn called out, as the two tall men started down the hall towards the living room.

Julian paused and turned to look at her, as though he had never seen her before. "What is it?" he asked loud enough to wake the girls sleeping in their tents.

"I'm going to order me a piano today, Julian," she told him.

Julian turned away, not having heard the woman, and he and Brother almost ran down the hall and through the parlor and out the front door. Evelyn pulled her bathrobe about her shoulders as though she were chilled from the conditioned air and, letting her head fall forward on her breast, stood in the middle of the hall weeping bitterly.

Riding break-neck through the countryside towards Milford with Gordie Blake at the wheel of the theater truck, Laura gazed out the window in silence of utter isolation. At one point, she saw children and dogs on a green lawn rolling away from the sun, the children laughing and the dogs lifting their legs at the bushes and barking for no reason, not thinking about rolling away from the sun—not even caring that the earth under them was saying good-by.

When they pulled up in the driveway of Susan's house, it looked as if everybody had moved out somehow, so empty. Laura was out of the truck and up the steps under the house before Gordie could even get the truck stopped.

"Oh, my God, hasn't she had enough?" Gordie said, as he turned the keys in the ignition.

CHAPTER TWENTY-FOUR

She promised Brother she would call Ned, and he took off around the corner of the house and left her standing there on the deck in her bathrobe without looking back. Susan thought probably Brother was a descendent of one of the magical knights of King Arthur's round table, and she thought he had left her to look all over the kingdom for King Arthur, who was probably lost in drunken slumber somewhere. But he had said he would find Julian, and she was perfectly sure he would. He was that magical.

She turned her back on the Coast Guard patrol boat and the early people gathering along the shore and went back into her glass house to wait for the men to come who would ask her questions and write down the answers and pretend something could be done. "I have lost a husband to the wars and a son to the seas," she announced to a possible adversary in her living room and felt a little foolish about losing Skinner to the wars rather than to the arms of The Other Woman—or rather to some dreadful hope that lived in his mind. However, it had a poetic ring to it, so she refused to disavow it completely.

She had closed the door on the mutter and clatter of the motors and the wash of the ocean and felt confident suddenly that she could go through with it now, since Brother was in charge and since she had left the cowardly woman upstairs sitting on the bed smoking Skinner's cigarettes. *Skinner,* she thought.

Oh, my God, Annie, she thought and went to the telephone. I have to call Annie of all people on earth. She would be able to look at Annie, because Annie was a woman. Women were used to losing husbands to the wars and sons to the sea and lovers to the arms of The Other Woman, but not many of them were used to losing lovers to the ghost of a dreadful hope.

She called Annie with flagging spirit, and halfway through telling her what she had to say, Annie had demanded out of dead silence, "Where Lark?"

"I called Bladens Beach and she's—"

"I'm coming," Annie interrupted and hung up fast and firm, leaving Susan standing with the receiver at her ear, having hoped for some vague reassurance from the woman whose job it had been to give such all her life. Then, she could imagine Mrs. Annie Davison, disregarding destiny, leaving her domain, her house on a dusty street with hanging plants under the eaves of the porch and potted plants on the railing, all intense green, moving in her direction, swift and unhurried, and there was great reassurance in that.

She called Ned Trivett, and she felt she had done it exactly as Brother would have wanted her to. She had come to like Ned Trivett better than she liked most people, although, for some reason, she still resisted saying as much. It seemed to her he had become Another Man, as she had become Another Woman, when he had understood at last what she was saying, starting and restarting her sentences.

"Is Jake dead, Susan?" he asked her.

"Brother said he wouldn't answer to his name," she said.

"Then, he's dead," Ned said. "I'll go to the hospital immediately. Thank you, Susan," he said.

"I hope to God he's dead," she said, taking revenge on him for some kind of selfish relief.

"It wouldn't be the first time," Ned said and hung up, and Susan felt she had been punished for her cruelty.

When Otho Harkness and the young officer from the Coast Guard with the skinned haircut and his cap in his hand arrived, she received them standing at the back door at the top of the steps smoking a cigarette like A Wanton Woman open for business. She had gone back up to the bedroom and found part of a carton of cigarettes among the abandoned socks and handkerchiefs in the top drawer of Skinner's chest. *Skinner,* she thought. The cowardly shadow of herself, too easily wounded for reality, still sat on the side of the bed with her legs crossed, and Susan left her there again, so that she might get through the day without knowing too exactly what had happened or what was happening or what was going to happen.

Otho Harkness as always looked like some harried bird, maybe a thin crow which had flown through terrible disaster, dressed up in his policeman's uniform as if it were a rented costume with the cap too big so that it pushed his ears out. His eyes were bead black and alarmed. He and the young man in the Coast Guard summer tans followed Susan into the house and stood close to each other for company in the middle of the living room. She sat down leisurely in her chair and put out the cigarette. Nobody knew how to get the investigation started.

"Sit down, Otho, and take off that damn cap," Susan said and realized the way she said it sounded as if she didn't care about anything. "You too, Mister—"

"Chief Petty Officer Knowles," Otho said. They shuffled sideways to the sofa and sat on it, ill at ease and erect, because of her nightgown and bathrobe perhaps, or because of the apology people feel in the face of tragedy.

"I see," Susan said. "Chief Petty Officer Knowles," she agreed and thought he was going to get up and shake her hand or even salute. "Take off that damn cap, Otho," she said to prevent his doing either. Otho took off his cap reluctantly and balanced it on his knee, however his ears remained bent out from long custom. There was another uneasy pause, as Susan lit another cigarette. She considered it might have been easier for all concerned, had she left them standing together for company in the middle of the room. Chief Knowles cleared his throat to get the investigation started, but Otho leapt into the breach.

"Ah—Mrs. Bates, could you just tell us what you know about this—" he began.

"I'm still Susan, Otho," Susan reminded him.

"Oh, well then, Susan," Otho conceded and was sorry she had felt it necessary to lower the tone of the proceedings. His cap unbalanced off his knee onto the floor. He studied it for a moment and then lifted it carefully with both hands and placed it on the sofa next to him, glancing at it reprovingly as if it had been insubordinate. "Could you just tell us what you know about this—ah—"

"Tragedy?" Susan suggested.

"—what happened," Otho said, rejecting the suggestion.

"It would be a help if you could tell us exactly what you know, Mrs. Bates," Chief Knowles said and at the sound of his own voice, he was no longer ill at ease. He sat back and crossed his legs. He assumed sudden authority, and Susan was relieved of another part of the responsibility. She considered he was A Fine Figure of a Man. She green-eyed him for a moment, but his questioning and earnest look remained steadfast.

"Yes," she said. "I know that my first cousin, once removed, a child of eight, has disappeared," she said, "out—" She pointed an accusatory finger at the sea without taking her eyes from his. "—out there."

"And how do you know that?" he asked.

"Well, Chief," she said and realized she was becoming insolent even at a time like this. *Skinner,* she thought. "I saw them swimming out very early this morning," she said and knew there was nothing but to submit to him, if things were not to be more hopeless even when they were already as hopeless as was possible. "I was standing on the deck there," she pointed again, "when I saw them come down onto the beach, there, and go into the water, there. He had swung Jubie up onto his back—"

"Who had? Whose back?" the officer said.

"The boy ain't right, Harvey," Otho Harkness spoke up. Susan glared at him and saw why it was he preferred to keep his cap on. A blade of hair, like a feather, stood as an exclamation mark at the crown of his head, denying him deserved authority.

"He cer—he most *certainly*—" she started and fell back to start again. "A Mister Jake Cullen," she stated to the officer, understanding suddenly that the defense of Jubie was no longer important. Besides, she found she didn't want to embarrass Otho further and was surprised at the impulse to compassion. "Mister Cullen was a visitor here in Milford," she informed the young officer.

"Ned Trivett, Harvey," Otho said. "He was staying at Ned Trivett's house along with that royalty woman who—" The "who" froze fast on his lips, and he sat absolutely still on the sofa for some seconds without changing the eager look in his black eyes, which shifted minutely in the direction of The Woman Abandoned, whom he had been on the verge of exposing right here in her own living room. It was as if he had played the wrong segment of tape at a hearing and was now running it fast backward to start it up again at, "He's the one we took to the hospital, Harvey," with no visible admission of the careless and embarrassing, mechanical error, except for a minute reshift of his eyes back towards Harvey

Knowles. "Brother Reeves found him washed up on the beach," he said and shut off the tape and shot a look at his cap to make sure it was still with him.

"Is he dead then?" Susan asked them, disregarding the inadmissible evidence. A clattering, flap-wing disturbance surged out of the distance and lowered over the roof of the house, silencing the investigation, rocketing like thunder, threatening to turn over the umbrella and table on the deck like a violent storm. Susan put her hands on her ears and saw the helicopter which could have struck shingles off her roof move sideways swiftly away towards the horizon, diminishing incredibly in size like a giant wasp with its sting extended. It seemed to her some strange, living, malignant mutation with a determination of its own. Its determination being that Jubie was lost forever, but that it must pretend otherwise. "I can't stand this any longer," she said and stood up in an attempt to keep the cowardly woman upstairs at bay. "You'll have to excuse me, I can't stand this any longer."

"Please now, Mrs. Bates," Chief Knowles said, and she thought he was going to get up and take her in his arms, but he didn't. He had just gotten to his feet with his cap in his hand. However, she felt the impulse had been there to take her in his arms, the desire to give her comfort was that strong on his face, although the cap in his hand gave the impulse the sanction of official duty. "We want to find the boy," he said, "we can still find the boy."

"No, you can't," she told him. "You won't even find his sweet little body."

"The boy ain't right, Harvey," Otho said, starting the tape up at the wrong place again.

"Oh, my *God,* Otho," Susan said.

"Well, Susan, he ain't," Otho insisted, justifying this second mechanical error.

"Wasn't," Susan said quietly and drifted aimlessly to the glass wall.

People were standing about in careless and immobile attitudes along the shore in inexplicable costumes, their skins slick with oil, women in black sunglasses and big straw hats, too fat and too thin and too old, bandy-legged men with bellies instead of chests looking out, as if there had been a shark warning and they were hoping for a glimpse of fin slicing the water. Rabbit Kendrick ran among them towards his house and his sad, anxious wife with all the money. He managed not to break his stride to insure looking his best for the summer girls. Susan felt a sudden contempt for men in general and Rabbit Kendrick in particular, wanting still to be God's gift. *Skinner,* she thought. The hovering helicopter and the rescue patrol boat with nobody to rescue were no concern of Rabbit's.

"Please, don't give up hope, Mrs. Bates," Harvey Knowles said in that gentle way men sometimes have, "we've succeeded many times in this kind of operation." Susan relinquished her contempt for men in general. Officer Knowles was standing beside her then, and she was grateful for his company and sorry he had decided against taking her in his arms. "I must ask you, Mrs. Bates. Why didn't you call us when you saw them swimming out like that?" he said.

"Oh, my *God!*" Susan cried, dumbfounded, and her contempt for men in general came back to her. "How could—how *could* I? They seemed so happy together. I tried to get their attention before they went into the water, but they were so happy together. They swam out and swam out without looking back to see how far out they had gone. How could I know—and I couldn't stand to watch any longer. I went upstairs to my bedroom to . . ."

"I see," Officer Knowles said, but she knew he didn't, or then again, she was wrong and he did.

"Is Jake Cullen dead?" she asked him.

"Yes," Otho said, and it was the shortest piece of tape he played all day.

"That was the least he could do," she told them. She saw him vividly then: his hair blonder than it had any right to be, standing under the moon at the corner of the deck like an apparition, and she saw herself in the deck chair with her arm over the back being as insolent as she knew how, which was plenty, and she saw him stark naked with a cigarette stuck in his mouth, falling heedlessly down the steps for another drink, and she heard the car—or rather she heard Ned Trivett's funny old car depart along the gravel drive, and she realized he had been offering himself as something beyond company in what he saw as her alienation. It was as if he had foreseen all of this and had offered himself as spiritual support here at the cathedral, so that she could give up making pictures in her mind and dividing into two women to avoid suffering. He had come out of the unexpected with the gift of sacrifice—well, not sacrifice really, because it was something he was anxious—*over*anxious—to give. And sacrifice wasn't supposed to be like that, sacrifice was supposed to be the amputation of a part of your life. *Skinner,* she thought. She wondered why there had to be so much leaving and regret and good-by and moments lost forever while you were living out your time. Salt tears caught in her lashes, and that was as far as they went. She stood up close to the glass wall, so there was a mist on the glass from her breath. Like Jubie. "What terrible mistake has that strange man made?" she asked. "God rest his lonely soul," she whispered.

"Ma'am?" Chief Petty Officer Knowles asked.

"You're not young enough to call me ma'am, Mister Knowles, why on earth do you skin your head like that?" she asked looking up at him sideways with the salt tears dry in her lashes.

Officer Knowles retreated into abashed neutrality. Not only had he been stripped of his rank, his demeanor and grooming had been called into question under extraordinary circumstances. "It's regulation," he explained to the young woman for whom he felt something more than just pity, a concern beyond duty in spite of or because of her long bony face and the rumpled bathrobe and the way she had of striking out at you for no apparent reason.

"I'm sorry," she said, "it's really very becoming. I'm not feeling. . . ." She heard somebody clambering up the back steps and down the hall into the living room.

"What the hell is going on here," Laura yelled, standing white as a sheet with her hand on her rising and falling breast. Otho stood up. "What the hell is going on here, Susan?" Laura demanded in the high, clear voice.

"I don't know, Mislark."

"You don't know Mislark!" she said contemptuously, her fragile crystal voice just short of shattering. "Otho, what are you doing here? Sit down and take off that damn cap, where is my child? *Where* is my child?" Otho sat—fell back down with his mouth open, but the tape had run out. He put his discountenanced cap on the sofa beside him again, not remembering when he had put it on. "And what are you?" she demanded of Harvey Knowles and strode into the room towards him, glaring at him with china-blue eyes, as if she could turn him to stone.

"We are doing our best to find him, Mrs.—" He canted his shoulders towards the sea slightly to introduce her to the patrol boat rising and falling among the swells and the helicopter hovering and darting and hovering again.

"Warren—Laura Warren! His mother!" she shouted. Susan went suddenly deaf, hearing nothing but a high, thin ringing in her ears, and a darkness obscured her vision, so that she could see only with difficulty and then only in dumb play. The color went out of everything. She found herself in a nightmare for which she was not responsible and from which she could not emerge by awakening into some less unfamiliar reality. She saw vaguely Laura move close to Officer Knowles, almost flat against him, glaring into his face with terrible eyes. And then, it seemed to her that Laura turned the glare on her for an instant, her mouth still saying scornful words, before jerking into a run out through the door and flying along the deck and down the steps into the sand. They watched, astonished at her headlong flight, as she flung herself through the gathering of curious people along the shore, throwing her limbs about, and not stopping until she was up to her knees in the surf.

Now, as if at a signal, a young man with startling black-fringed eyes emerged from the hall on some urgent mission and hurried through the living room and out the door without pausing and without looking at anybody in the room, but seeing Laura through the glass wall walking outward in the water with her hands on her mouth. Harvey Knowles stirred from some reverie of his own and followed the young man. They hastened without running, just under a run, along the deck and down the steps and then began to run and stumble in the sand. Officer Knowles in his crisp, regulation tans stopped at the water's edge, but the young man with the beautiful eyes waded in against a small wave and took Laura by the arms, and they fought desperately with each other in the early morning surf, until Susan saw—dim and distant—the young man, oh yes, that was Blake, Gordie Blake, probably, strike Laura on the face with the flat of his hand. Her head fell back on the stem of her throat, as though all the support had gone out of it. The cloud in which Susan stood darkened almost to completely dark. Her heart melted and her hands were feeble, her spirit fainted and her knees were weak as water. She sank to the floor. Her wide-eyed, almost smiling face didn't seem to know that. Otho Harkness stood up by the sofa, his black eyes and the exclamatory blade of hair making the very picture of alarmed concern, and came to stand over Susan, saying something she couldn't understand. He somehow persuaded—lifted—Susan into her chair. He lit a cigarette and put it in her feeble hand, and she knew enough still to be amazed that Otho Harkness would think of such a thing. He returned to the sofa to sit with his cap and observed her steadily with the curious and helpless distress of a child.

Now, the cloud thinned, but the day began to go in slow motion: even Laura's words and gestures—somehow they were all back in the house again, Laura and Officer Knowles and Blake, Gordie Blake with his startling eyes full of anger at someone or something, Otho Harkness looking desperate, trying to keep things orderly, as if he were directing traffic at a difficult intersection—which Susan knew to be quick and violent, were slow enough for her to study at her leisure. Laura was in the throes of madness, disengaged from true purpose. Looking back later, it appeared to Susan that Laura was in physical combat with first one man and then another, once even with Otho Harkness, who had long since parted company with his cap. They put her down on the sofa and she sprang back again, catapulted from a trampoline. Blake, Gordie Blake, she remembered, had taken her, still fighting, flinging her arms and legs, up the stairs in his arms and into the guest bedroom where she remained, mysteriously restrained, just long enough for Gordie to come back down into the living room, and then she came springing off another trampoline out of the bedroom door, and down the stair heedless of the steps, making quick, violent, defiant gestures. She flattened herself against the glass wall, gasping for air, but with her head resting against it in profile, not looking at the Coast Guard patrol boat idling on the swells and the helicopter swinging over in the limpid sky. But then, she sprang away from that too and ran to the telephone and picked it up and spoke contemptuous words into the mouthpiece, until Gordie took the receiver out of her hand and walked her back to the sofa again, where she would not bend to sit, only stand stiff and rebellious, starting her eyes from one stranger to another, ready to attack. All this ran slow and antic for Susan. She giggled, private in her chair.

And now, it was Julian Laura was fighting with, beating her tight,

white fists against his chest, and, Susan thought, spat into his face. Julian
didn't look like Julian. He looked like some worn and dispirited man
distantly related to Julian. He didn't seem to know Laura was struggling
against his chest or that there might be spit on his face, he just gazed
long-distance out over the top of her head at the helicopter veering sideways like a sea gull and swooping off to first one place and then another,
only to suspend there far out on the beating blades. You might have
thought the helicopter was an interesting new invention in which he had
some small personal interest.

Brother Reeves had come in behind Julian. He urged Laura away
from Julian's chest, still striking out, and supported her to the sofa again
and put her down on it firmly. This time she stayed there, folded over
forward with her forehead on her knees and her white hands resting lifeless
on the carpet, the fingers curled inward. Julian stood in the middle of
the room watching outwards still, and everybody in the room watching
Julian except Laura, who had retired from combat exhausted. Brother put
a glass in Julian's hand which Julian didn't notice for a while, but then
he lifted it and drank it off, whatever it was.

Susan began to laugh harshly from the chair, and the slow motion
machine turned off, and things returned to their normal time pattern
again, even though none of it meant very much to her. She was no part
of any of it. "Still drinking the water of affliction, are you, Julian?" she
asked in a hard voice and kept laughing until there seemed no point in
laughing any longer.

Now, "Where is that child?" Annie was shouting from the hall door.
"What have you done with that little child?" she demanded, taking them
all in with one terrible look and not liking any of them. She stood tall
and vast, blocking the doorway, taller even than Julian and as permanent
and immovable as a stone. "Oh, sweet Jesus," she said, seeing the helicopter with its bullet body and narrow sting-tail move swiftly close in
with a shattering sound as if it were strafing the shore. She surged into

the room like a mounting wave and contemplated the scene on the beach and at sea with her hands on her hips, understanding at last from beginning to end how it was, how it had all come about. She stood motionless and alien, accepting without a change on her face another great sadness and then swept the congregation with disdainful and superior contempt, swaying backwards to look down on them from a great height. "You white," she sang low and mournful. "Ain't you pitiful? Can't even take care of your own. Can't even take care of one of God's angels. Too weak and wore out and afflicted with your own selfs to make the sacrifice to save one sweet life." She studied them one at a time, and not one of them could look into the wrath of her darkening face. She paused, calling the roll of the damned, until Gordie Blake dared to look up into the black light of her unforgiving and forbidding eyes. "You, boy," she said to the Stage Manager, "you don't look like you belongs here. Help me with this poor creature, she ain't doing herself or nobody else no good flung down on the sofa in this house. Come on here, boy, whoever you is," she said to Gordie, "help me get her back home where she ought to been all along." She moved to the sofa and took Laura roughly by the arms, lifting her to her feet. Laura's head fell back again on the long, unsupporting stem of her throat, and she collapsed against Annie's breast. "Lark!" Annie shouted and glanced fierce-eyed at Gordie, who awoke suddenly and came swiftly to her aid. "Lark, come on now, stand up like the woman you ain't never been. Take that other arm, boy," she commanded.

"I'll take her home," Gordie said.

"No, you ain't," Annie said. "You help her into my car and go on back to where you come from. Annie Davison is taking her home," she said, "but it's the last time I'll take her anywhere. Ain't no reason to bother with her no more, I done all I could and what for? This is the last time I wants to see any of you pitiful creatures," she announced to the solemn and silent gathering. "I have throwed away my mean old life stepping after you. Stay with your own kind, the Lord say, and from now on, Mrs. Annie Davison will mind his word, late as it is."

The fire of rage had left Laura lifeless. Gordie put his arm around her waist and rested her limp, white arm over his shoulder and walked with her as if she were the life-size rag doll for a vaudeville comic dance act hanging against him through the door and down the hall. "How come you let the child die?" Annie asked them all, and nobody could answer. "Somebody put something into Mister Julian Warren's glass," she said. "He don't know how to run his life without it," and she left, and they knew it was for the last time. They all knew that definitely, including Chief Petty Officer Knowles, who was feeling he should not have seen what happened here. Annie Davison had confounded the moon and shamed the sun, and they would never rise nor set the same again.

Susan didn't care that much. She had seen the end of a number of things in the last few days. *Skinner,* she thought. And then she saw clearly that Skinner would not have cared in the least that Jubie was lost or not lost. He had never considered Jubie considerable, one way or another, hadn't seemed to be aware of him—hadn't looked at him even, when the two of them were left alone in a room together and Jubie had made an appeal for his attention. At that moment, she understood he had been an utter stranger all along. She had played the harlot with an utter stranger, but she couldn't regret that. It had been her time to play the harlot, and destiny had chosen her lover.

Through the scattering mist of memory, she saw from a distance the indolent figure of a man who seemed to have been waiting for her to pass. He smiled at her, a half-smoked cigarette clamped in his teeth. He had come out of nowhere wearing a faded vest hanging open on his sun-dark chest and a stained, bandless panama hat. But that was enough. Skinner died in her mind. One utter stranger died, but another was always living careless somewhere against the tide of death. A son lost to the sea and a lover lost to dreadful hope were never replaced, they were woven into the fabric. But desire could project life onward, if you were restless and beautiful and the harlot lived somewhere in your heart.

She smiled back at the indolent man. No. She smiled back at the possibility of smiling back at the indolent man.

Now, the rest of the day ran its course like a dream, until at last she and Brother were standing on the deck together, under the confounded moon and forgetful stars, watching the ocean claim its own and move without rest according to its natural instruction. The useless rescue operations had been suspended for the night, and people in their houses along the strand discussed at dinner tables about the Warren child and the man who had probably been a movie star. Rabbit Kendrick's wife was crying. Mrs. Stanley, wearing her green eye-shade under the harsh light on her screen porch, bid two spades at the bridge table, and her raggedy white dog slept at her feet.

Susan stood smoking in her nightgown and bathrobe. Brother, serious and refreshed at her side, didn't seem to need to breathe. The harlot and the soldier, still on watch, took their ease while they could.

"Maybe he'll sleep," Brother said after they had rested for a while. "I put the bottle on the table by his bed, and he got up and locked the door. He ain't got nowhere to go, Susan. He can't go back to that place he's been staying at."

"Poor old Mister Jukes," she said. "He'll never understand, and so he'll have to be on duty for the rest of his life, drunk or sober, probably drunk. Poor little Mister Jukes." Brother understood that. He turned to hear the rest of what she had to say, so she would have somebody to say it to. "In everybody ever born in the world, no matter what it looks like, there's somebody fighting to get out. I guess Jubie made it," she said.

"That makes two made it out in one day," Brother said.

"Yes," Susan said, and Brother loved her very much.

CHAPTER TWENTY-FIVE

Via degli Scipioni, 32
Roma, Italia
10 July

Dear Julian Warren,

I'm mad as fire. No, I take that back, it's worse than that. I've backed up from being mad as fire to being frantic, from the smoke to the smother, so to speak. Here it is ten o'clock Sunday morning with the church bells ringing all over Rome, and here I am sitting at my desk by the window in what used to be my library with a vodka in one hand and my pen in the other, writing to you of all people, probably the next to the last person on earth I ever expected to be writing to. That ought to give you some idea. To get right down to the quick of all this—somebody has got to come to my rescue. Somebody has got to save what is left of my sanity, to say nothing of my bank account, which is considerable but finite.

I think I ought to tell you right off the bat it's against my nature to run for help when the chips are down. All my life, before and since I was driven from my ancestral home in Mobile Alabama, I have picked up my own chips or let them fall where they might, depending on the situation. But this is different. You would have to see it to believe it. I realized just past dawn this morning, when the last uninvited guest left my premises, it was time for me to run for cover, sound the alarm—something. Anything! I have lost all control of the situation here. And although I understand what your feelings towards me must be as a result of certain unorthodox actions I have taken in regard to your ex-business partner and cousin by marriage, one Skinner Bates, you have turned out to be my last hope for cover to run for and the only person who might heed my alarm.

Ordinarily, I would have appealed to my once-loyal, ex-friend, Ned Trivett, an acquaintance of yours I believe—possibly even another cousin by marriage but certainly not his. However, Ned Trivett and I are no longer on speaking terms since he evicted me from his tiny house, bag and baggage of which there was plenty, and no place to go except to what is known as a motel for godsake, and because of his unreasonable and vindictive resentment of the unorthodox actions mentioned above. It astonishes me that he should care, he never has before. As a matter of fact, there was a time when the two of us   well, never mind that for now. We can go into all of that when I see you which I hope will be sooner than you might have thought.

Understand, Mr. Warren, I offer no apology to you or Mrs. Bates or Trivett or anybody else for what I have seen fit to do—although God knows I have had grievous cause to regret it. My intention was to save two lives at a stroke and—do confess—to enjoy the companionship of a charming young man as a sort of agreeable byproduct. I must admit here to having been for some time in the flux of a kind of crise d'amour, if you know what I mean, due to recent and tragic events in my own life, and at such times, a young man who is lost and needs finding is particularly appealing. Or rather, one who seems to need desperately to find something or someone he has lost, or both of the above. I was sadly mistaken. Never a good deed goes unpunished, as the saying goes.

Be that as it may, Mr. Warren, you are elected. Although from what I am told, you must get tired of being voted into this kind of office. My urgent plea is catch the next flight for Rome Italy, Mr. Warren. Skinner Bates is already in the *hands of the receivers and I am next in line. I am a woman alone, Mr. Warren, and I can see the vultures circling. My friends ha! ha! have abandoned me, and my resistance is low. I haven't closed my eyes for days.*

Skinner Bates is for the time being thank God upstairs dead to the world in drunken slumber following an interminable night of merry-making consultation with—what shall I call them?—his newfound business associates. Ha! ha! Mr. Warren, that's a good one! My house is a shambles, you would think there had been an earthquake very high on the Richter scale—toilet paper strewn everywhere, upstairs and down, but I couldn't even begin to explain that here—and the maids have quit or decided to go into show business, and this usually select and tranquil neighborhood is up in arms. I can see them standing in their windows from where I sit, staring at my house. Have you ever seen an enraged Italian stare, Mr. Warren? I tell you it will freeze the blood in your veins. I can only fall to my knees and pray they don't denounce me. Denunciation in Rome is no laughing matter. It used to be called revenge. They don't have those glittery black eyes for nothing, Mr. Warren. Oh my God, I'm fit to be tied.

Mr. Warren, I know the party in question holds you in the highest regard from the way he speaks your name and since, when I was putting away his suitcases, I found a snapshot of you on the beach in your bathing suit—what a shame we didn't meet before I was driven out of Milford. And I must tell you this. In the same suitcase, I found a receipt for the closing out of a joint bank account in the names of Skinner and Susan Johnson Bates. At the time, I was shocked by this revelation, but I am shocked no longer from sad experience. The party in question regards money as most people regard oxygen—free for the breathing and his just reward for having been born among us. As we both know, such is not the case. Moving up in the world, as he is wont to call it, is not just a matter of grab as grab can, now is it, Mr. Warren?

Anyhow, Mr. Warren—Julian, may I call you Julian? and, please, do call me Graziella. No, on the other hand, you'd better call me Gray. Anyhow, Julian, while I was staying with Ned Trivett (alas!) in Milford, I made the dreadful, possibly even catastrophic mistake of inviting Skinner Bates to visit me here in Italy. It seemed such a good idea at the time. But then, he had all the earmarks of being in a disturbed state of mind, to say the very least, and no one to turn to for succor. Besides, he is charming and everything else, as you may or may not have heard. At any rate, let me assure you he is. I even admit to this vision of myself running through my vineyards in Grecian veils, like Syrinx fleeing Pan. But (alas! again) such was not to be the case. It may be a woman of a certain age doesn't get to do much fleeing—although I most assuredly am not all that much older, for heaven sake. Do you know what a collapsing star is, Julian   well, never mind that for now. We can go into all of that when I see you which I hope will be sooner than you might have thought. But, Julian, nobody is all that charming.

    He arrived here with his suitcases full of Brooks Brothers shirts and hundreds of pairs of rolled up socks—what does he do with them all?—and the lovely, really quite charming snapshot of you, and the famous bank receipt. And that's when it all started. That was about the last I saw of his charm or anything else until around four in the morning for many days.

    I gather he spent his days and nights wandering the crooked alleys of Trastevere alone, presumably, searching for your brother of whom he seems to have been inordinately fond. Your brother, according to reliable report, vanished out of a window without a trace, leaving behind him a very strange history and a number of even stranger friends. I sincerely hope I am not the first to bring you news of these mysterious events oh my God, Julian, you should see the woman staring at me across the court now. Her eyes are like thunderbolts and she is just standing there stock still in the window like doom, as if she were a stakeout and has to make a report or something to headquarters.

    Do you see what I mean, Julian? I have had to draw the curtains and get myself another vodka. I understand now why they used to call it nerve medicine back in Mobile. I sometimes wish I were back in Mobile but not really.

    Chief among your brother's friends, also inordinately fond of him—what did or does the boy have? do let's hope we haven't seen the last of him—and now chief among Skinner Bates' friends is one Nico Milas, a second-rate Italian movie

star—*actually Greek, if you ask me—who has had considerable financial success
entertaining the maids and juvenile delinquents of this country by way of the silver
screen. I, for one, have never had the pleasure of seeing one of Mr. Milas' films.
I am told they are diverting. And now, to my dismay and consternation, not
satisfied with grinding the faces of the poor and ignorant as an entertainer, he has
suddenly metamorphosed into a screen writer and director. Think of that! And
your ex-real estate business partner and ex-cousin by marriage has even more
suddenly metamorphosed into—guess what!—a film producer. How's that for
moving up in the world? The two of them are thick as thieves, to coin an unfortunate phrase. Having been granted the privilege of reading one of Mr. Milas'
scripts, I should strongly advise, if asked and I won't be, that he stick to being a
spaghetti cowboy, or whatever it is they call them in show business. To say his
vision of the world is grotesque is begging the question. To say it is sick and obscene
is nearer the mark. Mr. Milas seems to have no patience at all with the general
enthusiasm for coupling exclusively with members of the opposite sex. In spite of
which, I think it only fair to report he has a devoted wife. I know very little
about her except that she has an endless wardrobe of alarming jewelry and in-
numerable fur coats fashioned from the skins of beasts fast disappearing from the
face of the earth. This information I have gleaned from pictures of her in newspapers
and magazines. She looks to be a vivid woman. Nonetheless, she has not been
present at the business conferences held here in what used to be my library but is
now referred to as The Office—forget about the signed eighteenth-century French
chairs and glorious Fortuny fabrics.*

    *I wondered for a time what my role, if any, might be in this thrilling
enterprise, aside from that of captive landlord and head maid. I wasn't to wonder
for long. As I recall, the money from the famous joint savings account was not
inconsiderable, but it was only just enough to get you-know-who set up as producer,
if you please—as the producer of Mr. Milas' nightmare extravaganzas. My role,
as it turns out, is an important one. It appears I am expected to come up with
the funds to back this venture and consider myself fortunate to be associated with
such geniuses. I won't and don't. I am a rich woman, Julian, as the result of the*

death of my late husband the prince, God rest his soul. However, I am not so rich and certainly not such a fool as to get myself tied up with this wild project and with these people who

Lord God! Just now a telephone call from the woman across the court with the thunderbolt eyes informing me she had been kept awake all night. I informed her I hadn't slept for weeks which didn't seem to diminish her fury. Thank God and my beloved husband the prince for my title—which here in Italy is some small protection—and thank God for nerve medicine. You do see what I mean, Julian.

Let's see now. Oh, yes. No, I certainly am not going to get myself involved with this wild project, but I get the feeling, like it or not, I am involved, that I have nothing to say in the matter. There is this assumption that I have no choice, I can't explain it. I am a prisoner on my own property. My house here in Rome and my place in the country have been taken over lock stock and barrel by strays from the Italian film industry.

Oh, Julian, Julian, I am in fear and trembling every time the bell rings, not knowing whether the maid—that is, when I have a maid—will usher in a thief or a dope fiend or some scraggy wisp of a boy with a beat-up guitar he can't even play. They tell me he writes music, well you could have fooled me. You should see him, Julian, he has the bruisey white skin and smudge blue eyes of Britain and the lank hair of an Alabama mill hand and not a word of English. Sweet and thirsty, poor creature, and God knows he could do with a good meal and God knows he gets it. Or a bevy of doe-eyed starlets who sit around in bovine silence grazing through my chocolates all night and do nothing but change the record on the Victrola and turn up the volume again after I have just that minute turned it back down. And a doe-eyed ex-bullfighter about to turn movie idol to hear him tell it and a tall, thin, doe-eyed personage with a long nose and little hair whose sole function is to sip cognac and look elegant which he does very well indeed, I must say. Everybody is either doe-eyed or ex-something or both. And another one. This Angelo (doe-eyed and an ex-nothing) who hasn't a shirt with buttons to his name or a pair of trousers which aren't several sizes too small for him. There's a whole lot of Angelo and don't you forget it. And, oh yes, an underground group, they say they are, and I do hope so. My sentiments are the deeper the better.

Oh, Julian, Julian, there's much more, but you would have to see what goes on here to believe it. They all gather at the beck of Signor Milas who is more hypnotist than actor. The boy missed his calling. Every now and then he has almost convinced me, and the producer smiles up into his dark face. His conviction stops the world in its tracks. There are no days, there are no hours, time doesn't register anymore. It turns dark, it turns light, but what has that got to do with anything? It's as if everything is about to catch fire. I can smell the smoke. Au secours! Au secours!

Well! And in the midst of all this confusion, Julian, bright-eyed and dazed, there's Skinner, speaking in tongues—words from somewhere else like a ventriloquist's dummy. He's no more the person I thought I had met in North Carolina than you would be, were I to meet you now. And I feel sure Mrs. Bates would have trouble recognizing him too, although I think the man who left her to come with me was not the man she married. So now, he's twice removed and removing further. It's as though his own soul had departed at some point and been replaced with the soul of an obsessed and vulnerable brother. He is on a collision course, talking loud and feverish about things foreign to his birth and his birthplace and believing them, Julian. Locked up here in the library hour after hour, being told by all those others he is something other than he is, using him to get to me to entice me into bankruptcy. And the boy was born to entice.

That, in the end, is the terrifying thing. Have you ever opened your bedroom door to discover a stranger in a friend's body, Julian? I have. And two times in one life is too many. Have you ever opened your library door to find your friend lying, easy and laughing, on the arm of another man, Julian? I have. And one time in one life is too many.

And so you can imagine all this talk of hundreds of thousands of my dollars and, Julian, his smile when I pass him in the halls that isn't a smile at all—

as if I were a body representing a means to an end that doesn't really matter—and lying down on the bed together at dawn with nothing to say or nothing to do but stare at the ceiling and maybe sometimes say good night and sometimes not, you can understand I am living with dread.

If I can survive this nightmare and get these vampires out of my life and get him into stronger and more capable hands than mine, maybe I can go back to the way I was living before, which wasn't much. But it was what I had come to at last and it was fairly safe. It has taken a long time to be fairly safe, where there is no need to move on again and no thunderbolt eyes with the threat of denunciation staring at my house and ringing the telephone full of hate and even death.

You must understand, Julian, in a way, I am what Skinner Bates is. The woman you see is not the woman in fact. I put on this show the way you light a lantern in the dark. It is my destiny and my obligation and I do it because I must and because I've got the daring. I believe it gets me what I want sometimes when I know what that is, and I believe it keeps me alive and determined and looking for what they say love is which it actually is not.

The difference is I know that. I choose to live the way I live even though it leaves me lonesome as a dog most of the time. We all of us pay the price for the life we choose to live, don't we, Julian? His is a spirit disembodied, gone astray. He is reaching for something that doesn't exist. I was reaching for a dream from the past when I saw him, for a warm and golden memory which was a terrible mistake and has brought me to this fearful situation.

I must close now. The party in question has just passed through my library—excuse me, The Office—on his way to the refrigerator in his customary morning costume. His skin. Doesn't Brooks Brothers make bathrobes? Goodness knows, under different circumstances I wouldn't complain, but it has come to that point where all the charm and everything else can no longer break my heart.

Well, Julian, I tried to save Skinner Bates' life and indirectly Mrs. Skinner Bates' life—granted for reasons other than the milk of human kindness—and now I ask you to do the same for me, for both of us.

The entire import of this letter can be put into one word.
HELP!

Graziella di Brabant

P.S. I am told that Mrs. Warren has left you for a life on the stage. I am very sorry, Julian. However, the idea that you have the talent to explain something to suffering humanity is an incurable disease which is certainly a credit to the species. Anyhow, we all have our little ways, don't we?

P.S. You will, of course, stay with me when you come to Rome, if, that is, ruin has not set in and my house is still my own. Please, give my regards to Brother Reeves. As for N. Trivett—well, never mind that for now.

CHAPTER TWENTY-SIX

In the sweet, fresh dawn of the day of memorial services for Jubie Warren and of the consignment of Jake Cullen's flesh and bone to the white flames of cremation, sweet, fresh-faced boys pitched the *Milford Morning Herald* onto porches all over town. Rising high to the pitch on the silver-spoked wheels of their bicycles, they had neither the time nor the inclination to glance at the flash picture on the front page of (from left to right) Nico Milas, actor, Princess Graziella di Brabant, a recent visitor to the city, both of Rome, Italy, and Skinner Bates, prominent Milford Realtor. (See story on page 6-A.) Nor did they pause in their flight among the leafy trees to consider SEARCH FOR MISSING YOUTH ABANDONED near the bottom of the same page, an account of circumstances surrounding the disappearance at sea of Julian Johnson Warren, Jr., age 8, son of Mr. and Mrs. Julian J. Warren, and the reluctant decision to suspend search and rescue operations. Memorial Services will be held at the home of Mrs. Warren, 814 Ransom Place, at

11 o'clock this morning. Friends of the family are requested not to send flowers.

"How come they ain't?" Annie Davison asked her husband.

The paparazzo's strobe camera had done small credit to Skinner Bates' dinner companions at the fashionable Elephant Restaurant in Rome Italy where they had gone to announce plans for a new film to be produced by Mr. Bates. The princess had been fast-frozen in what appeared to be a state of high fury, her eyes flared wide and her dark painted lips drawn back from her teeth, making what was either a terrific hiss or an obscene word. Mr. Milas was frowning with his mouth pushed forward in a profound sulk. Mr. Bates, on the other hand, looked to be blissfully happy leaning on the table on his elbows, smiling broadly into the camera.

"See story on page six-A," Annie Davison read out to her husband, "let's see what kind of story Mister Skinner Bates got this time to puff hisself up where he ain't meant to be . . ."

Citizens all over town, recovering from sleep, leaned out onto the porches in their bathrobes and took in the *Morning Herald* to morning coffee. Most of them were indifferent to or even offended by the flash photograph and didn't bother to turn to page 6-A. A majority were sorry for Mr. and Mrs. Warren and asked each other why such a terrible tragedy should strike such fine people.

At 11:00 A.M., thirty or forty people were easy-strolling in the dust of the balding, shady yard at 814 Ransom Place to pay their respects—probably last respects—to an unfortunate prince of the realm. They passed up the broad steps and across the gallery into cool rooms through tall double doors and sat around on rented folding chairs as if they had dropped by for morning coffee, taking up talk exactly where they had left off last time they had seen each other. Some of the talk had been funny, and they had laughed. There were no hats and no gloves and only one wheelchair with Caleb Johnson in it looking like an aged Sicilian thief. There was only one black dress, and crazy Sophie Talbert was wearing that as usual. The black lawn dress, come down from her mother and possibly even her grandmother, had seen a lot of use in Sophie's hectic life, familiar as she was with death and absence, since she was at least second cousin to almost everybody in the county and attended funerals with joyous grief. These were the only social occasions at which her dramatic, saucer-eyed presence was acceptable—acceptable in spite of the fact that she could not be restrained from repeating the prayers and scripture readings one split second in retard along with Reverend Wister, so that he had thought in his early days that there was a vivid and insistent echo in the chapel and would return to the parsonage with a violent migraine. He had since learned the eccentric rhythms of Sophie's delivery. Consequently, they had been more or less in unison for some years. "Neither death, nor life, nor angels, nor principalities, nor things present, nor things to come, nor powers, nor height, nor depth, nor anything else in all creation, will be able to separate us from the love of God in Christ Jesus Our Lord," Reverend Wister intoned standing before the marble fireplace under the mirror with the gold pineapple and bananas around it. "Amen!" Sophie hollered. It was one of their favorite passages.

At 2:00 P.M., Reverend Wister, Ned Trivett, Brother Reeves, and Susan Johnson Bates were gathered reverently around the wooden box containing the earthly remains of Jake Cullen in the chapel of the Thigpen Funeral Home. The Reverend had just finished delivering an uncomfortable and fragmentary eulogy followed by prayer. "Amen," they all murmured. The four of them looked harried and worn, having attended two unconventional and wounding religious rituals in one day. Susan could see that Ned Trivett was devastated. Nonetheless, he rose to the occasion. "I was present at the resurrection and am present now at a second death," he said, splaying his fingers out on the wooden coffin lid. "Perhaps he is sitting in the Presence of God at last. God will find in him a charitable heart and wonderful company indeed."

Susan was puzzled by this statement. She thought he had gone slightly balmy from the shock and wondered what she might say to comfort him or even to bring him to himself. Reverend Wister scented heresy in view of what he had heard of the circumstances, but he did his best to reserve judgment. Brother stood in a private silence, looking straight out as if he were witnessing some inexpressibly sad occurrence in the distance. They all of them went home to ponder. Immediately thereafter, the wooden box was removed to the white flames.

But that day went by and was over with, thank God, and then unnumbered days went by and they were all over with as well, and in the process, time drew up at a day which for some reason had the feeling of resolution about it, looking back some six or seven months later. The fever of summer and the anxiety of fall had reduced to what passed for winter. Nobody liked it much. Milford isn't meant for winter, they always said. Then paper boys had to circle among the black and leafless trees in the dark, disappearing like spirits into the luminous fog that sometimes rolled in from the sea, and the newspapers they had pitched last summer yellowed and were forgotten in closets and basements or were hauled away on trucks to be shredded and recycled and brought back again to herald other current events. Current events kept happening at more or less the usual pace, some of them remarkable, some of them probably not, some of them carried in the *Milford Morning Herald,* some not.

In the spring-conditioned air of her fine house, Evelyn Black was trying the action of her new parlor grand piano with the distant and unacknowledged thought of maybe going back into show business. The marine biologist had left off resting in her tent to recline in the curve of the piano's back and listen with awe to Miss Evelyn's ragtime rendition of a prelude by Serge Rachmaninoff.

Miss Lilly Atkins, the oldest living resident of the oldest family in Milford, N.C., breathed her last without knowing the difference. Her staunch kinswomen couldn't believe their luck.

Dorothy Bender, chopping onions in her steamy kitchen, was a remarkable woman. The value of her property was rising obscenely from
one day to the next, but she took no notice. However, a plaintive train
whistle in the distance reminded her pleasantly of Mr. Bender's absence,
God rest his soul.

Rabbit Kendrick, his libido cast many months forward to the arrival
of the summer girls, leapt along the shore in spite of the dismal weather.
He passed Mrs. Stanley's raggedy little white dog coming from the other
direction.

Mrs. Stanley, wearing her green eye-shade, bid two no-trump.

Millicent Kendrick was crying on the telephone to her mother who
told her to pack her bags and leave the son of a bitch, all he ever wanted
was your money anyhow. Millicent had no intention of leaving Rabbit
ever.

Annie Davison was spending a painful and awesome afternoon in
her kitchen with her grandson Robert. Robert was nine years old and took
full advantage. He hadn't seen fit to stop talking for a second until just
now. Annie studied his back with reverence and suspicion as he stood at
the window watching the fog move in. "Where Jubie at, Grandma?" he
asked her turning his face suddenly to watch the answer on her face. "Jubie
in the arms of sweet Jesus now, Robert," Annie answered. "Oh," Robert
said, "do Jubie know sweet Jesus too?" Annie's hope for the glorious future
of mankind increased dramatically.

Forty miles away in Grover, Doris Ann Hawkins was locked in her
bedroom writing a letter to Mr. Brother Reeves, Radio Road, Milford,
N.C., informing him that she was with child and that the child was his
beyond question. It took her two hours to get the letter exactly right, but
she never mailed it. However, she did mail a letter to Mr. Gordon Blake,
134 E. 22d St., New York, N.Y., regretting she could not accept the
position of assistant stage manager he had offered her for the upcoming

season of the Bladens Beach Playhouse. Her father, she wrote, had turned against show business.

DALLAS—A 15-year-old youth dressed in a wig and fur coat gained the release of his 13-year-old brother from the Dallas County juvenile detention home by posing as his mother, officials say.

Embarrassed officials admitted the episode Wednesday and said the 13-year-old was back at the detention home.

NEW YORK CITY—Mrs. Henrietta Worth, ex-telephone operator, had left David Worth's Third Avenue apartment under cover of darkness, taking her portable sewing machine with her. It was the only wedding gift she considered her own, married or unmarried. She was boarding the day coach from Pennsylvania Station for Bladens Beach, N.C., convinced that David Worth was stunning to look upon and God's gift to the acting profession but wearing on the nerves and that marriage was not what she had had in mind at the time anyway.

NEW YORK CITY—On Central Park West, Gordie Blake was helping Madelyn Haskins make plans for yet another triumphal foray on the summer circuit. "Should I do another Noel Coward this season?" she consulted Gordie, but decided, "No, I think not, I don't think I could stand another year of dear Noel, how about Blanche?" "How about Amanda?" Gordie suggested. "Amanda," Madelyn mused and glanced at herself in the mirror. "Or maybe I won't tour at all this summer," she said. "You'll tour," Gordie said.

SARASOTA—Luis Lopez in canary yellow leotards with a broad belt of flashing brilliants soared high up into the top of the tent, soared backwards downwards and back upwards folding almost double at the apex, soared forward downwards again and upwards even higher among the rigging, disappearing into the shadow, and flung himself from his trapeze into three tight somersaults and falling, opening out like a thrown cat, found and gripped the miraculous taped wrists of his brother and swung forward again in his brother's care in a swift downward arc and back up into a high midair pirouette onto his trapeze, come back to meet him. When his sister, also in canary yellow, caught him up beside her onto the landing platform, he had on his face the vague smile and distant eyes of a man who has flown into eternity.

ALGIERS—Dick Harteman, his stained, bandless panama hat pulled down over one eye and his faded vest hanging open exposing his bare chest, was punching a needle into the vein on the inside of his elbow. He rubbed his arm vigorously and lit a cigarette. He had on his face the vague smile and distant eyes of a man who has flown into eternity. The woman beside him on the unmade bed was naked and asleep.

ROME ITALY—Skinner Bates, after an exhausting day of wandering the crooked alleys of Trastevere alone, was discussing plans for a new cinematic production company with the brilliant and irrepressible Malvina Steinert for whom he had abandoned the Princess Graziella di Brabant. Malvina smiled but did not respond. Malvina owned a house in Beverly Hills with an attended gate.

Just across the Tiber River in Prati, Grace Jamison, vastly relieved to have been abandoned once again, was dressing to go to a party at which, she was aware, everybody would detest her, but never mind, honey, she was a collapsing star. All her clocks had come to a full stop and the firmament was the limit.

MILFORD—Julian Warren was packing his father's exhausted leather grip bound with buckled straps for yet another pilgrimage to the Eternal City. It was his mission to seek out family and friends for whose care and protection and retrievement he was convinced he had inherited the responsibility. He was still testing the waters of affliction.

MILFORD—In the drawer of his desk, Ned Trivett's passport expired without his noticing. He and Brother Reeves and Father Elvin Flowers, Pastor of St. Matthews Catholic Church, were sitting on the tiny front porch of the house on Hooper Street having a glass of sherry. A seasonal fog had moved in from the sound and the lamps were burning in all the rooms, so that the tiny house looked like a lantern set down among the bare trees by a lost pilgrim. Visibility was practically zero, which they didn't mind in the least. It enclosed the three of them in a soft and mysterious cloud, eradicating time and conducive to the speculation under way.

Father Flowers laughed merrily. He was delighted to be in such compatible company, having grown weary of solitude in this odd little town where a Catholic priest, or even a devout Catholic, was looked upon as a member of a foreign cult with secret and possibly unspeakable beliefs and rituals. "Let me say, Ned, I think we cannot think of Mister Cullen as in any way a saint," he said in his pleasant, counter-tenor voice. "After all, he took upon himself the responsibility not only for his own death but for the death of another human being as well, and both these things, on the face of it, are terrible sins. Be that as it may, I am sure he was a splendid man with the very best of intentions."

"No, sir," Brother Reeves said and put his glass of sherry on the porch bannister. "That ain't what it was. He and Jubie just went in the water together and swam out too far till they was drowned. Jake didn't kill nobody, not hisself and not Jubie and not nobody else."

"I see," Father Flowers said and felt that was as far as that should go. He was wary of this handsome young man who found it difficult to call him Father, having spent his life toiling in the hard Protestant soil.

"Then, if he isn't a saint, he is definitely an angel. Certainly, you could let him be an angel, Father," Ned said. "Don't you agree he might pass muster as an angel?—although he would have scorned such a thought."

"Well, that isn't for me to say, of course," Father Flowers said, giving comfort, "however, we know, don't we, that there are sinful angels?"

"Ah, well yes, Jake was undeniably sinful," Ned explained, "but his sins were of the most delightful and considerate kind—having to do, for the most part, with the flesh."

"I see," Elvin Flowers said again, feeling he had made no progress whatsoever in his instruction of Ned Trivett.

"Oh, Father, Jake was so full of light. I feel sure he is among God's angels," Ned insisted. "I found out through him finally and definitely that we are in the possession of some presence which exceeds ourselves. I know that now because of him, and I believe that not because I have been told to believe it, but because it is what I feel I must believe."

"Well, that won't do, Trivett," the young priest said, beginning to lose his ease. "It isn't all incense and Latin and Palestrina, you know. We're going to have to do better than that, if you are to be received into the church—and certainly, if we are to think about ordination in the future, as you have mentioned not once but many times." He left off abruptly, hearing his voice begin to rise in register which he knew to be a sign of rising vexation, and he did not want to lose this amiable afternoon to grim duty. "Or, perhaps," he amended, "that could be what we call the Will to Faith. Yes, that could very well be—"

"Jake couldn't help hisself," Brother interrupted, "and he went around trying his best to help God out."

"I see," Father Flowers concluded.

There had been a determination and a reproof in Brother's voice that warned he would not abide criticism of his friend by any measure other than the love of him. Ned and Father Flowers felt that this was as good a way to put it as any . . .

. . . while at the same time on the other side of the sound, it was beautiful indeed watching the leaden winter sea pitch and roll and spume, and it was exhilarating feeling the icy salt mist blown by an irrational and stinging wind into their faces—well, not so much a wind as a chilly, moist bluster moving restlessly over the water up onto the land and among the houses with the lamps already burning in the middle of the afternoon. The two women were bundled up in heavy sweaters in Susan's summer chairs like children with an overly-conscientious nurse. They gave the house and the deck the aspect of a ski lodge or maybe even more of an ocean liner making a crossing in bad weather. Laurie was wearing a red knit hat with a white ball at the peak pulled down on her forehead and a woolen scarf wound a time or two about her throat, so that there was nothing but a pale triangle of face with china-blue eyes to identify her.

A moment earlier, Susan had struggled to her feet to lift the fast-closed umbrella from its stand through the round metal table at her shoulder and put it away in a protected corner of the deck. It had seemed so captive and miserable shuddering in the relentless movement of the air like that. Ridiculous to open it now, as she recalled having done on other occasions to elevate the emotions and the bleak seascape. The great glass wall of her small cathedral house was rimed and runneled with salt spray. She lay back down in her chair and attempted to curve her arm over the back, as was her custom, but failed. She sighed (sigh). Laurie reclining alongside her (sigh) returned the favor. Susan sat up with some effort and adjusted her sweaters irritably and anchored the pins in her hair at the crown of her head and did her best to light a cigarette and failed at that too and fell back in her chair again (sigh). And sighed. Laurie (sigh) returned the favor again—rather too quickly, Susan thought. They regarded each other, blue eyes and green eyes clear and amused and then more amused, and then gave over to giggling which opened out into light laughter. Oh, what the hell, it was all very romantic facing the elements and very good for the skin and a fine cure for an ailing soul, they felt sure. However, it was chilly and damp and not all that much fun. The Pioneer Spirit had thinned and vanished over the generations. Dutiful discomfort had given away to psychic distress, as is the way with advancing civilization.

"I've had about enough of this shit," Laurie said, quoting some apprentices she had known last summer, and more girlish laughter shot out against the wind at that and was blown back into a bemused and lengthy silence.

"It has just occurred to me we are women without men," Susan remarked, "and why do you suppose that is?" Women Without Men.

"Fuck men," Laura said, quoting most women, and the women without men laughed together against the wind again, pleased with Lark's discovery that unacceptable words were a quick way to short answers and temporary satisfaction. They were a counterbalance to her fragility. It was strange, she thought, how they could make for a kind of courage under fire. She realized why some men liked them so much, men were not really the courageous soldiers they thought they were—or pretended to each other they thought they were. Men were only boys cursing against the night like everybody else, after all. Anyhow, that's what she felt.

She gazed out to sea for too long a time, and Susan knew from the intensity of the small, white triangle of face that it was too soon to suggest leaving the deck. They had withheld comment on the unfortunate and fortunate sequence of their lives for all these months now and no sign of grief except to come upon each other weeping alone now and then. Laura had taken up a kind of feeble attempt at living through the days consuming more courage than her frail spirit could spare. Watching her now, Susan felt the time may have come at last for the two of them to release the stricken bird from its cage, so to speak, so that what happened and failed to happen was not pain nurtured in the heart but tragedy accepted and survived. The flight of the bird set free might anchor Laura more firmly to the earth. Anyhow, that's what she felt.

"What is it, Lark?" she asked.

"I don't know, I don't know," Laura said and turned her face away from the sea which she had regarded for almost long enough to have forgotten where she was and turned back to Susan again. "I guess I'll never be a great actress after all," she said. The earnestness of the little peak of a face with the knit cap pulled down too tight on the forehead was so childlike and absurd and the sad appeal for reassurance so naive that Susan had to resist another laugh. She felt the sudden impulse to motherhood.

"Oh, Lark, you know better than that," the long-faced mother with stringy hair stretched back from her temples said, searching for just the right words for reassurance. "You already *are* a great actress. Not any— not *any*body could have acted that pitiful girl Alma any better than you did. Everybody said so. You already *are* a great actress," she insisted. "Besides, there is still plenty of time to—"

"Don't comfort me, Susan, I hate being comforted," Laura said, and they paused briefly to allow the comfort in the air to dispel. "I *did* have to try to die to do it that way," she took up again, indulging herself with the thought that she had risked her own life in order to create Alma Winemiller's. "I wonder why it matters to me so much," she said.

"Sometimes, it's the only available means of transportation," Susan said, quoting an old friend.

Alma Winemiller's china-blue eyes widened with surprise. "Oh, my Lord, Missook, I'm so glad you said that. Transportation, that's exactly what it is. For that remark, I'm glad we came out here." She cast a light laugh of relief on the wind.

They huddled down in the deck chairs, folding their arms across their breasts in the clumsy garments, and retreated into a miasma of consideration, surveying, each in her own way, the near and distant past. "The things we do to survive life this side of dying," Laura said, surfacing, and again Susan was struck by the depth of the appeal coming from the bloodless mouth of this wayward child of hers.

"Life is an arrest warrant," she declared, quoting herself, "so you damn well better learn to love the sheriff," she finished, surprising even herself with this latter half of the wisdom.

Laura examined the precise profile of her constant companion with undisguised admiration. "Why, that makes the second time in one afternoon I'm glad we're here," she said.

"I think you would find me invaluable company," Susan said, further quoting an old friend. It seemed to her somehow she was living in quotes.

"Now, just what in hell does that mean?" Mislark said struggling up on one elbow and looking at Susan with tempered anxiety, as if she might have found her replaced by a stranger. "What in hell do you mean by that, Susan? I have *always* found you invaluable com—"

"And a chest of inestimable value that has surfaced from the wreck of an ancient and beautiful sailing ship, only the locks have rusted shut," Susan quoted on, looking out toward where she had lost a son to the sea and a lover to the wars. "Proof that the treasure is still there."

"What on earth (gasp), what on *earth* has possessed you, Susan?" Laura asked, thinking it must be high time they got in out of the wind which, however, had subsided without giving notice. "Have you taken leave of your senses, Missook?" The depth of concern was considerably shallowed by the daft and fretful expression the knit hat forced down on her forehead gave her.

"I'm sorry, Lark, I'm only quoting from the past," she explained.

"Oh well, yes, the past," Laura said (sigh) and lay back in her chair. "There was much too much past last summer."

"Too much and too little (sigh)," Missook said, and again they withdrew into silence surveying what had happened like two women standing quiet at two different windows of the same house regarding the same sad landscape.

"Quoting who?" Laurie wanted to know at length.

Susan had to reconsider her thoughts and review what had passed between them some way back. "Oh," she said, "yes," finding the place. "Ned Trivett," she said. "I was quoting Ned Trivett."

"I might have known," Mislark said and let it go at that for a moment. "Which one?" she asked after the moment had passed.

"Which one what?" Susan said, having lost the place again.

"The available means of transportation or the chest of inestimable value, which one did Ned say?"

"Both," Susan said.

"Oh," Laura said. "I might have known."

"I thought up the one about the arrest warrant and the sheriff," Susan said, setting the score straight and demanding due credit.

"Oh, I realize that," Laura said, "it's the kind of too honest thing you always say." Susan wasn't absolutely sure for a moment that too honest was what she wanted to be, but then she decided Mislark had meant it as a compliment and that too honest was exactly the reputation she had always striven to establish.

They went back to studying the landscape from two windows. The ocean rose and fell, and the stinging bluster might never have existed. A bleak gray fog invaded from the sea and visibility diminished so that the two women, weaving away at the fabric of their lives, were left stranded on the deck of the cathedral house as if the rest of the world had fallen away. Susan's definite profile softened and Laura's face shone white and mysterious. It was like a dream. "He is taking instruction from Elvin Flowers," Laura said.

"Who?" Susan asked, lifting her head from the back of the chair. "What instruction? Who's taking instruction?"

"Ned Trivett," Mislark said and started a smile. "He is taking instruction from Father Flowers. He has given up being a nonpracticing poet and is preparing himself to be received into the True Church."

"I might have known. I expect it won't be too long before we will be attending divine services on Hooper Street," Susan said, and a laugh caught in her throat. "I wish he'd come on over here right now and listen to our sins and exorcise some of these damn ghosts," she said. She sat up erect in her deck chair and let the laugh fly. They laughed together at length and slowed down for respite and took up laughing again and didn't seem to be able to get it over with. "Oh, my God, Ned Trivett rushing around in a white collar and robes trying to redeem Milford," Susan suggested.

"Now, *there's* an available means of transportation for you," Laura said. That compounded their delight, and the way it would be came over them in waves, and every wave was more revealing and more antic. And more delightful.

"I don't dare ask myself," Susan said, and the laughing took up again. "Do you—do you (ha, ha, ha) get the feeling he will want us to repent?" she asked. This brought about a slowing of the hilarity, and they collected themselves, readjusting their scarves and sweaters, their summer bodies being ill-suited to winter garments. "I don't mind confessing," Susan argued, "but I have no idea of repenting until I've got more to repent for." She lay back down in her chair to rest, looking straight up into the gray void which should have been the sky, and Laura followed suit exactly. There was an occasional short spasm from one or the other of them. They had placed their hands quiet on their breasts and grown quite still. They could have been effigies. The fog increased as their silence increased.

"Somebody has got to redeem us all," Laura spoke straight up. "Maybe it will be Ned."

"Well, somebody has got to redeem Ned first," Susan reminded her.

"Maybe he can redeem himself, I'm not at all sure little Elvin Flowers is up to the job," Laura speculated. Her crystal-clear voice rose, cutting through the fog. "Maybe Ned can redeem me and Alma Winemiller and our foolish hope for life as it ought to have been and Julian, drunk most of the time, and his foolish hope for life as he thinks it ought to be and Skinner Bates running away with an artificial princess hoping to find some. . . ." The white voice trailed off into the thick silence.

"And me and my disdainful and lustful ways," Susan suggested, sailing on the breeze of inspiration, "and the savior from California with a worn-out voice, who could have been a movie star but most certainly was not—"

"—whose ashes are at this very moment on Ned Trivett's bookshelf in an Italian urn of inestimable value—"

"—a visitor and a hustler—"

"—reborn in a motel room in a little town in Mexico," Laura chanted, further inspired, carried away on the tide.

"Oh, really, who—" Susan interrupted the inspired song-fest and looked with strained fixity at her friend dreaming away in the chair alongside her own, "—who told you that?"

"He did," Laura crooned on, "come to save us all, come to save us all," she sang away.

"Oh, really?" Susan interrupted again, this time more forcibly. "When?"

"When what?" Laura said, breaking off the melody.

"When did he tell you about being reborn in a motel room in a little town in Mexico? He never told me that—"

"Last summer in another motel room in Bladens Beach much like the one he was reborn in," Lark said, picking up the melody where she had left off in an even sweeter and more penetrating voice which was definitely beginning to get on Susan's nerves.

"Oh, really?" she challenged with a shrill edge and thought seriously about this behind the shadow of a frown. "Under what cir—under what circumstances?" she wanted to know. "He never told me—"

"Come to save us all, come to save us all," Laura soared on in an increasingly irritating voice.

"Well, I cer—I most *certainly* would like to—ah—Under what circumstances?" Susan persisted, tensing in the chair.

"And who knows? maybe he did," Laura came to rest on a concluding cadence.

"Did what?" Susan asked, far from concluding, in a loud rude voice.

"Why, save us all, of course," Laura said, surprised anybody had to ask.

"I see," Susan said concluding quietly and suffered a small defeat in a motel room in Bladens Beach but decided not to give in to exploring the situation further, it being too late to do anything about it anyhow, God knows. She relaxed in her deck chair with an effort of will. "If ever he existed at all," she argued and took small comfort from this unsubstantial suggestion. This was no time for envy—no, not envy, no time for sour-eyed disdain of another woman's fortunate occasion and courage to sin. "Well (sigh), maybe he did in some way," she conceded at last.

"Did what?" Mislark asked.

"Why save us all, of course," Susan explained.

"Oh, I think he did, I think he did," Lark said quietly. "I think he saved Jubie from terrible and permanent exile from the world of human company and saved the rest of us from the hell of being his prison keep. That would have broken Jubie's heart, and I don't think poor old Mister Jukes would have survived it. We would have had to post guard on him day and night. As it turns out now, Jubie is one of God's soldiers."

Susan stood aside to permit another silence to confirm this last. It was the first time Laura had spoken her son's name since he had vanished, and she had spoken it with a show of great hope.

"Out there," Laura said, pointing toward where she could not see the sea, toward the endless, restless rushing, muffled by the thickening fog. "That's where he is. On the stream forever, and I think I understand that now, I think I can go on living with some hope now—even without the possibility of hearing the sound of his sweet voice." Susan thought she had said all she had to say, but she hadn't. "I have had to forgive God," Lark went on. "I have finally forgiven God for giving him to me and then taking him away from me. And I have had to forgive myself for something—I'm not sure what." She rested her cheek on the back of the canvas chair and regarded her companion with profound appeal. "Oh, Missook, do you think the angels choose to visit us from time to time?" she pondered. "Do you think some of them could be good-looking?" she asked.

"They would have to be, if they were invited to visit Ned Trivett," Susan said, thinking it was time to lift the fog a little.

"Praying away, praying away with poor little Father Flowers," Laura mused. "In the company of a possible angel's ashes in an Italian urn of inestimable value. Perhaps, he really will redeem us all, Missook."

"Missook," Susan repeated after her, as if it were an Amen, and her eyes stung with tears, but she denied them. "Well, while he's at it, I wish he'd pray me a certain dark-eyed, white-trash beauty with sideburns and a cigarette stuck in his teeth to fill in the time from now to what happens next."

"Give him time, give him time," Mislark said. "He's new at this thing, and he don't pray all that well yet."

The laughter rose up in them again, as the wind rises in the trees. It started out like an exchange, first one and then the other, and increased until they had to sit up facing each other on their chairs, each with a hand pressed to her breast. They laughed to tears again and beyond that, rocking forward and throwing back their heads on an invisible see-saw. My Lord, it was all so sad and all so funny, filling in the time from now to what happens next, and everything was almost all right and would possibly go on being almost all right.